Puck's Legacy

Katie Hall-May

Copyright © 2023 by Katie Hall-May

All rights reserved. No part of this publication may be reproduced, distributed or transmitted in any form or by any means, without prior written permission.

Published by **Paper Palace Print**
Printed by Kindle Direct Publishing

Author's Note: This is a work of fiction. Names, characters, places, and incidents are a product of the author's imagination. Any resemblance to actual people, living or dead, or to businesses, companies, events, institutions, or locales is completely coincidental.

None of the activities engaged in or risks undertaken by the characters are in any way recommended by the author.

Cover Design ©2023 by Claire Rutter

Puck's Legacy/Katie Hall-May – 1st ed.
ISBN 978-1-7394828-0-0

Trigger Warnings: Suicide references, dangerous or illegal activity, some bad language, some references to sex and sexual violence, mental health themes.

If we shadows have offended,
Think but this, and all is mended,
That you have but slumber'd here
While these visions did appear.
And this weak and idle theme,
No more yielding but a dream.

Puck's Monologue
William Shakespeare, *A Midsummer Night's Dream*

Prologue

Maybe the swallow knows.

I watch it, circling above the dusty playground, wings spread, neck stretched, beady eyes watching. There's nothing much for it to see, of course. I have made sure of that. We are only a handful of hot, squat figures dotted across the tarmac. Waiting.

I am wearing a rather tired brown jumper and faded black jeans which went out of fashion before I bought them. I have brown hair and a brown shopping bag. A pint of milk, a loaf of bread, a block of cheddar. I walked here in solid, flat, brown shoes. I have been wearing this costume for the last nine years and it is dissolving me slowly.

We stand in silence, mostly, except for Millicent, who has always been skittish. You notice a lot when you've been trained the way I have. You know the things normal people do which betray them. Millicent hums sporadically, a cross between Beethoven's *Ode to Joy* and *Yankee Doodle*. The rest of us remain quiet, except for the odd sigh or cough, and the continual 'blip blip' of the pelican crossing, which serenades us, blandly, in the distance. The humming fades. You can't expect much from someone called Millicent.

I *want* the swallow to know. It nears us now, circling downwards, considering a landing point.

"Well," says Mr. Adams, filling the silence, "I guess this is our summer then."

"Hope it lasts." says Janey.

"The thing is," says Millicent, "It's a bit *too* hot …"

The swallow despises us. But it lands anyway.

I am just another blob on the tarmac. I am a greyish-brown lump. Because of me two people are dead.

It only takes the thought in my head. Just a moment, a heartbeat and I am there again. Just for a second. The rush of colour, the heat of the lights, the smoky smell of nervous sweat. A sort of misplaced sensation, like going on holiday.

A woman, blank-faced and pale, holding her lover limp in her arms. Dust in the footlights. Blood on the boards.

There is a miniature commotion, and a stream of small life forms pour out of doors and rush towards us like jubilant water. All around me, other grey-brown figures are stooping, greeting, scolding, embracing. There is a crescendo of excited voices, a hundred mingled, mixed-up narratives.

She emerges, drawing a sort of involuntary cry from me by simply appearing, carrying a piece of paper carefully in one hand and her school bag in the other, looped carelessly over one small finger. It drags on the ground behind her as she skids to a halt, steadies herself on my shopping bag and looks up at me with eyes that are filled with stories.

"Guess what, Mummy ...?" she says.

She doesn't know my real name. I left it behind. I'm not sure I can exactly remember it myself.

If any of these parents, with whom I stand in a playground and discuss the weather, had any idea of the things I have done, of the people I have been, they would have me arrested. Perhaps, so will you.

But it isn't the police I am afraid of.

You should think carefully about which story you want from me. But don't be too hasty. There is a beauty in motherhood. There are complications. There is jealousy and resentment, love and exhaustion. And you have to admit that she *is* captivating. The brightest-eyed child ever to have graced any playground. It's been nine years now. We needn't wrench out old histories, dig into dark wounds. We could just listen to her chatter, we could try to 'guess what'.

No. I can tell. You would like to hear secrets. You are not interested in motherly love, warm rituals, brown jumpers, cheese sandwiches and sensible shoes. You want grit and violence, sex and drama. You would like to be shocked and scintillated and scared. You are, after all, not so different from me.

But still. Are you absolutely certain? Because that would be the story from *before*. It's old news.

"Mummy?"

That's who I am now.

The swallow takes flight. It circles briefly, and heads away northward, taking my secrets northward with it.

I will tell you. But don't worry. This is only a story. A clever succession of words and mirrors. There's no reason at all to believe it is real.

But you *want* to.

Act One

*"I talk of dreams,
which are the children of an idle brain,
begot of nothing but vain fantasy,
which is as thin of substance as the air,
and more inconstant than the wind."*

Mercutio
William Shakespeare, *Romeo and Juliet*

Scene One

(A small student theatre. The stalls are vacant. A lone figure sits hunched in the corner of the stage. There is a strong smell of lager.)

An empty theatre is never still, and that night was no exception. The place throbbed, quietly, populated with all the usual phantoms, departing characters with their fictional baggage, the hiss of burning dust motes in the spotlights, a lingering echo of applause. Ghosts. The only possible audience for this, most personal, performance.

I leaned against the backdrop, backstage left, and pulled the ring on another beer can, listening to the amplified ping and fizz rebounding across the deserted stalls. There was a shallow pool of spilled lager creeping its way across the stage, and it had reached my sit bones, seeping through my clothes. I felt the damp beneath me, and shifted, but without much effort. It was probably unavoidable, and not especially important.

The set was supposed to be the inside of a house, decorated conservatively in brown and beige, and when I moved, the wall swayed a little, wobbling its flimsy clapboard mantelpiece containing a battered carriage clock and a couple of ornaments.

The ballgown was lumpy and uncomfortable over my jeans, rucked up beneath me, trailing dust from the floor. It was sweat stained and stiff from years of usage and there was a wire loose in the bodice. It dug into the pale fold of my stomach, which had grown soft and doughy over the past few years, freed, deliciously, from the strictures of my father's health regime.

What your mother would have wanted.

I pressed my flesh against the wire, enjoying the sensation, wondering, idly, if it were sharp enough to cut.

Everyone else had long since discarded their costumes and left to immerse themselves instead in the after-party. I had told them I would lock up the theatre and join them. I had no intention of doing so. I hadn't quite decided, or wasn't ready to admit to myself, what my intention actually was.

"You can do anything if you put your mind to it," my father used to say, across a table made heavy with my unfinished coursework, my knuckles still glowing red from his ruler, "and the world will be your oyster."

But I had always thought oysters were small and sad, trapped all day inside their shells. And I never quite managed to lose the impression that it was somehow inevitable. That I would die, like my mother, at twenty-three.

If that were true, I still had two long years to go.

I sipped at the warming beer, sweating slightly in the heat of the lights. The others had left behind a twelve pack of lager, and for want of any concrete plan, and to delay the point where I would have to make one, I had begun to drink my way through it. This can was my fifth. I could feel the yeast coating my tongue, the gas escaping in tiny, irregular burps, smelling of alcohol and acid. I couldn't really taste it. I tipped my head back, closed my eyes and wondered if the solid lump I carried inside me had finally taken over so that eventually I would be unable to feel or taste anything at all.

If this was what it would feel like to be dead.

I finished the can in four gulps and trailed my finger around the sharp edge of the ring pull. It wasn't enough to draw blood.

"What doesn't hurt", my father used to tell me, "isn't worth it. What doesn't kill you only makes you stronger."

Even as a child, I couldn't help but agree. So did Tina Simmons, in my maths class. She cut weeping red diamonds into her forearms. Whatever it is she's doing now, the skin on her wrists will be viewed forever as if through the dull diagonals of our playground fence.

Liam Jefferson had a brother in prison. Jessica Clarkson's daddy blacked her eye. Benjamin Brandon's mum was dying. Tom Handley's friend's sister survived a car crash but lost a limb.

I felt something about these things which I did not understand. It clawed at me, fascinated me. At first, I asked endless questions about the minute details of the arrest, or the violence, the sickness or the pain. I stopped asking when I realised people thought it was weird. But these lives that other people were living, with disease, or with trouble or with fear - they stayed with me.

They made something burn within me.

There was a noise from somewhere in the theatre. I started and jerked upright, dousing myself further with beer. It was just a whisper of a sound, so subtle I couldn't be sure that I'd heard it. But it wasn't part of the usual groan and sigh of the building, the fizz of the lights or the creak of the boards. It was something else.

I didn't have my phone with me. I'd left it, deliberately, behind in my room because tonight was not a night for interruptions.

I sat very still on the stage and listened. Nothing.

Something clattered irreverently across the roof of the building. A pigeon perhaps, or an adventurous rat. The beer I had spilled in my initial alarm began to seep its way between the bones of the corset, pressing cold against my skin.

Still without moving, I ran my gaze across the stalls. Even in the absence of the electric strip-lights, which I had replaced with the spots as soon as I was alone, the theatre was too small to darken them fully. Whatever you did on that stage, you could always see the audience looking back at you.

The stalls were empty. On the third bench from the front, somebody had left a tissue. There was a half-empty bottle of something sticky and cherry flavoured lying on its side at the back.

I had auditioned for my first play in this very theatre with the same sense of dutiful plodding that I did anything else. It was a stone as yet unturned, that was all. I never expected the overpowering rush of it, the relief of being someone else. I had sustained myself, until then, with dark fantasies. War, death and bloodshed playing out silently in the back of my mind, while I rehearsed endless piano scales, went to chess club, passed my exams. I longed for something to fight for, something to feel. I had never imagined that the stage, with its rickety scenery, and its shuffling audience, could become for me so absolutely and totally real. I could never quite bear for the performance to finish.

And now the show was truly over.

I waited, but I could hear no further noises. The beer I had drunk had given me hiccups and my body was juddering with them, making the cheap painted chipboard of the backdrop sway with me. I should have locked myself in.

I looked for the keys which I'd dropped into my bag earlier. I'd left it somewhere on the stage. My vision dragged a little as I moved my gaze, and I felt a brief rush of nausea in the back of my throat. I swallowed, swore. If this was my swan song, it was disappointingly sordid.

I heaved myself to my feet, clutching the edge of the prop table, almost sending a clatter of bottles to the floor. I waited for the wave of dizziness to settle and imagined how I would look to an audience now.

My mother, I would tell them, *died for this*.

I let out a little, merciless laugh, which morphed gracefully into a fruity hiccough. Anguish is so much more eloquent when it's scripted.

My mother's heroic final sacrifice, her death in the act of bringing me life, *that* was the perfect theatrical set up. I could almost admire her dramatic timing. It was certainly my father's constant refrain. It was his life's work, his rationale for every decision he made – on my behalf and in her name – for every little loving cruelty. As if it was something she had actually *chosen* to do. In the dead of night, when the darkest of thoughts can be passed off as dreaming, I had often wondered which one of us, exactly, had been sacrificed. And for what? If she *had* made a choice, it wasn't worth it.

My bag was on the floor in the second spotlight, where I'd delivered my final dramatic monologue only a few short hours before. I moved towards it, stumbling a little, and crouched to feel for the keys inside. I pushed aside my keepsake programme, marked with all the traditional messages, (*Well done, you were so good! I loved working with you! See you when you're famous!*) and the letter from my father in its dogeared envelope. Opened. Crumpled. Smoothed. Replaced.

The blister packs crackled. I reached past them quickly, closed my fingers around the keys.

The pills were an option. That was all.

I had learned by then, as I know now, that people are satisfied with your mental condition, as long as you can keep putting one foot in front of the other. That is all anyone really wants from you, just to stay on the path. The exact same path they will tread for themselves, worn smooth already by countless others, and followed, without question, by everyone else.

Perhaps you think me melodramatic. But think of the stories you loved as a child, of your dreams, your nightmares, of the things you still imagine, darkly, in the shadier parts of your mind. The footfall of a murderer. The glint of a knife. The heroic encounter in a deserted backstreet. Is it only fear these fantasies grow from? Isn't there also a dark kind of longing?

I will stop. Partly because this is not your story, and partly because if I continue, I will feel the stirrings of old, forbidden passions, and at the end of it I might have recruited you.

And then Frederick will come and scoop you up.

It is dangerous for us both to think this way.

I stood up in the spotlight, keys in hand, then moved to the corner to set my empty beer can down on the floor, where it settled into the sticky circle that marked the position of previous drinks.

I heard it unmistakably this time. No ghost, no memory, not the creak and settle of a tired building. The sound of a person moving, very quietly, behind the backdrop. As if preparing to enter backstage left.

The alcohol seemed to leave my body in seconds. My heart dropped coldly towards the pit of my stomach, before picking itself up and thumping furiously. I felt sweat begin to prickle on my forehead. Propelled entirely by reflex, I gripped the keys tightly in my fist and threw myself towards the frontstage exit.

I heard somebody clear their throat.

I turned to look, despite myself. He wasn't standing where I had expected. He was in the entrance to the backstage area on the right of the stage, and he was so very still that for a fleeting and nonsensical moment I thought he might be a prop, some mannequin left over from a previous play that I hadn't noticed here before.

He was not a member of either cast or crew, and as I looked at him, I felt something shift within me. An odd, vertiginous feeling, as though my fear had dissolved very suddenly, leaving me curious and strangely hollowed out.

"Hey," I demanded, cursing the tremor in my voice which was mixing, disastrously, with the after-effects of the alcohol, "how did you get in?" But I felt my fingers relax around the keys.

He was tall and very thin, and he was looking at me intently.

"Well," he said quietly, "the door was open."

There was nothing threatening in his voice, if anything it was kindly, a statement of fact. But despite the stuffy warmth of the tiny theatre, I felt goosebumps prickling on my forearms. If I believed in ghosts, I might have cast him as one. But he was definitely real.

Without really thinking, I started towards him but as soon as I moved, he smiled at me, turned on his heels and began to walk out through the backstage area.

It seemed an odd thing to notice, in the circumstances, but there was something odd about the way that he walked. A sort of hitch in his movement, or a limp.

There was a fleeting moment in which I paused, confused, before hurrying after him, but I had only taken a few strides across the stage area, to reach the place he had initially been standing, when a voice behind me said,

"A very well-respected business. They remember your mother well."

It was a mocking voice, sly and amused. Male, but high, and slightly nasal. It belonged to nobody I recognised. But I knew the words.

I whipped around.

Another man, who I had never seen before, was sitting cross legged in one of the centre-stage armchairs, next to my bag, reading aloud from my father's letter. He was holding a cup and saucer, one of the props for the show, in a sort of parody of civilisation. He was not especially attractive, in fact he was a little odd, but there was something about him which commanded attention. His whole demeanour, from his voice to his exaggeratedly theatrical pose, made him seem as though he was perpetually on stage. Which, at this moment, technically, I suppose he was.

I looked at him just a little too long and, when I remembered myself and turned back, the other man, with the limp, who had met my gaze with such intensity, had gone.

Disappointed, my nerves still clanging, and rather short on patience, I focused again on the man in the armchair. He was wearing checked trousers, which had an air of vaudeville about them, and he seemed a little elfin perched there in the armchair, though I was vaguely aware even then that this was more an impression he had managed to give me than anything related to his physical build.

He had bare feet in close fitting shoes, something between slippers and ballet pumps, and ridiculously pale ankles against the brown drab of the sofa. He had paired all this with the same ribbed black polo neck jumper that was, at the time, the prevailing fashion among artists and actors, but on him it seemed a deliberate parody of affectation. In fact, he wore the whole ensemble not like normal clothes, I realised, but like a costume.

As I looked, he broke into an enormous and rather unsettling grin. He had a smooth face, pink, round and hairless, but animated, so animated I was reminded, strongly, of those rubber masks with finger holes in the back, that you can manipulate into a hundred different expressions in quick succession. I was annoyed by him and a little afraid, but I couldn't take my eyes off him.

Now, as if certain of my full attention, he arched his back, catlike, holding the cup and saucer in one hand, and releasing the letter so that it fluttered to the floor. He yawned and settled deeper into the armchair.

"Straight out of university," he quoted, his voice loaded with sarcasm, "how wonderful for you. Such a marvellous opportunity." He shrugged. "Of course, you're not going to take it."

He sipped his tea – just deliberately enough to make me realise it was real hot tea in the prop cup and wonder how he'd managed that – and gestured to the armchair opposite him.

Very briefly, I thought about those blister packs and the quiet finality of their contents. My exit, bathed in the warmth of the spotlight. There wasn't supposed to be anyone else.

And yet I found myself moving towards him, obediently sitting down.

When my voice finally emerged, it felt stiff and precise.

"Have we met before?"

He shrugged and raised his eyebrows, still grinning at me. "No," he said. "I know *you* though."

My voice deliberately low, self-conscious suddenly in centre-stage, I asked him what he meant. There was a small undercurrent of excitement inside me.

"Oh, not personally." he said.

I scanned the theatre for the other man. There was no sign of him, but I was sure he was still there. It occurred to me that I ought to be frightened.

I looked at the empty stalls, the flimsy backdrop, the dust motes drifting pointlessly in the lights. The letter on the floor which spelled out my future. My bag beside it which contained my escape.

They would have found me on the stage in the morning, I thought, seeing it all more clearly now that I had an actual audience. Cold at the scene of my erstwhile triumph, my virtuoso final performance, adorned with a dribble of crusted vomit. Reeking of beer and stomach acid and ingratitude. And someone would have had to tell my father.

When I looked back at the man in the chair across from me, it was as if he had been paused somehow. He had put down his tea and was looking at me, blandly, that mobile face naked somehow in its lack of expression. He stayed that way just long enough to be certain my attention had returned to him, and then he leapt into action.

"Yes," he said, "you are a very gifted actor. You make a very *clever* Ms Gabler, a very *cunning* Cleopatra, a very *manipulative* Mrs Macbeth."

I stared. With each character he mentioned he was moulding his face, his posture, just enough. I had never seen any of my own performances, but I knew somehow that he had me exactly right.

"A very, *very* filicidal Medea."

I wondered if he was a talent scout for an acting agency, there were rumours every so often that there was a scout or a prospective director in the audience, but these were almost always untrue, and he didn't seem to be behaving much like one. I wondered if he was a talent scout on some kind of drug.

He had raised his voice more in his last little speech, as if he had decided to play up to his invisible audience, and as I watched him, he suddenly changed tack.

"Want a drink?"

He jumped up and sashayed, effeminate now, over to the drinks table in the corner of the set.

"Fancy a cocktail, what'll it be?"

Before I could open my mouth to point out that the contents of the bottles were not what they said they were, that the table was a prop and the cocktail shaker tarnished and dusty inside, he was already picking them up, turning them, experimentally, into the light.

"I—"

"How about an Office Worker Mojito?" He held out a grimy cocktail glass. "Grey tailoring layered generously with fresh desperation, muddled with caffeine and topped off with tedium. Lovely over a measure of abandoned daydreams, and with a nip of stiletto just to give it some bite. Best enjoyed early in a packed-out commuter train with a side of depression when you're only half-awake."

He knew his script perfectly. He delivered it without hesitation, but he made every word ring out loud and clear. With each new image he wore his body differently. He became tense and exhausted, efficient and wired. He was preoccupied with his workload, checking his emails, and with one weary stretch of his shoulders I could see that he had been up for most of the night, unable to sleep, so nervous was he about the next morning's meeting.

I felt ice in my stomach.

"Or maybe you'd prefer a Nuclear Family Iced Tea? A *very* long drink, made of only the purest kind of slavish obligation. Complex, with overtones of sleep deprivation, balanced carefully with subtle notes of resentment."

He was moving now around the set, picking up the ornaments from the mantle, polishing them on his jumper and putting them back down. Every motion was imbued with dull disinterest. He was mechanical, resigned.

"Always best laced with guilt, that ancient companion of the imperfect parent, and held together with a spicy concoction of shattered illusions – and gin."

He grinned at the last part, but it was joyless, needy. He stumbled a little as if through intoxication or exhaustion, grasped at the mantle, displacing the ornaments, put his hand to his head.

I was standing facing him. I wasn't sure when or why I had got to my feet, and now I was rooted there, tortured, but unable to look away.

"Just to wrap it all up – and perhaps only the most experienced palate will detect this – a little hidden bitterness for balance – the delicate aftertaste of regret."

For a very deliberate moment, he met my gaze. The tears that had been welling in my eyes, unbidden, suddenly dispersed in the chill of it. It only made me focus on him better, to see my own secret terrors played out with crueller clarity.

He observed me in that moment, entirely without emotion, and, as if satisfied with the reaction he had caused, he nodded slightly. I felt a momentary warmth, a shared understanding. Then he turned suddenly on the balls of his feet, back to the mantel, delicately lifted a horrible ceramic figure of a gurning kitten which he had knocked over earlier and replaced it carefully the right way up. When he spun around again to face me, every inch of his face was sculpted, seamlessly, into an expression of sickening ingratiation. His performance wasn't over. He had made his point, and now he would hammer it home.

"I love your hair – did it take you *ages*? Let me get you a drink. I know what you'll *love* – a Rat Race Daiquiri. They're really good, honestly. I make them myself."

And he flicked back an imaginary mane of hair with such conviction I could almost see the shine in it.

"A heady concoction of temporary distractions, poured

over a watery base of crushed dreams."

He was actually at the drinks cabinet now, pouring coloured water from various bottles into the shaker with nervous flourish, all the time glancing back at me as if seeking approval.

"There's a little bit of the newest technology, just to give it a whiff of sophistication. Expensive stuff this, but I'll pour it generously, just for you. Only trouble is, it doesn't tend to hold its flavour. But that's alright, let's find something else, ah yes, how about a couple of spoonfuls of *money* – that'll do it, gives it a lovely brassy colour."

He tipped back the shaker and tasted. Dismay crossed his face, and I saw, in that moment, a myriad of renewed efforts. New looks, fresh starts, inevitable disappointments.

"Oh no, that's not it. That hasn't done it. It needs something else, how about a bit of an over-stretch on a house? A nice, big house always adds a bit of body, and there's that lovely peppery bite on the tongue, when the mortgage kicks in and traps you in it."

He paused, frowned.

"No, that's not it. Maybe a little glamour – yes that'll round it off, just a nip of Botox and a smidgen of face cream, mingled with some sours as you look in the mirror and you still look like … *you*."

He peered, despondent, into an imaginary hand mirror, imbuing the word 'you' with pained revulsion. It sounded like an expletive.

The cocktail shaker was almost full. When he wasn't despising his own reflection, he had been sloshing the contents of various bottles into it as he spoke, growing more and more reckless, talking faster and faster – and largely, it seemed, to himself – his voice cracking and rising until it was openly hysterical.

"Maybe a new job, perhaps more exercise, a little redecoration, or some new friends, a new hobby, something to drink, no, stop drinking, give up caffeine, get an iPhone, a new car, go vegetarian, go *vegan*, no that won't work, have a party, yes a party ... no ... oh *I* know."

And he thrust the cocktail shaker high in the air, as if toasting himself. It was filled to overflowing now with a variety of lurid coloured liquids, which had merged to create a noxious, black-grey sludge.

"DIET PILLS. THAT'S IT."

He froze in that position, shaker held high, a terrible mix of desperation and dead hope on his face, a tableau of a life spent searching.

There was a silence in which there would normally have been applause. He waited for it anyway, while the tears poured unheeded down my face. Just as I had gathered myself enough to breathe again, he visibly deflated, energy evaporating from him like an exhausted athlete. He brought the cocktail shaker down onto the drinks table with a bang.

"It's all just coloured water. Of course it is. Don't you want to taste something *real?*"

He dropped back into the armchair, round shouldered, glum and defeated.

I was silent and unmoving, partly because that seemed the only possible response, and partly because I needed some time to compose myself. I felt as though I had been skinned.

He said nothing further. He hadn't, I noticed, followed up on his implied offer of 'something real'. And for lack of any other obvious course of action, I found myself sitting down again opposite him.

After what seemed like a vast and echoing length of time, in which we had sat in silence, I ventured,

"Um ... are you okay?"

"I'm okay, *you're* the one dying inside."

His voice was too loud, and the cliché jarred. I was oddly embarrassed, despite the lack of audience, disappointed at this lapse in the quality of his script.

He looked at me, and, very deliberately, he nudged his foot against my bag. The blister packs inside it crackled.

I felt a rush of annoyance. This was *my* moment. He had no business being here at all. These were my last few hours with any semblance of choice, and I had wanted to relish them. This was *my* stage.

I sighed and stood up again. If I left now, I supposed I could still join the party. We could drown reality temporarily in beer.

"Hey." His voice was soothing now. "Hey, come on, don't fight it. Stay awhile. Just talk to me. I know this isn't what you want."

"*What* isn't?"

"To join the others, get drunk. Because you know that tomorrow it all starts again, the same thing, the same story, over and over and over."

Over and over. It echoed in my head. Over and over and over. I am not sure how many times he said it, or whether it only joined a chorus that had been reeling in my mind since I was old enough to think. Over and over and over. The same thing. The same story. Everyone in the country living exactly the same life. Over and over and over and over and over.

It's what your mother would have wanted.

I sank back down into the armchair.

"I know how it is," he said. "There are *some* other acceptable options. You could go travelling I suppose, and end up wandering about lost and pointless in Thailand, walking the same old tourist trail, getting drunk all over again with English travellers on watered down Guinness in

Irish pubs."

I had considered all this. There were other paths I could take but they all seemed overpopulated. And everything seemed inevitably to lead back to the same place.

"No," he said, as if reading my mind, and he suddenly thrust his foot out and this time he kicked my bag disgustedly away. It skidded into the front bench of the stalls with a thud and a crackle. "*That* isn't your style."

There was a pause. And then he said my name.

Slowly and deliberately, he said my full name. My first name, my middle name and my surname, and added, definitively, "you're not a quitter."

I will always remember the way he said it. Not my name exactly but the syllables, the rhythm of it. The way it sounded, so knowing, on his tongue.

What's in a name?

A lot. Too much.

I sat, a little stunned, in the armchair. He smiled a little, stood up, walked over to the drinks table. He stood with his back to me, while I tried to compose myself, and then returned with something in a glass. He handed it to me, and I took it and sipped it without thinking, and realised that it was real. A martini style cocktail, tart and crisp, and absolutely, inconceivably, real. All it was missing was the olive.

Before I could ask him how he'd done it, he suddenly picked up my father's letter again and sent it skimming towards me without warning, so that it collided with my glass, soaking my dress again in alcohol. I jumped in alarm and my foot jerked out and caught a discarded, half-filled beer can, sending its contents glugging in a lazy arc across the stage. The letter fell to the floor. It began, gradually, to soak up lager.

Both of us sat very still and watched it.

"*That's* your option," he said, bitter again now, "the only one you'll really take. Plod your way through the rest of your life, doing what somebody else suggested, miserable because you can't think of any alternative. What's wrong with that anyway? Half the country is doing it."

I drained what was left in my glass, crouching down to place it carefully on the beer sodden floor. I stood up. I wasn't thinking any more. I was so dreadfully tired of thinking.

"I do," I said, "I *do* want to taste something real."

He smiled.

"Was that it?" I said, urgent now, "A cocktail? *That's* what's real? What are you doing? Who are you? Why are you here?"

He stood up, mirroring my movements on the stage, and I saw pleasure in his eyes, and knew that both of us, in that moment, were consciously theatrical. We were acting.

"I'm Herm," he said, drawing out the moment, "and I'm your lifeline. I'm here to offer you Option Two."

Herm. Perhaps the most talented of all of us, and certainly the sanest. And yet that night he was only an oddity to me, a kind of fascinating annoyance, holding up a mirror to things I already knew. I sat in that armchair facing him for an hour and, most of the time, I didn't even really look at him. Instead, I stared dumbly into middle distance, at the greenish glow of the exit sign behind him.

Hermes the messenger. There to show me the way out. He played his part – as he always played all of his parts – perfectly.

I still cannot believe he's gone.

He told me that he was part of a theatre group. He said it

with an air of grandeur, sitting back down, crossing his legs, and leaning his head back into the armchair. The overall effect was one of enormous luxury. As though being part of a theatre group was a great phenomenon, a privilege afforded only to the few. I sat down again myself, a little disgruntled. I thought, rather sneeringly, that this explained his melodrama, his unreasonable flamboyance.

He met my eyes, warmth in his gaze, unperturbed by the chill in mine. I was so occupied with automatically steeling myself against it, trying so hard to resist being played by him, that I almost missed the crucial statement.

He told me that the theatre group he belonged to had one difference.

That they did everything for real.

Something shifted a little in me at that point, but I ignored it. I supposed that this meant that there would be real booze in the cocktails. Inside my head I gave a little scornful laugh.

"No," he said, watching me. "Everything."

Everything.

Perhaps there was an inkling, a part of me which was beginning to understand what he was telling me, a flare of excitement somewhere very deep inside. But I was also overcome by a general disappointment because it all seemed so normal now, the conversation reduced to a business proposition. I remember thinking, sadly, that this was just another job offer. Another *'marvellous opportunity'*. Just a slight twist on the same old path. I had already considered becoming a professional actor. But I couldn't guarantee the stage time, and my father would never have allowed it.

Besides, it wasn't enough.

The man in the armchair frowned. He elaborated. He told me that the troupe was a travelling company playing alternative venues – fields, or old ruins, or broken-down barns.

"Everything," he told me again, "is done for real."

I stared at the exit light behind him and his voice, still so quiet, so achingly gentle now, reached out in comforting waves and caressed me.

"There is no disappointment." he said. "There is no holding back at the point when you want to abandon yourself. You can *be* it. You can be everything. You can *do* everything. The alcohol is real, the tears are real, the laughter is real, the fighting is real. The sex," and he leaned forward a little towards me, "is real."

I heard the word 'sex' and, like a tittering schoolchild, I stubbornly ignored the swelling sense of longing which had been building in me as he spoke, and thought instead, with a twist of mixed repugnance and fascination, that this might be some sort of convoluted pick-up line. He saw it, smiled a little, and ignored it. I had the unnerving conviction that he was reading my mind.

He told me that the company had been preparing a play for an imminent performance, and that there was a role with my name on it. I already knew the script, he told me, it was one I had played before.

And I thought, after all this, that he really must be a scout.

"It's too late," I said. "I already have plans. I've got a job. It's what my mother …" I caught myself quickly. "It's what people do when they're starting out. And anyway, it doesn't have to be *that* awful. Life is what you make it, right? Maybe I'll be a famous CEO."

I laughed a hollow little laugh.

"Come on," he said, and I knew that he could see the part of me that was continually taking his words and deflating them, shrinking them into something more manageable. "You want something more. I know you do. I've seen it in you. It's in your performances, it's in your soul."

"Which performances?"

The actor's ego inside me had reached out with greed and without further thought, and groped around, hungrily, for praise. Or perhaps I was still missing the point.

"We've seen all of them."

I remembered commenting once to another actor, how funny it was that there were always a couple of people who left the theatre just after the final scene, before lights up. They had looked at me, puzzled, and it had occurred to me that maybe that didn't happen for every play. But I was certain it had in most of mine. I tried to think back to those shadowy figures, as the lights began to fade, excusing and squeezing their way out through the benches and disappearing outside.

We've seen all of them.

We.

I thought again of the tall man with the limp.

My companion was alert now, sitting straight up, forward on his seat, his eyes intent on me.

"This is your moment. Take it."

An instinctive longing rose in me. I ignored it. I forced myself to say nothing.

He explained that the performance – the one with the part with my name on – would happen tonight – more specifically, in the early hours of this morning. That it was an 'underground theatre production', put on in unconventional or unpermitted venues at unexpected times, advertised only by word of mouth between a few select people, who were in the know.

Everything refined itself into sharp focus. I felt my heartbeat quicken and my mouth turn dry in the same instant that the palms of my hands grew hot and wet. I became suddenly very aware of everything. I saw the cocktail glass on the floor, the growing darkness around us. I felt the silence of the empty lecture theatres which surrounded us, the distance from the bustling campus bars and clubs, the absence of anyone else within earshot.

I noticed anew the strangeness of the man sitting opposite me, the odd intensity of his words, his eyes on me, glinting in the semi darkness. The whole evening felt suddenly like the clumsy set-up of a predictable horror film in which the hapless protagonist is lured into a net which is clearly visible to everyone watching.

"That's ridiculous." I said, keeping my voice very steady. "It isn't practical. I don't even know what the play is, and we haven't rehearsed. If you really want me to join your theatre group, ask me again in the morning. If I'm still … if … you can find me."

It was a terrible performance. It rebounded flatly around the stalls.

Mentally, I tried to scan the building, considering my possible routes out. But my brain wouldn't focus properly, my thoughts kept slipping, tripping on those pernicious little phrases.

Over and over and over.

Don't you want to taste something real?

It was too late of course, but I *was* frightened now. And yet, beyond the rising fear, there was an unmistakable exhilaration. An inkling of a dozen sensational possibilities.

My senses prickled. I felt my blood surge and pulse in my ears. I thought of the darkness outside, the smattering of broken streetlights. I imagined sudden, rough hands over my mouth, at my throat, and I heard my own breath, quick and shallow in the silence.

I sat up, poker straight, every muscle held tense. I considered standing but wasn't sure of my balance. I saw myself, centre-stage in jeans and a ballgown, bound to the battered old armchair in the spotlight. I could almost feel the bonds digging into my flesh, nipping and chafing at my wrists and ankles.

It would, after all, an alternative exit. And there would be dignity in it. There would be no limp figure, soaked and stinking, no empty blister packs and vomit. No accusations of selfish whimsy. This man could remould me into a fallen hero. People would talk sadly of my wasted talent. I would be reborn, even as I died in the spotlights.

When I refocused, still breathing rapidly, I found he was still sitting there, amused. He shrugged and grinned at me, mock obliging. Opened his mouth as if to say something more.

"Be careful."

I looked up with a start. The tall man was back, framed again in the door to the backstage area. But his voice was stern, and he was looking hard at the back of my companion's head.

"It must be a choice, Herm," he said. "It must *always* be a choice."

He was so slender that his legs, inside his trousers, might conceivably not have been there. His face was angular, his cheekbones so pronounced it seemed as though the bones had been caught in the act of escaping his face and, rather than appearing fragile, it lent him a kind of imposing grace.

He was just outside of the beam of the spotlight, but he was lit very clearly where he stood, beneath the greenish glow of the exit sign, with the dim light outside shining through the tiny mesh window of the backstage door. It was as if he had paused there deliberately, to allow himself to be properly seen.

He was pale and his hair was very dark, he had dark, thick

eyebrows, and dark, thick lashes framing dark brown eyes. He was wearing a full-length black trench coat, not uncommon, and rather fashionable at the time, but on him it seemed authentic, as though it still carried with it all the fire and fury of the First World War.

He turned his gaze from the now silent Herm and met my eyes. I felt a quickening which was entirely separate to the mixture of fear and excitement already coursing through my veins and I saw a flicker of surprise on his face, as if he felt it too, and it was not something he had expected.

He was moving towards me, the limp in his gait made almost athletic in the length of his stride, kneeling in front of me to pick up my father's discarded letter from the floor. He examined it, and, with extraordinary care, began to wipe beer from it with the sleeve of his coat.

After what seemed like an unreasonably long pause, in which I barely breathed, and he absorbed himself entirely in cleaning my letter, he seemed satisfied, smoothed it on his knee, and offered it to me.

I didn't move.

He looked at me.

"Are you sure?"

I had not given either of them any definite answer. I had made no commitment to be 'sure' of, and still his question seemed unnecessary.

He knew, as I did.

I had always been going to select Option Two.

Scene Two

(A carpark. A camper van. Darkness.)

The outside world, when you leave the theatre, after the honey-dipped fuzz and warmth of the spotlights, is always disappointingly bland. The air, as I locked the theatre door behind me and followed my new colleagues through the carpark seemed to me unseasonably cool. It was darker, later, than I'd expected. There was even a smattering of tepid rain, making shallow, oily pools in the pock-marked tarmac. I stepped around them, hitching up my dress, and wondering, even as I did so, why I was bothering.

The truth was, I had felt that swell of excitement much more keenly in the theatre. Now that I had stepped outside it, had turned back, mechanically, to lock myself out, that exhilaration had been swept up into something more fearful. For every step I took across that gloomy carpark, I was making plans to stop immediately, or to run back inside. And yet my feet still moved me forward. The protestations and excuses I composed in my head still stayed there. I realised I was pressing my lips tightly together, as if some other, grimmer, part of me was determined not to let them out.

"Are you alright?" asked the tall man, turning to face me.

I met his eyes in the darkness. Swallowed. Nodded.

But I felt breathless, my chest stretched tight and straining. It was a feeling I associated with my childhood. Early mornings, bone-tired, muscles tensed, at the start of yet another long-distance race. My father spitting instructions behind me. I was always faster on the track loop out than I was on the return. I had always known how to run away. I had just never been sure where to go.

There were numerous moments when I could have turned back. When I realised I had only locked one of the doors to the theatre, and that the audience entrance remained unsecured. When it occurred to me that I was still wearing the ballgown over my jeans, that I should have changed clothes before I left. When I thought about my bag, left in the darkness by the edge of the stalls. And everything that bag contained.

I could have explained. That I needed to fetch something. My phone perhaps. That I needed more time. That I needed to run in the opposite direction. But I knew it would only take me back to the start.

If I had made another choice that night, would my life have been less pursued by ghosts? Or just significantly shorter?

I didn't know then, and I'm not sure now.

So I kept on walking. The wild and self-styled heroine within me, who had longed to feel and scream and fight, was a tiny, distant figure now. I must have left her in the theatre.

The rain slowed. The puddles glinted in the inadequate streetlights. There was an empty beer bottle in the gutter, a tightly folded crisp packet stuffed inside it. I could smell beer and sweat on my dress. Everything seemed so insultingly normal.

It was becoming rather hard to breathe. I saw Herm look sideways at me, as I panted a little, and they both politely slowed their pace.

By the time we reached Herm's vehicle, which turned out to be a medium sized VW camper van, incongruous and rather welcoming, we were barely moving at all. And neither man had been rude enough to comment.

It wasn't the first time I had done something reckless. During my termtime at university, away from home and briefly and wonderfully unmanaged, I had tried most things once, though I generally found them oddly unsatisfying.

When Herm opened the door to the side of the van, and offered me his hand, it wasn't the first time I had climbed inside a stranger's vehicle, though it might have been the first time he or she didn't join me, giggling, inside it.

"If it's a job worth starting," my father had said, standing sternly behind the piano stool, when I sprained my wrist running and begged him to cancel my piano exam, "then it's a job worth finishing."

Obediently, I found my way inside the van, and perched myself on a narrow bench opposite a wooden, flip up table.

"Thank you," I said, with my very best manners, as though to change my mind now would constitute an unconscionable rudeness.

"I understand if this feels wrong." Standing in the doorway, the streetlight behind him, the tall man became even taller and slimmer, a long, unnatural silhouette. I started to shake my head politely, then stopped myself so abruptly the bones cracked, audibly in my neck. I winced, felt my face flush hot in the darkness. But he nodded. "Of course. A last-minute performance is always exciting and if we could have put it on right there where we found you, believe me we would have done. But I give you my word, you are safe. I could call you a taxi…" He paused and I knew he was smiling in the darkness, and so I smiled along with him and then wondered what I was doing.

"But I'm not sure the driver would be able to find the venue. It's a bit out of the way. I don't think there's another way we can get you there, other than for Herm to give you a lift."

He seemed to be waiting for a response. I wasn't sure what to do, and so I nodded. There was an acid taste, tinged with beer at the back of my throat. I swallowed. A voice inside me was narrating my progress with crazed incredulity.

"It ... I mean ..."

My voice was very small and sudden. It had surprised even me. He had already begun to close the door and now he paused, still gripping the handle. He waited. A bird called from a rooftop, shrill above the dull noise of distant traffic. Towards the front of the van, I could hear Herm stop breathing, just for a moment.

"I left ... I mean I need ... I ..."

I could see myself stuttering my apologies, stumbling outside. I could picture the van rumbling off into the distance, leaving me alone in the dampened carpark. But I couldn't imagine what I would do with myself afterwards.

A bag. A letter. A packet of pills.

"Actually, never mind." In the darkness I could sense his expression changing, questions still lingering on his face. "This play – I really know the script?"

Something relaxed in the air between us.

"You do." he said, "Of course. As Herm said, it's fairly well-known, and you've played it before." He paused, as if weighing up his words, then added, "It's good to do something unrehearsed occasionally. It's actually a well-known directing technique, though I admit it's not done often. It keeps things fresh."

"Of course," I squawked. "Great. Okay. Let's do this." I gave a little, staccato, high-pitched laugh.

It echoed cringingly around the van as he smiled in the darkness, and gently closed the door. The little light that there was shrank to a sliver, then to nothing. There were blackout curtains at the windows. I clamped my teeth so hard together that it seemed I would grind them downwards into my jawbone, and I told myself it was too late. I was doing it now.

There was no turning back. What was there to lose?

I heard their footsteps, one regular, one slightly uneven, as they walked around the van and climbed into the cabin. There was a thud of doors, the rubbery squeak of the handbrake, the chug and roar of the engine.

I gripped the edges of the wooden table, with its smooth veneer, and my knuckles whitened in the darkness. I felt the sway and shake of the van as it left the campus, the whoosh of other vehicles as we joined a motorway, and the tilt and judder as we swung into what I guessed to be a series of country lanes.

I had no way of knowing where we were going, and I didn't think about what might await me when we got there. I let the alcohol and adrenaline in my system combine with the darkness to create something dreamlike and I mixed it with the motion of the vehicle, the fact that at least I was going *somewhere*, that I was doing *something*, until the force of it crushed the fear into a tiny, protesting insect at the back of my mind.

And so, I gripped the table. And we drove.

I don't know how long it was before the vehicle finally stopped. In the dark and the rush of it all, time had seemed to stretch and morph until I no longer had any concept of it.

I heard quiet voices as they climbed out of the van, and then the tall man opened the side door and held out his hand for me to grasp and climb down. I felt an unreasonable sense of relief, though I wasn't sure exactly what I had been afraid of, or why I was so convinced that it was no longer a threat.

I stood and squinted into the black, and I sensed him watching me like a cat in the darkness, waiting while my eyes adjusted to the faint moonlight. Herm had disappeared. We were in a field, surrounded, as far as I could see, by trees. I could smell the herb and pepper scent of damp grass. In the distance, I could just make out a cluster of dark oblongs of various sizes. Camper vans, some larger than others. There were no lights on inside them, and I could make out no movement, but I could feel the quiet pulse of people, like a sort of collective holding of breath.

He moved in front of me and took both of my hands in his.

"I'm Frederick," he said.

I felt again that frisson, sharply, through me. I had an impulse to grip his hands very tightly, to squeeze them and feel the knot of veins and tendons in his fingers, the bones of his knuckles, as if I could absorb him somehow into myself. I didn't do it, but I felt his fingers twitch, and I wondered if he felt it too, or if he somehow knew.

My heart was beating painfully in my ribcage. I had a vague desire to vomit. But it didn't feel like the same sort of fear anymore. It was closer to stage fright.

"Wait," he said, and, though he did not speak loudly, there was command in his voice. It made me jump a little. "Before we go any further, I need to know that you are sure." He looked at me with great intensity, searching for something in my face. "It is very important that you are sure."

He spoke so quietly that I had to concentrate hard to hear him. In all the time I knew Frederick, unless on stage, or making some dramatic entrance, he always pitched his voice just a little below the surrounding noise level. To communicate with him meant tuning out everything else around him, to be conscious of nothing other than him.

It was hypnotic. It was deliberate.

"This is the last time you have this particular choice. You can go home now, no questions asked, you can accept your new job."

Was I running from my life or just following him?

I didn't know then. And I don't know now.

"You understand," he said, "that everything is for real. *Do you understand that?* You need to want it. You need to be ready to accept nothing else."

I nodded, dry mouthed, and I felt his smile.

You cannot say he didn't warn me.

He led me across the field to a larger shape, which I assumed, in the dim light, was another camper van. I heard Herm's voice in the distance, and then his footsteps, following behind us. Frederick released my hand to open the door and I hesitated slightly, feeling an odd sense of loss, took a breath, then climbed, a little clumsily, inside. I saw Herm make a movement in the darkness, heard the quick click of a switch and I felt on my skin, for the second time that night, the unmistakable heat of a theatrical spotlight.

Lights up.

I stood, blinking. Small, blurry amoebas swam in my vision.

For a confused moment I thought I might already be on stage. I fought a rising sense of panic, and then my eyes grew accustomed to the light, and I realised I was standing in a cluttered backstage area, lit by a spindly, standing spotlight, crouched like a black spider in one corner. In its beam everything took on an unnatural brightness, casting colour and shadow across the walls and ceiling of what I now understood to be a hollowed-out vehicle, the size of a small lorry or a double decker bus.

Aside from the driver's cab, which was entirely closed off from the rest of the space, the whole back wall was covered with a forest backdrop, presumably from a previous performance, and the trees seemed to reach out from it and mingle with the clothes rails in front. Moss, bark, scattered sunlight. A monk's habit, a nightie, an assortment of masks.

The whole place had an air of unreality, as though it was,

itself, a set for something. There was a fake tiger-skin rug thrown over a coat rack, a tangle of wires and plugs over and around a pile of battered lighting fixtures. A skull wearing several hats and a blindfold balanced precariously on the side of a plastic bathtub, which was filled with a random assortment of household ornaments, kitchen utensils, and make up. It was like walking inside a surrealist painting, everything over-bright and too sharply defined.

At the far end of the bus there was a door, closed, and framed with heavy curtains to block the light and the audience's view. My pulse quickened.

An exit. Or an entrance.

Next to it was what I recognised as a prop table, incongruous in the chaotic surroundings, its contents ordered and precise, chalk outlines drawn around each item to ensure that nothing would be missed. There was a vial of clear liquid. An envelope. A dagger.

I stared at the dagger a little too long.

When I turned back to the two men, they were watching me and I was aware of a growing sense of tension, as though I had forgotten a line, or missed some imperceptible cue. Frederick met my gaze, but there was a sharp set to his jaw. Thin beads of sweat shone on Herm's forehead.

Something twitched inside me, and I took a step backwards, colliding with a large, transparent storage box full of assorted costumes. A pair of boots fell to one side, toppling an oversized black umbrella and dislodging a large metal bowl, which rolled away from us.

We all watched the bowl until it slowed and circled to a clanging halt in the middle of the floor.

I turned, just in time to see Frederick's almost imperceptible nod, and Herm reach across and turn the key in the lock.

I stood for a second, blinking stupidly. Then I made a sudden, useless movement sideways, banging my elbow on the wall.

I could have hurled my weight against the door, but that seemed laughably dramatic. And anyway, they were still standing in front of it. Making no move towards me but blocking my exit.

I faced them, and all the questions that I should have been asking, should already have asked, were lost in a thick-tongued, blundering fog so that the only words I uttered were a number of variations on, '… *what* …?'

They said nothing. Waited. I stuttered my abortive sentence to a muddled halt, shot a glance at the curtained exit at the end of the van.

"It's locked at the moment," said Herm, his conversational tone undermined by a muscle twitching in his temple, "but it'll be open for the performance."

My pounding heart slowed, a fraction. I turned again to Frederick. He smiled at me.

"It's where you make your entrance."

But he was uneasy. They both were. I opened my mouth and I saw them move, take a breath, as though in preparation for something.

"But what … I mean … when …?"

They breathed out again, audibly.

Herm checked his watch. It was the most normal thing I'd seen him do and yet it still seemed oddly theatrical.

"Very shortly," he said, as if vaguely surprised. As if at any moment he might talk about the weather. As though he might say, '*doesn't time fly?*'.

Annoyance snapped awake in me, and everything suddenly slid into focus.

"This is ridiculous," I said. "I still don't even know what

the performance actually *is* that I'm supposed to be starring in. I mean I know you want it 'fresh' but at least let me prepare before it starts. And why bother to lock the door? Just stop ..." I searched around for the words, "Just stop … *play-acting*."

I sounded like a fumbling student teacher. At the end of her tether with Class 2b.

I heard their collective intake of breath and I realised that, in some roundabout way, I'd finally asked the question they had been anticipating. Frederick was offering me something, holding out a flimsy, A4 poster and I took it mechanically and then everything stopped.

It was a single yellow rose depicted against a black background. It had one slender green leaf and a poisonous looking thorn, tinged with red at the tip.

The title of the play was picked out in gleaming red letters. *'Romeo'*, it said, *'and Juliet'*.

I had played Juliet for six nights in a student production. It hadn't even been very good.

I stared at the poster, aware of my mouth hanging open, the sudden silence in the van. I'd imagined they would pick something shorter, simpler. Perhaps a one act Pinter or a David Hare. I'd done quite a few of those, and I still knew the scripts. Or a two hander, played out fresh with an unknown co-star on an unfamiliar set. That would have made much more sense.

Juliet drinks a vial filled with a drug which will render her unconscious, so that she can escape an arranged marriage and elope with Romeo. She wakes in her family tomb, with Romeo dead beside her, because he, like everyone else, had believed her dead. Then she stabs herself in the tomb with her own dagger.

I stood, stock still. Then I turned, my throat contracting

violently, bile rising, and stared at the prop table.

A vial. A dagger.

It's all just coloured water. Of course it is. Don't you want to taste something real?

From outside, as if on cue, I heard the muffled sound of vocal exercises. A troupe of actors, warming up.

"No," I said, my voice high and strangled, and I could feel my eyes wide and wild in my skin.

I backed away but I was already standing against the wall of the caravan and there was no further room for movement. I planted my hands against the wall for support. I looked at Frederick.

"You said I had a choice." It came out in a whisper.

He looked back at me and the expression of sadness on his face made my breath hitch.

"You do," he said, "You do have a choice. But it's a different choice now."

The adrenaline in my body won over against the crippling fear and I catapulted myself off the wall. In the corners of my vision, I saw them quietly step aside as I hurled myself at the locked door between them. I slammed against it, yanked at it, pounded on it with my fists. I shouted as loud as I could, until my throat closed, and my voice cracked. Neither of them tried to stop me. Only when I had paused, spent suddenly, breathing in great, sobbing gasps, and leaning on the door of the van, more for support than in any continuing effort to open it, did Frederick speak again.

"You have a dagger," he said. "You are armed. Against us. Against yourself. But there is an audience out there. And they're waiting for you. It will be the performance of your life. You can go out in a blaze of beautiful glory. Or you can simply go out. It's up to you."

It was deathly silent. Somewhere amid my shouting and

flailing, the sound of the warm-up exercises had ceased. I could hear nothing. Even the intermittent creak of the van, the drip of the tap into the tiny, paint-stained sink, seemed to have stopped for his words.

Then, into the silence, as if on cue, so very well-timed that I was almost convinced I had imagined it, came the sound of trembling violins.

Recorded music of course. A soundtrack. The opening music for the show. But I knew the piece. Richard Wagner's *The Ride of the Valkyries*. We'd used it in countless student plays.

Still, none of us moved. We stood together, listening as the music swelled, wind instruments joining violins and trumpets. I could almost see the Valkyries, glorious and fierce, riding that trumpet call up and out and into the night. I could see them speeding through the sky towards some bloody Nordic battleground, ready to choose the fates of the mortals, select their dead and carry them away.

As the trumpets grew louder, repeating their refrain, I heard Frederick's voice beneath the music.

"Your props are there, you've got costumes on the rack. You can skip your early scenes if you're not ready, Cat will sub for you. We've written out a few of the lesser parts, servants, and constables, but otherwise all your cues are exactly as they are in the original, with one exception. When you make your entrance at the ball where you and Romeo first meet, I want you to come in a bit earlier than usual, at the end of Mercutio's Queen Mab speech."

I was staring at him, my stomach dropping and churning, following the strings of the violins as they replaced the trumpets.

He was so practical now, so in control. I could almost believe I was simply preparing for another performance.

And wasn't I?

Something dark and tantalising was creeping and spreading in the back of my mind.

I looked at Frederick, still unable to respond, but captive to his instructions, noting them despite myself and storing them away.

"That speech is all about Mercutio. Queen Mab is only a fantasy figure he's made up, but by the end of the speech he's in thrall to her. Queen Mab is a threat, she *owns* him. And just before he is interrupted, when he says, '*This is she*', then *you* come in. You join the party."

He paused for breath, and I saw the fanaticism in his eyes.

"It follows, doesn't it? You enter on *'This is she'*. YOU are Romeo's version of Queen Mab."

I saw it. And I understood.

He looked at me a little longer, then he nodded, as if satisfied, swung a long cloak off a hook, swept it around him and strode to the stage entrance.

I was still unable to move.

The trumpets were back now, building and climbing. Frederick paused, hand on the door, his body shrouded in the heavy, velvet curtain.

"Remember," he said, "you're just an innocent young girl. A bit nervous. At a party. You enter when Herm says, *'This is she'*."

And with that, while my insides tumbled and flipped and all I could think was '*Herm*?', he disappeared behind the curtain. And the music swelled as the violins and the Valkyries descended together.

To choose those who will live.

And those who will die.

I took an impulsive step towards the place where Frederick had disappeared, then stopped in confusion, the movement pointless. I swung round to face Herm. His face was shining with sweat. I could smell it. But his eyes were calm, and his gaze met mine. I looked past him and saw my own face, reflected in the peeling, full-length mirror which was leaning against a standing spotlight. There was something unhinged about it. I felt brittle and broken, as though some essential part of me had recently worked loose and was rattling around inside. I opened my mouth to speak but as I did so, the music rose into its bold crescendo, and I heard Frederick's voice from the stage, timed perfectly, his first word booming in the wake of the final, triumphant note of the music as he spoke the famous opening lines.

"*Two households, both alike in dignity…*"[1]

I had not imagined his voice could carry so far. The sound from the stage permeated the enclosed backstage area with ease. It seemed to weave through the forest-painted walls and ricochet off the lamps and the costume rails and the general detritus.

"*From ancient grudge break to new mutiny, where civil blood makes civil hands unclean...*"

I had been staring, wild and blind, towards the stage but when I turned back Herm was already squatting in front of the mirror. There were costume racks arranged around it, with curtains draped over them, and a muddle of make-up and hairbrushes on the floor.

He hadn't bothered to draw the curtain. He frowned at his reflection, selecting from the scattered grease sticks on the floor. The epitome of concentration. But there was a quiver to his hand.

"*You* are playing Mercutio?" It was no more than a whisper. He nodded. The make-up was slick on his face.

"*The fearful passage of their death-marked love …*"

Mercutio. Romeo's friend. The vivacious inventor of the

notorious 'Queen Mab'. He would die in a street brawl at the beginning of Act Three.

"...*and the continuance of their parent's rage ...*"

Frederick's voice was inescapable. It marked out our remaining time with every new, relentless line.

"*... which, but their children's end, naught could remove, is now the two hours traffic of our stage ...*"

We both had less than two hours to live.

I backed as far as I could away from the entrance curtain and began again, in a kind of panicked trance, to tug and rattle and thump at the locked door. In the back of my mind, I ran through the play, counting entrances. How many until my initial cue?

How many until my final exit?

My eyes stung and blurred with sweat and tears. I banged at the door, the walls, any available surface. And yet what, asked a voice at the back of my mind, would have been my other choices?

A letter. Or a lot of pills.

I drowned out the thought, hurling myself at the door, and pounding my fists against the metal walls. The audience outside must have heard it, and yet the actors' lines kept coming. Samson and Gregory, servants of Juliet's father, swaggering onstage and looking for a fight.

Were the spectators aware of what they were watching? I felt cold strike through me. An invited audience, clued in, expecting blood?

Behind me, Herm drew the curtain across the makeshift dressing room and began to get changed.

"*Quarrel, I will back thee.*"

"*How, turn thy back and run?*"

I felt the scorn in the words from the stage as if they were aimed at me personally. I bit my lip, hard, punched at my tears with the heels of my hands, and took a deep, angry breath.

"Do you bite your thumb at us, sir?"

The antics of Samson and Gregory seemed even more pointless and puerile than Shakespeare presumably intended. I set my teeth against it, unable to stop myself from listening.

I was avoiding, for the moment, Juliet's dagger, the only weapon I knew I had. I wasn't sure what I would do with it – it was too large to pick the lock and too small to pierce the walls – and besides, I didn't really want to look. Instead, I climbed over upturned crates and picked up heavy light fittings, weighing them in my hands, imagined myself smashing them against the door. I ran my hands along the top of painted backdrops, felt behind stage blocks. I upended rucksacks and bags full of props and poured them all out on the floor, searching for something I could use as a lever.

From outside, the taunting escalated into its inevitable violence, and I heard a sudden gasp, a rush, and the sound of metal clashing hard against metal.

I felt my stomach churn, bile rising in my mouth. The world grew suddenly black and hazy and the sound from the stage became muted and muffled, as though I was hearing it from some quiet space deep underwater, and for a moment I sank into that feeling, felt my legs begin to give way beneath me.

"Part, fools."

Benvolio. Romeo's peace-loving friend. A woman's voice. There was concern in her tone, panic even, but also an authority which cut through the air and pulled me, panting, back to my senses.

The van looked ravaged. I felt a tiny pang of remorse, as though I had desecrated something important.

There were shouts from onstage. New voices, hot and angry, bent on the pursuit of blood. Benvolio's calm was never destined to last. I heard once more the clash of metal and I swallowed, steadied myself on the wall of the van.

Herm was sitting on the floor against the opposite wall, staring past me into middle distance. He had finished changing and was wearing a pair of slimline flannel trousers and a simple jacket. He looked like any actor, preparing his role. I tried not to look at the sword, its hilt a cold right-angle in his belt, glinting in the spotlight beside him.

I felt something terrible stir inside me.

A shimmer of excitement. A spark of concentration. Even, at the very sharpest depths of it, a glamour, a kind of rising joy.

The way an actor might feel at the start of a performance.

I smothered it.

"Rebellious subjects, enemies to peace."

A new voice. The Prince. Frederick? I wasn't sure. But I could hear in that voice all his character's frustration, the years of continual management of these two families and their ancient, never-ending quarrel. He made me feel his weariness, the effort involved in retaining his dignity.

I ignored it.

I would not admit their talent. I would not acknowledge the truth that even then I must have been beginning to realise, that the urge to take my place in this unforgettable performance was rapidly becoming the most powerful instinct in me.

Instead, in the comparative quiet that followed his words, I finally approached the prop table.

Juliet's dagger.

It was small, a slim black hilt sheathed innocuously in plain grey metal. I had expected something more frivolous somehow, something girlish and decorative, with swirls and flowers. A pretty affectation. More fashionable than fatal. This coldly functional item seemed too understated.

I picked it up.

It was heavy in my hand. I hesitated for a moment, feeling it cold in my palm, then, my fingers growing slick with sweat, I pulled at the sheath and shivered, hearing again the grating scrape of metal.

The blade was silver and surprisingly narrow, tapered into a wicked looking point. I stared at it.

I registered Herm's gaze on me, his intake of breath and stiffening of limbs. I paused for a long moment before I pressed the very tip of the dagger against my finger.

The pain was minute, but in my exaggerated state of tension it made me start and drop both dagger and sheath so that they clattered loudly to the floor. I listened, but the players were too accomplished, and the audience either wilfully unhearing, or too spellbound to notice. I stared at my hand. At the tip of my finger there was a tiny, swelling bead of blood.

"If ever you disturb our streets again, your lives shall pay the forfeit of the peace."

Could I use the dagger to defend myself? I tried to imagine holding it, pointing it. Plunging it into soft, warm flesh. Acid rose in my throat. Perhaps I need only posture with it, use it, somehow, as a threat. But who would I threaten? An entire audience, possibly already aware of the nature of this performance, and who had paid to view it on that basis? A whole troupe of players, willing to die for their art?

At the other end of the van, I could still feel Herm's eyes on me. He had not moved from his position against the wall, and his sword was sheathed and discarded at his side.

Would I have a hostage in Herm? Could I do that? Hold

the knife at his throat, hands slippery with sweat, terrified at any moment that I might accidentally slip and pierce his skin with that razor-sharp point and murder him through lack of skill?

And would it hold any weight, even if this wild bluff were taken seriously? Whoever these people were, they had already given Herm up to his death.

"Away from light steals home my heavy son, and private in his chamber pens himself, shuts up his windows, locks fair daylight out, and makes himself an artificial night."

I started, focusing once more on the progress of the performance outside. My time window for escape was narrowing. The scene had already changed again. Somewhere amid my frantic planning, the Prince had made his pronouncement, and the chaos had dissipated. Now only Lord Montague, Romeo's father, remained, confiding in Benvolio about his concern for his son.

They must have written Lady Montague out, I thought.

Aside from the pedestrian nature of that thought, the immediate conclusion I should have drawn from it, was that perhaps this theatre troupe contained only a limited number of people. That, therefore, there might just be an outside chance of somehow fighting them off. But success would have been very unlikely and as it happened, I didn't think of that at all.

Instead, I thought about how clever it was to have Lord Montague take this scene with Benvolio, undoing his portrayal as a squabbling lout, expressing his tenderness in his concern for his son.

I was thinking all the wrong things. I was wasting time.

I shook myself, picked up the dagger from the floor where I had dropped it, replaced it in its sheath and closed my fingers around it.

Perhaps I could run, now, out of the stage entrance - and sprint as far as I could away from the vans and towards the nearest road or house. But it had been almost entirely dark when we arrived here, and we had driven off-road for quite some time before that. I would struggle to find my way back to the main road from here.

It struck me, cruelly, that I had spent my whole life desperate for something to happen. That earlier that evening, I had been ready to die in circumstances much less meaningful than this. Now I could think only of ever more unlikely strategies to escape this opportunity and live.

And for what?

Tears of self-loathing sprang to my eyes.

"Good morrow cousin."

Benvolio's voice was bright, too bright. She sounded like a nurse in a geriatric day ward, compensating too eagerly for her friend's mood.

Despite myself, I listened, tensed for the answer, for Romeo's unprepossessing first line. I wanted to hear his voice.

"Is the day so young?"

Romeo, like me, was not satisfied with living, but Romeo would be redeemed. He would be poetic and dignified, even in death.

Theatre is infinitely better than life.

"Herm?" I said. He looked at me.

"They're going to kill you," the words scratched painfully at the roof of my throat. "Why are you doing it? Did they make you? Why?"

"Nobody made me," he said, "everybody has a choice."

If it sounded as though he had been brainwashed, he at least repeated it with genuine conviction.

"But why?"

He shrugged. "Everyone has their reasons. What are yours?"

"I'm not—", but I paused. Not what? Not doing it? Was that true?

"Not ready?"

"Not quite."

It was instinctive but it was not what I wanted to say.

"Not doing it." I corrected and ignored the fact that it might just be a lie.

He looked surprised, but his voice was still gentle.

"Really?" he said, "but isn't this your moment? Your time to stray off the same old trail? Part ways with the rest of them and get out there and really feel something?"

Exhausted suddenly, I leaned against the painted forest, closed my eyes. It was growing more real by the second. I could almost feel the rough bark of the tree trunk as I let myself slide down it to sit next to Herm. He shifted a little to make room for me among the slew of items I had strewn across the floor.

You can go out in a blaze of beautiful glory. Or you can simply go out.

When I opened my eyes, Herm was waiting.

"What exactly are you going back to?" he asked, "If you decide to escape?"

I looked at him, but I saw only the question, and a flicker of anxiety.

"*Is* there something? Did we get it wrong?"

I felt my father's breath in my ear, full of hot, sharp plans, more statement than aspiration – *'when you marry', 'when you get the top job', 'when you win'*. I saw him roasting pumpkin seeds with rosemary to improve my concentration, funnelling them into tiny bags for me to eat instead of crisps. His hands bruising my shoulders. His fingers tearing up my French homework in front of me because in one sentence only, I had declined the wrong verb. His letter, as much a command as a congratulation, to a daughter who existed only to make her dead mother proud.

And then I saw him, for a moment, all alone.

I shook the images away. I listened, instead, to the sound from the stage. I heard the subtle pause of the scene change, the breath of the audience, the hum of the lights. I smelled grease paint and old leather. I saw the bright technicolour of Juliet's lifeline, so short and intense, so dangerously young.

"No," I said, "You didn't get it wrong."

In the pause that followed that admission, we listened in silence to the County Paris, talking with Juliet's father, as though she were merchandise to be purchased.

"Younger than she are happy mothers made."

By the end of this conversation, Lord Capulet would have agreed, on his daughter's behalf, to her marriage. And in doing so he would set in motion the chain of events which would lead her to her death.

I was still gripping the dagger, cold in my hand. I stared at the vial of liquid, Juliet's 'medicine', waiting on the prop table. It looked small and innocuous, like a pretty perfume bottle. A meaningless trinket. It was only half-full, the liquid inside it pale and slightly milky.

What was it? Had they really found something which would knock me unconscious? How did they know how long it would take to have an effect? How long it would last for? Had they tested it? How sure could they be that they could wake me up?

And if whatever was inside the vial actually worked and I awoke when I was supposed to? What then? Romeo, or whoever it was that played him, would be dead beside me.

And when it came to my turn? When I stabbed myself,

lonely in a tomb beside my dead lover, would it hurt? How would I know where to place the knife? How hard to push? Would I be screaming in agony if I somehow got it wrong?

Did I want, did I *really* want to die that way?

I was crying now, squeaky, gasping tears, like a mewling animal or a frightened child.

Did I want to die the other way?

My whole body was shaking. I buried my face in my hands. I felt Herm's arms around me, and I realised it was the first time that he had actually touched me. He smelled of sandalwood and sweat.

We stayed that way for some time while I sobbed the fear out and he held me in silence, until the flood of emotion slowed to a trickle. I breathed into the damp white cotton of his armpit. My fingers steadied around Juliet's dagger.

I felt emptied. I felt ready.

I pulled away from Herm and stood up. He watched me in silence. I turned and walked to the other end of the van, replaced the dagger on the table. I took a simple white dress from the costume rail and carried it into the makeshift dressing room, drawing the curtain closed behind me.

The scene with Juliet's father and Paris was over. Invitations to a Capulet family party had been issued and, from the stage, I could hear Romeo and Benvolio preparing to gate-crash it.

The next scene would be mine.

The dress fitted perfectly. I kicked my other clothes to the side, pausing for a moment to look at them. Jeans and a sweat-stained, crusty ballgown, from another reality, another life. I smoothed the fabric down over my hips and surveyed my tear-streaked face in the mirror. I walked to the tiny, paint-spattered sink and bathed my eyes, until I no longer looked as though I had been crying.

I moved towards the entrance, Benvolio's voice growing louder as I approached. I stood beside the curtain. Felt the weight of it where it brushed my body.

"… *let there be weighed your lady's love against some other maid that I will show you shining at this feast …*"

I needed to think. I needed to be thinking Juliet's thoughts. But my mind was like a barrage of white noise, nothing in it but vibrations. My blood, thundering in my ears.

Romeo and Benvolio made their exit.

Dimly, beneath the roar in my head, I heard Juliet's mother enter with her nurse. There was a palpable change, a heightened tension.

"*Nurse, where's my daughter? Call her forth to me.*"

I could think of nothing, paralysed with fear. It occurred to me that there was something ironic in this lack of feeling, faced finally with something approaching high drama, and I considered whether I should laugh.

"*I bade her come. What, lamb. What, ladybird.*"

They were calling me. I realised that. But I was distracted by a feeling that there was something I was forgetting, something I had to do, or to say, it was as though there was something on the tip of my tongue that I knew but could not immediately access. Like a speech or a word.

Lines. My lines.

"*God forbid, where's this girl? What Juliet.*"

I stood at the entrance quivering, sending tiny, velvet currents through the heavy curtains.

Outside, there was a tense silence. I felt the silent hiss of anticipation, a shiver in the air. The banging pulse in my head was unbearable. I could hear my blood being pumped around my body. And yet my hands and feet would not move.

"*God forbid, where's this girl? What, Juliet.*"

The repeated line was an exact match of the first in cadence and tone. Only the tiniest edge in her voice betrayed the tension.

Every limb in my body felt sunk in concrete.

From the other side of the van Herm stood, very still, watching me. My breathing seemed very loud, even over the roaring in my ears, and the edges of everything had grown fibrous and fuzzy. And as I waited, frozen, poised at my entrance, I heard a new voice.

"How now? Who calls?"

In that moment, the roar rushed away and the scene outside continued without me.

Cat will sub for you.

What would happen if I never entered? If Cat, whoever she was, took my place entirely? If I froze on every cue, would they kill me at the curtain?

I lifted my head to look at Herm, and only in doing so, did I realise I had been hanging it in shame. He met my gaze, and I saw the understanding in it.

"Tell me, daughter Juliet, how stands your disposition to be married?"

"It is an honour that I dream not of."

She was good. I felt it even as I felt the preposterous stirrings of jealousy. Her Juliet was demure, obedient, but I could hear, beneath it, the subtle stirrings of the fire and spirit which would awaken later. I felt the edge of fear in Juliet's feelings for her mother, her love for her nurse so much less complicated. I knew that she sensed that this conversation was important, and yet was unable to quite grasp why.

A hand on my arm made me start and cry out. Herm.

"I have to enter soon," he said. "Will you be okay?"

It was a ridiculous question, in the circumstances, but I nodded, nonetheless.

She would not steal my moment. I would not fizzle out.

"What say you? Can you love the gentleman? Tonight you shall behold him at our feast."

I moved away from Herm, away from the entrance, felt his eyes follow me as I went back to the mirror. It was just that I had not been ready. I wasn't prepared. After all, this was a party. I would be meeting a man who might one day marry me. I could not do that without at least a little effort.

I picked up grease sticks, replaced them, rolled up lipsticks, shook my head.

It needed to be right.

I breathed. Refocused. Applied a single smear of a pale pink blusher stick, across my lips. A little Vaseline to wet my lashes and tame my brows.

I shook my hair, ran my fingers through it, and listened to the voice from the stage. The voice that was my mother, speaking only to me.

"So shall you share all that he doth possess, by having him, making yourself no less."

I felt a little flutter of excitement, though there was of course some nervousness. After all, I had barely met this man. How would I know how to act? What if I made some wrong move and appeared cheap or unsophisticated?

"No less? Nay bigger: women grow by men."

I heard the bawdy laughter in my nurse's voice and bile rose in my throat. I swallowed it.

"Speak briefly, can you like of Paris' love?"

I piled my hair up on top of my head, held it there. And I spoke Juliet's line with her, silently, into the mirror.

"I'll look to like, if looking liking move, but no more deep will I endart mine eye than your consent gives strength to make it fly."

I held my hair in place, and stabbed grips into it, one on each side. Immediately, strands came loose and curled a little into the damp of my neck.

Perfect.

I stood back a little and surveyed the effect. There was a flush on my cheeks. I looked sweet.

And scared.

When I emerged from the dressing room, Herm was poised at the entrance.

"Goodbye," I whispered.

He smiled. "See you on stage," he said.

He opened the door, stepped out, and was gone.

I followed him as far as the door and listened. Romeo, Benvolio and Mercutio were laughing and fooling, ready to gatecrash the party. Romeo was still hedging.

"Nay, gentle Romeo, we must have you dance."

Herm's voice. I could only recognise it because I knew it. Otherwise, in all aspects, he was Mercutio. He was feverish, nervy, burning too bright. He was perfect.

I would be perfect too.

"I dreamt a dream tonight."

"And so did I."

"Well, what was yours?"

"That dreamers often lie."

"Ha. In bed, asleep, while they do dream things true."

"O. Then I see Queen Mab hath been with you."

I felt my feet rehearsing, quietly, the steps of the dance. I would remember my lessons, my footwork and my manners. Should I dance with the gentleman my father had picked out for me? What would I say to him?

"… o'er ladies ' lips, who straight on kisses dream …"

Perhaps I wouldn't have to talk much. Would he expect something else? What *did* a gentlemen expect? I was excited. I had to admit that too. This final shiver on the edge of womanhood, with all the mystery it entailed. I smoothed my gown again and reminded myself, always to smile.

"... this is the hag, when maids lie on their backs, that presses them and learns them first to bear, making them women of good carriage ..."

Just an innocent young girl. A bit nervous. At a party.

"This is she – "

I opened the door and stepped out.

Scene Three

(A darkened field, lit by a faltering campfire. Figures are silhouetted on the grass, their backs to the fire, facing a grassy stage area. Nobody is focused on the performance. They are watching the door at stage right.

There is a hushed moment.

Then the door opens and a girl, rather timid, makes her entrance. She is, every inch, Juliet.

The audience bursts into rapturous applause.)

The first thing that struck me was the lighting. It was too dark. I registered a few scattered audience members and the fire behind them. I hesitated, but then something in me reassembled. In the empty space before me, I constructed for myself the goblets, glinting in the firelight, smelled, beneath the woodsmoke, sweetmeats and cake. I scanned the party for my mother.

Mercutio was like an animal, pacing, sweat on his forehead, eyes gleaming. I realised, in a rush, that there was no one else on the stage. I heard, as if from a very great distance, the sound of an audience applauding.

At first, I barely reacted. I was still hoping that my mother might sweep over, all jewels and carefully practised smiles, and mutter instructions under her breath. Beneath that I was wondering whether I might have been too hasty with my cue, or whether Romeo had missed his, and beyond all of that there was – there *must* have been – a faint stirring of understanding.

When Frederick stood up from among the audience, and walked across the stage towards me, I stumbled into a confused sort of curtsey. Frederick looked at me, then paused, turned to Mercutio, and laid a gentle hand on his shoulder. He twitched and whirled round, wild-eyed, like a sleepwalker awoken too soon.

"It's okay, Herm."

I stood up, wobbling out of my curtsey. I heard Mercutio say angrily, "I talk of dreams", but Frederick was already turning back to me, his dark eyes burned orange in the reflected campfire. He took my hand. His fingers were long and slim and smooth.

"Welcome," he said, "to my Company."

Time stopped. I didn't move or speak for what must have been seconds, but they were seconds which warped, stretching and looping around us. My head was empty.

At the end of a long, befuddled tunnel, I heard Mercutio say again, "I talk of dreams," and I saw that he had slowed his pacing. His voice was flat now, resigned, and as I watched he added, with a sense of great tiredness, "the children of an idle brain, begot of nothing but plain fantasy."

He sighed again, and in that moment, as though a child had wiped him from a giant blackboard, all of the various versions of Herm that I had known that evening faded into scattered, chalk-dust ghosts. And in their place stood a middle-aged, slightly balding man with a bland face and, beneath his jacket, the vague outline of a paunch.

"Congratulations," he said and smiled at me, and there was genuine warmth in his eyes. Then he sat down on the grass where he stood, rubbed his forehead and the bridge of his nose, produced a pair of spectacles from somewhere, and put them on. Someone very petite, pale and freckled, who looked about fourteen but with a fierce tension in her face which must have accumulated over decades, appeared next to him, and took his arm. She looked at me out of wide, feline eyes and I saw suspicion there, and a touch of judgement, before she dropped her gaze and turned it back to Herm.

My blood, which had been pumping in my ears, seemed suddenly to rush away. The scene, if it was a scene – reality was slipping from my grasp and I wasn't at all sure I wanted to welcome it back in – began to swim a little at the edges.

"Sit down," said Frederick, gesturing towards the campfire, where the 'audience' were now gathering, throwing logs onto the embers and warming themselves, their skin dyed amber in the light. "I'm sorry for the – er … *playacting*," his mouth twitched, "but we had to know. We had to know you were really ready. We can't take anyone who isn't sure."

Dazed, I allowed myself to be guided to the campfire, which turned out to be a large bronze firepit, tarnished and cauldron shaped. I sat down, cross-legged, on the grass, still fighting the conviction that I mustn't stain my dress, and I felt the slight damp of the early English summer seeping through the thin material.

My face was reflected in the firepit, concave and distorted in the curve of the bowl. I stared at it. It might have been my face, or it might have been someone else's.

"Just sit down here and take a moment. Catch your breath for a second."

A muscular woman with a striking, lined face and tattooed birds and dragons taking flight across her arms, was sitting next to me.

"Give her some space," she said to Frederick, and he moved away immediately.

"Thank you," I said, with a politeness reflex which still belonged partly to Juliet.

My heart was thumping, not fast, but loud and deep, as though beating a rhythm from an alternative world. I could almost see the pulse across my cleavage, my dull skin dancing in the firelight. Juliet would have been embarrassed. I crossed my arms across my chest.

"You're welcome," said the woman beside me and I felt her hand, heavy and reassuring, on my shoulder. Her voice was very precise and it surprised me. I had expected something gravelly, rough at the edges. She turned and shouted so loudly the fire faltered in the rush of it. "Would somebody please get this poor girl a bloody drink."

I sat dumbly, while everything blurred around me, and it seemed as though it was only the woman's hand on my shoulder that anchored me to the spongy ground.

In fact, in the end, it wasn't the campfire, the woman beside me, or even Frederick, that finally brought me back to myself. It was Herm.

Herm.

Do not think for a moment that it is not painful for me to tell this story.

He was sitting across from me, staring into the fire, his spectacles wonky and his eyes unfocused. Gone was my charismatic messenger, sharp and relentless, mixing me his toxic cocktails. Gone too was the quiet dignity of my companion backstage, the stoic hero awaiting death. And the feverish Shakespearian partygoer, delirious, lost to his own invention. In comparison now, he seemed utterly featureless. I could have passed him a hundred times in the street.

As I looked at him, I felt Juliet fade out and leave me. I let the damp soil make its claim on my dress, and I knew that Juliet's beautiful trajectory, of sex and poison and tragedy and death, was hers and not mine.

Somebody passed me a brandy bottle and I tipped it, quickly, to my lips.

"Weird feeling, isn't it?" said the woman beside me. I spluttered a little in reply, feeling the liquid prickle at my throat. "The comedown I mean. After the show. Worse than drugs if you ask me. It passes eventually. Everyone gets it."

I was unable to answer.

She looked at me, and nodded, as if confirming something, "Yes. The first time's always bad."

I was swimming in a haze so thick with questions that I didn't have the faculties to prise them apart. I took another gulp of the brandy and felt the alcohol warm and bite at my insides.

Frederick was suddenly behind me, bending, his hand held out towards me.

"Here," he said, "your key."

I placed the brandy bottle on the grass, where somebody immediately snatched it up. Frederick replaced it with a cool metal object.

"Your camper van key," he said, "it's the one over there."

I felt my eyes widen and he smiled. "We'll take you shopping tomorrow," he said, "for the rest."

"The rest …?"

"Clothes." It was not Frederick who answered, but the girl beside Herm across the fire. She was looking at me, her green eyes narrowed in her small, pale face. With a sort of exasperation, she added, as though this point was obvious, "Well you can't bring your old ones."

There was a pause. I stared at her. She stared back, as if daring me to disagree.

"Alright, alright, calm down over there," said the woman next me. "Give the girl a break. She's spent." She gestured across the fire at Herm, "So's he. Give it a rest for five minutes."

The words were as affectionate as they were blunt, but

there was warning in them, and I saw a quick, sudden flare in the other girl's eyes, before she turned back to Herm.

"He gets it bad," said the woman with the tattoos, "Herm I mean – I'm Emily by the way – he's always done in after he's been out recruiting." She met my eyes then, frank, but without judgement. "It's a lot of effort."

I looked at Herm, the new Herm, with the spectacles and the thinning hairline, who was sitting opposite me, eating something now, out of a plastic carton. He did look exhausted. Next to him, the pale girl was watchful and quiet. She seemed to look at everyone with the same sense of guarded aggression, as though poised for a fight. Later I would learn it was her habitual expression. I would never learn what sort of horror had created it. There were unspoken rules in the Company. There were things you didn't ask.

On the other side of Herm was a young man with a face and physique so strikingly beautiful that even in the dim light of the fire, he genuinely made me catch my breath. I remembered, dimly, that he had smiled at me earlier, had offered me his hand and introduced himself as 'Colm' with a sort of timid formality, shortly after I had sat down. He was talking now, quietly, to Herm, his skin gleaming darkly in the coppery light.

"Recruiting is tough. They were preparing for ages." Emily looked at me sideways. "Rehearsing, I suppose you'd call it."

The brandy bottle appeared again at my side. I took it.

"Rehearsing?"

She nodded. "They've got to get it right."

I thought of Herm's entrance at the party, his apprehension backstage. I thought of the dagger. The blood on my finger. A chill ran through me, and I took a needy swig of brandy.

Yes. They would have to get it right.

"How long does it take? The … rehearsal?"

She shrugged and slapped my hand from the brandy bottle, so that she could reach across me and take it for herself. It was as if we had been bosom friends for years.

"It depends. On who it is and what they need." She swigged straight out of the bottle, coughed and wiped her eyes. "Shit, that's foul. I forgot how bad it was. Like bloody battery acid. Fuck."

I waited while she recovered herself, wondering if the real me was floating somewhere, looking down at these proceedings and thinking about the weather, or what to have for lunch.

"Bleurgh. Yeah. Anyway. It depends on when you count it from as well. If you start from when Frederick starts to stake you out it can take years. Well, we think it can. He doesn't tell us. But we all remember him from somewhere." She stabbed her finger at the younger man across the campfire. "Colm reckons he was four." She snorted. "Bless him. It's probably bollocks."

I had seen a man in a book shop once, watching me, when I was fourteen and my father was busy paying for textbooks. I was sliding a fantasy romance thriller into my pocket, but I lost my nerve. There was a man in a club at university who met my eye as I snorted white lines of nothingness, recklessly and openly on a sticky side table. A figure in the audience, in countless productions, slipping out of the theatre under cover of the applause.

Could they all have been Frederick?

The more I considered it, the more moments I thought of, when he may or may not have been there in the background. By the end, I had painted him into the shadows, the corners, the backs of rooms, the silence of my father's back garden at night. And the more I painted, the less clear was the picture.

None of us ever knew exactly how long Frederick had been watching us. He was there enough to *know*. But that was it. The rest of it we fabricated.

That is what Frederick is like. He's part man, part fantasy. He gathers your wild imaginings about him, wraps them around himself like a garment. Until eventually he is a figure made mostly of the mystery you endowed him with yourself.

And you don't try to unravel it. Because you're afraid that all you'd have left is a pair of brown eyes and a limp. And by that point, you've already given him so much.

"Most of the stuff we do is old," said Emily, producing a packet of hoop-shaped crisps from somewhere in the pockets of her trousers. She opened it, threw one into her open mouth, offered me the packet, shrugged when I shook my head, and began to crunch. "You know, out of copyright. Too much hassle to keep applying for rights and too risky to perform stuff without them." She glanced at me, sideways. "No point in attracting unnecessary attention, if you get what I mean. It gets a bit hackneyed after a while, and so Frederick writes a lot of it himself. Something with scope. You know, a bit of action."

Action.

It covered a myriad of things. Fighting? Drug use? Drunkenness? Sex?

And death?

But surely that wasn't frequent. After all, I told myself, it was a tiny company, with only five members. Six. I felt the cold metal camper van key in my hand.

Still, there weren't a lot of people to spare.

Unless the Company had once been larger.

Emily delved noisily into the bottom of her packet. "Bastards are definitely making these smaller. I swear most of it's air now. Even the bloody *crisps* have a hole in them. They're too good though." She tilted her head back and shook the last few hoops into her mouth, with a heady, effortless sensuality. "Yeah. Frederick's not a bad writer. But you never forget that first one."

"So …" I was hesitant, but growing braver, something about her casual frankness lending me strength. "Do you always do this? When somebody joins?"

She paused in her crunching and looked at me, surprised. "Well, yes," she said, as though it was obvious, "As Frederick says, you've got to be sure. He doesn't take anyone who isn't ready. He doesn't take anyone who doesn't need it somehow."

I looked at Frederick, across the campfire. He looked up, as if sensing it, to meet my gaze, and I saw a flicker of something I couldn't quite place in his eyes. I held his gaze longer than was strictly polite. I looked straight into those dark eyes, glowing in their borrowed firelight. I saw the surprise in his face, and watched it turn to intrigue.

The fire crackled, and by some unspoken rule or some instinct, we both looked away.

When I glanced up again, he was gone.

"But you normally have audiences, don't you?" I asked. "I mean, aren't you worried they'll do something? Intervene or report you or call the police?"

Emily looked across the campfire, met the eye of the small girl still sitting beside Herm. They grinned at each other,

"Puck's legacy", they said in unison.

Emily laughed.

"That's what we call it," she said. "I mean, obviously we're careful, we move on fast if we have to, and don't do too many long runs, but usually, you know, it's like that speech of Puck's in '*A Midsummer Night's Dream*'."

"*If we shadows have offended, think but this, and all is mended,*" the pale girl joined in, waving her hand like a conductor as she recited the words. Everyone was listening now, smiling and nodding. "*That you have but slumber'd here ...*"

Emily grinned, but cut her off. "Basically," she said, "it's like there's a contract with the audience. If something in the play upsets them, they're allowed to just assume it's not real. They want it as realistic as possible, but they don't want to be responsible for it. We call it Puck's legacy. No one ever leaves a play and wonders whether the injuries actually happened. They leave the play wondering where exactly the actors got all that really great fake blood."

I laughed. The sound was high and thin beneath the crackle of the fire.

Conversation opened up after that, everyone reminiscing about their first times. They had all had a variation on my experience, although with a different play, and as they sat up into the night, swapping stories in which they had expected to die, it seemed as though we were only a bunch of teenagers, discussing our sex lives.

Colm and Emily had been recruited together as Iago and Desdemona in *Othello*, though they did not know each other at the time.

"That was some bit of theatre," said Herm, smiling.

"You slept for a week after that one," replied the girl with the green eyes, and there was love in her voice, and accusation.

"Colm was Iago?" I said, confused. "But Iago doesn't die. I thought that was the whole thing."

"Ha. Spare a thought for me," said Emily, "Othello smothers Desdemona with a cushion. I was bricking it."

"Spoilers," said Herm, laughing.

But Colm, across the firelight, was sombre.

"Sometimes," he said, and his voice was deep and, surprisingly, tinged with a very slight Welsh lilt. "It is just as bad to bring about the death of somebody else."

"Why?" said the pale girl sharply, "Were you thinking he'd be Othello just because he's black?"

"No …" I stammered a little, "No, it wasn't that, it was just the death thing, I—"

"Yeah right."

"That's enough now." Colm's voice was soft, but there was a flush on his face. He gave a little, mirthless, half-laugh and looked down immediately at his hands. "I just … I don't need a bunch of white people discussing my ethnicity."

There was a silence.

"Good on you," said Emily quietly.

"I was Julius Caesar," said Herm, "I actually got into it quite quickly – didn't even take me all that long in the dressing room. I thought, I may as well have a bit of power and get to stride about a bit before all my friends kill me." His tone was light, but I saw his fingers reach for the girl's and entwine themselves. I watched her face lose a little of its tension. Still, she leaned away from him, as if to prove her independence, and met my eyes.

I looked away.

"I was Faustus," she said, "I was the first." She laughed, tightly, "I made my pact with the devil. But I didn't go to hell, I left hell and came here."

I met her eyes then. She was staring straight at me, keen-eyed and fierce. In the periphery of my vision, I could see Colm shifting, Herm watchful, but unreadable. As the silence continued, and I held her gaze, I felt the slightest ripple of something between us. A burgeoning respect.

"How did you play him?" I asked her. "Faustus, I mean?"

I watched her relax, her eyes soften.

"Hungry," she said. "Desperate."

I nodded and I felt the gathering tension flicker and disappear with the smoke.

Beside me, Emily was holding her empty crisp packet to the heat of the fire. I watched, we all did, as she angled it carefully, just near enough to the flames for the packet to melt, but not enough to set it alight. As she turned it in the heat, the edges began to curl, and the lurid lettering to shrink.

"We need to name you," the pale girl said, suddenly. She turned to the others. "We need to name her." Again, that hint of accusation.

"Good point," said Herm and may have been about to say something more, but he was cut off by Colm, who had moved beside me the moment the naming was mentioned.

"She is right," he said to me, "We always give a name. You have to have a new name for the Company. It's like a rule." He flushed again. "Only, not really. More like a …" He hunted around for the words, and I looked at him, searching for fear in his face, for some threat that might be hanging over him, some cult ideology to make him compliant. "An escape," he said. "… Like witness protection." And I looked and found no trace of fear, only earnestness.

"Everyone gets a new name for the Company," said Emily, "it's just sensible. Gives you a new identity, doesn't make us easily traceable, helps you forget. For those of us who have something they need to forget." Her gaze travelled over the assembled people, resting just a little longer on Colm, and the girl next to Herm.

"There's usually a logic to it," said Herm, sounding practical, as though he was explaining how a washing machine worked, or outlining a bus timetable. I felt a sudden thrill. How long would it be before I used either of those again?

"Yeah," said Emily, "so I'm Emily, because my play was Othello. You know, Emilia is the wife of Iago."

I was a little confused. "Not Desdemona?"

"Ha." Emily snorted. "Seriously? Desdemona? Can you even imagine that? No way. At least Emilia's got some guts. And anyway, who the fuck's called *Desdemona*?"

I laughed with the others and in that sound a part of me broke off and fell away, and I felt light without it. Like a cinder in the air.

"So who the fuck's called Herm?" I said and I heard my voice daring and bolder than I had been before. I felt a hiss of danger and I grabbed it and pulled it close to me.

Herm smiled. "I had another name," he said, "before. But no one remembers it. And then I started to go out recruiting with Frederick and doing a lot of the stuff to get the audiences in, you know, in the towns, drumming up gossip. So, everyone started to call me Hermes – like the messenger. And then it stuck at Herm."

"He's amazing," said Emily, pulling the crisp packet away from the fire to examine it. She touched her finger to the edge of the packet, hissed at the heat, grinned a little and put her finger back. "Ah. It's gone cold now. Pathetic. Yeah – I reckon he changes more than any of us. When he's acting. That's why Frederick takes him recruiting. You wouldn't know him twice."

"Herm is very talented," said Colm, smiling at his colleague from where he had resumed his position across the fire. There was always a hint of formality in his words, a touch of shyness which I sensed had not and would not diminish, however long he'd been with the Company.

"I agree," I said, sounding grave and a little over formal myself.

There was a short pause. Emily held the crisp packet over

the heat again. We watched as the edges shrivelled and melted.

"And Colm?" I said. I wasn't sure whether I was trying to put off my own naming, the concept of which sent a shiver of unease and excitement through me, or to understand theirs.

"Colm means peace," said Emily, smiling at Colm over the distorted crisp packet. I saw the flush rise again in Colm's skin, like a flicker of flame. Muscles twitched on his arms. He looked down at the ground through thick, black lashes.

"It means Dove. It's Irish. Frederick named me. But it's not a character."

"Neither is mine," said the petite, fierce girl at once, and I saw, for the first time, the loyalty behind the challenge in her voice.

"Colm didn't need to be named after a character," said Herm, "it was enough for him to be named after himself. 'Peace' works perfectly."

"I'm Thea," said the girl. "First few letters of 'theatre'. I was the first."

It was the second time she'd told me that she was the first member of the Company. I looked, instinctively, round at the other faces, expecting to catch some hint of eye rolling, an indication that this was an obsession of hers, that they'd heard it all before. I saw nothing. This was a company who hung together. They moved as a body. I looked away again, ashamed.

"But everybody calls her Cat," said Herm, lovingly, "because she looks like one."

He was right. The wide green eyes slanted a little at the ends. She had lithe, pale limbs, and a certain way of moving, quick and darting, yet somehow graceful.

"Scratches like one too," said Emily, under her breath, but loud enough to have been intended for everyone, then laughed at her own joke. Colm smiled, but he was eyeing Cat. Herm was chuckling, squeezing her shoulders. And, when I dared to look at her, I saw that Cat was grinning too, and there was pride in the grin, though I thought I saw a quick flash of uncertainty in those sharp, green eyes.

"Are we naming this girl or what?" demanded Emily. "Only I don't know about you lot, but I'm knackered."

Four pairs of eyes turned to look at me, and I felt myself flush, staring at the crisp packet, now blackened and barely the width of Emily's thumb. She brought it back towards her, briefly, as though I had drawn her attention to it, then shrugged and flicked it into the fire. It disappeared.

"Juliet?" said Colm.

"No. Too obvious. Anyway, she doesn't look like a Juliet."

"Leah?" suggested Herm, "like Julia. So, it's not Juliet but it's related?"

"Nah. That's not quite right."

"I agree – unless we spelled it L I A?"

"What possible difference would that make?"

"I dunno. Just seems better, somehow."

"What about Willa? As in Shakespeare?"

"Not bad … no though."

"I don't think Willa. How about Mia? From Romeo?"

"I think," said Emily, snorting, "you're just clutching at straws now."

I sat, while they discussed me, and I felt my whole body flushed and blushing and very much alive. I thought of cults and horror stories, people forced to give up their identity and assume a new one. But I wanted a new life, and I was willing, too willing, to dispose of the old.

"Mabel? From Queen Mab?"

"Ooooh, clever … sounds a bit old though."

"Raj? As in Romeo And Juliet?"

"Raj? Are you serious? *Raj?*"

A wave of laughter.

"Verona – Vera?"

"I still can't believe you said 'Raj'."

And so, it continued, Cat's eyes and nostrils flaring dangerously, but calming just in time, whenever she made a suggestion that wasn't taken up. Emily poking fun at the more unlikely suggestions and throwing in a couple of her own for good measure.

The newness of the situation made me nervous. I wondered if naming new members was always this difficult. Did I just not fit in? How long had it taken the others? Eventually, the flow of suggestions faltered, and everyone fell silent, staring into the fire or, unnervingly, at my face as they sought inspiration.

"Oh well," I said, shrugging with painful nonchalance, "*what's in a name*, eh?"

"Ooh, good idea." Emily was suddenly alight with enthusiasm. Around the fire, I could see everyone nodding and smiling. Befuddled and still a little caught up in self-doubt, I didn't understand what I had said that was so helpful until Colm finished the quote.

"What's in a name? That which we call a rose, by any other word would smell as sweet."

He spoke the words with a shy, slightly forced, cadence, like a child reading poetry. I wondered if his acting would be as impressive as the others'.

"So. Rose then." said Emily. "What do we think?"

There was a general swell of approval, until someone said, "Is that a bit twee? Should we adapt it a bit, maybe Roz or Rosalie?"

"Rose is perfect."

I looked up, startled. Frederick had reappeared, and was

standing, tall and slim, in the shadowy light, looking at me with that strange half-smile he had, as though the other side of his mouth was shielding some other, different emotion. I had no idea how long he'd been there.

And so, I became Rose.

We drank again, to celebrate my naming, and gradually people began to leave for bed, Emily and Colm first, and then Herm and Cat. Frederick had disappeared.

Herm, who still looked tired, but seemed to have recovered somewhat, ruffled my hair on the way past.

"Good playacting tonight," he said, and grinned.

I flushed. "Thanks," I said, and then, because I couldn't help it, "you did *say* you did everything for real."

"We do." He'd caught the shade of sullenness in my voice. Despite all the stories I had heard this evening, of everyone else's first performances, I still had not quite shaken the vague notion that they were somehow laughing at me, that my 'initiation' as they called it, had only been some sly trick, a matter of entertainment.

"Put it this way," he said, "there are a lot of weapons in that van. Ever heard of Chekhov's Law?"

If a pistol appears on the wall in Act One, it must be fired in the final Act.

A chill flashed through me, but he grinned again and strode away. I couldn't be sure whether or not he was joking.

I sat for hours by the campfire that night, watching the approaching dawn and listening to that very human sound of sleeping, which carries in the air at night. I held the key to my new camper van in my hand, sweating metallically into my palm. I couldn't quite imagine myself climbing the steps to it, plumping the pillows, closing the door. My father's presence seemed to hang in the shadows.

"Can't sleep?"

I jumped.

Frederick stood behind me. He was still fully clothed, silhouetted in his long coat. Perhaps he never slept. It seemed faintly possible that he might be some kind of vampire. He was acting even when he wasn't. I wondered if he knew that, or if it had become so much part of him now that he no longer knew what he had once been beneath it. I wondered if, eventually, that would happen to me.

"I don't know," I said, "I haven't really tried yet."

He smiled, but he hadn't yet sat down. Some instinct in me held my ground, and I resisted the temptation to feel intimidated, or to stand up to greet him, and instead tipped my head back casually, to look at him.

I waited for him to sit down.

He didn't.

There was a long pause. I turned my gaze, though with some difficulty, back to the fire.

We stared at the flames in silence.

"May I sit down?" he asked.

I shrugged. "If you like."

He smiled. I grinned. He sat down.

We stayed there for some time in companionable silence, something sparking in the air between us, an energy which had nothing to do with the fire.

"Frederick?"

"Yes?"

"What would you have done?"

"If what?"

"If I'd done it. If I'd used the knife."

There was a pause. He looked confused.

"If you'd used the knife?"

"Yes. If I'd used the knife. What if I'd attacked Herm? Or

killed myself in your camper van?"

He shrugged, a lazy stretching of his limbs.

"Then you would have attacked Herm. Or killed yourself in my camper van."

There was a long silence.

"Really? You didn't have a plan B?"

He stood up, as if to leave, but paused and looked at me. I felt my pulse quicken, but his face was unreadable.

"We don't need a plan B," he said. "Nobody ever makes that choice."

Act Two

"Within the infant rind of this weak flower
Poison hath residence and medicine power:
For this, being smelt, with that part cheers each part,
Being tasted, slays all senses with the heart.
Two such opposed kings encamp them still
In men as well as herbs."

Friar Lawrence
William Shakespeare, *Romeo and Juliet*

Scene One

(A field. A campfire. A van.)

Humans shed identities like skin cells. From context to context, year to year, we are all, continuously, subtly adjusting ourselves. Judge me if you like, but I did not pause to be subtle. I shrugged off my skin, left it there whole, papery and ghostlike, blowing feebly in the wind on the grass of that field. I trampled it into the mud as I walked, and I tried very hard not to look back at it. For those first few weeks though, it still pursued me, and it accused me with my mother's eyes. I would wake up sweating in the middle of the night, certain that I had heard a car pulling up outside my van. My father in the darkness, come to bring me home. As I lay there listening to the silence, the relief I felt was always tinged with sadness.

My debut performance would be a double bill of two one-act plays, both of which I would star in. Frederick announced it by the brittle ashes of the campfire in the morning, and then Herm took me shopping. I dyed my hair a brighter colour, and took to wearing flimsy ballet pumps or, when I could get away with it, bare feet. I bought long, flowing skirts and blouses, and decorated the inside of my modern campervan like an old-fashioned Romany gypsy wagon. Or the way I imagined one might be. If it occurred to me that this in itself was an act, it didn't bother me.

By the time Herm drove me back to the university a few days later, to collect my belongings and provide my excuses, I had at least three identities already established, and no time to consider the implications.

I wrote to the company who had offered me a job, to tell them very politely that I had been offered another opportunity and would regrettably be unable to take up the role.

I returned to my university lodgings and packed up the clothes, kitchen implements and books that had made up my life. I would give them to Herm later, for him to dispose of.

I telephoned my father.

He sounded gruff and business-like.

"What do you want?" he said, "It's eleven in the morning."

I felt my fingers tighten around the phone. I had been tortured by the prospect of this phone call, struck with awful pangs of guilt, stabbing at the depths of my stomach. Now I wanted to hang up on him and walk away.

"I just … it's nothing actually, I …"

I caught Herm's eye. He had been sitting in the corner of the room, occupying himself politely by flicking through one of my textbooks, but now he lifted his gaze and shook his head.

I cleared my throat.

"I'm joining a theatre company."

There was a long pause.

"It's a travelling theatre company. It's very well thought of … I mean …" I searched my brain frantically for the right phrase to fill the silence. "… It's a marvellous opportunity." My voice cracked on the last word.

My father seemed to be waiting for me to explain myself further, or perhaps to apologise. I couldn't speak. Eventually he sighed.

"I see. And what about your job?"

My job. Already mine. Mapped out and bagged and delivered. Like me.

"I didn't … I didn't take it, Dad."

I never called him Dad.

"You didn't take it." It was a flat statement, not a question. I whispered. "No."

This time the silence was so interminable I thought he might have left the phone. Finally, he said, very quietly,

"Your mother would be disappointed. I gave up a lot to get you that job. They remember your mother, you know. She worked there when she was—"

"I know, I *know*. She worked there. They loved her. She died because of me." I heard the sharpness in my voice too late. My heart started to race. On the other end of the line, he sucked in breath.

"I'm sorry." I said, "I …"

In the back of my mind, I saw myself catapulting up from my start position, race number pinned to my chest, running through fields and forests and footpaths, away from him.

A muscle began twitching compulsively in my thigh. I smoothed my skirt down over it, gripped my leg, squeezed hard.

"I have done so much for you." He was speaking calmly and clearly, every word precise and clipped. I reminded myself shakily of the four-hour drive it would take for him to reach me. "I have done everything, *everything* she would have done. You were all she ever thought of. Right from the moment she knew she was carrying you. Right until her final breath."

"Yes." I said. There didn't seem any other appropriate response.

"And you're joining the circus?"

"A travelling theatre company."

"Same difference."

In the corner, Herm raised his eyebrows. I turned down the volume on the phone.

"Do you really think that's what she would have wanted for you?"

"Wouldn't she … would she maybe have wanted me to be happy?"

The minute I had said it I wanted to snatch it back. It was too large a question and it had been too long unasked. But he only laughed.

"Oh come on. You can't be that naïve. Happiness doesn't come from chasing fluffy bunnies in meadows, my girl. It's about hard work. Hard graft and discipline to get what you want. It's what I did, it's what your mother did, it's what every other sensible person in this world does."

"I'm sorry," I said, "I have to go now."

I threw the phone hard at Herm and it hit him in the chest. I burst into tears. Herm looked at me quietly for a moment, then retrieved the broken phone from the floor, opened the back and extracted the sim card. He handed me a pair of scissors, squeezed my shoulder, and walked away.

I cut my sim card into tiny pieces and threw away my phone. I emptied my bank accounts and gave my passport to Herm, who sealed it into a padded, brown envelope, and labelled it '*Rose*'.

I made sure I 'bumped into' as many of my university friends as possible, and, on Herm's advice, I told them the nearest thing I could to the truth. That I had joined a theatre company, that I would keep in touch, if I could, but that we would be on the move, or in places with poor signal, so I couldn't guarantee it. When pressed for a name for the company, I provided something bland and subtly different to each person I spoke to. I did not deviate once from my script.

Yes, I agreed with everyone, it was, indeed, very exciting.

We left the campus within three hours, well before my father could possibly have reached it. I still don't know whether he ever bothered. Or whether I would have wanted him to.

There was no time for reflection when we got back. There was never any induction period. The only thing made clear to me was the manner in which I should disappear. The excuses I would make to friends and relatives, the carefully staged exit in plain sight.

"We don't," said Frederick, "want anyone worrying about you."

Or making missing person reports.

Even the 'training' I did receive, which was in fighting – fencing mostly, as that required skill in addition to instinct – was entirely unstructured. People would attack me without warning. I would be eating, or talking, or half-undressed, and find myself ambushed. And aside from Colm, who was a little gentler, they did not hold back. The only allowance anybody made was that the swords or daggers, if they used them, were the handful of blunted stage versions we kept backstage in case of inspection. At least they were to begin with.

"For now," said Frederick, with that maddening half-smile, and I knew that when the weapons were switched, I would not be warned beforehand.

I was covered in bruises, sore and sometimes bloodied, but I learned either to keep a weapon near me, or to improvise with whatever came to hand. I became more alert, learned to balance my body weight. I fought desperately at first, and then with more awareness, gradually absorbing moves and tactics. The bruises healed and my muscles tautened.

For the first time in my life, I felt truly happy. I gained freckles and colour from all the time spent outside, and I always sat too close to the fire. I can still see the gleam of the firelight on the sweat of my bare thighs, my skirt hitched up, laughter and chatter around me. I can smell the woodsmoke mingled with Cat's strong coffee, Emily's herbal cigarettes. I can feel the damp grass between my toes, the sting of sparks on my skin, the brandy burning my throat.

There are days when I think I could go back there tomorrow. There are nights when I dream I never left. And I wake up shaking.

Once I had the leisure to investigate it properly, I learned that the entirety of Frederick's van had been remodelled so that the front could be removed to create a stage. It fascinated me to think that, locked inside that van, on that first, terrifying evening, I had always been inhabiting a set. The true production had not been my eventual entrance as Juliet, but my panicked journey to reach it, a virtuoso performance without an audience.

We had several portable theatrical lights on tripods, a handful of heavy ceiling spotlights and a couple of speakers, rigged up with timers for musical cues. That was the sole extent of our setup. But once the backstage paraphernalia was cleared, the floor swept, and the appropriate backdrop slid into place, that van could became anything we wanted it to be. And yet, through all the performances we played out on it, in the heart of all the characters I inhabited, there would always be a core, a kernel within me, which still remembered Juliet. And whenever we used the 'forest' backdrop, I felt once again the cold fear of that evening, and the tangled limbs of those insidious trees seemed to reach out and claw at me.

There were three others. There was an 'interior' scene, deliberately non-committal as to time or place, with brick walls and hanging frames, into which Colm, who I learned had created the backdrops in the first place, would paint a mirror, or a portrait, or a window, depending on the demand. He showed me all of them one afternoon.

"They're not very good," he said.

They were astounding.

Despite being intentionally bland, so that they could be manipulated to suit the production, something about those backdrops was deeply unsettling. Every one of them managed to create an effect that went beyond a simple indication of place. They evoked an atmosphere, they insinuated something.

Aside from the 'interior' and the 'forest', there was an 'institution' version, with white walls and noticeboards. It could represent anything from prison to hospital to orphanage, and it gave me a cold feeling in the pit of my abdomen whenever I looked at it.

There was a 'street' scene – with walls and moss and, depending on the show, graffiti or streetlamps. When I touched it, I expected to scratch my palms on rough bricks, to snag my fingers in old chewing gum, smear myself with the ashes of stubbed-out cigarettes.

In front of those backdrops and under those lights, we played out what are probably the greatest moments of my life. A heady stream of alternate realities and rotating scenery, punctuated by crumpled theatrical flyers, discarded identities evaporating in the fire.

Double Bill:
'Porcelain and Pink' and
'If I do'

I had waited, after Frederick announced the plays, for somebody to announce rehearsals. At first, I assumed the delay was an uncharacteristically merciful gesture to help ease me in, that they were concentrating on my absorption as part of the Company, my training. I waited for the scripts.

The first piece, *Porcelain and Pink,* was a lesser-known play by Scott Fitzgerald. I would play 'Julie' and would spend the entire performance sitting in a bathtub, from which I would carry out a farcical conversation with my neurotic sister's innocent suitor, in the belief that he was talking to her, through a small high window from which he could not see the bathtub.

In our case, the play's appeal would revolve less around the mistaken identity, than the fact that the girl in the bathtub, of whom the audience could only see head and shoulders, might or might not be naked. It would end with my sister (Cat) rushing in, seeing her lover's head at the window, and fainting in alarm, causing him to leave the window to rush in and rescue her.

Which of course would leave 'Julie' with no choice but to exit the bathtub. This much I knew from Frederick's impassioned outline (as much a performance as the show would be) around the ashes of the campfire that first morning.

Without the script, I had no idea whether the play ended there, though I suspected a modest dimming of the lights, at least in the original version. But I was under no illusions about the way this company would stage it.

The second play would be written by Frederick and as time wore on and the script did not materialise, I assumed perhaps it wasn't finished.

I was told it would be a little more serious in genre, about a girl named Jenny, trapped by her own obsession with appearances, having second thoughts on the night before her much reported-upon celebrity wedding.

She would bid goodnight to her fiancé, then become increasingly drunk as she confided in her disapproving mother-in-law. It would end with her abrupt exit to throw up offstage.

I noted, at the time, how calculated were Frederick's choice of plays, allowing me a little exhibitionism and a little risk. The significance of the themes, being naked and vulnerable, but still playing a game, and the fear and wonder associated with making a long-term commitment, were not lost on me either.

I was not stupid, you can judge me as you like, but I was never stupid, and I was never blind. I only chose to look away. I understood that this company, of all companies, would not approach rehearsal in the ordinary way. But I did expect *something*.

Instead, the plays were never openly mentioned. Emily, who would play my mother-in-law in the second play, took to sitting up with me on the steps of her caravan, drinking into the early hours of the morning, always pressing me to have another, to have just one more, to follow it up with a chaser. I stumbled into bed as the light came up each morning, my head already banging, and I was frequently sick. Emily, somehow, never was.

There was a period in which there was apparently some sort of repair needed to the interior of my van, though no one ever quite explained what it was, and Frederick instructed me to move in with Cat, who would play my sister in the first play. It would have seemed far more logical that I move in with Emily, and I found Cat an irritating, obtuse companion, who seemed to have become, in addition to her natural tension, overly correct, stiff, and patronising.

Colm, my 'suitor' in the second play, started to invite me out for walks with him, talking to me with a diffidence imbued with a new, unsettling, sense of preoccupation, always straightening his clothes and flexing his muscles, scanning the trees for paparazzi. For which of course Frederick, as the only person among us allowed access to photographic equipment, obliged.

By the time we opened, I would have developed a mutual sibling exasperation with Cat for the first play, *Porcelain and Pink*, plus a paranoia about cameras. I knew Emily would have an exact knowledge of how much alcohol it would take to achieve the desired effect on me by the finale of *If I Do* and I'd have enough immunity to cheap white wine to be able to reliably deliver my script. If I ever had one.

I knew what they were doing, and I played along, but, coming before I had really established who any of them were when they weren't in character, and juggling several half-formed identities of my own, it was probably the most brutal thing they did to me. Worse even, than the sudden switch of the fencing weapons, sprung on me partway through a drinking session with Emily, when I could barely see.

I started having terrified, sweaty dreams about walking out on stage without knowing my lines, made worse by the alcohol burning in my veins and the panicked sense of guilt I always felt in the morning for breaking character in my sleep.

I spent the mornings applying make-up to cover my hangover in front of Frederick's ubiquitous camera, the afternoons in stilted conversation with Colm.

The evenings on Emily's steps were a relief, her mother-in-law character was not as disapproving as she appeared, and I think she allowed a little of Emily through in addition, a measure of sympathy. I relaxed with Emily even without the wine and, beneath our inhabiting of our respective roles, grew a carefully unacknowledged friendship.

Until, inevitably, each evening I reached the point of no return and stumbled back to the van to find Cat waiting, arms folded, to lecture me again about my irresponsible drinking.

Herm had already been into the nearest town to drum up excitement about the show. He would give out flyers, spread rumours, and use his charismatic magic to weave from hurried passers-by a loyal audience in thrall to him. Time after time, town after town, he always managed to bring them to our stage.

A week before the opening night, I tumbled through the door of the van in the early morning to find Cat asleep. And two innocuous A4 ring-bound scripts neatly stacked on the table.

I fell on them of course. I knew by then I could not rehearse them out loud, and it would be out of the question to ask anyone to test me. I learned them hungrily, sinking them into the characters which, for weeks, I had already been living. I read and re-read them, focused on Frederick's play in the early mornings, when the alcohol was still fresh in my veins, Fitzgerald's while I showered or when Cat had annoyed me.

I was still a little new, a little hungover from the customs of traditional theatre. But, over time, I would grow to perfect this as the others had, the ability to learn lines almost unconsciously, so that on the night that we spoke them for real, we felt them as sudden impulses, occurring to us only in that moment.

"Have another one," urged Emily.

"You need to grow up and take responsibility for your actions" said Cat, as I fell, head spinning, fully clothed, into bed.

"Be careful," warned Colm as I stumbled on a tree root, Frederick's camera flashing in the shadows. "People are watching. You can't show me up."

"I've come to take Cat out," said Herm, peering through the window of my van while I was trying to get dressed. "Is she there?"

"Wow. I've got a great one here." said Frederick to an imaginary newspaper boss as he gazed at the shot he had just taken of me, hunched over, sobbing, throwing up despairingly into the ditch.

By the night of the performances, I didn't walk out on stage so much as gather all the disparate parts of myself and explode with them onto it.

Play One - Porcelain and Pink

(Interior backdrop. A girl sits in a bathtub.)

I sat there, submerged in cooling bubbles, my exposed skin tingling in the evening air. My nudity, under the gaze of the audience, was all the more thrilling because I knew they could not see it, and that they would not believe it. It was my secret.

I tripped through the dialogue, eager for mischief, mocking and trouble-making, ignoring Cat's impatience, and playing Herm's staid romanticism against him. I had goosepimples, which had nothing to do with the chill, and a sense of heady, building excitement. I openly flirted with the audience, and they giggled back at me from their camping chairs on the grass. They were as flirtatious with me as I was with them.

It was a game. And I was winning.

When, finally, the penultimate moment of the performance arrived, and Cat appeared and duly fainted, leaving me, as Julie, with the necessity to emerge, at last, from the tub, I shivered, a mingled fear and joy running through me like icy fire. I placed my hands on the side of the tub and there was a moment of hesitation born equally from a genuine last-minute panic, and an actor's instinct to prolong the most significant moment.

The towel I was supposed to wrap around me when I made my exit, was very much smaller than I had expected. I was unsure whether this was because Cat, whose trust I knew I had not yet wholly earned, had chosen to test me, or if it was only Frederick's glint-eyed manipulation of the props, providing me with an excuse. Certainly, nobody had dimmed the lights.

Either way, it was a challenge I rose to. I pushed myself up with my hands and stood, for a moment, glittering and dripping, while the audience gasped, before I stepped out, picked up the tiny towel and dithered with it for a moment, as if unable to decide which part of me I should use it to cover. I felt the rebellious pull of Julie, and I grinned, shrugged, dropped it – and ran.

(Blackout)

I sprinted, enveloped in darkness, out of the same van whose exit I had so tentatively emerged from once before, and around the back. There I whooped and skipped, barefoot and damp in the grass. I was silver plated in the moonlight, the rustling fields before me, the van behind, and beyond that, an audience, laughing and cheering in fervent applause.

Adrenaline lifted me and, just for a moment, I flew.

Play Two - If I Do

(Interior backdrop. Bright lights. Stern-looking portraits frown from the walls. 'Jenny' pours herself her sixth generous glass of white wine. Her hands shake a little.)

"I think maybe you should stop drinking. You need your beauty sleep for tomorrow." Emily's voice was careful, overly cheerful, her character trying in vain to undo all the terrible confidences I had divulged on-stage throughout the evening. I swung round, dousing myself in wine and immediately turning back to top up my glass.

"Pah. Tomorrow. I *am* beautiful."

There was a pause, and in it I heard suddenly the truth of that line. And its curse.

"I am a star. In the sky..."

My voice wobbled, and I felt my throat close, and my eyes burn. I swallowed and felt my face crumple, mascara smudged and blurry. I began to cry.

"… and Jeremy's the moon …"

I did not get to celebrate that performance. I spent the night hunched over a plastic washing up bowl, vomiting acid splatters of bile and alcohol, while all the scarves, tassels and dreamcatchers which hung from the roof and the surfaces of my van (now mysteriously repaired) shuddered with me.

The curtain call, which the Company largely hated, but held anyway because it gave the audience their cue to go home, meant that, after my hasty exit, Emily was still on-stage. To my surprise, it was Cat who turned up instead to stroke my forehead and hold back my hair.

Armed with a bowl and a glass of water, she met me behind the curtain rail we had erected to provide some backstage privacy, and she put an unexpectedly strong arm around me and helped me around behind the van where she had a blanket already laid out.

I collapsed onto it and through a fug of nausea, I watched her, angrily protective, instructing the others to 'get rid of the audience', 'fetch more water', and 'leave her alone'. I saw in her the remaining vestiges of her character, and overlaid with it, a sibling love, which Fitzgerald's play had not necessarily made explicit.

She spent that whole night with me, despite the mutual frustrations of the previous weeks of enforced cohabitation. She stayed in my van, enduring the little frills and hangings, which she must have found excruciatingly twee, breathing in the hard yellow smell of sick, grimly emptying the bowl, washing it out, bringing it back. Tucking blankets around me against the midnight cold.

In the morning, when there was nothing left to expel from my body, she helped me into bed, turned the lights off and tiptoed outside.

"No. I said *no*, Colm, leave her alone, she needs sleep."

She stayed there on guard for the rest of the day, dispensing threats and warnings to anyone who dared approach, until I'd finally slept it off.

"Good, you look better. But don't go pushing it. You've been at it for weeks now, you're probably well on your way to alcoholism. You've screwed up your system."

That note of accusation, so familiar in Cat. I wondered what it was like, being caught as she was in the epicentre of her own aggression. And as I wondered she widened her eyes at me and asked me what I thought I was staring at.

Cat was back, but the sisterhood we had established would not necessarily disappear. We emerged from each performance with permanent shadows of our respective characters, and we simply weaved them in. Our reality was so close to fiction, it was an easy set of lines to blur. So, whilst Colm and I were glad to be rid of our courtship, and Frederick his camera, Emily and I continued to meet on the steps of her van, while she smoked her herbal cigarettes and brewed us big, chipped mugs of tea.

    I loved those people. I love them now. And I fear them.

    And I am so very sorry for all that I did to them.

Scene Two

(A field, dotted with caravans and bordered by forest. The smell of sweat and crushed grass.)

Emily shielded her eyes from the early evening sun.
"Yes. Good. Now do it again."
We were preparing for *Benched*, a play by Frederick about an injured athlete recovering in hospital. We had drawn the usual lots for the parts, Frederick producing a black velvet draw-string bag, lined with red, from which we had each taken turns to withdraw a slip of paper. Colm had the main part. I was the supporting role, the nurse to his patient.

Emily pushed strands of sweat stiffened hair back from her forehead so that they stood up oddly, like gleaming spiders.

"Excellent work Colm. That was very effective."

Colm flushed with pride and repeated the movement. The other three of us, though with rather less of a natural grace, did the same. We had been at this for weeks, or at least Colm had, the rest of us were joining in mainly for fun.

Emily had suggested, very casually one night, that she could teach us a martial art. And we, just as casually, took her up on the offer. Nobody ever commented on the intensity of the training, or the obvious focus on Colm. And, in just the same way, nobody discussed the change in the way we talked to Colm, flattering him continually about his athleticism and prowess, until neither he, nor we, discussed anything else.

And nobody questioned Frederick's decision to ask Herm, who was far less artistically gifted, to make the relevant changes to the institutional backdrop.

"I want to work more on my sparring." Colm said, sweat

and concentration mingling and gleaming on his face. "I'm still not as fast as I want to be."

His Aikido gi was covered in stains, as though it had bruised on his behalf. He was the only one of us other than Emily, who wore one.

We had made this his identity. We had removed everything else. And if I had felt a little pang as I watched it happen, if I had wondered a little about the ultimate intention, it melted from me now as I watched him.

"Right. Yes, agreed. More practice. Let's go. Yes, like that, much better. Watch your feet. Watch your centre. Right. Good. Better."

Emily was a blunt and powerful teacher. She stepped forward, demonstrated a new move, stepped back again, watched. Colm, under her tuition over the last seven weeks, in preparation for the play which would open in two days, had become a genuinely formidable fighter.

Herm was puffing a little. We had all become a lot fitter over the past weeks, though we, unlike Colm, were not adding to the regime with lengthy early morning speed and fitness training sessions. Still, we were flagging.

"Herm needs a break," said Cat, "we're off to get dinner."

"He would, he's a lightweight," said Emily, her gaze never leaving Colm. "Good. You need to strengthen your posture. Ramp it up. Come on Colm, you need to strike like a snake."

I hadn't known Emily was a martial artist, though the discovery hadn't surprised me. Now that she wasn't busy preparing me for *If I Do,* I realised that, for all her efforts to congregate us around the campfire in the early evening, she would often leave once the rest of us had trailed off to bed, and head to the nearest town. She would return in the early hours, and there were times, if she wasn't in recovery or heavy preparation for a show, when she might be gone all day too.

"You name it," said Cat, "and Emily's done it."

"She's a free spirit," said Colm, wisely, eyes dark and serious, "she lives everything to the full."

These pronouncements hadn't done much to satisfy my curiosity. In the end it was Herm, with his gift for distilling everything we did into something which vaguely resembled logic, who gave me a straight answer.

"Emily collects experiences. If we're near a town, she'll take a class or just go straight for an exam, just to see how she does. She'll go sky diving if it's on offer, she'll go out, take a drug, take a man, a woman, whatever's on offer. She's got a couple of open university degrees, though she never claims them, just learns the subject. She's a third Dan Black Belt in Aikido, and she's run so many marathons I've lost count. And ultra-marathons. Unregistered of course. If it's on, she'll do it."

In some ways, Emily was the only one among us who was not here to escape something. Attaching herself to something that might one day demand death was just another way for her to feel the rush of life. Perhaps it was only because I loved her, but I had always felt I understood it.

"Suit yourself," said Cat, when I said I would stay a little longer, attempting to follow Emily's instructions. If there was an edge in her voice, or a warning in her tone, it wasn't unusual in Cat, and I chose not to heed it.

My hair was wet and plastered to the back of my neck and my face was slimy. Emily ignored me, her entire focus on Colm.

"Was that better?" he asked her. "It felt better." For once, he didn't blush at his own pride. I smiled at the back of Emily's head. Aikido was perfectly fitted to Colm's natural personality, his careful manner, his self-control, and that passion, that virulent need for rules.

I had the impression that there had been something in Colm's family life before, some dysfunction, some cruelty, I couldn't quite make it out. But from his change of expression, the flicker across his face when the conversation at the campfire ambled into certain topics, I think that his mother cast a very long shadow.

There was a rule, unspoken, but fervently applied, that we would not talk about our lives before, or what it was that had led us here. Inevitably, of course, in those early days with the Company, I found myself absorbed with curiosity, mentally playing out potential scenarios for all of them, tragedies and sorrows which might have driven them to make their entrance on this particular stage. But even while I burned with curiosity, my speculation brought with it a vague sense of displacement, as though my own sense of self faded a little in the face of my companions' colourful and wholly imagined identities. It made me feel itchy and it drove me to add whole new layers to the part I was consummately playing, so that I began to forget what was real in my own history. And that made me wonder if any of the others honestly remembered theirs.

"It *was* better. Let's try to put into practice," said Emily, but with none of the warmth I had expected. I felt a chill of knowing flush through me. She was steeling herself.

"Just one more time," Emily said, and she turned then to me, and I read the warning in her eyes. My stomach clenched.

"Rose. Leave them now."

Frederick.

There was something in the way he always said my name. Quietly but as if, somehow, the name itself was a full sentence. I wasn't sure he said anyone else's name like that. If he did, I hadn't noticed.

I turned. He was standing just behind me, so slender it was as if he could be blown over in the breeze, and yet, he was, and remains, one of the most commanding figures I have ever met.

I hesitated.

There was an odd compulsion, a sort of addiction I had been developing with Frederick, a mysterious sense of push and pull that made me want to resist him, just to feel the force of it. It was like a magnetic force-field, or an electric shock. I wanted to move towards him and push him away all in the same movement. It made me want to defy him, in order to be compelled.

I met his gaze, defiance still arranging itself on my face, and a prickle of something ran through me.

Cat and Herm had vanished.

He reached out and took my hand. His grip was strong, I felt the skin across my knuckles roll with the force of it and my eyes widened as I looked up at him. Frederick's power was in the quiet assurance of his voice. He very rarely touched us. Fear and excitement rose in me.

We stared at each other for a moment, breathing quickly. There was a fleeting movement across his face, a flicker of a smile, a hint of a grimace. That uneasy mix of passion and cruelty. I recognised it because he awoke it in me too.

With a precise little flick of his wrist, he pulled me closer to him, then let go of my hand and, in the same movement, took my arm, trapping it through his so firmly that I gasped a little as I allowed myself to be led, rapidly, away.

Behind us there was a crack, loud and sickening in the darkening light and a cry.

Benched

(Institutional backdrop. It is clinical and too bright. Colm occupies a bed at centre stage, his ankle bandaged, shivering slightly. Rose, his nurse is leaning over to adjust his pillows.)

"There, that'll be better."

I said it with a cheer which rang false, even to me. His pupils were tiny, his face damp and clammy, and there was something wild in his eyes. I touched his forehead, "You're still very hot. How are you feeling?"

"Fine." It was a deadened monotone.

My heart ached.

"I know it's hard," I said, "really, I know. But you have to eat."

I reached for the tray of food behind me. It was good food, I'd made sure of it. It was a plate full of everything he liked. I held it out to him, trying to imbue the action with confidence, a sense that I expected him to take it. He'd ignored two meals already.

Colm said nothing, but, in a single violent gesture, he reached up and knocked the tray out of my hands.

Hot coffee, undiluted by milk, splashed, stinging, onto my forearms. Pasta stuck to the front of my dress. Behind me I heard the audience gasp as the plate hit the floor and smashed, the stage becoming slippery under my feet. I felt my breath and my heart quicken.

There was a silence.

In the script, Colm was supposed to accept the food without looking at it and leave it there for the remainder of the scene without bothering to touch it.

For a moment I stood there dripping, skin burning, staring into Colm's eyes. I saw nothing of him there.

"I ..."

We were supposed to end the play with a reconciliation. After several fruitless attempts to engage him, I would almost lose patience with his sullen lack of co-operation and then, at the last minute, make a crucial connection, and our relationship would become at least a partial replacement for the hope he had lost.

I shook myself into action, summoned my borrowed nurse's instinct, and reached across him again, with the idea of removing the duvet and replacing it with a clean one. But he grabbed my shoulder and pushed me away, with all his athlete's strength and power, so that I staggered backwards, colliding, painfully, with the coat rack we had rigged up as a drip.

There was an excruciating silence. I looked at him, wide-eyed, and felt my calves tense as if readying to run. The script, so carefully unrehearsed and yet such a comfort to me still, in those early days, fell away from us, useless in the face of these developments.

I opened my mouth to say something suitably professional and stern, but he threw the duvet off, so that it dropped to the floor and began, slowly, to soak up more of the mess.

"Is this what you wanted?" he shouted, his eyes wild with anger and pain. "This?" he gestured to his leg, "to see the 'great athlete' brought down? To ogle? You want to see?"

He reached down to his ankle and started to try to pull the bandage off. I leapt forward to stop him and he waved his hand, catching me in the side of the head, so that my vision blurred briefly, and I flinched away.

"Here you go, this is what you wanted isn't it? Have a look. Have a good long *fucking* look."

I had never heard Colm swear. He was still scratching and pulling at his dressing, but his flow of words had faltered, and I saw the wet on his face, not sweat now, but tears, as he began to cry in gulping, angry convulsions.

Getting a grip on myself, I stepped forward again and, this time, I took both his hands in mine, gripped them, and drew my face close to his. He smelled of something sick and sweet.

"Stop," I said. "Stop."

And as the fight went out of him, as his shoulders dropped and he half-lay, half-fell, back onto his pillows, I fixed his bandage and changed his sheets.

When I left the stage, I could still feel my heart racing, my head throbbing. Herm had made his entrance and Cat was backstage, watching me.

"He often does that," she said.

"Ignores his lines?"

She laughed. "No. *That*."

"Oh." I was still trying to gather my senses, what had happened out there had been something I had never before experienced. "Yes, he um ..."

"Goes a bit wild."

"Yes ..."

"He's good though." She was looking at me, as if expecting me to attack.

"Yes." I said. "Yes. He's good. We're all good."

And we were.

We formed, as was often the case after a performance, a subdued group around the fire that night. A few of us attempted the usual jokes and ribbing, by way of over-compensation, and there was plenty of alcohol flowing, but Cat had broken a plate earlier, then burst into senseless, angry tears, Frederick was notably absent, and Herm was quiet and watchful. Even Emily seemed to have sensed a lost battle.

Colm had his ankle up on a camping chair and was clearly in pain. He seemed quiet and embarrassed, unable to meet our gaze, and muttering 'sorry' every so often to no one in particular, until it became a sound which routinely emanated from him, like a cough or a breath. He was unable to drink the alcohol as it would interfere with the painkillers, and he twisted and fidgeted in his chair, as though he had been put there on show and wished only for privacy.

After a while, unable to bear it, I got up and brought him a cup of tea. I brought one for myself too – I was still a little wary of alcohol after *If I Do* – and sat down in front of him, my back to the campfire, shielding him, at least partly, from view. That nurse's instinct, borrowed or stolen from my character's identity, still pulsed within me.

"Thanks," he said. "Sorry."

"What for?" I said, sipping my tea. "That was an amazing performance. You got three encores."

"I know." He grimaced. "I just … I wanted it to end. I wanted them to go away."

It was something we often remarked upon. The more we weaved a spell for the audience, the more they lingered, unwilling to leave us, but more often than not, we were exhausted, facing the inevitable comedown and still wearing the torn vestiges of the characters we had spent too many weeks inhabiting.

He smiled, and then, as if catching himself doing something terrible, corrected it. "Yes, but I'm sorry. I could have really hurt you. *Did* I hurt you?"

"No," I said. It was only partially a lie. "And I don't need you to apologise."

He looked as though he was about to say something else but then he stopped himself, blushed, and started to lever himself up from the chair. "Sorry. The painkillers. I think I'll just go to bed. Can you … I'm sorry … can you help?"

I helped him to his van. He was heavy, he was tall and

broad, and he had been muscular even before the training. Now, leaning on my shoulder, he was a dead weight and I had to fight to stop my knees from buckling. He paused at the doorway and insisted that I needn't help him further, that he could get himself into bed. I stood a little distance away and waited until I saw the lights in his van go out, then turned back to the campfire.

"He likes you."

Out of nowhere in the darkness. I jumped.

"Cat. You scared the life out of me."

She ignored this, looking at me, eyes glinting in the darkness. For all the world like an actual cat.

"He's a nice guy," she said, "there's nothing wrong with him."

I felt a surge of anger. I wasn't in the mood to deal with Cat's particular brand of aggressive loyalty, and I had joined the Company to get out of this rat race, the continual striving for someone to sleep with, followed by the continual striving to marry them, to make money, to buy a big house and fill it with children. All those things my mother would have wanted.

I opened my mouth to say so, but Cat was gone.

I hesitated for a moment, fizzing with some unplaced anger. Then something in me resolved itself, and without further thought I turned and strode across the darkened field, towards Frederick's bus.

Being also the stage, it had its windows blacked out, so that it was always almost impossible to tell if he was there. And we never intruded. None of us. We didn't visit. He always came to us.

I suppose it wasn't that unusual. None of us really opened up our vans for visitors. I had been inside Cat's van only as part of our preparation for the previous play. And I suspected she had packed away anything of personal value beforehand. I had been in everybody's driving cab – it was one of the rules of the Company that we were all licensed and able to drive each other's vehicles in case we needed to move on quickly and somebody was incapacitated after a performance, but the cab spaces were deliberately bland and impersonal. Herm's van served as short-distance transport when we needed it, but I had never been inside Colm's van, and Emily and I had only perched on her steps.

Our vans were our backstage. Our place to be who we were. Or whatever vestiges we cared to remember of who we were.

It was different with Frederick. There was something more to it. His bus, despite being the boards of our stage, was forbidden in some way that I did not understand. Night after night, when he left the campfire, I would drift away from the conversation around me, and watch his retreating limping figure, and wonder how that vehicle, which was capable of being so open, could be, perpetually, so closed.

I banged on the door. Almost as soon as I'd started, I pulled my fist away again. Fleeting memories of that first night, when I'd pounded on that door from the other side, mingled with a sudden sense that the others shouldn't know about this visit – and that familiar rising of contrary impulses which I had come to expect from my encounters with Frederick.

I breathed. Once. Then I yanked the door, hard. To my surprise, it swung open, and before my brain had really caught up with my body, I was up the steps and inside.

He was standing in the middle of the stage, still set as it had been, the bed in the centre, the hospital backdrop still in place. The coat rack drip stood, waiting, tubes hanging, poised like extra limbs, ready to embrace another patient. The spotlights had been dragged back inside on their tripods, and they aimed their beams at him like alien creatures, setting light to the ends of his black hair and his black eyelashes, bleaching his pale face paler.

He hadn't turned the main lights on and the spotlights made the interior uncomfortably hot. There were piles of backstage paraphernalia all around the far edges, but none of it was placed so as to obscure the backdrop, or to clutter the stage.

I stood and stared, and he stared back at me. He looked frozen and furtive, as if he had been caught doing something intensely painful and private.

"You'll …" I trailed off and gestured at the bed, words failing me, the question seeming suddenly abhorrent and intrusive. Neither of us had moved or broken our gaze.

"Yes." His voice was very quiet. "Yes, I'll sleep here, Rose."

I thought of him. Alone, in his bus, on his own private stage. It wouldn't be scripted, this night. It would not even be a performance. He would simply slide into bed and go to sleep, in character, as the injured athlete he had created. Would he hook himself up to the makeshift drip? Would he sleep, all night, beneath the lights?

"We all have to come down Rose. We all have our own ways."

I thought of us all, around the campfire. Connected, even if only by a shared sense that we were lost. But Frederick's athlete would not have a nurse.

Something swelled inside me, and I wanted to step across the stage towards him. To touch him. But I remained exactly where I was. Dust motes floated in the lit air between us.

There was a reason why none of us ever visited Frederick, why we waited for him to come to us. It was called respect. I should never have intruded. I had forgotten why I'd come.

But I didn't leave. Instead, the silence seemed to grow and bind us, and slowly, I summoned the nurse within me, gathered her together, and stepped onto his stage.

The density of the light and the moment seemed to thicken the air, as I made my way across the floor towards him, still motionless, watching me.

I reached out. As the ends of my fingers touched his skin there was a moment when we both stayed still, eyes locked, and there was a collective intake of breath which seemed to reverberate around the vehicle. I lifted his wrist and took his pulse. His skin was cool, despite the lights, and as I counted the beat of the blood in his veins I felt it again, that strange, alternating current that connected us.

I watched it swim back into his face abruptly, that power he could summon even now. He moved free of my hand to sit on the edge of the bed, characteristically straight, skin stretched across every, perfectly aligned, knot and bone of his spine. I stepped back and walked away, leaving the spotlight. I sat down, consumed by a kind of emotional exhaustion, on a box of costume accessories. I felt my face flush.

The box was uncomfortable, it had a sharp, raised edge around the top of it and it dug into my thighs. I pressed my weight down onto it, let it ground me in a reality which seemed to be tipping and sliding.

"Hello, Rose."

He was smiling.

"Hello, Frederick."

I smiled back, and it turned into a little half-laugh. I saw his smile deepen.

"What brought you to see me?"

So much, it seemed, had happened in the few brief moments since I first walked through his door, I had almost forgotten what I'd come here to say.

"It's Colm." I said, and then, gaining momentum, "Are you deliberately casting Colm and me together? The lots just … well they seem to keep falling that way."

He didn't reply. He didn't even try to protest. And his silence galvanised me.

I didn't know exactly why I was angry. I had a handful of surface reasons, but it seemed to me that there was some other, distant issue that I either couldn't or wouldn't access or admit. It made me defensive.

"Is that what this is? Frederick? Are you trying to run some sort of twisted lonely-hearts agency? Because I don't think … I mean … Colm's not …" I was losing track of my own objection. "He's *vulnerable*. You can't. You shouldn't…"

There was a pause in which he simply looked at me, patiently, as if to be certain that I had finished before he spoke again.

"He's a powerful young man Rose, physically and emotionally. Don't patronise him. But yes. I cast you in those roles deliberately. Because I knew you would do that."

"Do what?"

"Be kind to him. You're kind, Rose. And Colm needs a bit of kindness."

Later, the cool of Emily's steps seeping through my skirt, my hands wrapped around a mug of tea, surrounded by the thyme-scented fog of her herbal cigarettes, I told her only of the very last part of that encounter, and without mentioning my visit to Frederick's bus.

"I mean, he kind of implied that Colm didn't otherwise *get* any kindness."

Emily's face was thoughtful in the moonlight. She drew on her cigarette, considering. "I don't know," she said, after a while, "I suppose we're not especially kind."

"What?"

But she was unmoved, shaking her head. "Fierce. Loyal. But not kind."

"I'm fierce too." I said.

She looked at me. "It's not an insult. And it's okay to be different. That's the whole point. Anyway, you're not *that* kind. You're just more kind than us."

I felt annoyance rise in me, and just as quickly, subside. Emily could see things other people didn't notice, and she was never afraid to expose them. It was maddening, but it was also why I loved her.

"But don't you think Frederick is somehow … I don't know … pulling strings?"

Emily stubbed her cigarette out on the steps, then picked up the butt and aimed it at the mouth of a plastic bin liner propped up against the side of her van. It missed.

"Ah bollocks. Oh well. Yes of course he is, you idiot. It really took you till now to know?"

I flushed and looked out into the trees at the edge of the field. Somewhere, on the edge of that treeline, was the log which Emily had thrown Colm onto, having negotiated him into exactly the right position for injury. Creatures were moving there, heading for safety and sleep, or just waking up. The light was changing. Below the horizon, there was the burgeoning glow of the early sunrise. Emily laughed and slapped her thigh for good measure.

"Oh, come on. Of course he does. He gives Colm rules, which he needs, and he casts him in roles that allow him to break them – which he needs. Obviously. It's what we joined for."

"But he's not supposed to cast us, we draw lots for the parts."

Emily only grinned at me. "Yes," she said, lighting another cigarette. "Of course we do."

Scene Three

Carte Blanche

(A blank, black backdrop, scrawled with white chalk. A spotlight acts as a grimy streetlight. Two groups of people stand at opposite sides of the stage, eyeing each other with palpable hatred.

A heaving, unmelodic soundtrack, no more than a collection of long, purposeless notes played on base instruments, groans overly loudly into the silence.

The figures at either side of the stage seem to grow and swell together, as if in one last act of unity. And then, with a kind of part-cry, part-scream, they launch themselves towards each other.)

I charged the short distance across the stage so filled with frustration and directionless anger that at first, I simply ran into the midst of them, catapulted myself against other warm bodies without any definable purpose.

It had been stultifying – the past three hours on that stage had felt like a lifetime. The play, written by Frederick, was an endurance test both to watch and to perform in, about a society ruled over by a faceless regime, which manifested through a cloaked, hooded figure who appeared in brief silences, the only pauses in the endless soundtrack, to chalk new 'laws' upon the wall.

It lasted three, gruelling hours, at a crawling pace, and at the end, the characters, having gradually lost the last vestiges of their freedom, seized upon the only power they could still wield, against the only enemy they could fight on an equal ground – each other.

Frederick played both hooded figure and oppressed citizen and had begun subtly preparing us for weeks beforehand, while we learned our lines and otherwise went about our business. Gradually, he had restricted our habits, prohibiting Cat from sleeping with Herm in his camper van, imposing curfews, forbidding Emily from leaving the site. Once again, Colm was denied the small, creative pleasure of designing the backdrop, forced instead to paint over his own street scene, line by cruel line in flat black paint, while Frederick stood over him, silent and watchful, pointing out sections he had missed.

The small stipend Frederick usually paid us out of the takings was cut, first a little, then completely, and without explanation. The other provisions, food and fuel, bought by Frederick with money that we all understood he had inherited and suspected was plentiful, dwindled to the very basics. Lighting the campfire was prohibited. We were not permitted to congregate. Eventually even speech was forbidden. It seemed it had been decades since I had touched another person.

I was filled with wasted adrenaline, fear of a force which I loathed and despised but was nevertheless deeply in awe of, sick of the wall and the laws and the constant grate and tickle of chalk-dust in my nose and my throat. I was hoarse with shouting lines above the drone of the music after weeks of near silence, and I hated all of them. I even hated those who were fighting alongside me.

At first, I struck out erratically, flailing like a child in a tantrum, too far out of control to co-ordinate my body, but then I felt someone's fist collide with my shoulder and the pain and the shock of it forced me into awareness.

I focused and saw Herm, to the right of me, looking wary and bitter, blood on his mouth. He met my eyes with a cold, miserable kind of anger and I poured all my frustration into my fist and swung it, wildly, at his head. He ducked and moved towards me, and behind him I could see Cat, fighting dirty, nails and teeth and small fists flying.

Colm, rage twisting his beautiful face, was powerful and elegant even in his passion, and I felt a pang of relief that his new-found fighting abilities were directed away from me, and towards Emily, who was struggling and panting with the effort to maintain her equilibrium. I thought of the grim look on her face when she was training him. I heard again that sickening crack at the edge of the woods and I felt a brief, conflicting swell of emotion, a fleeting remembrance of who we were and what we had been. And then someone pulled my legs out from under me, and I hit the stage with a crash and felt the vehicle shake beneath me.

Winded, I gasped and then rolled, away from the approaching footfall. Stumbling to my feet, I recalled my own training, and I placed my weight on my back foot and prepared myself to strike.

Frederick.

I looked up into his face and caught my breath. He was pale and tall, so commanding and yet so familiar, but his brown eyes as he met mine were filled with hatred. There was nothing beneath it. He was entirely in the moment. He knew nothing of our Company. He knew only this place.

But I hesitated and, as I did so, I saw his face change.

And then something barrelled into me from behind and I stumbled and whirled around.

It was Cat. She was fast and lithe, and relentless. She had me doubled over, winded, and then she brought her knee up under my chin so that I bit my tongue and tasted blood. I yelled and turned, hooked my arm beneath her elbow and flipped her, easily, onto the ground. She hit it hard, she was lighter even than I had expected, and I saw anger and pain on her face as she scrambled, limping slightly, to her feet. I felt a pang of remorse and then, as I paused, she launched herself at me, knocking me backwards, her elbow in my neck and I squirmed and kicked her hard in the stomach.

Then the soundtrack, the music which had been so loud and relentless for the entirety of the performance, stopped – and we limped from the stage.

This was the final scene. We collapsed together behind the bus, wounds and bruises suddenly felt. I saw Herm cradling his wrist, Cat, on her knees, coughing up chalk-dust, Frederick, clutching his jaw. Colm was massaging the foot he had broken before, but otherwise seemed to have escaped uninjured. I looked around for Emily but felt blood in my mouth and bent over instead to spit onto the ground.

Behind us, hesitantly and a little shell-shocked, the audience began to applaud.

Colm stood up. Emily reappeared, staggering slightly. Herm caught my eye and winked at me, grabbed Cat by the arm.

And we followed Frederick back onto the stage.

Curtain call.

"Oi. You can pass some of that up here."

Herm was grinning at me, half-way up a ladder, wires looped over his arm, fiddling with a spotlight. I was mopping and coughing, sweeping chalk-dust off the stage, pausing every so often to groan a little and self-medicate with some of the strong brandy we seemed to have an unending supply of, and which had made a mysterious re-appearance the moment the show was over. I grinned back, screwed the lid on and threw it up to him. He caught it by the neck, raised one eyebrow.

"Easy, tiger."

That we were all working that same night to take the set

down was unusual. We often did so when we needed to move on quickly because something we'd done had been especially illegal, or we had a sense that we were under suspicion. This play had been nothing if not controversial, but was unlikely to cause us a visit from the police, though admittedly it might be difficult to explain away such a collection of actual injuries.

The fact was, getting rid of that set was proving very cathartic. It vanquished something, taming that chalk-dust into grey-white smears. I'd noticed Cat pulling the wires out of the speakers with relish. None of us wanted to hear that soundtrack again.

Or perhaps it was only the lingering need to obey. Frederick hadn't told us to get to work. He was Frederick again, our gentle leader. But still, nobody wanted to step out of line.

"Mind out, I've got a box of … some sort of assorted crap … and it needs to go on that floor if you ever finish mopping it."

Emily was approaching, carrying a box full of props to load back into the bus. She was limping and one eye was almost swollen closed.

I shook the mop out, flicking chalky water at Cat, who squeaked and whirled round in annoyance, then relaxed and grinned at me.

Somehow, despite the somewhat frenzied cleaning, there was none of the usual difficult comedown. If anything, the fight seemed to have been cleansing for us. Even Cat was relatively calm in the wake of it, as if she had purged a little of that continuous anger, and Frederick too, had relaxed his guard and was striding unevenly about, moving boxes and laughing. Every one of us winced and drew in breath as we moved, and we all, with the exception of Colm, wore in some way the violence of those last few minutes, on our limbs and on our faces. I had brought out my nurse's kit, which I kept in my van, though I could barely remember now when I had acquired it, and done my best to patch everybody up, but there was only so much that I could do.

Emily put the box down, then sat on it. Herm shimmied down the ladder and handed her the brandy, then gave me a quick hug, squeezing my shoulders and ruffling my hair, before bending over a pile of dismantled spotlights and packing them carefully into a box.

Emily took a large swig from the bottle, then winced and felt around in her mouth, "Fuck. Broke a tooth. Bloody Colm."

She said it indulgently, and almost as soon as she'd spoken, Colm appeared and sat down next to her. With immense tenderness, he tipped up her face with his finger.

"Let me look."

Emily said something garbled, her mouth open, and he smiled. "It's not broken. You just chipped it a bit."

"Oh well great, that's fine then. When did you get your sodding dental qualifications?"

But she laid her head against his shoulder, and he pulled her close.

"Come on, old lady," he said, and I turned, shocked, to Frederick who was standing behind me. Colm was never rude like that, even in jest. The rest of us jibed, ribbed, and laughed at each other, but Colm never did. He was always respectful. Frederick simply smiled and gestured towards them and when I turned back, I saw Colm supporting Emily, who was limping, walking her back to her van.

"He'll drive her on tonight," said Frederick. I nodded. I wasn't sure I could imagine us sitting around the fire in this field. There had been too many restrictions and for too long. Moving on quickly was part of the reset. Emily was the most injured and Colm the least. Herm would drop Colm back afterwards to collect his own van. We'd done it like that before. We did it that way for Colm. After Emily broke him.

"I see they've made sure to take the brandy," said Cat, and we laughed. Then, for no particular reason, we laughed a bit more, until we were all of us laughing, wincing and holding our sides in the joy and the pain of it. And I thought how much I loved these people, whose marks I bore on my body, and with whom I had fought so violently, hours before.

In the early hours of the morning, when we'd finally packed up, and only Cat and I were left, I gave up on my idea of catching a few hours' sleep before driving myself on, and so I made a cup of tea to prepare for the journey and wandered out, wincing, into the dewy wet of the field.

"I'll have one, if you're making," Cat was sitting in the darkness by the unlit campfire. There were no longer any restrictions on our freedom, but I knew we would all wait for a new location, a new play, before we dared to break them. And we'd think twice about it even then.

"Coffee. Really black. Really strong."

I grinned. I knew how Cat took her coffee. It was a standing joke in the Company. I sometimes wondered if that, and not some ancient fury, was what made her so unpredictable, and kept her from sleep.

Frederick had left with the others, though not before I, remembering the night after *Benched*, had slipped inside his van and, heart racing, chalked some commands for him on the newly-scrubbed backdrop.

'You may not speak.'
'You may not read.'
'You may sleep for four hours exactly.'
'You will drink only water.'

He would never mention it. But I suspected he would obey. It sent a surge of power through me. And something more tender, but more obscure.

I joined Cat in the semi-darkness, handed her a second mug. It was chilly at that time of the morning, even in summer, and we both wrapped our fingers around the ceramic and bent our faces over the steam.

"So how was it for you?" She took a sip of her coffee. "The play I mean."

I wasn't sure how to answer.

"Fine. I guess." I frowned and thought a little more, "I mean it was such a grind and then such a release. It reminded me of exercise."

I thought she'd laugh at that, but she didn't. Encouraged, I carried on. "You know? When you sweat and it hurts and afterwards you feel calmer and happier. I used to do it to stave off … whatever. Stuff."

I remembered those early morning runs, the long-distance races, the swimming club. I always imagined I was running away, that I was swimming to freedom, that I would not, at the end of the pool or the racetrack, be turning around, and coming back. That I might be able to outrun that constant heaviness, which I had never identified, but which, back then, had never left me.

It had gone now. I almost couldn't remember how it felt.

"Hmm …" Cat was nodding. "For me it was school."

"School?"

Any hint of Cat's past, of anyone's history, always sent a prickle through me. If that was what school was for Cat, perhaps this explained a part of who she had become. But she was smiling, a faraway look in her eyes, gazing into the fire as though recalling a treasured memory.

"We used to have gang fights. That's what we called them.

It wasn't really gangs, just two rival schools. We'd meet in this park on the edge of town. It was brilliant."

"What? Proper fights? Or just posturing?"

I knew my incredulity was dangerous.

"Pretty much proper fights." She laughed. "I remember Rebecca Charles made a knuckle duster. Out of nails and bits of wire."

Horrified, I turned to look at her.

"Really? But weren't people seriously hurt?"

"No," and there was a sense of disappointment in it. "No, she just waved it around a bit. Wimped out of actually punching anyone. I told her she should or what's the point. She wouldn't though." She shrugged, "I suppose if we'd been older. But we were just kids."

Whatever happened to Cat, whatever the damage, it had been done long before school.

"I told her to hit me with it. I said I wouldn't sue or anything. But she wouldn't."

"What would you have done if she had?"

"I don't know." She shrugged, the defensiveness returning. "Hit her back, probably."

There was a silence. We watched the dead ashes in the fire bowl stirring, ghostly, in the breeze.

"This is better," said Cat. "More real than at school. We were just kids then. Just …"

"Playacting?" I grinned.

She laughed. "Yes. Playacting. That."

We sipped our drinks, and the atmosphere grew a little warmer. I was about to make some remark about Colm when she spoke again, a new intensity in her voice.

"This is what saved us. From all that. This. This Company."

She turned to me, eyes bright, like green fire in the semi-darkness.

"Frederick began this because it makes sense. It just makes *sense*. All the time you're supposed to care about stuff, you're supposed to feel stressed and upset or work hard or be in competition or something – and all of it's just nonsense – it's *nothing*. But you feel it all the same and you're not allowed to do anything about it. You can't scream and kick and destroy things – even if something actually *happens*. I mean even then – even when it actually does – you have to *'get over it'*." She was spitting the words out now. "And all the time you've got all this instinct. All these animal impulses to run and fight and you're not allowed to use them. So what's the point?"

She shifted suddenly closer to me. I could smell the coffee on her breath.

"There is literally no point in life except death. And this is the only thing – it's the *only thing* that's real. We march out there on stage ready to fight or love or die. That's how we wake up in the morning. And so does every single other person in the world. But they don't admit it to themselves. And they're not even allowed to express it. This –" She gestured across the field and I saw in that gesture the stage, the shows, the sacrifice, the terror of initiation, the preparations, the campfires, the comedowns, the pain. "This is pure. It's honest. It's the *only* honest thing."

She was sitting so close now, she was almost on top of me, her skin flushed, her eyes, too bright with emotion, boring into mine, so that I struggled with an urge to pull away. I saw the fervour of the zealot in her, and inwardly I shivered.

"Frederick saves us," she said, "he sacrifices himself for it. It's his money we live off, it's his living space we use for the stage. And he has to stay distant, be cruel if he needs to, or be angry, or be kind. He's always, *always* got to be the leader." She looked at me. "He was the lawmaker *and* the people tonight. Can you imagine the strain of that? Can you imagine how hard it must be? To never completely let himself go?"

If I hadn't known, hadn't witnessed the depth of feeling between her and Herm, I might have suspected her of being in love with Frederick. But this was an ardour that reached much higher. It was a deep, even disturbing, devotion to the cause.

Perhaps she read what I was thinking, because her eyes changed a little, as if coming back into focus, and I saw a flush of shame across her face, that familiar defiance. Her breath slowed and she stood up, gave me a small smile and a quick, painful, squeeze on the arm, tipped the remains of her coffee into the grass, and walked away, rapidly, towards her van.

I felt for her then. I sent wordless reassurances after her, but she didn't turn back.

It occurred to me, as I got up, with some difficulty, tipped the campfire ashes into the bushes and prepared to drive to join the others, that I wouldn't want her as my enemy.

And that whatever else this Company might be, it wasn't the sort of club you could leave.

Scene Four

(A field, muddied and yellowing in places. A scattered set of figures. A campfire, strewn with bottles and rubbish and largely abandoned. The stale smell of old whisky.)

I have to admit, there were times when I doubted him. That Frederick pulled the strings of our puppet theatre was clear, and generally accepted. That he did, at least on the surface, appear to have a plan – that one play would be an antidote to a particular individual, and the next an antidote to that play, was also clear, though largely only with the benefit of hindsight.

But sometimes I just wasn't sure. It was a lonely sort of feeling, and I had learned not to express it to the other members of the Company. There were times though, when I looked into those brown eyes, and I saw something else behind all that secretive wisdom, something hot and wet and human. It was as if he was a hypnotist, and the hypnotism hadn't worked on me, so that I, alone, remained conscious among them. At the same time there was a pull in him so strong I sometimes physically struggled to keep away. I would walk to my van and find myself taking a strange, curving path, bending towards his bus. And I didn't notice anyone else doing that. I *was* hypnotised. Just in a different way.

We were mid-way through preparing for Eugene O'Neill's tragically beautiful *Long Day's Journey into Night* and it was proving to be a miserable production. Emily, as the morphine addicted Mary, her furtive habits and unpredictable moods gradually breaking the heart of her family, needed to become inured enough to morphine to both understand the addiction and remember her lines. Herm, Frederick and Colm, as her husband and two sons, were drinking more and more whisky in the evenings, for the same reason, and becoming, along with their characters, increasingly belligerent and bitter, so that the campfire was no longer a pleasant place to be. On top of that, the morphine had to be procured, which meant Frederick and Herm were taking unknown risks, and were often out in the day, making Cat uneasy. She had not been cast at all in this play.

I would play Cathleen, the maid, appearing only briefly, but it gave me the opportunity to look after Emily. I went into her van, and cleared up the awful mess I found there, which I suspected was Emily's natural habitat and nothing to do with her preparation for this character, and made tea and dinner for her, but her half-glazed state was disturbing and depressing, and I worried for her. It seemed to me that the casting was unfair, Emily having suffered by far the most in the last performance.

Cat, denied her twin passions of both the performance and Herm, paced round the site like a poorly-caged tiger, seeking out quarrels and baring her teeth. She saw plots in any conversation which did not involve her, read insults into every passing remark. She was convinced there was malice in the way we looked at her, mistook concern for disdain, and frequently dissolved, on some insignificant event, or some slight inconvenience, into fits of alarming, angry tears. More than once, I had caught Herm watching her, and his efforts to be with her whenever he wasn't offsite or round the campfire preparing, were valiant but not enough, particularly given the after-effects of the whisky, which he was suffering on a daily basis. When she began, after a while, simply to disappear for long periods, I met Herm's eyes, and read the warning. After that I contrived, continually, to be with her.

She was not an easy companion. It was exhausting for all of us.

Although I knew this was part of our accepted lifestyle, I did question why nobody ever really objected to Frederick's choices. I suspected, in this case, the lingering effect of the previous performance was making us more willing to fight each other than to resist authority, but the thought made me uncomfortable. Partly because it threw doubt over whether any of us still had any real identity, but mostly because it made me wonder whether Frederick had planned the sequencing of plays with exactly that effect in mind.

I still can't be sure that all that happened later had not been planned by Frederick from the start.

Either way, Colm was nervous and perpetually hungover, spending hours on the interior backdrop, painting black and white family photographs with uncannily lifelike faces onto the wall in sharp-edged, gilded frames, declaring them not good enough, and painting them again. It was as if he was serving some kind of penance. Somebody, possibly even Frederick himself, had suggested in passing that there might be some question over whether the play was out of copyright. It was. We reassured Colm of this constantly, but he continued to fret about it. He was perfectly okay about the morphine. Perhaps, it was simply that the drugs had a place within the boundaries of the Company, a rule within a rule, whereas a copyright infringement would break both the rules of the world and the rules of our troupe. Whatever skewed logic existed behind it, he was unhappy and shifty, increasingly withdrawn. He still exercised in the mornings (he had done ever since *Benched*), but he was pushing himself further now, disappearing on punishingly long runs when he was already dehydrated, his skin growing dull and tarnished with lack of sleep. I joined him sometimes, used it as a release from the increasingly difficult atmosphere at the site, but I could never run as far or as long.

It was a bright afternoon, in the cooling air of the late summer, when I found Emily wandering about in the adjoining field. She was vague and befuddled, twisting her hands in her shirt, which was buttoned unevenly, and looking for something on the ground.

"Emily?"

She looked up at me without recognition, a flicker of fear in her watery eyes. She seemed to have aged and swollen all over. The dragons on her arms and shoulders no longer looked capable of taking flight, they were somehow simultaneously engorged and shrivelled. The sight of her wrenched at something so painfully inside me that my throat closed a little, and when I spoke, my tone was unintentionally waspish. "Emily what are you doing?"

"I'm looking for something," she said, smiling at me, speaking partly as Emily, partly as Mary, her lines muddled in with her blurred reality. "Let me see, what have I come here to find? It's terrible, how absent-minded I've become, I think I've lost the bloody …?" she frowned, "the bloody …" Her face suddenly lit up in relief and conviction, "Tea. That's it. The bloody tea …"

I'd asked Emily once why she chain-smoked herbal cigarettes, and not actual nicotine. She'd looked at me, horrified. "Are you kidding? Those things are really bad for you."

Given the kind of risks we took daily, on stage and off it, in the name of our art, I had found her answer quite funny at the time. But I thought of it now, as I looked at her ravaged figure, and I felt the humour die inside me.

I walked her back to her van, sat her down and boiled the kettle. She'd fallen asleep in the chair by the time I had made the tea, and I left it, cooling, on the table next to her, marched down the steps and, after a quick check to make sure that Cat was still with Colm, straight around to the back of Frederick's bus, where I waited, seething and pacing, until I heard Herm's engine, returning from town.

I confronted Frederick the minute he rounded the corner, looking tired, his keys in his hand. He was even paler than usual, sporting the same dark circles beneath his eyes as Herm and Colm, and he looked for all the world like he might really be dying of consumption, to match his character in the play. *The lawmaker and the people. Imagine the strain of that.* I felt a quick dart of compassion, which I immediately smothered.

When he saw me, he looked resigned and weary, walked past me to unlock the door, gestured me in. But I stayed where I was at the bottom of the steps, forcing him to stop and turn to acknowledge me. I didn't trust myself to touch him.

"Frederick, really – why *this* play? Why this one? There must be hundreds of others." I took a breath, tried to compose myself because time in Frederick's presence always seemed unnecessarily charged, and I needed to focus. "Look," I said, "I understand what we do here, I'm not completely naïve. But why put the idea in Colm's head that it's not even something we can legally perform? Why? I mean, other than deliberately to cause pain?"

There was a pause, and I felt my anger grow to fill it.

"Or is that the whole point Frederick? You think you can break us just so you can put us back together? Frederick?" I felt the realisation grow, horrifying, within me. "That's it, isn't it? It is. You break us. Just so you can put us back together."

They were bitter words and there was a hot flicker of truth in them. But even as I spoke them, I knew also, that it was, ultimately, exactly what all of us were seeking. It's what we expected him to do for us. He stood and waited, watching me realise it, his dark eyes unreadable and red rimmed with drink.

"It's a good play," he said.

"Yes but ... I mean – couldn't you ... at least for Colm ... you lied to him."

When he spoke again, it was very quiet. "We don't lie, Rose."

"Yes, we do."

But I'd blurted it out without thinking. He had only suggested something in passing, planted a seed in Colm's mind to produce an emotional state which would be truer to his character.

We *never* lied. We did everything for real, we didn't even pretend to our audiences. We didn't lie even when we were expected to.

I looked into his face. In a split, fleeting second, I imagined myself walking, dreamlike, up the steps towards him. I imagined reaching out with my hand, very carefully, brushing my fingers across those dark eyelashes, touching the taut white skin at his temples. Splaying my palm lightly across his chest, feeling the throb of his heart in its ribcage. Tracing carefully, the square of his jawline, the nape of his neck, pressing my forefingers, at first gently, then with greater pressure, into the smooth hollow between his collarbones.

I blinked and we were both still standing there, neither of us moving, a flood of wasted adrenaline, dissipating between us into the air.

"No," I said, and my voice seemed to scratch at my throat, "maybe we don't lie. But there are things we don't say."

Long Day's Journey into Night[3]

(Interior backdrop. The living room of the Tyrone family. Herm, Frederick and Colm, as the father and his two sons, in various states of miserable inebriation, stare at Emily, who cuts a pale, bewildered figure. She is wearing a dressing gown and carrying what looks like a wedding dress over one arm, so that it trails behind her on the ground. She frowns vaguely.)

"Let me see," said Emily, heartbreakingly unaware of the tension, "what did I come here to find? It's terrible, how absent-minded I've become. I'm always dreaming and forgetting."

"What's that she's carrying, Edmund?" whispered Herm in a strangled voice.

Frederick looked up at her. "Her wedding gown, I suppose," he said, without expression.

Herm sprang to his feet, standing in front of Emily, anguish twisting his face, "Christ! Mary!" he said, "Isn't it bad enough?" His words caught and he paused, controlling himself with an effort, and taking a careful, persuasive tone. "Here, let me take it, dear. You'll only step on it and tear it and get it dirty dragging it on the floor. Then you'd be sorry afterwards."

Emily let him take it, regarding him without recognition and as though from a long distance.

"Thank you," she said. "You are very kind." She looked at the wedding gown, with a detached, rather puzzled interest. "It's a wedding gown. It's very lovely, isn't it? I remember now. I found it in the attic …"

It took a long time to recover from that play. We had to move ourselves on in a hurry, immediately the audience had left. We could not be sure that Emily, furtive in the throes of the addiction we had created for her, had not hidden small stashes of the drugs in places we would not be expecting, and we couldn't risk a visit the next morning by a suspicious police officer.

Cat and I spent an exhausting night driving first Emily, then Frederick, Herm and Colm to the next location, leaving them there to sleep off the various after-effects, and returning together, taking turns to retrieve the other three vans.

Emily was still, to some extent or another, out of action for weeks afterward, as she had to be gradually weaned off the morphine, and her addiction made her desperate and deceitful. Months later, we were still discovering half-consumed packets of pills, hidden inside prop boxes or the pockets of costumes.

We rattled about on the new site, in various stages of comedown, all of us restless and exhausted and irritable.

And then, just like that, Frederick announced the new play - and put us all back together again.

Scene Five

A Winter Without Elves

(A group of people lounge around a campfire. There is a sense of great luxury, even of decadence. Behind them, there are scattered flyers and chairs still left out for the audience, who have long since left the venue. The stage has been abandoned, sprinkled with props and bits of costume, against a twinkly forest backdrop.)

The play, by Frederick, was about a young woman reluctantly choosing to leave the bohemian free love commune she was born into, in order to make her way in the city. It was gentle, and bitter-sweet, and focused more on her fond farewell than on the inevitable culture shock which would come later. It featured, predictably, rather a lot of sex.

It was a tonic. We embraced and touched and, when the time came, we writhed and rolled and we felt the tension, the leftover resentment, the shadows and ghosts of our previous roles drift upwards and dissipate, until they were only specks of dust in the spotlights.

Frederick had not cast himself. I had a strange, hollow feeling when I thought about that choice, about the fact that he would fight with us, but he would not love, and I smothered it.

Everybody else had been given equal share of the stage, almost to the point of self-indulgence. Even Cat and Herm were not separated, or paired with others, and there was at least as much in the way of gentleness and kissing as there was actual sex, because Frederick was never pointlessly shocking. Even so, I had rather enjoyed myself with Emily, and, to an extent, with Colm, though Frederick had given

Emily most of the fun in that department.

We barely waited this time for the audience to depart, before we arranged ourselves around the fire, still wrapped, happily, in a glow of intimacy. Like many of our productions it had only been a one-night run, Frederick sensing perhaps, that the magic would wear thin with repetition. None of us had bothered to clear up. We were relying, rather recklessly in this case, on the rule of 'Puck's Legacy', and Frederick had positioned the audience quite far back, and introduced a fair amount of 'mist' into our forest scenes, so that aside from the obvious nudity, which we had signposted dutifully in the flyers, I supposed it *might* not have been entirely clear to them exactly what was and wasn't real.

"They won't care," said Emily, lazily, "they won't go away thinking 'ooh, I wonder if they actually had sex', they'll be too busy going at it themselves."

"They'll think," said Colm, though he blushed as he said it, "wow, what a load of sexy actors." He giggled like a small, shy little boy.

"With bodies to die for", said Emily warmly, and he blushed again.

Colm certainly fell into that category, increasingly so now that he spent every morning in intensive conditioning sessions. He looked after himself painstakingly, perfecting his physique. The regime came from his time in *Benched*, but I wondered sometimes, whether it had started earlier, when he played my celebrity spouse-to-be. It made me a little uneasy, as if we had somehow defined him to himself by his looks. But it did make this particular play rather enjoyable for the rest of us. He looked like a character from a superhero comic.

Frederick did not try to join us at the campfire. Instead, he surprised us by turning up with a whole crate of very good red wine. He had bought it, Herm told us later, on one of their trips into town to secure morphine in the previous run, much to Herm's confusion.

Self-excluded, he had placed it on the ground next to Emily, with the words, "Good work tonight," and that maddening half-smile, then turned, and limped away.

I watched him go, but his figure was stiff and tall in the dwindling light, and he didn't look back.

We dug into the wine with relish. It wasn't often we had such luxuries, and a few hours later, there were already several empty bottles scattered around us, glinting in the firelight.

"This stuff," said Emily, giving the side of her wine glass a smacking kiss, "is actually decent."

"I know," Cat was nodding, lips smeared berry-red, "beats the battery acid brandy."

"Why *do* we drink that?" asked Colm with such apparent bewilderment that everyone dissolved into giggles. I spluttered a little and grabbed Colm's knee, pulling myself up by it. Herm, who was lying, his head in Cat's lap, put his foot against my spine to support me.

"I don't know," I said now, once I'd caught my breath. "I don't even know where we get it. Herm probably brews it in his sink or something."

"Oi, watch it, you." said Herm, poking his toes into my back.

"Ow!" I said. "Oh, that's quite nice actually, carry on. Ouch. Not that hard."

Herm laughed, stretching his arms up above his head to circle Cat's waist. She leaned down, grinning, and kissed him on the lips.

Colm mock groaned. "Hey, enough of that. The show's over."

"Says who?" demanded Emily.

The build-up to this show had been rather fun. I suspect that Emily, at least, had indulged in a bit of bed hopping, and I had found myself slapped hard on the backside by a grinning Cat as I walked past, felt Herm's arms around my waist, giving me a quick squeeze as I stoked the fire, and once, Emily had reached across suddenly as we sat on the steps of her van, grabbed the back of my head and kissed me forcefully, her tongue tasting of cigarettes and brandy, pulling away after a while to comment casually on how I might improve my technique.

Only Colm was too polite to take the cheerful, offstage liberties the rest of us did, but I had felt his eyes on me across the firelight, and late one night there had been a tentative knock on my door, which I had pretended not to hear. I was afraid of Colm's feelings, which I suspected ran more deeply than performance related libido, and I didn't want to hurt him. Even so, for my part, I had found myself eyeing him as he stretched, shirtless, after the early morning runs for which I joined him, running until the barely remembered shadow of my father grew ever smaller and fainter behind me. I had found myself noticing the way that Emily smelled, of musk, herbal cigarettes and sex, the glint in Herm's eye, the pert, sharp edges of Cat as she moved.

"I don't mean to be impolite," Colm said now, propping himself up on one elbow, and gently dislodging Emily, who had wriggled around to lay her head on his chest, "but you don't normally seem to mind the brandy."

It was daring for Colm, and I honoured it by grinning at him, twisting away from Herm's foot and leaning over to ruffle his soft, curly hair.

"That's different, that's when we don't have the good stuff."

He smiled back, moved his head so his cheek lay in the

palm of my hand. I felt a wave of tenderness. It was more maternal than lustful, but I reached down anyway and kissed him, very gently, in the middle of his smooth dark forehead.

"Get off," said Emily, pouring herself more wine. "He's mine."

"Aw," said Herm, "you keep all the best ones."

I smiled to myself and lay back down, looking up at the stars. I felt the warmth of Colm's body next to me, Emily, mock angry, fussing around with my feet, moving them out of the way of her wine.

I thought, with a little rush of warmth, that for all my wrangling, for all my pushing and fighting against Fredrick's decisions, there was indeed a remarkable, in fact an astonishing, wisdom to him. I could see that it was, after all, not the sex in this show, but the trauma of those we had been through previously, that bound us together, and now made us whole. Cat was right, it was the fight and not the victory that Frederick worked so hard and so selflessly to provide for us. And didn't I always know this? Did I not long for it all of those long, hungry years, when I lived alone in my head with my battle-strewn daydreams?

I didn't go straight to bed that night, though I pleaded tiredness. I left them at the campfire and walked to my van. But I didn't go in. Instead, I worked my way, carefully, slinking in the darkness through the trees at the edge of the field, to Frederick's bus.

He had drawn the heavy curtains across the stage to allow himself privacy, though he hadn't yet slid the front panel back across it, a task which required at least two people. For some reason, perhaps because it was clearly visible from the campfire, and perhaps moved by some actor's instinct never to cross the curtain, I walked around the back. The wine and the recent performance combined hotly inside me, and made me daring and brazen, and I walked straight up the steps and pushed the door without knocking.

It was locked.

I stepped back in surprise. This little ritual, in which I would visit Frederick in his van, would fight with him against some new rule or idea, had become our way. An acceptable little act through which we could dissipate, or perhaps more truthfully, indulge, some part of the tension that stretched between us.

Through the blacked-out window towards the front of the vehicle I thought I could see a faint silhouette, tall and thin, looking back out at me. I stood and stared back at it. Somewhere inside me I knew that he would not let me in tonight. Frederick was our leader, and he must keep himself distanced if he was to maintain this precarious dynamic, to continue to win this high-stakes card game we played with our bodies, and our hearts.

"Eurgh," said Emily fidgeting about and pulling at her jeans. "I hate those bloody cap things. I swear I can still feel it in there for days after."

We were seated, as always, on Emily's steps, the early morning light just lifting above the treeline. I nodded, though my part in the performance had not required contraception. This was the only exception the Company made to its commitment to reality. Children, it was fervently agreed, should not be raised in this environment, it being unfair because this strange, harsh lifestyle was something that we had chosen, not them. Frederick was always adamant about choice. This meant, in reality, that any intercourse which took place on stage required some sort of intervention by the women, so that it could be arranged backstage, beforehand. The more long-term alternatives tended always to require some sort of identification, or a registration with a doctor. Compared to the other things we did, however, inserting a diaphragm was a minor inconvenience.

I yawned and rubbed at my forehead. "That wine was good. I think I'm getting a hangover."

"That's because you were boring and went to bed."

The others, after my thwarted attempt to visit Frederick, had stayed up most of the night, chatting and laughing, and only drifted off to their vans in the early hours. Emily had not yet been to bed. I had returned to my van from Frederick's, feeling unfulfilled and a little flat after the heady heights of the past few hours, but I hadn't slept much. I should have gone back out and joined them. But I still struggled whenever I drank nowadays with a terrible urge to drink much more, although, since *If I Do*, I had never, ever touched white wine.

"Did I miss anything good?"

She shrugged, "More of the same. Colm had to apologise to everyone about four hundred times, of course. Once the afterglow had worn off."

I laughed, "Poor Colm."

But her expression was dark. "Yes. Poor Colm. Poor, bloody Colm. That woman did a proper number on him."

"Who? His mother? I always wondered … but how do you know?"

"Come on Rose, you know the drill. We don't talk about these things."

There was a pause. She sighed. "Our initiation plays. Colm and I were in *Othello* together, remember? He was Iago and I was Desdemona. Well, you do strange things when you're rattling about backstage, thinking you might kill someone or thinking you might die."

I thought of myself, holding that dagger, imagining plunging it into Herm, and flushed with shame.

"So basically, I tried to shag him, and he tried to confess."

"Really?"

She snorted. "Well obviously, have you *seen* Colm?"

"No. I mean – he told you about his mum? In his confession?"

She frowned again, blew smoke out from her nostrils. I fought the urge to cough. After the morphine comedown, cigarettes had been the lesser of two evils for Emily, but I missed the old herbal scent and I hoped for it back. She'd told me she was cutting down on the nicotine, but I hadn't seen any sign of that yet.

"Well, I'm not going to tell am I, priest confidentiality and all that. Suffice to say he grew up in rural Wales and he didn't have anyone much to confide in. And *she* was a violent, religious maniac. 'Free Church' or something. Didn't sound very free. He'd been to prayer meetings and sermons and bible camps and had his soul saved more often than he'd been allowed hot dinners, and everyone was very keen on discipline but not at all keen on intervening. And nothing was good enough for her and nothing ever will be."

She took a swig of her tea, put it down and stared out across the field. "You know he's the only one that Frederick expressly forbids to contact home, don't you?"

I did not. The majority of us kept our contact to a minimum, I more than most because I dreaded the taut, disappointed interactions with my father, but a certain amount of economical truth-telling once in a while was necessary to avoid suspicion.

"Well, he does. And Colm still goes and begs him. Not all the time but at least once a show. Still hopes he might be able to get her to – I don't know what – watch a performance. Something. And finally approve."

"And would she?"

Emily stubbed her cigarette out on the steps by my knee.

"How would I know? Do you think I've met her? I got the impression there was something else, something he thought was too awful to tell me. From what he did say though, I don't think she'd approve of anything. Unless we did the *Passion of Christ* or something. And crucified Colm."

There was a very long pause. I scrambled about for something to say, but no words were available. I felt an urge to get up at that moment and go to find Colm, and knock on his door, and take him in my arms. But that would change nothing.

"So, did you?"

"What?"

"Shag Colm?"

It broke the ice, as I had meant it to. I felt ashamed that I had asked, regretful that she had told me. It was a rule we had broken, a rule that Colm himself so fervently adhered to. I wanted to un-know it.

"No," said Emily, "he's incorruptible. Or he was then …" She looked sideways, mischievously, at me, "You know I really think this play was one of Frederick's best."

Scene Six

(A ruined barn set to the side of a quiet field. It is a beautiful late summer evening, and the sun is low in the sky. It fills the barn with gold-tinged shadows, piercing the cracks and holes in the brickwork and casting patterns of light on the grassy floor.)

We were preparing for Edgar Allan Poe's dark masterpiece, *The Fall of the House of Usher,* and the barn would be perfect, though we were generally much safer when we performed in the bus. There were fewer complications, less chance of suspicion, or of scrutiny beneath the furrowed brows of health and safety officials.

Once again, we would need to move on as soon as the performance finished. The barn, though we had tested it rather perfunctorily, for safety, was nonetheless falling apart. We would not be revealing the play's exact location, only the field it stood in. The audience would not know about the barn until they were ushered inside it.

It was made of large slabs of grey stone, with jagged holes along the sides, as though some large and terrible creature had mauled it. A wooden door, missing several of its slats, hung drunkenly from the door-frame at the top end, held precariously in place by a couple of wicked-looking nails, bleeding rust into the stone. The slight breeze made it sway and creak, and, occasionally, slam itself angrily against the brickwork, scattering a confetti of rust and wood splinters over the ground. Some of the roof had been half-heartedly repaired at some point, covered by sheets of rusty, corrugated iron, but this tailed off half-way across, as though whoever had started the work, had declared it unworthy part way through.

The remainder of the roof was topped, rather spectacularly, with a complex network of exposed beams, reaching up in triangular splendour and casting long, tangled shadows on the grassy floor inside. An insistent, creeping ivy clung along the outside wall, above the door, red-tinged and spidery. Moss grew in the cracks of the stonework and weeds reached their long fingers up from the gashes in the walls. Old broken roof tiles lay partly buried in earth and foliage, waiting to crunch under the feet of any person or creature moving around the perimeter of the barn. In the low light of the early evening the building had a sort of terrible beauty.

Inside the barn, and towards the back, there was a mezzanine hayloft, accessible by a rather rickety wooden ladder, missing several rungs. Above that, we had tied a thick rope over one of the beams, both a route up and a pulley system.

I was lying, face down, across a horizontal beam, the creaking boards of the mezzanine hayloft far below me, thighs gripping the wood, arms tensed around a heavy spotlight.

"How's that?"

I craned my neck around to look upwards, wobbling a little and pausing a moment to re-secure my position, before glancing up again.

Frederick was holding the other spotlight higher up, against the join of two of the higher, diagonal beams, aiming it downward. He was stood on the beam I was lying across, his arm and one leg wrapped carefully around the central vertical beam for balance. He looked, in the dusk light, like some alien vine. I turned my head downwards again to survey the hayloft and the floor of the barn.

"Yes, that's it."

We were trying to position the lights in such a way that we

could recreate the same light effect we were experiencing now, but which would fade, quickly, into darkness as the evening advanced. We had a couple of lights positioned on the ground outside too, poised to shine through the holes in the wall, and the slats of the wooden door. The overall effect, reminiscent of some grand but neglected cathedral, would lend the barn even more of a majestic deathliness.

Frederick nodded, satisfied, and began securing his light, hooking the metal grips around the wood, and securing them there with tension ties, clamps, and a thick black chain. I grunted and shifted, changing my grip. It was heavy work, but I had volunteered to do it.

We worked largely in silence, concentration being paramount both to our safety and to the preservation of the lights. But there was a pleasure in our shared breath, in this lofty, shared space. There was a pleasure in everything else being so far below.

"That should hold for now," said Frederick. "I'll secure it better later." He surveyed the barn. "Yours is the last. We must get that one right."

I nodded, my shoulder muscles beginning to cramp, but I smiled a little. It was always essential to get everything right. This was the third time in three days that he had rearranged the lighting.

I felt his eyes on the back of my head, and I twisted and met the search in his gaze. There was a hint of defensiveness along the set of his jaw, but he said nothing. I raised my eyebrows at him, and, despite the protest of my arm muscles and my precarious balance, shrugged and grinned. For a long moment he didn't change his expression. We only stared at each other, and I felt my own grin fade. Then, slowly, he gave me that habitual, half-smile.

"You're okay to hang there for a moment, aren't you?" he

said, and I read the challenge in his voice, and beneath it that strange, indefinable something that we shared. A frustration made cruel.

My muscles were screaming, and I could feel the sweat on my hands, slick against the metal.

"I'm fine thanks." I said.

He held my gaze for a long time. "Excellent." He said, finally, and his voice was quiet, and suddenly hoarse. Then he coughed and made his way to the end of the beam and down the rope, "Just hold on for a while. I'm checking something. I won't be long."

I knew he would. He would delay deliberately.

But I waited until he was outside the barn before I shifted or changed my cramping grip. Something inside me bubbled up so quickly I wasn't sure what it was until it emerged from my mouth as a kind of wild laughter, and I lay there, tears of mirth misting my eyes, shouting with laughter in the beams.

The Fall of the House of Usher is a disturbing short story about Roderick and Madeline, strange and isolated siblings in their huge, dilapidated house. When Madeline falls ill, her brother, mistakenly believing her dead, stores her body in a tomb below the house. Days later, there is a terrible storm, during which Madeline breaks out of the tomb where she has been trapped and reappears, a deathly apparition. Only then does she die, and as she does so, falling into the arms of her brother, simultaneously killing him with fright, the house around them finally falls.

In Frederick's version, the house would be the central character and, apart from Cat's Madeline and Herm's Roderick, we would, all of us, be part of the house. Cat and Herm's final 'deaths' would take the form of their reabsorption as part of the building. Frederick would narrate the story as a ghostly, pre-recorded voiceover, and he and the rest of us would swarm and creep over the barn until the audience felt it was alive around them.

It would be us that formed the tomb that poor Cat would need to break free from, entwining ourselves over and around her to encase her tightly, like powerful vines, and, at the moment of 'death', she and Herm would unite as part of the house with us, until the whole troupe eventually fell. The risk, this time, was not in the story itself, but in the way we would stage it. Harnesses and safety nets would not be used. We either truly became the *House of Usher*, or we risked falling off it. And either way, as Frederick pointed out, it fitted nicely with the theme.

When Frederick re-entered the barn, the evening sunlight had all but gone, and I was illuminated only by the spotlights, lying quietly now, and calm, my muscles numb and cramped into place. I watched his long shadow enter, and then pause for a moment to take in the effect, which was indeed spectacular. We had finally got the lighting right. When he climbed the broken ladder to the hayloft, and looked up at me, I could see the tenderness in his eyes.

I did not adjust my expression.

"That was quick." I said.

I watched the half-smile spread across his face and I almost dropped the light then and there, for no reason. "It's exactly right, isn't it?" I said, feeling a sudden need to move past this moment, and he turned and surveyed the barn again, his satisfaction palpable.

"Yes," he said, "it is exactly right."

He scaled the rope, moved across the beam and sat down next to me.

"Do you think you can hold it in place for a little longer while I secure it?" he asked, his eyes on my blue, cramped fingers.

"I can hold it," I said.

He paused. His fingers brushed over the length of my arm, travelling coolly along the taut muscles. I felt a sensation of sudden warmth, and a sense of panic, as though I might be suddenly not in control of my body. Confusion combined with physical strain made me grit my teeth.

"I can hold it," I said again, and, just like that, his fingers were gone. For a second, I felt his eyes on me, and I stared down, my face burning. Then the weight of the light lifted slightly as he began, wordlessly, to secure it to the beam.

I continued to hold the spotlight until he had finished his work, and I waited even then until finally he said,

"It's done now, Rose. Thank you."

I released my fingers. I moved my hands to the beam to push myself up with my arms but as I put my weight on them my muscles quivered, and I wobbled and cried out. His hands were like lightening, on my shoulders, and I felt that strength I'd noticed in him before, belying his slight frame.

"Breathe," he said.

I was panting, quick and sharp, my heart pounding against the beam.

"You need to use your stomach muscles instead," he said. "They've rested, they're still strong."

I frowned in concentration, slowed my breath and, with an effort, used my abdominal muscles to drag myself up into a sitting position, straddling the beam and shuffling backwards until I could lean my back against a vertical join and release my knotted legs. Pain flooded through me as the blood flow resumed.

Our preparation for our parts, as the collective *House of Usher*, had focused entirely on our bodies. We avoided being in the barn too much together, for fear of accidentally conducting a rehearsal and corrupting the freshness of it, but at any given hour of the day or night, one of us at least would be there. We learned the location of potential footholds, or of gashes and creaks in the beams. We created ever more inventive, ever more dangerous, ways to move ourselves up and around and under and over, until we began to feel, truly, like a living piece of the building.

I became keenly aware of my body. I had learned to listen to its impulses, to indulge it a little in the last play, now I tested it, pushed it, isolated and identified every muscle. I understood myself, at that time, as a mechanism, I knew which tendons moved which bones, and which parts of me were the strongest, and I mercilessly punished the parts which were weakest until I had beaten myself into taut submission.

In the mornings, Colm and I ran together silently, each focusing on our own body until our leg muscles were in spasm and our toes were numb. We spent hours, afterwards, stretching in the grass, each limb pulled and tightened and lengthened and manipulated.

I had entered the barn on one occasion to find Emily hanging by her feet high above ground level, from the highest of the horizontal beams, adrenaline and effort streaming from her face. I'd already encountered Cat trying to move along the walls like a spider, using hands, feet, and teeth. I had become aware, again, of everyone's body, but this time with a distanced, detached sort of surveillance, like a buyer inspecting a machine. Colm's strength, Cat's lithe agility, Herm's paunch, Emily's easy, swinging way of walking.

I closed my eyes and leaned my head back against the beam up against me. I reached upwards, slowly, caressing the wood and snaked my arms around the vertical beam behind and above me, feeling the change in blood flow, the relief of my muscles as they flexed the other way. It felt luxurious.

Frederick's voice, when he spoke, seemed to come from a long way away, and I could hear the amusement in it.

"You need to drink. I'll get water."

He was back much quicker than he had been earlier, carrying two flasks that he had filled from the drinking water supplies in his bus – and the brandy bottle. I opened my eyes and laughed.

I remember I felt so free in that moment. So happy. Life by then, had grown to have a value I had never thought possible, made all the more potent because of the way we lived.

I could have drunk the water, had a sip of the brandy and then made my way, quietly, back to my van. He could have continued to test the lighting. If we had done that, might I still be drinking tea with Emily, running with Colm, laughing around the campfire? Or was our destruction always inevitable, the house collapsing in around us? Extremism, by its very nature, must always go to its extreme.

"Frederick? Do you ever wish you didn't have to be in charge?"

I had drunk my water in huge gulps, splashing it down my chin and wiping it off with my sleeve. I'd sloshed some of it deliberately down my neck, enjoying the gasp of the cold of it on my hot skin, and relishing the chill it would bring as it dried in the late evening air. I'd taken a similarly enthusiastic gulp of the brandy and the question had come when Frederick had taken back the bottle. Getting drunk up here was pointlessly dangerous. And we were never pointless.

He didn't answer. I hadn't expected that he would. I stretched out my legs, tested my body for strength, then swung them over the side of the beam and leaned back, hanging from my knees, hands dangling in the air, enjoying the sudden heat of blood as it rushed to my face.

"I mean, don't you ever want to just relax for a moment?

Be told what to do? Let somebody else be the big, wise leader – just kick out for a bit and do what you're told?"

The whisky burned in my throat, my digestive tract being suddenly upended, and I swallowed and breathed slowly to prevent a stitch. Above me, the stars were a speckled, silver carpet.

"You know. Just be able to do what you want?"

It was a contradiction, but he didn't point it out. The fact was, we both understood. Frederick's position made him simultaneously all powerful and utterly constrained. He was, in many ways, our captor, but he was also, of all of us, the least free.

"What makes you think I don't do what I want?"

I swung myself upwards, using the momentum to catch the beam again with my hands, and pulled myself back up to sit beside him.

"Well, do you? Do you always?"

I turned to look at him, slightly incredulous because we both knew the answer, but he was staring into middle distance with an expression which made the words die a little on my lips.

"Frederick?"

"No." He spoke so quietly I could barely hear him. "I don't always. Who does?"

Below us, far away, I watched the tiny figure of Cat walk across the field towards Herm's van. I saw the flickering of the campfire in the distance.

"But with great power," I said grandly, trying to disguise the intensity of the moment, "comes great responsibility".

"Churchill," said Frederick, to my surprise, "not Spiderman. Churchill said it in 1906."

"I never said—"

"No," said Frederick, "but everyone thinks."

I swung my legs around again so that I could lie back along the beam, facing the stars. My head was inches from where Frederick was sitting. I could reach out and touch him. I kept my fingers locked together on the underside of the beam, anchoring myself.

"Does it matter?"

"Who's the quote is? No."

"Oh."

There was a pause.

"Except that Spiderman was a fictional character. And Churchill was leading the country through a war. So yes, two people said it. But only one of them was killing people."

I shivered. The night was rolling in, and it was colder and meaner than the summer evenings had been, a precursor to the winter we would have.

"Pass the brandy," I said.

"No. You'll fall."

We stayed, exactly still and in silence, for some time after that. I felt the weight of him through the beam, his breath mingling with the air, the warmth of his body near my head. Below us, some small creature poked around in the longer grasses, before retreating, alarmed at the unseasonal lighting.

I heard the distant bang of a camper van door, Colm or Herm off to bed, Emily either going out, or returning from town. I felt oddly disconnected, perched up here with Frederick. As though we were, for a moment, out of space, and out of time. I considered reaching for him, but gripped the beam instead, shifting, restless, and began to climb up to the next level, planting my feet and pulling myself up with my arms, until I lay on my stomach on the beam above him, staring down at the top of his head, at the stiff, angular set of his shoulders. It was an oddly intimate vantage point. Frederick's height meant that his body, viewed from this angle, seemed exposed and vulnerable. I could see the hollow at the nape of his neck, the first, pale knot of his spine, his cheekbones, sharp below his forehead, the dark precision of his brows.

I draped myself over the beam like a snake and let my arms dangle. They hung in the air, a hair's breadth away from him. If he moved his head just a little, I would be touching his face. He stayed there, staring ahead, perfectly still.

"Did you read it? Spiderman? When you were small?"

I couldn't imagine it. He smiled.

"You don't have to be small. But yes. I read everything."

"Really?" I was intrigued. Frederick never spoke about himself like this, usually he deflected the conversation to others, or turned it somehow to teach us something, or to make a point. Perhaps, like me, he was enjoying this moment, outside of what scraps of reality we still adhered to. Where the rules, spoken or unspoken, might, just possibly, not apply. My breath quickened at the thought of it.

"They called me a changeling child. Odd. Always at the edge of things. Always reading. I wasn't interested in either sport or studying and whatever was happening, most of the time I wasn't paying attention."

He gave a small, mirthless sound, more a sudden outlet of breath than anything else.

"I lived in another world. A better one."

I thought of my own lurid fantasies, played out in my head against a backdrop of college and grey streets and work.

"I understand." I said.

"Of course you do."

There was another pause. Below me, Frederick picked up the brandy bottle, hesitated, his long, slender fingers on the stopper, then tightened it again and set it down.

When I spoke my voice was gentle.

"So, you've made that world now. You've made it real. Or something like it. You can relax. You can be free."

"Rose."

He lingered on my name.

"Rose. I can't."

"You can." I was indignant, angry about this for reasons I could not collate in my mind. I started to scramble about to sit up on the beam with a notion, only half-formed, of climbing back down to his level.

"You can. Why can't you?"

But at that moment, I lost my grip and slipped. I had one leg looped awkwardly over the beam, but the rest of my body flailed in panic, so that I would have fallen if it wasn't for his arm, shooting out to steady me, holding my elbow, hard, squeezing it painfully as he hissed in my ear.

"Because I'm holding you."

I knew that the 'you' he was referring to encompassed not only me, but all of us.

We were both breathing heavily. I hung there, his hand still gripping my elbow, and then I lifted my head and looked into his eyes. He met my gaze.

For a long time neither of us moved. I tensed my stomach muscles and pulled myself up so that my face was inches away from his. We were barely breathing.

Briefly, and so lightly I could almost have convinced myself it hadn't happened, our lips brushed.

We pulled away, and for a split second, I met his eyes, wide and uncertain, like mine. We stared at each other, his hand still gripping my elbow, and then, unable to hold my position for much longer, I reached up and gripped the beam above him.

In the same movement, he released my elbow and reached his arm up and around my waist, caught me mid manoeuvre and pulled me down beside him. I landed on the beam, bruising the backs of my thighs with the impact, reaching behind his head to steady myself on the vertical beam he sat beside. His grip on my waist was hard and the pressure of it made me gasp, struggling a little to catch my breath. I reached out with my free arm around the back of his head, buried my hand into the dark of his hair. I squeezed a little. Pulled tufts of it between my fingers, felt my knuckles graze the soft skin between the tendons of his neck. There was a tiny pause, barely a fraction of a heartbeat, in which we simply held each other so hard it bordered on violence, and then we gave ourselves up.

It was just a kiss. The whole thing lasted less than a minute. We pulled apart, alarmed by our own insistence, by the suddenness and the urgency of it.

Our grip on each other had moved, somehow, beyond embrace. Our knuckles were white, the flesh we gripped would blossom purple and blue by the morning.

As if on some unspoken cue, we released each other, wobbling a little as we adjusted our balance. He looked at me and I saw love and regret in his eyes, and then he swung himself, rather more heavily now, off the beam, down the rope and out, a silhouette, graceful even with the limp, striding across the field in the distance.

It was a long time before I climbed down from those beams, and by the time I did, the light was breaking into morning and my limbs were numb and blue with cold.

I walked through the field. Emily was sitting on the steps to her van, drinking tea, a second mug prepared beside her. She raised her hand in expectation, a greeting on her face, but I only smiled tightly and walked on past. I felt her gaze on my back, but she made no comment.

I know that one stolen moment in a ruined barn cannot, on its own, be the source of so much. That everything that happened after, and every person that we lost, cannot be traced back to one ill-advised kiss. There was more that was simmering beneath us all, perhaps even then. There was more than one canker in the blood.

Even so. That night was a marker for something. It was the beginning of the end.

Act Three

*"These violent delights have violent ends,
And in their triumph die,
like fire and powder,
which, as they kiss, consume."*

Friar Lawrence
William Shakespeare, *Romeo and Juliet*

Scene One

(An empty field. The remains of a campfire.)

He announced the new play the next morning, before we had finished the current one, moving us on after a single performance. When, amid the ripples of surprise from the others, I dared for the first time to meet his eyes and felt the shared knowledge sparking and spitting between us, there was a rush of giddy pleasure in it, before we both, very quickly, dropped our gaze. Even so, when, later that day, I made my way rather overtly back to the barn and stayed for longer than was necessary, I was still disappointed when he did not join me.

Those were the rules. *This* was our reality - the *House of Usher*, with its ghostly, crumbling visage and its ghostly, crumbling inhabitants. We had turned our back on the rest of it. Marriage and sex and death.

It's all just coloured water …

But I couldn't help thinking that we should have stayed there for longer that night. Should have played for the encore. After I finally left, I saw him standing, stiffly, outside his bus, every bone in him angled towards that barn.

And so, when Emily protested, surprised, that surely we didn't need to leave so quickly, that as productions went, the *House of Usher* wasn't especially risky, that we could at least stay the night, I was silent because I understood why we could not.

If Frederick and I did not leave now, we would never be able to will ourselves to stop. We would keep returning to that barn.

Over and over and over and over and over.

Arms and the Man[4]

(Interior backdrop. Situated, somewhat unnecessarily, inside the actual interior of a house. A long, low room, filled with a selection of lounge and dining chairs for the plentiful, if rather elderly, audience, and a stage made of blocks at one end. On-stage Nicola and Louka, played by Frederick and Rose, are arguing)

"The way to get on as a lady is the same as the way to get on as a servant, you've got to know your place, that's the secret of it …"

I wasn't really listening to him. We were tripping through the lines for the eighth night in a row, and any feeling which had ever been in me for my character arose only when her frustration corresponded with mine.

"… and you may depend on me to know my place …"

It was penance of course. This play, so full of affectation, in which passion waged war with slavish obedience, with its too convenient ending, and its stifled, stifling characters, escaping their narrow confines, and thinking themselves heroic, not realising that their victory was still only possible because it remained within the social rules. The domesticity of it. The repetition. Even the continuously drizzling rain.

He was making a point.

"Oh, I must behave in my own way," I said. As I met his eyes, I felt again that energy between us, so unsuited to Nicola and Louka. It flared briefly before it fell, unspent, onto the empty stage between us. I turned away from him, spoke the lines, fuelling Louka with my own frustration. "You take all the courage out of me with your cold-blooded wisdom …"

This was the 'vanilla play', the annual house run when we would visit Frederick's property to deal with the dull necessities which kept our cover, like DVLA registration and MOTs, and perform something safe and, for us, desperately boring, confirming our status as nice, normal, travelling theatrical players, just the way we were listed on the insurance.

I knew of these runs, but it was the first one I had experienced, and despite my dislike of being predictable, I was hating every minute of it. I even hated the audience, the cooing inhabitants of the surrounding countryside who had known Frederick's father and who flocked, nodding and smiling, through the doors like good-hearted peasants greeting the squire in some second-rate historical drama. They were moneyed, all of them, soaked and dripping with it. I was being bitter and unfair of course. This was the local event of the year. They probably actually looked forward to it. I don't know why I hated them so much. Perhaps it was simply because they witnessed the aching need between us and did not know that they were seeing it.

At first, I had been excited to see Frederick's house, because it represented some new knowledge of him. The shadows of my performance in the *House of Usher* had not entirely left me, and I almost expected to touch the paintwork and feel the heat of him. I wanted to press the curtains and the cushions to my face and inhale him. As if it might somehow replace all those lost moments when we moved so carefully away from each other, afraid to brush past each other backstage in case it brought everything crumbling down around us.

In fact, though the building was large, it was unremarkable, and it held nothing of Frederick. It represented only the life he had removed himself from. It was just an inheritance, part of the structure that allowed us our lifestyle, and to which we were obliged to pay annual homage.

The sudden displacement of our transitory habitat into a house and four walls had put everyone off balance. The vans stood outside, empty, pelted by the rain and driven away in turns for repair or maintenance. He had some arrangement with his tenants whereby they left each year for the duration of our visit, so we had a bedroom each if we wanted one, and a large, shared kitchen, but there was something unnerving about the solidity of the structure. When the wind blew, I missed the slight tilt and sway of the van which accompanied it, when the rain pounded it sounded unnaturally muted. I felt as though I was living in some kind of isolation tank, everything warm, impulsive, and human inside me being gradually stifled. Which was, of course, the intention.

"I guess it's just you and me then," said Herm, toasting me over the top of his glass. I grinned.

"Salut. The last man standing."

The firepit, tarnished and redundant, was languishing somewhere in somebody's van. Without it, the troupe felt uncoordinated, as though we were not a troupe exactly, but just a number of people who happened to be milling around. Tonight, by some unspoken agreement, corralled and managed, I think, by Emily, we had all congregated on the stage after the show, and sunk several bottles of another case of wine which Frederick had miraculously produced from somewhere.

"His cellar, probably," Emily had said, and I recognised in her tone that instinctive resentment that seems to overtake people when they stand eye to eye with money.

"Probably," said Colm, who was drunker than I'd seen him before, "there's probably hundreds of bottles down there. It probably stretches the length of the town. One bottle of every kind of wine in the world."

Emily snorted. "Once you step over the bodies."

I was uncomfortable suddenly. Frederick had made himself even more absent than usual throughout this run. I sensed he was uncomfortable in the house. I think it brought with it lonely, sad, little memories, and I suspected he was secretly sleeping in his bus. But the troupe never normally talked like this about Frederick, drunk or otherwise, and, as far as the play was concerned, we'd done worse.

"All feels a bit different, doesn't it?" said Herm and I pulled myself back into the moment to find his eyes fixed on me, shrewd and bright. I'd forgotten his uncanny ability to read, if not minds, at least faces. I felt a flush of guilt as I wondered what else he might have read, what other moments his eyes might have caught me in.

I took a gulp of the wine to cover my confusion and felt it acid and harsh at the back of my throat. The others had all gradually trailed off to bed, even Emily, and I knew I didn't really need any more alcohol tonight.

"This run," said Herm, though his eyes were still intent on me.

"Yes," I said, breathing out suddenly and hard, "Yes." And then, made too honest by relief, "It's awful, Herm. I hate it."

He laughed, lay back a little among the nest of throw cushions he'd arranged around him. He looked like some ancient ruler in his lair.

"Yes, it is. It always is."

"But we have to do it."

He nodded. "But we have to do it." There was a pause. "This one's worse though. I don't know why. It's not the length of the run. I remember one year we did four whole weeks of the damn thing. Frederick's bus broke down and it took ages to fix it." He shook his head. "That was hideous.

Can't even remember the play. Something tedious."

"This one's pretty tedious," I said, with feeling.

He laughed again, "It's not that bad. We've done much worse. There was some awful performance poetry thing one year. I don't know how we survived it."

"Maybe it's the rain?" I said, though I knew it wasn't.

"It's rained before." He looked serious again. "There's something else."

"We just need a new play," I said gesturing rather wildly to the side, sloshing wine over the side of my glass. If he noticed, he didn't comment. I was reminded, suddenly, of that night in the student theatre.

Would you like to taste something real?

It seemed so long ago.

There was a pause in which the rain tried to hammer its way through the windows, but the double-glazing, cruelly, kept it at bay.

"A new play, like what?" asked Herm.

"I don't know. Something dramatic." I said, sitting up to stretch my back, then settling back down, leaning back, feeling the knot of my spine against the dusty wood of the stage.

He laughed. "Be careful what you wish for."

There was a movement upstairs, a bang and a creak and we both stopped and listened. Sound in this house was muted too and given the contrast against the thin walls of our vans, I had found myself missing sounds that I hadn't previously known I was hearing. Taps running, beds creaking, Herm and Cat making love, toilets flushing, Emily returning from town.

"Cat, I think," said Herm, still listening, "she was quite drunk tonight."

"We all were," I said. "It's the boredom."

Herm raised one eyebrow. "Really? I thought it might be

the wine."

I took my shoe off and threw it at him. He caught it, without spilling his drink, and tossed it back at me. We sat for a minute in companiable silence.

"Do you ever miss it?" I said, "All this. You know. Houses, heating and walls and stuff."

"No," he said. There was a pause. "But I never really hated it either."

"You didn't?" I had largely stopped second-guessing my friends' histories, they had become to me somehow less important as my own began to recede further, the ghost, ironically, not of my dead mother, but of my living father still followed me, but it was gradually losing detail to the grainy film of time. Even so, I was immediately interested.

"Don't get so excited, there's nothing much to it. I was a bit bored, nothing huge, and I didn't really have any other direction. I was annoyed by the fusses people made about small things, that's all. Then I was annoyed by the fusses *I* made about small things. I tried to stop caring about stuff that didn't matter, but I couldn't. I concluded that my world was too small, so my concerns were too trivial, and I thought I'd give myself something serious to fuss about."

"Like multiple stab wounds," I said, remembering Herm's initiation play, *Julius Caesar*.

He shrugged and laughed. "Yeah. Like that. Like black eyes and bad trips and fire and injuries and climbing about in death-trap old buildings. Whatever."

"A bit drastic though, if you weren't really that bored."

He was silent for a moment. "Do you know what it was, the final straw? The thing that actually triggered it? A sofa. There was a radio programme in which a woman was calling in to complain because her new sofa had taken a long time to be delivered. She had her old sofa, she had a house, she had something to sit on, but to her and the radio presenter and to everyone else who phoned in to commiserate, it was a disaster. Like she was in danger, the sofa company was out to get her." He shook his head in mild disgust. "And then just after that there was a piece on an earthquake in which thousands of people had lost their homes or their lives. And nobody else seemed to see the irony."

I nodded. I knew what he meant, though my own motivation had been rather more selfish.

"And so … multiple stab wounds?"

He grinned. "And so multiple stab wounds."

"I considered stabbing you. In my initiation."

I had never admitted this to anyone before, but he only smiled. "I guess I must just attract it. Why didn't you?"

I was shamefaced, "I wasn't sure I could. But … mostly … I didn't know if they would care. I thought you were going to die too anyway."

He laughed outright. "Well you were right. I am going to die. At some point."

"But not now." I was confident, sure of myself. "I mean, in all the stuff we perform – the actual stuff – not the initiations – has anyone ever actually died?" I spoke in the certainty that nobody had. But he was looking at me closely, his laughter gone.

"Yes," he said, eventually, "yes, Rose, they have."

There was a silence. I dropped my gaze in confusion. When I walked out of Frederick's van that first night, I had not decided to join a theatre company. I had decided to die. But that was then. I wondered, suddenly, whether I would really be ready to make the same choice now.

There were plenty of things I had done, there were plenty more things I would be prepared to do for this Company, but the fact was it had given me a reason to survive. I finally had a life I would fight for.

"There was a young guy, joined us quite early on. He was pretty much alone in the world, been in and out of foster homes, rattling about in various soulless care structures till he hit eighteen, never really settled since, and he wanted a good send off." Herm's eyes were on me still, focused and steady, despite the wine.

"And you …?"

"We gave him one. We gave him one *hell* of a one." He spoke quietly, there was never anything about Herm that was overstated, unless a performance required it. But I heard the break, unmistakable, in his voice. I had never seen it in him before, offstage, and I wasn't sure what to do with it. Just as I was opening my mouth, trying to coerce my thoughts into some sort of order, so that I could say something sensible, he sighed. "He was terminally ill."

"Oh." I felt a rush of relief. "Well then. Obviously, that's different."

He looked at me, frowning, and was about to say something when we heard an almighty retch from upstairs.

"Cat?" I asked.

"Cat," he said. He stood up. Cat's voice sailed down the stairs, a little shaky but still strident.

"I'm fine Herm. I don't need looking after."

"Okay. Sure." he called back, winking at me over his shoulder, without breaking his stride. But at the doorway he stopped and looked back at me.

"Night," he said.

"Night."

"And Rose?"

"Yes?"

"Never say never."

And with that he was gone.

That conversation should have been a reminder. It should have illuminated for me the parameters of the set I inhabited, refocused my vision, made me see once again the beauty of it - and the cost. But I was in a strange and floating zone at that time, detached even from our particular dreamy version of reality, my mind always with Frederick. I had forgotten exactly what it was I had signed up for.

I ignored Herm that evening, put his words from my mind. I carefully avoided the knowledge I still had, the understanding I was trying so hard to unlearn – that the fabric of our lifestyle was woven together, not by Frederick, not even by the bonds we had with each other, but by the ever-present threat of death.

Scene Two

(The stage is set, though the actors and spectators are not easily distinguishable. The audience are standing now, but they hesitate. Occasionally, small sections of their number split away and begin to exit, uncertain and more than a little disgruntled.)

"The audience *never* leaves," said Cat, peering, furtive, out of the door of Emily's caravan, where I was sitting on the steps. She glanced back inside, checking on Emily.

"She okay?" I asked.

"Getting there. It's been three nights now. I think it builds up."

I nodded. "I think that's why he repeats it. We'll be doing it every night until it's the most real we can get it."

"Or we've made enough money."

Our audiences, unsurprisingly for a largely outdoor theatre setting, grew slimmer as the weather grew colder. We had a marquee erected, which kept out any rain, and the campfire in the centre, winding smoke up and out of the narrow opening into the sky, lent it a certain novelty, which meant audiences never quite dwindled to nothing. Despite this, and although Frederick's funds still bought us the basics, there was not much left for frivolity. In this season, we all had to tighten our belts.

Cat made an exasperated sound, staring towards the marquee.

"Oh, come *on*." She said, hissing with impatience, "Just *go home*".

I sympathised. But in this case, the audience's reluctance to leave us was unsurprising. Frederick's adaptation of Thomas Hardy's short story, *The Fiddler of the Reels*, played on the original's unsettling, unsatisfactory ending. Emily was playing Car'line, to Frederick's viola-playing Wat Ollamoor, seduced and enchanted by him, though the spell seemed to be cast less by the man himself, than by the sound of his music. I had never seen Frederick play before, had noticed the instrument and assumed it was a prop, but certainly he managed, somehow, to elicit melodies which, even to me, held a certain fascination. It was simultaneously toe-tapping and sinister, and to Emily's character, a hopeless addiction.

In the story, Wat reappears, fatally, after a long period of absence, in which Car'line has managed to rebuild her life, marrying the simple, reliable Ned (Herm). Ned's love for Car'line is jaded, and rather dubious, but he has grown to love her illegitimate child (Cat), as though she were his own.

All this security is lost to Car'line as she falls, once again, to the lure of the music. She dances until, part entranced, part hysterical, she collapses, and in the ensuing confusion, both child and musician disappear. It is an unsatisfactory ending at the best of times, with Ned's return, his casual lack of concern for his wife stark against his terror for the fate of his beloved child, presumably kidnapped by Wat. The young child is never seen again, a fact made all the more ominous by the casual speculation of the villagers that Wat had no doubt found in her a 'highly desirable companion' and that he had probably trained her to dance for money.

In Frederick's version the child was a little older, but the blur of reality, between audience and players, made it much more disturbing.

We played the early scenes, inside Car'line and Ned's house, on the stage, but the climactic scene of Wat's return took place in the centre of the marquee, around the fire, and among the audience who were seated cabaret style around little 'tables' made of stage blocks. We whipped them into a false sense of celebration, getting them to their feet, and dancing with us, so that, in the final moment when Emily collapsed, they were entirely unprepared and it was they, as well as we, who created the confusion, running to help, unsure of where the acting ended, and the emergency began.

It was easy for Frederick and Cat to slip away unnoticed, Frederick heading back behind his van to sit quietly, staring into the cold of the night, and Cat to hide in Emily's caravan. I would help Emily away, while Herm weaved his panic through the audience, questioning them urgently about whether they had seen his daughter.

And, as they began to realise this was part of the production, Colm would move among them, spreading grim insinuations like poisonous seeds for them to carry home with them. Herm and Colm remained in character until the last paying guest, finally understanding that there would be no finale, took their leave. It was a triumph of cruelty. And we had done it for three nights.

I watched the audience dwindle. They left in pairs or groups, Herm still pursuing them, begging them to come back, to bring news of his daughter.

Frederick would be sitting behind the stage. Forearms resting on his knees, viola discarded beside him, his spine against the van, head tipped back in the moonlight. He wore an open-necked white shirt and no shoes for his last scene, and he would be shivering patiently, staring into the darkness, the dark hair at the top of his chest black against his skin, his feet half-buried in the wet grass.

I felt something rise in me and swallowed it down.

We all had our reasons to wish the audience gone.

After the vanilla run finally closed, and we gratefully resumed our nomadic existence, Frederick and I had continued simply to avoid each other. There was the

Company to think of, with its already precarious dynamic, and the sharp taste of normality we had just experienced was enough to reinforce in me the importance of maintaining our own, unconventional status quo.

But the scene on the beams played over and over again in a whirling loop at the back of my mind. And each time it seemed to subtly change genre. Sometimes I was shocked at our actions, our mutual trespass onto unknowable ground. At other times it was a secret pleasure, a treasured memory, fuelling fantasies. There were times when I had come very close to retreating into my own imagination, my outward self on autopilot, the way I had lived all those years before I joined the Company.

And then, one night, for the first time since the encounter amongst the beams, we had found ourselves, perhaps by accident, but probably, I suspect, by furtive design, alone together at the end of a night around the campfire. We had sat in silence while the air burned between us, until it was all I could do not to spring towards him. Instead, with a sort of wordless agreement, we both stood up and left, separately, and a little apart.

After that we became stealthier. We found reasons to touch each other. Passing the brandy, lighting campfires, erecting backdrops, carrying props.

Brushing past each other in the darkness.

Cat shifted and tutted behind me. "I hate this waiting. It must be the weather."

"It's the play," I said.

Cat had been given very little character of her own, Emily's child being literally a bargaining chip, and she was as hidden on stage as she was now behind it.

"Yeah," she sighed, understanding. "It's not exactly satisfying. At least Herm's pleased to see me at the end of every night."

"He's *always* pleased to see you." There was an edge of bitterness in my tone, which had crept in unexpectedly, and which I had not quite been able to cover. I snatched at it now, tried to bury it, smiling. If it had been Emily, she'd have heard it. But Emily was passed out still, on the bed in the van, and Cat only looked defensive, made an exaggerated retching motion. And I felt a pang of jealousy so strong I had to turn away for a moment, because Cat had the luxury not only to have her partnership, but to openly deride it.

The Fiddler of the Reels
Night Five

(Backstage, in the shadows behind the bus, the audience noise gradually receding in the distance. Frederick and Rose stand together. They don't touch.)

Emily had been weaker again tonight, leaning heavily on me as I guided her back to her van. She'd said something to me in the dark on the way, something about being exhausted, something about not being able to keep it up. But it was colder that night, too cold for such early winter, and the thought of Frederick's thin shirt and bare feet, his stoic waiting in the chill of the moonlight, was claiming all my tenderness. I had said something distracted and placatory. And if, as I helped her lie down on the bed, I noticed the swelling in her ankles, the bruises on top of bruises, where she had fallen each night, I had only filed it away, promising myself I would care for her better the next night, maybe even talk to Frederick about ending the run.

But I didn't talk to Frederick. The structure of this play and its staggered exits granted us just a little privacy, and the rarity of that made me selfish. I muttered some excuse to Cat and stole Emily's spare blanket, taking it with me, away, into the night.

"Careful," said Frederick, his voice deep and his breath quick.

We were both standing very still and very close, the proffered blanket forgotten somewhere between us. I could feel the heat of him. For a while, neither of us responded, and then, with a terrible creaking effort, I stepped backward, away from him.

"We have to stop this," I said, but my voice lacked conviction. You cannot stop something you haven't properly started.

He reached out but stopped before he touched me. "Rose."

I would give anything to hear him say my name one more time. And anything not to.

I looked at him. But he shook his head.

"No. Rose, you're right. We need to get back to the campfire with the others, they'll be looking for us once the audience has left."

I moved towards him, pressed the blanket to his chest. I felt the beat of his heart in the sharp of his ribcage.

"The audience never leaves," I said.

The Fiddler of the Reels
Night Seven

(It is very late at night. The stage is lit but the campfire is dark. Frederick stands in the middle of the empty marquee, the entrances to which are closed. Around him is the detritus left by the audience, the chaos of the final scene. Behind him the camper van stage is still set to 'interior'.)

He was standing with his back to me, staring into middle distance. I stood for a moment, watching him, riding a surge of conflicting emotions. *This was what you always wanted,* a voice told me, smugly, from deep inside, *to feel something. Now you do. Offstage. Not on.*

What I felt was not simple. Emily had cracked a rib tonight. I, along with the others, accepted Frederick's brutal wisdom, and the choice we had made to follow it, but we weren't above anger. And he knew it. Only now, when Emily had been cared for, and everyone had gone exhausted to bed, had he emerged from hiding. I wasn't even sure where he had been. To refit the front of his bus so that he could sleep for the night was a two-person job, but everyone had been busy with Emily, and the fact that nobody had offered was either genuine distraction or a deliberate punishment. I felt a pang of pity for him.

As if sensing this shift of mood, he turned then, unhurried and unsurprised, as if he had known I was there all along. He probably had. Despite the cold, he was barefoot still, in his costume, the white shirt fluttering in the slight breeze.

He had his viola, dangling from one hand by his side. The sight of it chilled me a little. I thought of Emily that evening, gasping and clutching her chest, fear running through me in that initial second, when I had thought she might be having a heart attack. The alarm, echoed on Herm's face, looking across at me as she came to, sat up and clutched at herself in pain, and Colm, by our side in an instant. I felt again the relief, and the tenderness, as we had realised together that it was nothing more serious than a cracked rib, and then the anger that followed naturally in the wake of it.

Colm had walked with me back to Emily's camper, his rumour-mongering could wait. Emily had been in too much pain to talk, she took small, shallow breaths, wincing each time she breathed in.

I stared at the viola with something approaching hatred. He followed my gaze, his dark eyes meeting mine when I looked up. We gazed at each other for a moment in silence.

"I'm not …" I broke off. "I only came to … I thought you might need help with the front of the bus." My words were a sharp, staccato rush.

He smiled.

For a moment, neither of us moved, and then I jerked myself, graceless, towards the van. There was a pause. He began to follow. I stopped.

"You won't need the instrument." I said, without turning round.

There was a long silence. I heard him shift, heard the vibration of the strings as he put the viola down on a table, a low, mournful wail.

I still didn't move.

He approached me, his feet light and soft on the grass, pausing just behind me, so that the only part of him which touched me was his shadow, long and slender in the lights.

"Rose." I turned and looked up at him. He spoke very quietly. "It's okay. It's over. This was the last night."

I nodded, but I did not speak. My throat felt tight and scratchy. I stood for a moment, met his gaze, and then, wordless, we turned and walked to the bus.

We unfastened the marquee where it met the vehicle, collected the front section, lifted it between us, and slotted it back across the vehicle. We did not speak, only moved, each sensing the other. The only sound we made during the whole operation was a slight, simultaneous intake of breath with the initial effort of lifting.

When it was done, we paused, uncertain, now that the immediate task was over. I busied myself with the clasps which attached the front section to the bus, fiddling with them more than was necessary, securing, unfastening, re-securing. I felt his gaze on my back. Then I heard him move away.

I stopped.

The long, low opening note of the viola rang out through the marquee. It was sorrowful, quivering at the edge of the note as though it was trying hard not to cry. I turned slowly. He was standing in the centre of the marquee, his white shirt luminous in the lights. He held the viola up to his chin and was drawing the bow lovingly across the strings, like a caress. His eyes were on mine. I felt myself move towards him.

I stopped.

"Frederick," I said, "I'm not going to dance for you."

But I knew – as he put down the viola, as we moved together, as we shed our promises, our restraint and finally our clothes, that this time would not be the last – and that what I had said was a lie.

I *was* dancing for him. I would dance until I died.

Scene Three

(Frederick's van. Lit by a single, glaring spotlight. The windows are blacked out with tape. In the centre of the van Rose sits. She is bound, at wrists and ankles, to a chair.)

I shifted, trying to ease the tension in my shoulders. The action made the sweat on my forehead drip, stinging, into my eyes but with my arms secured behind me, I couldn't wipe it away. I shook my head, feeling the tape chafe at my skin as I moved.

Frederick's bus, stripped of its props and backdrop, had become a very different place. The spotlight was a sinister parody of itself, rigged specifically to shine into my face. I blinked and shook my head, trying in vain to escape the heat of it, while the rest of my body shivered with cold. They had not afforded me the luxury of a coat.

A shadow fell across my face, and I looked up quickly, a fresh shiver of fear running through me. I had always noticed Colm's beauty, the smooth gleam of his skin, his dark eyes, the strong black curl of his hair. Now, when I looked at him, my eyes watering and blinking in the sudden absence of the light, I saw only his power.

He held a tumbler of water up to my lips and I gulped at it noisily, the chill of it burning my throat. My joints ached from hours secured in this position, my limbs and torso brittle and frozen.

Colm's voice, when he spoke to me, was gentle, coaxing. I opened my mouth as if to speak and saw the flash of anticipation in his eyes. In that moment I wanted to tell him everything. The things that I knew, and the things that I didn't. Things done and undone. Real secrets. Stage secrets.

But they had blurred in my mind into an indistinct bundle, a tangle of monsters too jumbled to articulate.

Emily's voice came, sounding irritated, behind me.

"Give up, you know that doesn't work."

And I heard the rest of them murmuring agreement, dark figures around me, made tall and imposing by their coats and their shadows and the fact that they were not tied to a chair. I saw the disappointment, then the anger on Colm's face, as he stood up, paused for a second over me, then turned and moved towards the sink. The light flooded back into my eyes as he moved away, blinding me, and I heard the slosh of water against the side of a bowl. Behind me, I felt Frederick's long, slender fingers, cool and uncompromising, on the back of my neck.

I was under no illusions. From the moment that Frederick had announced this play, I had known exactly how the lots would fall.

The play, by Frederick, centred around a group of desperate people in desperate circumstances who have captured a woman inside a rotting old campervan, convinced that she has information which, if they could only persuade her to reveal it, might be their salvation. It is not clear whether she really knows anything. If she knows nothing, as she continually, but rather unconvincingly, protests, they have no hope, and will probably kill her. If she has the information and chooses to reveal it, they will be saved and might spare her, but she will most likely be found and killed by the 'others', the people for whom she is keeping the secret (if indeed she really knows it), and from whose iron grip her captors are hoping to escape. Her only chance of survival is to ensure that her current captors continue to believe that she knows something, without revealing it. But to survive this way is a dubious privilege and there is clearly a limit to how long it can be done. The play ends with dark irony when her captors, hearing the approach of the mysterious 'others', suddenly flee, leaving her to the mercy of a new set of strangers. These, in turn, are desperate to confirm whether or not she knows their secret and whether or not she has revealed it, leaving her, as the performance concludes, in precisely the same situation as she began.

Days of Dim Lighting
Night Six

Emily, having secured me to the chair, moved around to the spotlight, and switched it on. I blinked but said nothing. She paused for a moment. Then, very slightly, she shifted the light so that a little of the beam missed a little of my face. Neither of us spoke. She walked to the bed and sat on it.

The performance would not open until seven and so the audience would not arrive for hours, but in the play my character would have already spent several days and nights in that chair, and so we always started early, each member of the troupe taking turns to collect me from my van, escort me to the stage and secure me, staying there to guard me until the performance began. By the time we opened, my limbs would be cramping and screaming, and both I and my captor would be bored and chilled to the bone. It was brutal. But real. It had been my idea.

"I'm bloody freezing. Fuck it. I'm getting a cuppa." Emily stood and walked over to the kitchen area, filling the kettle, dropping a teabag into a mug. She paused and turned back to me.

"Want one? Go on, I can hold it for you. It'll keep the chill off."

"No." I said. "No, but thank you."

I smiled at her, and she held my gaze.

"Suit yourself," she said, shrugging and turning back to the kitchen, but I knew from the sound of the teaspoon in the mug that she was, at least, frustrated.

When she returned to the bed, she sat down, mug in hand, leaning forward, as though she was a girl at a sleepover, swapping make-up tips and face packs and gossiping about film stars.

"So this is how I get to speak to you," she said, mock lightly, though I heard the emotion beneath. "I have to tie you to a chair now. Time was, you used to come willingly."

I felt a pang, tears springing to my eyes too easily, the accumulated tiredness and the brutality of the run was, at that point, just beginning to break me.

I hadn't sat with Emily on her steps for months. I didn't know how to talk to her without talking about Frederick. And then, as I began to spend more and more time in his van, to exit it and approach Emily in the early hours, would be to give away the fact that I wasn't sleeping in my own bed.

She was still looking at me, unblinking, shades of the play blending into her demeanour, her character sharpening the natural lines of her face.

"Rose? Are you okay? You've been weird recently." She paused. "You've been weird for a while. Well, more weird than normal."

The joke fell flat. I stared into the light, letting the glare of it sting my eyes, providing a neat explanation for the salt water which still threatened to spill from them. The themes of this play, the untold and untellable secrets, were an obvious story, in the circumstances. But I knew it wasn't just a test. Frederick was not that simple, nor was he that vindictive. I understood the play and its casting exactly for what it was – an open question to us both.

I had never quite managed to explain to myself why the relationship between Frederick and I had to remain secret, and we had never talked about it. But somehow, instinctively, we had each gone to some effort not to reveal it. Perhaps it was his self-inflicted absence from *A Winter Without Elves*, or the aftermath of his dual role as oppressor and oppressed in *Carte Blanche*. Perhaps it was Cat's words that same evening about his untouchable leadership. Or his own on that night in the barn.

Or maybe it was simply that we enjoyed the excitement of it. The drama.

Whatever the reason, valid or otherwise, neither of us had really known how to raise it with any of the other members of the Company. And now it was too late. We had deceived them too long. If there were cracks already in the walls of our *House of Usher*, a revelation of this kind might serve to widen them. This was an ensemble. Trust was everything.

"I'm okay," I said. "I'm fine."

Her posture softened, hunching her into herself so that, for a moment, she looked like an older, a weaker, woman.

"I've missed you," she said, in a gravelly whisper. "I still make you a cuppa every morning. Come and claim it sometime."

"Okay," I said, and for a moment, hope moved in me. Maybe if I could endure this play, I could return to something like our former friendship. I could meet Emily for a cup of tea in the dawn-light. Maybe I wouldn't even need to find a way to tell her. I could sneak out from Frederick's van under cover of the treeline, loop back and approach her from the direction of my camper. Talk and laugh with her. Watch the sun rise. Avoid the subject of love.

I heard the creak of the bed, as she shifted her position, so that she sat with her legs tucked beneath her, hands cupped around the mug for warmth.

"I could murder a fag," she said. I laughed. It turned into a cough. The long hours sat on this chair in the cold were taking their toll on me.

Emily's expression darkened. She watched me until I had finished coughing, turning to wipe my mouth on my shoulder.

"Rose," she said, "seriously now, will you tell me what's

wrong?"

The run would end whenever I said so. Frederick had made that very clear. But the play was a question. And I wanted to be certain of the answer.

"Emily," I said, "you're breaking character."

And that, if nothing else, meant something among us. She pursed her lips, gulped her tea, moved the lamp back into place, then returned to her post on the bed in silence. And so, when the audience began to trickle in ahead of the start time, and she busied herself with small tasks to give them something to look at, if she checked my bonds a little more thoroughly, and tightened them a little more cruelly, it was not clear whether she was angry, or simply taking me at my word.

Days of Dim Lighting
Night Eight

It was always Frederick who finished it. He alone had permission to untie me after each performance was over, to bring me, gently, back to my van. Every night he seemed to arrive earlier, the moment the last audience member had left, sometimes barely before they'd exited the marquee. He never took his turn to secure me.

Perhaps the others assumed this was part of the preparation, that he was protecting them from the necessity of breaking character, preserving the integrity of the play. I looked into his eyes and knew better. It pained him, this play. He had not intended it to run for so long. It had been only a kind of thought experiment, a necessary catharsis. He wanted it over before it had begun. But incongruous though it was given my current position, I was in charge.

I felt him move around behind me, his hand gentle, and light on my shoulder, his fingers, very gently, tracing down the length of my arm to begin, delicately, to remove the tape.

"Careful," he said as I began to pull my hands away, "do it slowly."

He put his hand to my shoulder, as if to brace me, and eased my arms out of their locked position to place them, one by one, in my lap. Then he knelt in front of me, massaged the muscles in my shoulders, fetched a warm cloth from the sink to soak off the remnants of tape from my wrists. The skin there was red and raw from repeated binding, broken in places, irritated by the sticky coating of the tape on exposed skin. He held the cloth against them, and I winced.

"Rose," he said. "I think this has to be the last night now."

"No," I said. "I'm not done yet, we could do more. The audience are still coming."

"Stop." I saw the flash of command in his eyes, the pressure on my wrists temporarily increasing. "Rose? Stop. Okay? You've done enough. If you're trying to prove something, you've done it. You win."

Tears filled my eyes, my voice came out in a tiny, childish squeak.

"But *I'm* not. *I'm* not done yet. I don't know, I—" I trailed off. I didn't really know how to explain it. This play felt like punishment. And it felt like confession.

Days of Dim Lighting
Night Ten

Colm crouched down in front of me once again. Behind me I could feel the others shifting and fidgeting. They were all pushing me harder now, trying to bring it to an end, this circular play with its nasty undertones and its raw, uncivilised desperation. Humanity at its worst. Everyone wanted this run to be over.

"Give up, you know that doesn't work."

The line came, as always, from behind me, but they had waited longer tonight. I saw Colm's grim resignation, his eyes trailing over my face as, once again, he stood and turned towards the sink.

He had hesitated, earlier, when he walked me to the stage and took his turn in securing my wrists to the chair behind me. I had felt it, his pause, and his intake of breath as he surveyed the red marks on my wrists. Then his hands were on my arms, a little further up, avoiding my wrists, binding the tape onto healthier skin.

"Do it properly," I had snapped, and felt, rather than saw, the quick flush on his face, heard his stammered apology for breaking the rules. His hurried adjustment of the tape. I knew them so well. I knew them all. And I knew how to play them.

I knew too, that this run was meant to draw us together, in darkness and drama, the only way we knew how. But somehow it was only serving to pit me against them, to isolate us all a little further. I should have stopped the run long ago, but I had reached a sort of numb hysteria. I hated the play, but I couldn't let it go.

Everyone had tried, in their own way, to persuade me. Everyone except Cat, who wore on her skin her own busy network of self-inflicted scars, and who probably, of all of them, understood the best. When they failed with me, they had approached Frederick, a tentative but growing mutiny.

They met only with his gentle, but firm repetition that the run would end when I decided, no earlier and no later. But afterwards, when I had found my way to his van, and we were lying together, my head on his pale chest, his arms around my shoulders, on the creaking bed beneath the warmth of the spotlight, the hated chair seeming to watch us at the edge of my vision, I saw a new vulnerability in his eyes. A shadow of fear. It was the first time I had ever seen him challenged. And the first time I had ever seen him unsure.

Colm turned with the bowl and advanced towards me. I flinched at the sight of it. The water inside it had been cool when it was filled and had been sat out all day. It would be shockingly cold now, only just short of freezing. This was the coldest winter this side of Christmas I had ever experienced. There was even talk of snow.

Colm knelt again, in a cruel parody of his earlier, gentler stance, and he held the bowl up to my chest. Frederick's fingers flexed on my neck, pushing my head downwards. I made myself open my eyes. Inside the bowl, the surface of the water was covered by a thin jigsaw of ice.

I had run with Colm as usual that morning. He had stretched with me afterwards for much longer than normal, coaching me, massaging, and extending my aching muscles which had been tethered into one position for so long at a time.

"I don't think Emily came home at all last night," he said, breaking the usual silence between us. We rarely spoke as we ran, just enjoyed one another's proximity. It was a welcome change from Emily's questions, Herm's searching gazes, Cat's sharp looks. Colm was easy, gentle company. I felt supported by him, without asking for support.

"That's nothing new," I said, willing the conversation to cease.

"No but it's much more often now," he said, staring out across the field and missing my tone. "There's something up with us, Rose. I think. Something's not right somehow."

"It's the play," It had become my token answer, and I waited for him to ask me to cease the run. But he didn't. And he didn't change position or begin the next stretch. He just continued to stare into the middle distance.

"It's not the play," he said, "well – not *just* that. It's like a ... I don't know ... there's something gone wrong." And then, with that rare and striking way Colm had sometimes with words, he said, "It's like a bruise. A bruise that looks worse under make-up."

If we were bruised, I felt sure it was Frederick and I, at least in part, who had dealt the blow that caused it.

Frederick's hand on my neck pushed my face into the bowl and I felt the ice crack against my forehead. Through the fug in my head, I heard them arguing, the familiar lines made blurry and strange. My hair floated a little in the edges of my vision. Soon I would struggle. There was a point at which my body would do it simply as a reflex action. For now, I let my face float half-submerged in the water, felt the freezing slap of it against my ears and the back of my neck, the cold on my chest where it had spilled there, pasting the neckline of my top to my skin.

Secrets breed other secrets. That's how they work.

Days of Dim Lighting
Night Fifteen

(For the third time, Rose's head is pulled up, dripping water. She gasps for air but there is a glitter in her eyes, a kind of manic calm on her face. Her captors exchange an uncomfortable glance. Then one of them, the man who has been kneeling, holding the metal bowl in front of her, suddenly stands up, hurling it violently to the floor.

"This is pointless," he shouts, and his anger is wild and filled with frustration. Then he strides to the door of the bus, opening it and slamming it furiously behind him. The vehicle reverberates with the force of it.)

It didn't take long for the few audience members to leave that night. Even so I was shivering in my chair by the time that they came to me. Not just Frederick this time, but all of them.

They entered from various parts of the marquee and the stage, as though preparing some sort of ambush. Initially, my befuddled, fevered mind couldn't quite distinguish the play from reality, and I wondered, wildly, whether they would try once again to interrogate me, in the privacy of the darkness, without the public present to bear its static, ineffectual witness. Even then, as I refocused, I reminded myself that the play was not real. I didn't have the information they needed. I had other secrets. But nothing that would save them.

I was aware I was not thinking clearly, and so I pressed my lips together and bit them to stop myself from speaking. But they did not speak either. Instead, in silence, they climbed onto the stage and took their places around me. Herm at my wrists, cutting through the tape, Emily bringing water to bathe my skin, Colm at my feet, Cat crouching next to him, waiting, holding bandages and dressings.

There was a grimness to their ministrations. They were

careful, but there was tension in the air and Frederick, whose job it usually was to release me, had stepped quietly back as soon as they arrived, waiting in the shadows of the stage to the right of me, watchful and silent.

For a long time, they worked in silence, no one speaking, even to me. They removed my bindings, bathed my wrists until the last of the residue of the tape had been soaked away. They applied something cool and soothing to the swelling on my ankles and wrapped them in bandages to secure it in place. When they had finished there was a pause. Everyone seemed to be waiting.

"You have something you would like to say."
Frederick was still standing in the corner of the stage. It was a statement, not a question, and addressed openly, to everyone. I looked at him across the heads of the others who were still crouched around me, and I saw the hidden fear in his eyes.

"Yes." It was Emily who spoke. "Yes, Frederick. We're not doing this anymore."

"No more shows," said Herm, and his voice, though more controlled than Emily's, contained a steel beneath the calm which would allow for no argument.

"No more of *this* run," said Cat, as though rescuing something, catching it before it fell around her. I wondered if she felt as strongly as the others. I wondered whether, if it had been her, she too would have opted to carry on.

"No." Emily's voice was raised, and she did not try to calm it. "Not one more night. We won't turn up. We won't do it. Look at her, Frederick, she's had enough."

Frederick turned his face to mine. He was a little paler than usual, but perfectly composed. I met his gaze. We had done, I was certain, harsher plays than this. And the Company, to my knowledge, had never questioned him in this way. I felt a rush of cold through my blood. But in the last few days, my mind had swirled into a strange, shivery soup. I stared at Frederick, and I did not know what message to send him.

Eventually, he moved towards me, the others instinctively stepping away. He knelt at my feet, close, but not touching me. I felt the slight warmth of his breath in the cold of the night. I remembered suddenly that very first evening, Frederick on his knees in the theatre, handing me my job offer, my ticket to another life.

"Have you Rose?" he asked. "Have you had enough?"

"No." I said, but, despite myself, I felt my throat swell and my eyes fill. I brought my hands, with their raw red wrists, up to my forehead and I buried my face in them. Sobs erupted without my permission, spilling out in salt and mucus through the lace of my fingers.

"Yes." My voice seemed to come from a very great distance, high and cracked and indistinct, as though I spoke to him through a mouth full of glass. "Yes. Please."

It wasn't a clear instruction. But it was enough. I felt relief flood the stage, and, making room for it, some of the tension drained away, though there was still a crackle of anger in the air. Frederick nodded. He put his hand up to my face, still covered with my fingers, as though to comfort me, but then he seemed to think better of it, and he put his hand back inside the pocket of his coat, stood up, and stepped back.

"The play is closed," he said. As if in testament to the remaining loyalty he commanded, no one moved until he had said it.

There was a whirl of activity then, and I felt myself conveyed, somehow, back to my van, where I was tucked into bed, and given tea, and cool dressings beneath the bandages on my wrists and ankles. There was a warm hot-water bottle between the sheets, and I felt a towel in my hair, gentle, teasing at the knots which had formed through the course of the play.

They took turns over the next few days to keep a continuous vigil at my bedside, but at the time I was only vaguely conscious and feverish, so that my understanding of the situation blurred a little, in my overheated mind, and the bandages become bonds and the figure by my bedside a jailer.

Frederick did not join them. They had left him on the stage. Not forbidden, but palpably unwelcome.

Scene Four

(A damp, icy field. A campfire, lit and, for the first time in weeks, well populated. It is a small patch of warmth.)

It was probably the worst thing he could have done. Oscar Wilde's popular comedy, *The Importance of Being Earnest*, with its fluffy triviality and farcical wit, was a perfect choice for audiences over Christmas, but superficial and deadening for us. Frederick chose to resolve this by layering in the truer story around the edges of that play, of Oscar Wilde's pursuit through the courts by John Douglas, the outraged father of the man he had loved. It led, at the peak of Wilde's triumph as a writer, to his arrest and imprisonment for homosexuality – after which he never wrote a play again.

It was genius. It should have been beautiful, a tour de force, playing two plays at once, striking that wonderful discordant note, emotions swinging chaotically from one spectrum to another, and the clever exposure of the real farce at play in Victorian London, the tragedy buried beneath.

He cast Herm as Wilde, preparing for the performances by denying him and Cat the right to express their love openly, so that they too had to creep and dissemble, and could be together only in furtive, snatched moments.

He had hoped, I think, to mend a little of our increasingly fractured lives, to recreate some common feeling. Maybe, I allowed myself to wonder, he even considered that it might pave the way to a more honest relationship between us, to emerge from the shadows with the Company's blessing, without jeopardising his status as leader. I was both excited and frightened by the prospect.

In reality, it had been a bold gamble, and his status as

leader was already in crisis. The play drove great wedges through our cracking sense of community. With two thirds of us nursing 'secrets' from the others, the essential recovery time around the campfire, already endangered, dwindled to nothing.

It was exhausting. Colm's casting as John Douglas, the villain of the piece, meant that he too, would creep about in the darkness, hoping to catch Cat and Herm in the act of transgression. The field at night grew ever more populated and ever lonelier, and mine and Frederick's own attempts to snatch time with each other became doubly difficult.

On-stage it would have been hilarious.

But everything always looks better on-stage.

Christmas day arrived like an oasis in the vast and frozen landscape of this run. It was the first Christmas I had spent with the Company, but it felt at once like an indulgence and a treasured memory relived. I was nostalgic for it even as we celebrated it.

We huddled close around the fire, both for warmth, and because the physical nearness of each other, having become in recent times such familiar strangers, simply felt good. Emily had an apparently unending supply of biscuits and marshmallows, which we toasted on sticks throughout the morning. Frederick supplied several large bottles of port and Herm and Cat managed to rustle up a full Christmas dinner on the four tiny hobs and two microwave ovens they had between them in their camper vans.

I felt a brief pang, a slight, guilty sense of disappointment, that this should be so pedestrian, a couple sweating over hobs and ovens, hosting friends for dinner. I was not sure what it was I would have preferred, for us to cook dinner together, perhaps, over the fire? Hand-caught pigeon? Or squirrel with handpicked wild mushrooms? I knew I was being ridiculous, but the fact remained that something in me sank a little at the sight of the supermarket pre-wrapped, half-cooked, pre-stuffed chicken, and Herm in an apron, boiling carrots. And, as I removed my outer pair of gloves to lean down to scratch at a chilblain on my toe, a legacy from the extreme cold in the previous show, I thought that there were many aspects to this life I had chosen which were not quite as romantic as I might once have imagined.

The Company had a tradition of buying small tokens for each other, related to a play performed during the year, or otherwise symbolic in some way. Colm bought me a very large fluffy bath-towel, recalling the tiny one which had been supplied in my very first play. The merciless teasing which followed this gift made him flush to the roots of his hair, and he mumbled an unconvincing explanation about it actually being to dry my hair with, after it had got wet so many times in the last play.

Herm bought me a set of kitchen knives, delivered with a wink – 'to facilitate your stabbing tendencies'. I laughed with the others as I received them and I appreciated that he had, in typical Herm style, managed to incorporate something practical into his gift, because I'd commented in passing that I needed something decent to prepare food with. But the block was solid and uncompromising, the knives themselves plain and silver and the whole thing somehow seemed only to reinforce the falseness of the 'danger' that had characterised my initiation. It seemed to me as though he had taken something wild and crazy and reduced it to something basic and necessary. I felt my secret ingratitude like a lump in my stomach, and I covered it over with disgust, adding it to the growing pile of secrets, the things I no longer expressed to these people, my beloved companions, and one-time confidants.

Emily bought me a pair of fluffy handcuffs.

"Because you clearly like that sort of thing."

"Now all you need is somebody to try them with," added Cat.

I looked at her then, but I saw no hidden meaning. I realised, to my surprise, that Cat, for all her suspicions and watchfulness, really didn't know. Somehow, in the back of my mind, I had assumed that someone must, by now, have guessed. I suppose the idea was so very alien, Frederick so very unavailable, that the possibility simply didn't occur. And I couldn't place exactly how I felt about that.

"Why," I said, with bright, brittle levity, "are you offering?"

"No way," said Cat, shaking her head, "nobody ties *me* up."

Frederick bought us all little luxuries, expensive equivalents of props or items which we would never have managed to afford for ourselves. Specialist whisky for Colm and Herm, a whole case of wine each for Emily and me, a selection of fancy coffees for Cat.

It was a tacit apology for the harshness that characterised our existence sometimes, and for the fact that we did not earn money we could save or lavish on trinkets. But I was concerned that it only served to underline the distance between us. The fact that he, alone among us, could afford one day to walk away.

Or perhaps he wanted to emphasise it.

I had made Cat a miniature house out of children's building bricks, built and painted to look like a barn. If you pulled a string attached to one of the little plastic figures inside, it tripped a hinge which brought the whole lot crashing down.

I'd bought Emily a pair of red ballet pumps to which I had attached ribbons, in reference to the similarity in plot between *The Fiddler of the Reels* and *The Red Shoes*.

I bought Herm a cocktail shaker, and I wrote out, from memory, a list of ingredients for an Office Worker Mojito, a Nuclear Family Iced Tea, and a Rat Race Daiquiri, realising only later that my gift related far more to my own experience, than to his.

I should have bought him a sofa.

For Frederick I bought a chalkboard and a set of white chalks, which made the others groan in remembrance of that play, but produced from him a beautiful half-smile, full of a meaning which could be understood only by me.

I had rescued Colm's old white gi, scrubbed at the grass stains until it almost resembled its former colour, and found him a black belt, presenting it back to him so that he would remember, however it ended, that he was once something approaching an Aikido master.

All of these gifts had taken effort, but it had felt good to work at something I would eventually present to them, rather than worrying at something I had hidden away.

Somehow, although it was wonderful to sit there, surrounded, albeit temporarily, by laughter and smart comments, I couldn't help feeling slightly sad. I looked at my bath-towel, my knives, and my wine, and, apart, perhaps, from the handcuffs, they all seemed so normal. As the group began to slip away from me, and me from it, I wanted to grasp at the roots of it all the more firmly, feel all the more keenly the aspects of our existence which were, to my mind, not sufficiently extreme.

It was some time after the swapping of gifts, when everyone was overly full and comfortably drowsy, that Cat caught up with me.

I was on my way to my van, and she appeared out of nowhere, startling me so that I dropped the plate I had been carrying back to wash up. It bounced on the damp grass. She grabbed my forearm, her sharp little fingers digging painfully into my flesh, and I felt a sudden irrational panic rise in me, swift and short-lived, as I whirled round to face her.

She was holding something behind her back.

"You haven't had *my* gift."

"Sorry," I said, "I …"

"I've checked with Frederick." Her voice was defensive, arming herself against some imagined objection. "And you can keep it. We have others we can use. To you, this one means something."

She pulled her arm out from behind her back, grabbed my hands and pressed something into them. Then she nodded once, a quick staccato movement, and disappeared.

I stood in the darkness, plate forgotten, tears pricking in my eyes.

A slim black hilt sheathed in plain grey metal. The blade, silver and surprisingly narrow, tapered into a tiny, wicked looking point.

I was holding Juliet's dagger.

(Lights up. The campfire is not burning now, and has been enclosed once again by the marquee, set up against the now open front of Frederick's van, and lit by the spotlights. Chairs are arranged for the audience, but the performance for tonight is over. Frederick and Rose lie together in his van, warmed by the spotlights, her head on his chest.)

"We need something. We need something soon."

It was the first time I had spoken in a while. We often lay for hours in this way, my warm skin against his cool, sharp angles. My hand on the surprising soft of his stomach, his arm around my waist. It felt like a conversation, as though we could somehow absorb each other's thoughts through our skin.

"We *do* need something," he said, sounding pensive, "there is a … disharmony, and this run is quite mild."

"Something stronger," I said, lifting my head to look at his face, pleased that he was confirming my point. But he was quiet, his eyes far away, though his grip on my waist tightened. "A better play," I said, pursuing my need, "something more extreme … a shared danger … or—"

"A return to form." He said and I saw, again, the light of the zealot behind the gentle brown of his eyes.

"... Yes ..." I said, though I was unsure whether he was quite pursuing the same point. "Maybe—"

"Rose." The way he said my name. It made me sit up fully and look at him. But he stayed where he was, lying on his back, bathed in yellow light on the stage. "Rose, we can't just keep scaling up. That's not the point of us. That's never been our meaning."

I flushed, feeling rebuked, but his eyes on mine were soft, and that half-smile was playing at the corner of his lips.

"Well, what then?" I demanded, that defensive instinct which had been building in me recently, rising and making me argumentative. I understood Cat more and more. "We need some—"

"We need something," he agreed, and the half-smile broadened then, his hand up to stroke my cheek, his fingers rearranging the tousle of my hair. "We do. You're right. Things are not quite on track."

This seemed like rather an understatement to me, and I wanted to discuss my suspicions that part of what was not right stemmed from us, from this, but I was afraid to voice it, and make the culpability real.

"Rose, we need to recruit. I'm going to take Herm with me. I have someone in mind. Two people actually." He smiled again, and the smile seemed to me incongruous. "They're brothers."

I couldn't quite respond.

Frederick would take trips away, usually while we were preparing a run, but they were generally short-lived, an appearance perhaps, in the shadows of someone's life. An observation. A suspicion. Often, he would investigate a potential recruit and it would come to nothing, some little detail would not be right, some qualm he wasn't willing to override. He never approached anyone unless he was already certain. And he hadn't, in the time I'd travelled with the Company, ever reached that stage before.

"Really?" I said, eventually. "Are you sure?"

He shook his head. "Not yet. Not sure enough. But nearly. I need to spend more time. I need to go away for longer, take Herm with me, in case we need to test the water."

I nodded, though my emotions were in turmoil. The others had told me that Herm and Frederick sometimes engaged with a potential new recruit in some other guise, before they reached the point of finally offering that gilded, fatal invitation.

"You don't like it." He said it as a statement, and his tone, which contained no real surprise, belied his frown.

"I just. I don't know. It'll be ... different."

I sounded pathetic even to my own ears, and I couldn't quite pick apart what it was I was trying to say. But he nodded. Sat up to join me, propping himself up on his elbow.

"You think we're not quite right as a Company, so it might be dangerous. To bring in someone new. It might disrupt things further."

I wasn't sure that was exactly what I meant, but I nodded, while my eyes told him other things, and his fingers strayed through my hair until his palm laid flat against the nape of my neck and he pulled me towards him and laid his forehead against mine.

"We'll be fine. It won't happen yet anyway. We have a few more runs to get through first." He paused, "And yes, Rose ... we do need a bit of a shake-up."

If I had some influence over Fredrick that the others did not, if that game of push and pull which still fizzed between us, was clouding his judgement, I did not choose to think about it.

"We need a better play," I said stubbornly.

He paused, his fingers back in my hair, tugging a little, then, very gently, he kissed the top of my head where it pulled and through my hair, I felt his frown.

"Better?" he said. "Or worse?"

Scene Five

(The darkening interior of Rose's camper van. Rose sits rigidly on the very edge of the bed, her fists clenched. Alone.)

We performed Shakespeare's *The Taming of the Shrew* for one night only, and it was simply too terrible to describe. Even now the memory of the actual performance is hazy, swimming just out of reach, as though I have somehow medicated myself against it. I know it only by its aftermath.

Frederick had taken me at my word. His staging was brutal. Where directors usually played down the sexism, emotional abuse and gaslighting, Frederick had exaggerated it and added new layers.

I don't remember the curtain-call, if indeed any of us were capable of doing one, only that the performance finished and I found myself alone in my camper van, door locked, rocking and shivering, the ghosts of the show still circling in the air. Katharina, ('Kate'), still raged within me.

Colm, as Petruchio, had been a master manipulator but also brash, brittle, and violent. My skin was bruised, and my emotions ragged. My own loss of control had very possibly resulted in a broken jaw or nose for Cat, as Bianca, my gentle, long-suffering sister, and the final scene of forced submission between Petruchio and Kate, interpreted sexually by Frederick, had been dark and terrible.

It was a black blur in my mind from almost immediately afterward, but that did nothing to anaesthetise me from it. That Colm had not been Colm in that moment, that I was not myself, did not help me. I was always someone else. That had become who I was.

In my camper van I stripped naked, ran the water as hot

as a camper van shower can muster, and scrubbed every inch of my skin until it burned. Guilt ate at the fraying edges of me. I had walked into this depravity. Wasn't it, fundamentally, what I knew I had agreed to when I left that tiny university theatre and climbed into a van and travelled with strangers into the dark? And the more I thought, the more I scrubbed until long after the water ran cold.

Sometime after, when I was sitting on the bed again, dressed and shivering, my hair hanging in wet strings, there was a soft knock on the door.

I swivelled my eyes towards it without moving any other part of my body. Frederick. I knew his breath. I knew his shadow. There was a pause and then the knock came again. I saw his hand move to the door handle, test it, try again. He called to me, softly, spoke my name. I watched his silhouette, listened to his voice, my hands very still in my lap. He was persistent, gentle, but Kate had still not fully left me, and I was frightened and desperate, paralysed with conflicting emotions. Eventually, he went away. The moment he left I wanted him urgently, but I didn't move to call him back.

There had been a silence when he had announced his treatment of this play, quietly, but brokering no argument, citing the need for a 'return to form'. The faces around the fire were pale and set, but nobody argued because everyone understood.

The only slight mutiny had been over the lots. Emily insisted on preparing the little velvet bag herself, checking it carefully, turning it inside out in front of us, Colm writing everybody's name on carefully identical slips of paper. This time, the casting had truly been left to chance.

Frederick conceded, but, when I pulled out the tiny slip of paper with 'Katharina' printed on it in Colm's careful handwriting, he read the result in my face, and he blanched so shockingly, I thought for a moment that he might pass out.

I dropped my gaze, and by the time I had found my voice and announced my character to the rest of the Company, he had recovered sufficiently to avoid suspicion. We were all solemn that day. We knew we were pushing against even our boundaries. But the thrill of the draw and the enhanced sense of life whenever we turned up the dial and increased the volume of our lifestyle, was addictive. Of course. It was probably what finally killed us.

Knocks at my door were frequent that night. Emily was next, alternately wheedling, coaxing, and bullying. She was bolder than Frederick had been, talking to me through the door, ignoring the fact that I did not answer. She was rational, direct. Now, more than ever, we needed to gather around the campfire, to regroup and to heal and to forgive each other. To remember who we were. I knew she was right. Once upon a time, I might even have acted on it. But it had already been too long. Those days were over and there had been too many performances after which we had already neglected to do it. I don't think she managed to rouse anyone else either. It was very quiet once she had left.

I sat for a while, my mind circling idly, in emotional lockdown, my responses shut off and stored away. It wasn't until much later that Colm arrived. His shadow outside was twitchy and anguished, his apologies only partly coherent. He pounded on my door, dark flames of Petruchio still flaring within him, and I understood that it was only I, as Katharina's alter ego, who could grant him the absolution he wanted. But I hadn't fully managed to escape her yet, any more than he, as he wheedled, then grew more aggressive, had fully escaped Petruchio. I waited on my bed, very still, until the knocking and shouting finally ceased, and I heard instead a small, defeated sob.

I nearly moved then, but it had been so long since I had shifted from my position that my body didn't seem to be able to respond immediately, and by the time I shuffled to my feet and opened the door, the field was empty, populated only by the silent vans and the distant rumble of thunder.

Later still, I was shocked out of my stupor by Herm, appearing suddenly outside the door, and asking whether I knew where Colm was. Something in his voice made me suddenly cold and it galvanised me into opening the door. Herm looked me up and down in silence and then, his voice soft, said, "I know it's hard. We can sort it later, but we've lost Colm and he's probably in a state."

"We should have been together."

Cat stood beside him. Her face was still marked from my earlier violence, her nose strapped up with plasters. I felt defensiveness rise in me, and concern, just as quickly, overtake it. I couldn't quite find the words to admit to my interaction, if it could be accurately called that, with Colm earlier. But Herm's knowing eyes were on me, and he nodded.

"We didn't let him in either," he said.

"We assumed someone else would," said Cat, close to tears, "but Emily went out – no one seems to stick around here anymore."

"Frederick's already out looking," said Herm, his urgency slicing through the shades of accusation that were creeping into the conversation like grimy shadows.

I pulled my shoes on, hunched myself into an anorak and stepped outside to join them, the rain beginning to hammer on the rooves of the vans, and the wind rising.

"Where would he be?" I shouted over it, "we're in the

middle of nowhere, how does Frederick even know where to look?"

Herm was already striding off.

"His mother," he said over his shoulder grimly, "I suggest we check the nearest phone boxes."

We looked until we found Colm hunched in the corner of a battered old phone booth, still holding the phone. Frederick was already with him, but Colm was unmovable. He was fervently shaking his head, his eyes bloodshot with tears, knuckles tight around the receiver. I was shocked at the state of him. He was wet and shaking, mutely hysterical, rocking slightly so that his head banged, dully but repeatedly against the glass.

Frederick, turning to greet us, met my eyes, a thousand unspoken words flooding the spaces between us, whipped into silent arias by the storm. I wanted to slap him, to stroke him, somehow to touch him, but Colm was in trouble and there wasn't time.

Everyone tried to help, but in the end, it was Cat who managed to bring him home, pushing us impatiently out of the way until we backed off and cleared her a path. She sat down next to Colm, made no attempt to take the phone from him and simply took his hand, as though there were no urgency in the world, and this was merely a nice place to admire the view. She started to talk to him, not especially gently, but with a sort of blunt practicality. Cat knew how to deal with these moments specifically because she had been on the other side of them.

As Colm was persuaded to release the phone and walk quietly back with us through the rain, I wondered, not for the first time, if what Frederick provided was really the therapy he hoped it would be, or only a kind of exploitation.

We set up the campfire in the marquee and, for the first

time since Christmas, we sat there all night, keeping vigil with Colm.

Emily did not come home.

Eventually, Colm, still murmuring apologies, but much calmer, went to bed, and, with relief, the rest of us did the same.

I lay for the majority of the frozen morning, dry but fully clothed, in Frederick's arms in the single bed in my cramped little van, both of us aware that there was no way in the world I would spend any more time that day on his stage. The numbness was beginning to give way to a sense of weariness, Katharina retreating into the distance, though I knew she, like the other ghosts I carried with me, would never truly leave.

We lay in silence for a long time, and then, turning a little so that my face was buried against his neck, I asked, "What do you think she said to him? Colm's mother, I assume that's who he was calling."

"Yes." He sounded grieved. "It's usually a case of not granting permission. For his own sake. And you know he responds to that. But tonight ... tonight he didn't even ask."

I didn't respond. But I understood the implications.

Frederick sighed. "Nothing," he said, "she didn't say anything. He didn't get through."

"What?" I pulled away from him in surprise, but he only looked at me.

"Sometimes, in a situation like Colm's, he doesn't need to speak to her. It's not so much what she says, it's what he imagines her saying, or what he remembers. Even her not picking up the phone, to an unknown number in the middle of the night, to Colm it's still a kind of rejection. She could have died or moved away. He'd still call. It would still affect him."

I was shocked. "Shouldn't we try to unite them then? Give him some kind of closure?"

He looked at me. "How?" he said.

I was silent.

He sighed. "Rose," he said, his hand stroking my hair, "it's not ours to give."

I sent him away. Gently but firmly. After the final cruelty of *The Taming of the Shrew* (I never quite called it rape), I wanted to sleep for the rest of the day, maybe for the rest of the week, on my own. I watched him leave from my van window, a tall, slender figure, receding gradually into the distance. There was something different about the way he moved. It struck me, just as he reached the door to his camper, that he wasn't limping, but before I could catch my breath and refocus, he had disappeared inside his van.

And I could never be sure that I hadn't imagined it.

Emily did not come home until late the following evening. She'd gone rock climbing in the darkness and got stuck on a ledge in the storm.

If she'd fallen that night, we would never have found her.

The Merry Wives of Windsor

Frederick's timing remained impeccable. We opened *The Merry Wives* with minimal preparation, just as the aftermath of *The Taming of the Shrew* began to subside, but long before it had gone completely. Cat's nose would never again be entirely straight, Colm was subdued, and I was still getting flashbacks of the submission scene, suddenly and without warning, making me retch with the shock of it. On a couple of occasions, I had vomited, violently and miserably onto the grass in the wake of one of these moments, until, at Emily's suggestion, Colm and I sat round the campfire one night and got hopelessly and rather unhappily drunk. We were both sick after that, but it had, at least partially, cleared the air.

I spent every night with Frederick, his imminent departure with Herm making me fierce and hungry and rather more desperate than I liked to believe myself. I set an alarm to return to my own camper van in the same way I had once set an alarm to meet Emily. And I always left the back way, skirting out through the tree-line, slipping into my van to lie wakeful, listening to the sounds of the morning. It seemed to me that we had, all of us, somehow inherited Frederick's limp, real or otherwise, and were dragging ourselves painfully through the thorns in the path we had chosen to walk, no longer remembering why.

And then Frederick cast Cat and I as the eponymous 'Merry Wives' and we all engaged in a bit of Colm baiting. As the chauvinistic buffoon, Sir John Falstaff, (just similar enough to the chauvinistic bully he had played in Petruchio), he peered at us from above his ridiculous white ruff, deliberately cut and fastened rather too tightly, so that at the end of each performance, he had a reddish indentation where it had cut into his skin. We entered into the barely disguised cruelty of *The Merry Wives* with abandon. We tipped him out of the laundry basket in which we had tricked him into hiding, into the freezing stream that ran around the edge of the site, chosen deliberately by Frederick for this feature.

Night after night he crawled out again to make his entrance, soaked and shivering in the February temperatures, for our amusement and to the delight of the audience.

When he was beaten out of the house by Mr Ford, played by a grim-faced Herm, who still remembered Cat's face in the wake of *The Taming of the Shrew*, we played it for laughs but the blows, inflicted by his carpet beater, were real enough.

In the final scene, when we surrounded Colm, laughing and teasing and pinching, I looked into his eyes and saw our reflected cruelty, the unfair anger we'd released without compunction. And, beneath the layers of him which were taken over by Falstaff, I saw his acceptance of this, his need for it. It wasn't exploitation, I thought, I had been wrong about that. It was more a complicated form of collective self-harm.

We tortured Colm for five nights, at which point Frederick, observing our waning enthusiasm for it, a gentler light in our eyes, quietly called it to a close. He would leave with Herm early the following morning.

Scene Six

(A scattered audience gaze impassively at the stage. It is lit with a warming, homely light but the backdrop is clearly that of an institution, veiled only partially by the presence of twee cross-stitch pictures, and the overly soft furnishings. The play is in full swing, but it doesn't have the pull of some of the Company's previous performances. There is something off about the atmosphere.)

It was hot in the wings, despite the still wintery weather outside and it felt oppressive and airless. The heavy curtains hung close around me and seemed to sweat into my skin. We had never had a lot of space backstage, but tonight I felt smothered in velvet.

"A plumber would rob us blind. Murder us even. In our beds. Or worse …" On stage, Colm took Emily in his arms. "We'll make do and mend my darling. Even if the house falls down around us …"

I swallowed and closed my eyes, the tiredness that had been growing in me over the past few weeks suddenly sweeping over me, as though I might fall asleep on my feet. I stopped myself, just in time, from leaning my weight against the curtain box I stood inside, and landing with a crash onto the stage.

For a moment, nerves jangling, I had to re-orientate myself, half-convinced I had actually fallen, but Emily and Colm had made their exit on the other side and Cat's monologue remained magnificently unbroken. The audience was sparse, but she was fully absorbed in her character, eyes wide, blanket pulled up to her chin, staring fearfully out into middle distance.

"Imagine a house where the house fell down and all the

walls went missing ..."

I felt a sudden pang for her. She was beautiful in this role, wondrous and terrified. We never usually cared about the audience but this time, as I surveyed the scattered figures, I knew we hadn't done Cat justice. We were supposed to drum up talk and gossip, spread rumours in bars and coffee shops and clubs. But we'd only half-heartedly handed out flyers. Herm and Frederick were still gone at that point, and had returned for the performance tonight, too late. They would have done more.

"... and the sky came in, and the birds flew down and all the bricks were broken ..."

The play, *This is the Place Where the World Must End*, was designed especially so that we could prepare and put it on with two of our number missing. Written by Frederick, it was a lyrical, wistful piece about a pair of isolated siblings, Hallie and Clarissa, trapped in their house by their overly protective parents.

The children obsessively make up stories to populate their narrow world, simultaneously scared and excited by their own creations. While the younger sister, Hallie, becomes increasingly unable to disentangle the fiction from her bland reality, her older sister grows restless, realises her situation, and finally escapes. But she is unable to persuade her sibling to join her.

It was easy to prepare for, we only needed to avoid public spaces and stay together, which was almost certainly part of Frederick's design. Perhaps that too was why we had tried so little to drum up an audience.

The others had lived their parts exactly. Emily, as our mother, had been the epitome of prim from the moment we began preparing. Cat had embraced perfectly Hallie's terrible mixture of fear and longing. Colm had been smothering all of us for weeks with an alternating pattern of love and control. But I felt distant somehow. I had prepared the older sister's character with my head and not my heart and now I was running through the lines with an automatic reflex. There was always something shifting in the back of my mind, a nebulous shadow which I refused to examine openly, but however hard I had tried to prepare for the performance, it continually pulled me back.

I told myself that didn't matter, perhaps even that it could be part of my preparation. Clarissa was doomed to be different. She was separated from the world by her closeted family and set apart from them by her belief in 'the outside'. The play concluded with her escape, but whatever happened to her afterwards, she would remain, always, a little distant, haunted by their fearful ghosts.

That was the one aspect of my character I truly felt. It was a little too close to the truth.

There was a split-second silence on stage and some subconscious instinct rose in me, my feet moving me before my mind recovered. I stumbled out of the curtain into the light, barely remembering the toothbrush which was my prop. I joined Cat beneath the blanket,

"Imagine a house where the house fell down and the sky became a doorway …"

The lines poured out but even as I spoke, I felt sick of this play, which I had barely begun to engage with, and it came on me with a wave of what I realised, with some alarm, was actual nausea. I swallowed, stuttered a little and felt Cat tense beside me.

Frederick was a vague shadow, silent at the back of the audience. I could barely see him through the glare of the lights, but I could feel him. He was a watchful figure, in his consummate role as director, but I knew that he would have the same acute sense of my presence as I did of his. I wanted to run through the audience towards him.

There was a time, before, when I used to feel this same urge as an audience member. It seemed that I would be unable to control myself, would at any moment stand up, clamber over the anonymous heads of the audience in front of me, and claw my way, gasping, towards the bright white comfort of the stage. Now I wanted to run away from it, to trample the audience as I pursued something else.

I felt Cat's hand squeeze my forearm hard, and I realised that the lights had faded, and the scene was changing. I shifted, feeling my way off the stage in the darkness, Emily pushing past me to take her place.

The performance continued and I seemed to sleep through it, only waking every now and then to hear myself delivering a line and realise, with some surprise, where we were in the script.

I entered and exited, spoke, and gesticulated with exactly the right amount of expression and none of the feeling beneath it. My stomach still felt unaccountably queasy, and I was hot, even beneath the minimal lighting.

The automatic sentences springing from my mouth reminded me, horribly, of the conversational autocue I used to employ, back when everything I did and said seemed meaningless, so that I responded to Colm's paternal questions with an undertone of sadness which my character, at this moment in the play, should not have had. It was the first time I had ever stood on stage and remained entirely myself. A hot, defensive anger burned inside me. Who was Rose anyway? Who were any of us?

"Good girl," said Colm, and there was an uncharacteristic note of warning in his voice, or perhaps it was only his role as my father. It didn't matter. I heard the lines through a sort of muted haze, as scant in detail as the field in the darkness, made darker by the lights.

A small titter from an audience member, amid one of my speeches, at a point when they should have been fearful and tense, brought me temporarily back to my senses, and for a while I managed to pull myself together.

I channelled my anger into my character. I strode onto the stage to confront Cat in the climactic scene and spat my lines at her.

"Imagine a life where you don't have to pretend it. Imagine a life where there's blood and breath. Imagine a life where you actually live it—"

"Clarissa, you can't …"

"We can. We are old enough."

"We don't know our age."

There was panic, and genuine confusion in her voice, and I softened a little, felt her sadness.

"Hallie," I said. "I think we might be older. Older than we're meant to be."

"It will be dangerous."

"It will be free."

I faltered and, somewhere within me, the bony, fragile little effigy of Clarissa I had been building, sputtered and died. I thought of the freedom I had pursued when I left that tiny university theatre, my tiny, mechanical, narrow life. I thought of the joy that rose within me in those early days when I breathed the fresh morning air of a grassy field, watching the sunrise from Emily's steps. The release as I ran and punched and screamed and cried on that rickety stage which was also the backdrop to so many snatched moments, so much furtive, urgent love. And I wondered how this bright, open freedom had become, so quickly, another cage.

"Imagine the ghosts," I said, mechanically, delivering what should have been climactic lines, "imagine the ghosts that haunt this house. Ghosts made of fear and buried futures. Ghosts laying ghosts like bricks and mortar. A house made of ghosts. And faulty wiring."

It got the tense laugh it was supposed to, but I was disembodied, floating. Perhaps this me that stood here now, was only a ghost itself, white and sweating on a cardboard stage.

"The sky will come in," said Cat, as Hallie, clutching at me in panic.

I evaded her and reached out towards the backdrop for support. Nausea still heaved within me, and I felt faint and dizzy. The lights were too hot. Perhaps the wiring really was faulty.

"What's all this noise about?" said Emily, entering with a kind of indulgent menace. "Be good now, you girls. It's past your bedtime. It's late."

I climbed onto the bed. The slight sway of the stage was making me seasick.

"It's late," Emily said again, and I thought it was odd that she had repeated that phrase. The repetition wasn't in the script and she, unlike Colm, was not given to embellishment.

I felt her hand on me, squeezing my shoulder with a motherly twist and, somewhere beneath it, an anger which I realised suddenly, blinking, was directed towards me from Emily herself.

This had been my cue. I was supposed to say something sad and rueful, about being late. About being *too* late. Bile rose in me as the stage blurred in panic. I groped blindly for the line, but my brain seemed to have emptied itself. I knew this was an important moment, and I should have been able to draw on my character, to make up the words I could not call to mind. But everything in me had turned to ice and I could only perch there, filled with a horrible sense of nakedness, frozen with horror, staring wildly up at her, my subconscious script gone, my mind simultaneously urgent and blank.

Somewhere, silhouetted at the back of the audience, Frederick snapped the lights off.

Scene Seven

(Rose and Frederick sit silently inside Rose's van. It is covered in baskets, streamers, and dreamcatchers, and a very slight breeze is causing the paper bunting to shift and rustle, and the string of tiny bells above the door frame to quiver noisily. The furnishings provide the only sound or movement.)

I sat on the edge of my bed, one hand wrapped around a mug, the other hand clutching Frederick's, my knuckles white. He was sitting across from me, watching me intently.

When I squeezed his fingers, he didn't flinch, only responded in kind to grip mine tighter. Somehow, he had made the tea, almost without me noticing and certainly without letting go of my hand. I suppose it was only a small caravan, everything more or less in reach. But even so, Frederick had a gift for seeming to be everywhere at once. Maybe it was only that the world we inhabited was small. Every day, it seemed to me, it was shrinking.

I had been crying hysterically since I tumbled off the stage. I had begun to run almost before my feet hit the grass, gasping for breath, the tears blinding me. Frederick had met me at the steps of my caravan, where I had come to a sudden halt, doubling over, waves of nausea returning with renewed vigour, my body reacting to the violence of my sobbing, my mind spinning.

He had scooped me up, carrying me carefully inside the van. It was a typically theatrical gesture. My breathing had only recently slowed, the sickness beginning to settle inside me. I had not yet managed to speak.

I fought the bile now as I tasted it, rising again in my throat, and forced myself to sip my tea. Frederick's eyes did not leave mine, but for the first time, I found myself struggling to hold his gaze. Instead, I winced sharply as the tea burned my mouth, put the mug down on the table with a shaking hand. He frowned, his fingers tightening around mine, his hand a bundle of cool white bones against the sweaty flesh of my palms.

He reached behind him and produced a bottle of the brandy we used to pass around the campfire so many, many lifetimes ago. He poured it into two glasses and handed me one, but the smell of it brought a new wave of nausea and I put it down and pushed it away from me.

He did not respond, only continued to watch me, and in the end, it was his silence which finally managed to calm me down. His eyes were too knowing, and I didn't want him to see it, to understand what I knew by now, that secrets really did breed secrets, before I was sure what I felt about it myself.

"Frederick," I said. It was not a loaded statement. It was simply hello.

"Rose." he said, and my heart swelled. I gave a little panting laugh and bent my head towards his so that our foreheads touched, and we sat like that for a long time, in silence. My hair fell forward around my face so that all I could see in my circle of vision was the space between us, and our hands joined across it. The sharp swell of his knuckles, the blue-grey of the veins on the back of his hands. The dark hairs at his wrist.

He had still not asked me what was wrong. I wasn't sure I knew the answer. Like the seasoned actor that I was, I searched for the next line in this situation, for something which would express this with the dignity and poise which deserts us so cruelly in real life. But I couldn't find the energy. I felt hopelessly, terribly tired. In the end I pulled away.

"I missed you."

He smiled, but there was sadness in it, and he did not comment. He only watched me, waiting for more. I felt irritation rise in me. All I wanted was to sleep. When I spoke, my voice was childish and sullen.

"I hate this," I said. "It isn't working. *We're* not working. Not any of us. It's broken." I paused. "I couldn't concentrate," I said, and with that admittance, my voice broke again, and tears spilled anew onto skin already raw and tight with crying. I realised with surprise, and slight disgust, that my flawed performance was still the thing I cared about most.

If it's a job worth doing, it's worth doing well. My father. I hadn't heard his voice in months.

"I'm sorry," I said, and my own voice was small and tinny. "I just couldn't get into Clarissa. I froze. And I didn't know what to do."

My hand was shaking. I squeezed my fingers into a fist. I thought of Juliet, preparing herself to meet Paris, of Julie in her bathtub, playing games with her sister's suitor. Of Katherina. I thought of myself as a nurse, calm and capable, as an oppressed citizen, fighting back. I thought of myself as bricks and mortar, the *House of Usher*, knitted and gnarled around its occupants.

I thought of us all falling down.

Finally, I met Frederick's eyes and he looked fatherly and sad, the weight of the world, our tiny, brittle, little world, on his shoulders. I grabbed him, pulled him to me, and held on.

"Frederick," I said into his neck, "it's still not right. There's something wrong with the Company. There are too many secrets."

I felt his arms around me, the palms of his hands spread flat and tight.

"There is only one secret Rose," he said.

He was wrong. But I said nothing. Just stared at the tiny hairs on the nape of his neck, the slight indentation of his weight on the bed.

He sighed, releasing my shoulders, and leaning back a little.

"What," he said, "do you suggest?"

I was not sure that was really the question he was asking, but I answered it anyway, dully. I didn't want the solution. I wanted to complain. *A woman, on a radio show, whining about a sofa.* I clenched my teeth.

"Why don't we just tell everyone?" I said, "Why not just say?"

The anger in me had grown as I spoke, but the pain on his face cooled it. I put my hand up to his cheek, felt the smooth of his cheekbone, held it there. For a moment, the intensity dulled in his eyes. He looked tired. I felt a subtle change, a surrendering in him, the weight of his head against my hand. But he only said,

"We are a Company, Rose. This is an ensemble. We can't carve out sections. We live by the group."

"Herm and Cat," I said it without intonation and without bothering to elucidate further.

"Not the same." He matched my brevity.

I sighed, felt something spike within me. "We should have told them when it first started," I said tonelessly, "it's too late."

We were treading old ground.

"It's not just the fact of us." His voice was quiet. "There are other things Rose. I don't seek advice from anyone else. But I've announced plays just because you've asked for something more serious. I've let runs go on longer because they gave me more time with you."

He reached out and gripped both my arms at the elbow. It steadied me and at the same time I wanted to push back against it.

"You cast me as Katharina," I whispered, and realised the stupidity of it before I finished the sentence.

"Emily and Colm drew the lots." He said. "A case in point. We've lost trust in each other. All of us. I'm supposed to be a leader." I felt his grip tighten on my elbows.

"Are you really that arrogant?"

I stood up suddenly, so that his hands fell from my arms, and I felt the floor of the van rock with the suddenness of it, felt again the precarious tilt of our lives.

"You really think the Company would fall apart if you're not the god of it? If you don't stay untouchable?"

His hands hung limp at his sides where they had fallen, as if in surrender. He raised his head and met my eyes.

"Yes," he said.

I said nothing.

"Do you want to know about the two new recruits Herm and I have been watching? The two brothers?" I didn't answer. Seated as he was, he was stealing my moment, making his speech while I stood over him, turning our positions so that he held the power, and I became awkward, exposed in my role. He needed it, I realised. He needed that power.

"They grew up in the system," he said. "It didn't work for them. They've been doing a bit of acting, a bit of light crime. They're getting by, but that's all. They're both young still, late teens, early twenties, but their birth mother had a degenerative brain disease which they're very likely to inherit, so they've not got a lot to look forward to right now."

He looked up at me meaningfully, waiting for some reaction. But I was staring at him, breath shallow, nausea rising again in my belly. He was telling me the new members' backstories. He was breaking the rules to support his point.

"I think they're ready," he continued, "although I am a little bit more worried about one of them. He's convinced the disease has already set in." He trailed off, frowned a little, then, like a master, he caught his own argument and seamlessly, he carried it through, "But these are the people we're here for. These are the people we *want*, the ones nobody else does. The ones who don't even want themselves."

I was silent.

"People do not join this troupe because they're happy, Rose. I don't abduct people from their lives, I create lives for people because they feel they have nothing. It's not a kidnapping, it's a rescue. Think about it. Think about the members of this Company. What would they have done if they didn't do this? Rose? Who? Who can you point to who'd have been absolutely fine? Who can you point to who would even still be here?"

Colm, lost and beaten, in the shadow of his mother. Cat. I didn't want to think about Cat. She was strong and fierce, but her anger grew inward. She'd have taken matters into her own hands long before. Emily, adrenaline junkie, would her need have finally overwhelmed her? Would risking her life have grown old eventually, until simply risking it wasn't enough? Maybe Herm would have been fine, but would a sad Herm, a deflated, depressed one, continually dissatisfied, really have truly been Herm at all?

Maybe all of them would have found some other way. Maybe, given time, Cat might have had some kind of therapy, Colm's mother would have died of old age and freed him. Herm might have found another path. And what about me? Where would I be?

An Office Worker Mojito. A Nuclear Family Iced Tea.

"I gave them another way, another life. One that gives them what they need, a better alternative to what came before." He was watching me, softness creeping back into his face. "I'm responsible, Rose," he said, and I saw the truth of that statement, but, beneath it, I felt the immensity of his pride in it, his enormous investment in his own position.

And I felt the danger of that.

His voice turned sharp, perhaps sensing the turn of my thoughts. "I'm not deluded. I know the life I started with didn't work out for me either. I made it for me too. But now I have a role to play, and other people depend on that. I have to live up to it."

There was a silence. My van, so lovingly decorated, seemed to me suddenly tacky and cheap. A piece of staging for a badly written play, clumsy improvisation by an ill-informed child. My feet felt as though they would sink through the cheap vinyl floor, the cracks in it disguised by a rug made of rags. A mass-produced item masquerading as something homemade, its cheap dye only imitating colour.

Would you like to taste something real?

"Rose." It was not a question. It was a call to attention. His voice was very quiet now, forcing me actively to listen. "Rose, you know how it works. People *believe* in this. The people who join this Company walk out onto that stage the first night because they are ready to die. *That's* what they prepare themselves for, not a place in a travelling theatre group. They give themselves up to a cause, because, either way, they have given themselves up. And what they get, Rose …" He stood now, took both my hands in his, the warmth of his breath on my face. I saw again the fever of the fanatic, his words growing mystical, an actor warming to the climax of his speech. "… what they get is not an exit, it's an entrance." He paused, as if to allow his audience time to absorb the weight of his words. I stood, immobile. I wondered if he had rehearsed this and at the same time, I knew that he wouldn't have needed to. This was his truth. Everything he did was staged.

"Rose. Please. It's precarious, what we have, it's built on absolutes, it's something created, new and bright, out of other people's hopelessness. We can't risk anything that would destroy it."

"But it's falling apart."

I had spoken without really considering it. The words, harsh and unmistakeably accurate, had simply escaped from me. I wasn't even sure, for a moment, whether I had spoken them aloud. But his shoulders slumped, and he sank down again, suddenly dejected, on the edge of my bed.

"Yes. Now it's falling apart."

Remorse filled me. I moved towards him, steadied a violently swinging dreamcatcher which he had brushed with his head as he changed position, and sat very close to him. I felt the warmth of him through me, ran my fingers across the back of his hand, took it gently in mine. I leaned my head on his shoulder and felt his kiss through my hair, the weight of his head as he rested it on mine.

"Yes," he said. "We are falling apart. Something needs to be done." There was a grim quality to his voice, and I moved my head sharply to look up at him.

There was nothing, at this stage, that I would not believe him capable of in the name of the Company.

"So, we just make sure you stay impartial," I said, and my voice was more measured than I felt. "The others will hold you to it, they already do, you pointed out yourself, they drew the lots for *Shrew*. We just tell them we're together and then we work through it. You said yourself half the problem was the secrecy? Maybe, if we just came clean about it, we could rebuild."

He shook his head.

"It's too late now. Maybe we could have done that before. But we've deceived them too long. There would be too much fallout. And anyway, it would only solve part of the problem."

"I know." I said, "but we'd just work through it. Wouldn't we? Isn't the Company built on something bigger than this?"

Desperation. Power. Frederick himself. A chill ran through me. If we were a cult, he was its leader. I scrutinised him, trying to silence my love for him enough to reveal any monster that might be hiding beneath. But he only looked tired and sad.

"I think," he said, "that we've forgotten what we're built on."

"We've talked about this before," I said, "something drastic, a return to form, we've tried that. *Telling them* would be drastic. Frederick, we do *everything* for real. Everything. This is the only lie we've ever lived. That's got to be part of what's eating us."

But he wasn't listening. His eyes were far away.

"That's the trouble," he said, partly to me, partly to himself, "we need to get back to it. Reconnect with our core. Put the right things front and centre and burn away the edges."

Something heavy dropped with a jolt into the pit of my stomach.

He turned to me, smiled, leaned over to kiss me, and I could not read the look in his eyes.

Scene Eight

(A group of people sit stiffly around a campfire. The flames sputter a little and falter in the damp air. Nobody speaks.)

The field the next day was very quiet. I don't think any of us left our vans. It wasn't until Frederick lit the campfire that we gradually emerged, trailing across the grass to join him. I was the last, and the most reluctant. I had spoken to none of them all day, but anger and unanswered questions about my thwarted performance had seeped through the windows and the cracks at our doors, so that now it swirled like fog around us. I took my place in silence and looked hard at the ground.

We waited. He didn't speak initially, only stood, and surveyed us, as if measuring the extent of the damage.

"How did the recruitment go?" asked Emily, characteristically the first to break the silence. Colm strained forward a little, as if to taste the answer, as if maybe, within it, there would be some resolution.

"It went very well," said Frederick, "there are two, and they're brothers. We've spent enough time with them now and I think we can be fairly sure. We'll make the final approach and hopefully bring them over for an initiation performance soon."

There was a silence.

We had all expected more. Herm frowned, then spoke into the pause, his eyes on Frederick, as though repeating a cue, or feeding a forgetful actor his lines. I cringed at the analogy. Was it also for my benefit? It would be unlike Herm to be so oblique, but I was tense and hyper-aware that night, a prisoner waiting to be judged.

"They're both very talented," Herm said, "really very

good actors. Naturally born to the stage."

There was a sort of collective nod, as though Herm had finally spoken the magic words, and then we all lapsed again into silence.

"Pays off for them too," Herm added, grinning, though the smile was thin, and no one returned it, "the odd con here and there, a bit of charm, a bit of trickery. It's a way to get by."

Herm trailed off. There was a long silence. I was wondering if this might be it, whether we might simply all get up and walk away. Whether we might continue walking, all of us, far away into opposite corners of the field, over the fences and out into the night. But where would we go? What would we do if not this?

Nobody moved. We were waiting for Frederick to fix us.

Eventually, he cleared his throat. There was a perceptible shift in our collective breathing. Emily was looking straight at me, Colm down at the floor, as though about to be reprimanded.

"I think we need a new play," Frederick said.

Anticipation, mixed with a little disappointment, rippled through the group. People nodded again, but it seemed a foregone conclusion. We had expected more. I felt something scratchy and hard in the back of my throat. *I had expected more.* I dropped my gaze to the ground, my face hot. But Frederick was warming to his cause.

"We need a new challenge. We've drifted, recently." For a moment I felt his eyes on me, but I didn't lift my gaze and he continued, after a barely perceptible pause. "We need to reconnect with our purpose. Something bold. Something strong."

"*Yes.*" I could hear the passion in Cat's voice.

"We are actors," said Frederick and his voice was powerful. He was proclaiming now, trying to whip us up with him. He was trying to save us by reminding us of who we were. "We do this because we believe in it."

I felt the others begin to stir and murmur agreement around me. I felt nothing but heavy and dull. I stared into the fire.

"We walk out onto that stage, and we inhabit those characters and there is not one shred left in us which is anywhere other than *that* world, *that* life."

"Yes. *Yes.*"

Cat was spilling over in her enthusiasm. This was vital to her. She believed absolutely in this cause. Acting was her purpose. *This is the Place Where the World Must End* must have killed her. I shifted.

"This is what we have forgotten," said Frederick, "and this is what we must recapture."

"We *have* forgotten," said Cat, "haven't we Rose?"

I was waiting for something like it, longing almost, for the topic to be broached so we could all get it over with, but when it came, I still flinched. Her voice was not unkind, but it was sharp, characteristically aggressive. I could feel her eyes on me, and I burned in shame. The others were watching me too. They were all angry, I knew that. The group would forgive anything as long as we always brought everything we had to that stage. I had let them down. In the silence that followed Cat's pointed remark, nobody, not even Emily, spoke. I may have had their sympathy, but there was also accusation. They were waiting for an explanation.

In the end, it was that which did it. It wasn't a considered decision, or a cry of pain, it was a petty act of self-defence.

"We're sleeping together."

The words came out muddled and unclear and at first the only response was confusion.

I hadn't intended to home in on the sex, that most basic

part of it, as though that was all it was, some casual bed hopping, preparation for a play. But then, I hadn't planned it at all. After all those months of furtive loving – this, in the end, is how it happened. A lashing out, my voice loud and unnatural, reducing everything to sex.

"Frederick and me. We're … together. Like a couple. Like Herm and Cat."

I said her name, deliberately, the way she had said mine, fixed my gaze on her shocked face, heard the intake of breath around me with a cruel, spiteful sort of satisfaction. I felt a sense of release, immediately followed by a rush of fear.

"We're together," I said, but now my voice did not sound dramatic, only sulky, and scared, "we have been for months."

In the immediate aftermath nobody said anything. Time seemed to hang, and I felt a strange, floating sense of dissociation, as though I hadn't actually said it, but was only imagining myself saying it, and would be brought back to reality any moment by somebody passing me the brandy. There was a thundering in my ears, like a sudden head cold, and a creeping, eerie sense of calm.

What was done was done now. I knew I should never have mentioned how long it had been, that I could have revealed the love without the extent of the lying, but it seemed smoother somehow, easier to have the whole truth of it out there, without any loose ends or open questions.

I suppose, in that silence, I really thought that it might just blow over, might drift into the campfire, and burn into dust, and we would all simply nod, even laugh a little.

But then I looked across the campfire at him, and I saw his face, made pale gold in the light of the flames, eyes dyed black in the moonlight, and I knew that he loved me. And that I had destroyed him.

The silence ended abruptly, as though everyone had been

suddenly re-animated at the same time.

"Fuck, Rose," said Emily, under her breath.

There was an onslaught of questions, demands, accusations, flying across each other so that I could barely pick them apart. How long exactly? When did it start? Had we lied outright or simply kept secrets? When were we planning to tell them?

I felt a rush of annoyance at these people, who felt they had a right to my life, and then remembered that they did, that this was exactly the arrangement. Our lives were signed over when we started. We were all of us here on borrowed time.

Colm looked stricken, his face furrowed and worried, a rule broken and restitution uncertain. He couldn't cope with other people's transgressions, he preferred to punish himself with his own. If he could have somehow made it his fault, he would have done. Then he could have done the penance.

"It's OK," I tried to say to him, but my words were lost in the general flurry, and everybody was talking at once.

"Couldn't you have just had sex once and moved on? If you really had to?"

"Or written it into a play and been done with it?"

"How serious is it exactly?"

"Are you in love?" That was Colm.

"Yes," I said, but I didn't look at Frederick.

"So, this has been going on since when, *Arms and the Man*? Earlier?"

It was Herm's rational, matter of fact tone which pulled everyone to their senses. I looked at him and I saw him put it all together, the disjointedness, the nature of the recent plays, the lack of time around the campfire, my forgotten cues. I nodded.

"Around then."

My answer prompted another swirl of noise. The words blurred and mingled in my ears, but I could hear the accusation, the anger as people began, rightly or wrongly, to identify our relationship as the corrupting force beneath the critical disintegration of their lifestyle.

I scanned their faces, Emily, angry but sympathetic, mindful perhaps, of all those undrunk mugs of tea. Colm, quiet and shocked, alarmed at the barrage of noise around him. Herm was asking questions but looking carefully at Frederick, as if trying to read there the answer to some other, unspoken enquiry, while Frederick remained silent and very pale, surveying the carnage. But it was Cat who alarmed me. She was sitting, stiffly, staring at me. She had not yet spoken, and her face, as I stared back at her now, across the questions and the campfire, was filled with something that made me shiver.

We deserved it, I thought. Frederick and I, together, had trespassed on and damaged something vitally important to her. I had been brought into her refuge and had destroyed it from within. Won her trust only to hack through her lifeline. Her eyes were unnaturally bright and her cheeks vivid.

"Cat." I mouthed, stricken, across the firelight. "I'm so sorry."

Frederick stood up, and we fell immediately silent, everyone watching as he unrolled himself, gracefully, to his full height, assembled his dignity, drew that old charisma like a cloak around his shoulders.

"Later," he said, and his voice rang through the field, perfectly projected like the actor he was, cutting through the confusion in the air. "We will do this. Later."

He turned and began to walk away.

But he couldn't do that anymore. Frederick, who could melt into nothing, disappear, and reappear like some terrible magician, had lost his power.

He made it two steps before Cat caught up with him.

"You're not so gutless." She grabbed him hard by the elbow, spinning him round, caught by surprise more than force. "You broke it. So you fix it." Her voice was low and controlled. She spat out the words, but slowly, enunciating them with excruciating precision.

Everybody was sitting very still. Herm was hunched forward, tensed, watching her warily, crouching a little on his toes as if poised to spring. Frederick put up a hand as if to stop her, or to signal peace.

"Cat …"

"No." The word exploded out of her as though it had been boiling quietly for some time. "No you don't. You don't. You do NOT get to do that. You don't *calm the situation*, you don't tell *me* how to be."

Her voice was rising, dangerous. "You risked this; you risked *all this*. Frederick, *our great leader*." She soaked the moniker in sarcasm, and I felt a terrible pang of sadness, because at one time, I knew, she had believed in it fervently. "You knew what you were doing when you set up the Company. You did it because you believed in something. Or you did then. Maybe even you cared."

"Cat—"

"You *named* me. You named all of us – you made us into something else and we can't go back, and we wouldn't want to," her voice broke, tears spilling, fast and hot, down her cheeks. She swiped viciously at them, as though they belonged not to her body, but his. "Who *are* we?" she shouted, gesturing violently behind her at the frozen group around the dying campfire. "Who would any of us be if we weren't … this? No one would give a shit about us. No one gave a … shit … before." The words were higher in pitch now and the tears made them blurred at the edges, her speech becoming less distinct, morphing towards a howling scream, frightened and frightening. "What are we – an overgrown kid, still ruled by *his mummy* ..."

Emily put a hand on Colm's arm. He snatched it away. Cat was still shouting,

"... An ageing daredevil trying to prove she's still got it. A depressed teenager barely finished with school. A middle-aged man running ... running to fat," On the last she paused and turned to Herm, her voice softening.

"Sorry," she said. Herm shrugged, his eyes still on hers.

"It's okay," he said.

She turned back to Frederick, the tears taking prevalence now over the anger. "And me," her words were imbued with a terrible loathing, "a *nut job*." She was crying in earnest now, her last words like a child's howl, "I'm *crazy*, Frederick. That's what they told me. More or less. What else would I do? What would any of us do if we don't do this? Where else would we go?"

His face twisted in anguish, Frederick put his hand out to touch her arm. She whipped it away. In my peripheral vision, I saw Herm look at him, shake his head, warning. *No.*

Cat pushed both her trembling palms into her face, pressed into her eye sockets, dragged at the skin across her cheekbones, as if pushing the tears back inside. When she looked up at Frederick again her eyes were clear, her voice steadier, determination replacing hysteria.

"I get it", she said. "You love her. But is that actually more important? Really? Than all this? The fact is, you *can't*. It won't work. Look what it's done to us – *look*." She gestured wildly, the sweep of her arm encompassing the field, the caravans, us, and everything that had gone before "Look what it's done."

"It wasn't just that," said Emily, flatly. It was the first time anyone else had spoken. But she didn't follow it up and neither did anybody else.

Emily was right, I told myself. There had been other, more complicated matters at play. It had taken more than the fumbling of two furtive lovers to bring this Company down around us. But it was the only easily identifiable cause. Everything else was made of shadows and impulses, forces too nebulous to be explained.

Cat did not appear even to have heard Emily's comment. She was focused, laser-hot, on Frederick.

"You started this, you brought us here, we were going to seek truth. Not lies, truth. Something which made sense. And we can't go back." Her voice had begun to rise again, passion and emotion vying for stage time, so that she had to pause to breathe.

"I'm sorry that you can't have a normal life, Frederick. But none of us can. You brought us here. You have to be in charge." Frederick started to turn away, pain on his face, but her hand shot out to pull him round to her.

"Where are all those high ideals now Frederick? Where everything was honest, everything for real? Where is all of that now? We're forgetting lines, forgetting cues – if the performances break down, we have nothing left. Don't you understand that? *Nothing*."

There was something, actually. There was something in me. But I wasn't thinking about that, as far as I could avoid it, and I certainly hadn't admitted it to anyone else. Still, I couldn't help agreeing with her. Around me I could feel people stirring slightly. I felt the old excitement swell in me, the exquisite luxury of stepping into another person's life for a few hours, experiencing their love, their pain, their passion, all just a little more glamorous, more worthy than my own.

And it seemed an irrefutable truth. That preserving the lifestyle that he had created for us really *was* more important than anything else.

Cat's face was flushed, her fists balled, white knuckled, at her sides.

"You betrayed us, Frederick. "You let us down."

"Fine."

His voice was loud, louder than necessary, and we all started, Cat stepping back a little, uncertain. He turned to face us. Then he strode back to the campfire with a strange, stiff effort, his face blank and unnatural. He stood for a moment, breathing, as if gathering some arsenal within him.

Everybody watched him. Nobody moved.

"I need to announce our next play," he said.

There was a brief renewal of the general clamour then, he seemed to be somehow missing the point. Cat was tense behind him, still poised for a fight. But Herm was looking directly at Frederick, and his face had grown suddenly very watchful.

"We'll do *Romeo and Juliet*," said Frederick.

His voice was still unusually loud, and at first, I thought he was simply reacting angrily, that he would reconsider in a moment, or was using it only as a threat, to shake us out of this hysteria, so we could return to normality and work our way out of this together.

He said it again then, more quietly, and I could see, as he spoke, his conviction growing. I realised that he must have had this idea previously, must have been turning it over in his head, fighting against it and struggling with it. And yet I could see how rich it was in its simplicity, how perfectly orchestrated.

My heart seemed to stop. Then, without warning, in the midst of the shell-shocked silence, it began to pound again feverishly, as if trying to break its way out.

A reconnection with our centre. A reminder of what the Company had been built upon. It was a horrible suggestion, and yet it represented a reformation, uniting us again with our truest selves. It was the only solution. It was cruel. But it would bring us back to our roots.

He turned to me, and I faced him, my tongue dry in my mouth. I saw the love in his eyes, a hunger only part-masked by zealotry, but there was resignation there too, and a bright spark of something else. A director's fervour. A passion formed deeper and earlier than mine.

When he spoke, he spoke quietly, and directly to me.

"*Romeo and Juliet*, Rose. It's the play you were named for."

Act Four

"O serpent heart, hid with a flow'ring face.
Did ever dragon keep so fair a cave?
Beautiful tyrant, fiend angelical,
Dove feathered raven, wolvish-ravening lamb."

Juliet
William Shakespeare, *Romeo and Juliet*

Scene One

(The interior of Colm's camper van. Everything is spotlessly clean and tidy, but every last inch of wall space is crowded with painted faces. They stare out at Rose. She is alone.)

It was Cat's expression that stayed with me. In the echoing silence that followed Frederick's announcement, she seemed to be the only one still breathing. Her face was flushed, tears barely dried from her earlier outburst, but there was a light in it, an odd sort of triumph. This was her dream, the perfect realisation of everything the Company stood for. Strictly speaking, it should have been all our dreams. But Cat had always been the purist amongst us.

It occurred to me that if Frederick had fallen in love with Cat, it would have been easier. The issue with our love had never been that it was forbidden, but perhaps instead, that we were unequally engaged with our cause. Had I joined the Company that very first night, fooling myself that I was seeking some purpose, but in reality, only following Frederick? How different was I really, from those Office Worker Mojitos, those Rat Race Daiquiris, seeking only to partner off and settle down? I felt my hand move, unbidden, to my stomach. I snatched it away, pressed it instead to my chest.

And into the silence, Frederick spoke.

Shrewdly now, he dropped the dramatics, lowered the pitch of his voice. Tender, he reached across the shock wave his words had produced in us and grounded us in practicalities.

He would abridge the play enough to allow us to double up on parts. He would write out the servants and Lady

Montague and give her lines to her husband. We would use the new recruits to help make up the numbers. We would stage our performance in a barn not too far from here, which he assured us would be in better repair than the last. He had originally earmarked it for Strindberg's *Dance of Death* because it was dark and enclosed, and suitably claustrophobic. It even, and his voice took on a delighted note here, contained a raised walkway that ran all along the back of the wall, where we could stage the famous balcony scene.

For how long had he been planning this? I imagined him weighing it up in the night, torn between passions, while I slept beside him. Did he bring it out now as a last resort? Or had it always been his strategy? Had he ever truly thought it might work out another way?

We would seat the audience, he told us, on stepped haybales with blankets. We would paint brand-new backdrops for this production, and they would be set in just enough from the wall of the barn to create a narrow backstage passage, through which we could move between exits and entrances.

Despite ourselves, we actually concentrated. We began to imagine it.

A split in the lighting. Balcony and stage floor as light and darkness. Good and evil. Day and night.

Frederick was ringmaster again now. We were wild animals tamed, beasts in thrall to him, cringing and compliant. When he had given us enough of a taste for the production, he wheeled on his heels with such charisma I could almost feel the sweep of a dark cloak, the flash of red velvet, the sharp crack of the whip. He spoke over his shoulder, almost as an afterthought, drowning out Emily's strangled "Frederick—"

"We will meet again. Here. In one hour. We'll draw lots for the parts."

And he was gone.

How I ended up in Colm's van is unclear even now. We were still and silent, watching Frederick stride away to his van. He owned it now, his new exposure. He had made it his limelight. I was unable to look away. There was a horrifying allure to him. When he was out of sight, as if we had been released, there was a sort of commotion. I was vaguely aware of Cat starting towards me, then a blur of people moving quickly between us and Colm gripping me suddenly, pulling me away, and up the steps of his van. There was a brief moment when Colm and I faced each other. I opened my mouth to speak to him, but I didn't know what to say. Then he shook his head, turned, and exited without a word, closing the door behind him.

He didn't lock it. He might even have left the key in the ignition. I had an hour in which I could have been revving Colm's engine, turning the wheel, speeding out of the field. But I did not. None of us did.

Instead, I stood in the middle of Colm's caravan, and stared. I had never been inside before. He was secretive about it, the way all of us were.

I felt my throat catch as I looked.

The walls were filled with hundreds of tiny, exquisite portraits. Cat's small features, pale but vivid, her green eyes bright with challenge. Emily's strong, lined face, her frizzy, brown hair, a sharpness in her expression belied by the warmth of her eyes.

There I was, looking softer than I imagined myself, my dyed hair unnaturally bright, as though wearing a costume. I tried but I couldn't read myself in my eyes. There were more portraits of me than there were of the others. Herm, in most of his, was grinning, that rubber face, stretching open, honest, and wide. I could see his laughter, his japery, that sense of maturity mixed with play. He wasn't wearing his glasses. I couldn't see his paunch.

And Frederick. I couldn't look at Frederick.

Colm had painted himself too, though with none of the generosity with which he had depicted the rest of us. He had under-estimated the gleam of his skin, his tight black curls, the softness of his lips and eyes.

Why did he paint these portraits? Why hang them this way? Was it simply that he wanted eyes on him, to extend the sense of theatre, the same way I liked to sleep with Frederick on the stage? Or were they his jurors, there to watch him, judge him, keep him honest?

There was one face I didn't recognise, that appeared far more often than any other, which I guessed was his mother. A slender dark face, with none of the gentleness of Colm's. The skin seemed to hang in disapproval, the eyes were severe and full of judgement. Even from the shoulders up, I could feel the tension in her limbs. She seemed to stare from her small frame with terrible alertness, as though scrutinising my actions. There was nothing in her face to suggest she liked what she saw. In some of the paintings, there was a slight smudge around the mouth, as though he had tried to paint a smile, but been unable to envisage it.

She stared at me from every wall, from every angle, but the faces of our Company were peppered amongst them, warmer in comparison. Was he gradually replacing her? My heart ached. How many years would that take? How many years did he have?

Colm could be Romeo, Mercutio, Tybalt, Paris. Excluding Lady Montague, because Frederick had written her out, there were five deaths to choose from.

I began to pace the van, shock giving way to speculation. How would the lots fall? Who would play who? There were too few of us, even with the new recruits. At least one of those dead characters would have to double up.

Maybe no one would die at all.

I put a hand to my stomach. A few seconds later, as if a little late for its cue, I felt a slight cramp, a renewal of the nausea I had been feeling on and off for weeks now.

The hour was very nearly up. I realised, with horror, that I had been looking forward to it. I *wanted* to live out this moment of high drama. Even now.

I felt sick at myself. The eyes on the walls blurred in my vision, losing clarity and colour, faces shedding skin and sinew. Until they became a mass of cold, grey skulls, dead in their frames. Emily, Herm, Colm, Cat, Frederick. All dead.

I gave a small cry, the bile rising, and I stumbled out of the camper van, doubling over to heave onto the grass.

Then I made my way to the campfire.

Scene Two

(Five people sit in frozen silence around a campfire. The night is dark. The fire is smaller than usual, and nobody has thought to stoke it.

There is a sound. A camper van door opens and shuts. Footsteps approach in the darkness, deliberate, though a little uneven. In the silence of the night, they seem unnaturally loud.)

Frederick made a big entrance. Of course. If we did not indulge the drama in this, of all moments, what were we sacrificing so much for?

He wore his long, black coat, as close to a cloak as he could get without crossing the boundary into the ridiculous. Beneath it he wore all black, as if in respectful, pre-emptive mourning. But I knew it was also because he had considered the effect it would have in the darkness.

Frederick always considered the lighting.

He stepped into the firelight, out of nowhere, making everybody jump, even though all of us had heard him approaching. He had one hand behind his back, like an old-fashioned gentleman, and in the other, he carried three identical black silk bags, each with a red drawstring at the top. He stood quite still at first, scanning our faces. Then, with a sudden movement, he drew his other hand from behind his back to produce a small fold-up table, and, with a flick of his wrist, flipped it open so that the catch fell into place with a loud cracking noise.

It was like a gunshot in the night.

He placed the three bags in a line on the table. I watched him in fascination, marvelling at him. He had abandoned the ringmaster's whip and rhetoric, and now he was a dark magician, smooth and terrible.

I stared at the bags. I knew the lots were manipulated somehow but I had never realised he had more than one of them. How often had he used these duplicate bags? Some of the time? *All* of the time? And now? Would the lots be fixed? Or had he, by bringing them out to us quite so publicly, showed his hand, implicitly promising that this casting, at least, would be left to chance?

I shivered. The longer I looked at them, the more those bags, with their black noose and their thin line of red at the opening, seemed to conjure up images of death.

He began by clarifying the details.

"We will, for the performance, have two new recruits."

He picked up the bag nearest him, and held it up, between thumb and forefinger, pausing to check our attention. He needn't have bothered. We were all of us staring at that little black silk bag.

"This," he said, "contains only the more serious male parts. We will need to pick the new recruits' roles from these for obvious reasons. An initiation requires a certain gravitas." His dark eyes moved across us all, fixing us one by one as though examining us for mutiny. I wanted to look away but curiosity drew me and I found myself searching his gaze in return. I found nothing. It was as though he had drawn down a blind. "*They* won't die this time," he continued, once he was satisfied, "because we're not murderers, we're artists, and everybody gets a choice. And a decent chance. We all had our plays stopped before the moment of truth. They won't have that option, but an initiation is not supposed to be an ending. We'll tell them the truth just before the big scenes. Any weapons we use on them will be blunt."

He looked around the group, eyes narrowed, daring us to contradict him. Nobody did.

We're not murderers, I told myself. *We're not murderers. We're artists.*

For a moment I dared myself to hope.

"The rest of us, on the other hand …" He paused for effect, surveyed our faces grimly, "have made our choice and survived our initiations. Whatever we pick, we play. To the end."

Romeo, Tybalt, Mercutio, Paris.

We were, all of us, mentally listing the contents of that bag. We all knew the play well, but I would have bet my life - the life I was now preparing, quite literally, to gamble - that all of us, in that hour of waiting, had mentally tallied up the deaths.

"Would you do the honours?" Frederick was holding out the bag, offering it to us.

Nobody moved.

He frowned. "Please." It wasn't a request. There was an authority to him which could not be contested, his voice, solemn and clear, brokered no argument. He swung the bag towards Colm, who shrank from it. Frederick's face softened but he moved the bag, insistent now, and held it out to Herm. I watched the two men meet each other's gaze, and, with that silent understanding that seemed for so long to have existed between them, Herm nodded once, and then reached, slowly, into the bag and drew out a folded piece of paper. He did not take his eyes from Frederick's.

"Another," said Frederick.

Herm reached into the bag a second time. He sat, hands open, the slips of paper resting on the palm of each hand, as though he were offering them to some unearthly authority. I wished fervently that the wind would take them, burn them to ash in the fire. But there would be more paper. And there were more bags.

Frederick did not hurry his movements. He had the unswerving attention of this audience, and he knew it. He had an actor's instinct for timing, for the power of silence and stillness.

He turned back to the table, opened the bag at its drawstring, and tipped the remaining contents into the third bag. He laid the empty silk bag down next to its compatriots with that odd gentleness normally reserved for the dead. Then he swiftly took the papers from Herm's outstretched hands, opened them both simultaneously and nodded to himself.

"Romeo and Tybalt," he said, a grim smile of satisfaction, entirely without humour, stretching the pale of his face in the firelight, "Okay. Good. They're the right age. And in fact, the parts rather suit them."

We remained silent. All around the fire, faces frowned in concentration. We made the deductions.

Two deaths down. Two reprieves. But there were more to go.

Paris. Juliet. Mercutio.

"Right." Frederick's voice was raised, sharp. It called us from our calculations. Our heads snapped up to look at him, like obedient puppets or trained, domesticated animals, responding to the voice of their master. I hated all of us in that moment.

"You know we are writing out servants, bit parts, and Lady Montague. We'll be doubling up on some of the others. We're also going to write out Paris' death scene outside Juliet's tomb."

I felt the hope thrill through the group like sparks from the fire. And I felt the confusion beneath it, the parts of us which held, still, to our purist values, that could not conceive of such literary surgery, such admittance of compromise. But the fact remained that there weren't enough of us. It couldn't otherwise be done. And none of us could deny the chill in the air. The parts of our brains which were still responding to the words *Juliet's tomb*.

"No one particularly cares about Paris," Frederick continued, dismissing Shakespeare as though he were an amateurish child, "he's not built to be liked and he's not bold enough to be a villain. The audience has no connection with him, and it dilutes the effect of the other losses. Having Romeo kill him in a fit of pique makes Romeo less likeable and detracts from the poignancy of his grief. It's a waste of stage time."

He paused, scanned our faces for signs of rebellion. There were none. Whatever our personal response to this artistic decision, it was hardly the biggest issue here.

"And it means we can double up on his part." concluded Frederick, admitting the more practical aspects of his decision only now.

I stared at the two remaining bags. By my calculation there were only two deaths left – Mercutio, and Juliet.

As if on cue Frederick swept up the second bag, holding it aloft.

"You'll all be aware that we don't normally make distinctions between the male and female parts," he said. "Generally speaking, anyone can play any part. And, for the majority, that goes for this production too. Anyone can be Mercutio, or Benvolio, or the Friar. However, there are a handful of parts, that will for this performance be best played by the gender which matches the character. Lady Capulet, for example." He paused. "And Juliet."

I looked up, automatically seeking out Emily and Cat. Emily met my eyes, her lined face very serious. There was no bitterness in her gaze.

Cat was staring directly ahead, ignoring both of us. I wondered if she wanted to play Juliet. If she, of all of us, was actually rooting for it.

"This bag contains both those gender specific parts," said Frederick, "and one other, selected from the remaining parts at random. The girls will draw from this bag first, and then we will pass the remaining bag around the rest. Is that clear?"

Nobody answered.

"Is. That. Clear?" his voice was harsh and loud. It cut through our collective stupor. He was taking no captives. For the first time since I had known him, he was openly dangerous.

We mumbled and nodded.

"Good," he said. "And is that fair?"

There was a pause then, but again we nodded. We could not fail to admit that it was. At least within context.

"Okay," and now his voice was gentle, reassuring. It reached towards us, caressed us. Comforted us. I felt a brief wave of calm, and then the black silk bag was in front of me, and I was reaching inside it, feeling three, innocuous, little slips of paper, selecting one, pulling it out. I gripped it in my fist, feeling my fingernails pierce my skin and the damp of my palm begin to seep into the paper.

One by one, Emily and Cat reached into the bag. Nobody spoke. Nobody opened their paper. Frederick returned the empty bag to the table and held out the third.

To Colm. To Herm. And then finally, himself.

We sat, all of us, in absolute silence.

Emily was staring at her folded paper, held between her finger and thumb, as though it was something she did not really want to touch. Colm was looking straight down at his knees, cross-legged as if in meditation, twisting the paper between his fingers, sweat gleaming on his smooth forehead.

Herm was watching Frederick. Only Cat sat upright, her face calm and impassive, the paper lying quiet in her open, cupped hands.

"If this," said Frederick, holding up his own unopened slip of paper, his voice so quiet now I strained to hear him, "if this is Mercutio, I won't be able to direct you. I'll need you to select someone to take you through the rest of the piece. After that," he shrugged, "after that, it's up to you."

I felt, rather than heard, the collective breath. Nobody had imagined it might come to this point. None of us had engaged with this possibility. And now nobody could meet anyone else's eyes. We stared, all of us, at our slips of paper.

Mercutio. Juliet.

Perhaps it was Frederick's words, but something rushed in me, a rising anger, a terrible frustration. I could not stomach the waiting any longer.

I unclenched my fist and grabbed at my paper, opening it, reading it, and shouting out its contents almost in the same movement. My voice was too high and too loud, as if my mouth, entirely disengaged with my mind, was desperate only to remove the taste of the word.

"Juliet."

I think we all already knew. It had been clear from the beginning.

Later, I would rail against that casting, would protest it and wrestle with it, and it would raise goose pimples on my skin. I would feel a sharp tightening at the back of my throat as though the knowledge of it was gradually strangling me. There would be a terrible, paralysing sense of panic, wracking my body with sudden sobs, or with quivering anger. It would wake me, screaming, in the night.

And yet, in that moment, around the campfire, I felt only the release of that awful tension, the relief that comes with finally knowing. I dropped the paper into the grass, where it lay, twitching slightly in the breeze. My heart thundered in my ears, I felt the blood surge in my head, but my mind, sluggish with the impact of the last few hours, simply moved on. I began to wonder about the other characters.

I did not look at Frederick. I did not look at anyone.

It was Emily who broke the silence first. She opened her paper without ceremony, a sense of stubborn practicality in her delivery, a down to earth impatience I had seen in her before. I thought suddenly how frustrated she must be with our melodrama. That it was just one of the fissures and cracks in our 'oneness' which must have been there even before I joined. I was learning so much about this group. So much and so late.

"I'm Juliet's nurse, Lord Montague, Balthazar and a few incidentals." Emily said, and then, as if to move us on, "Cat?"

"Benvolio and Lady Capulet, Juliet's mother".

Cat said it defensively, as though this was a decision she had made and must defend. I felt a flash of anger because she had, she *had* caused this with her provocation and her fighting and her fanaticism. Was that cruelty I had sensed in Emily's voice when she spoke Cat's name just now? Did the others feel the same? I tried to smother the feeling in the darkest corner of my mind that Cat ought really to have picked one of the deaths. That she had got off lightly. Did she resent being Benvolio, the peacemaker, I thought, could she really pull that off?

But when I looked up, almost afraid to do so, as if my feelings might be written on my face or in the firelight, everyone was looking at Frederick, his paper open in his hand. He was looking straight at me, still in control, still in character, but his eyes full of sadness.

"Friar Lawrence, Lord Capulet, and incidentals," he said, without dropping his gaze.

I stared back and felt my eyes burn with a relief which surged through me so fast it left me light-headed. Somewhere, beneath a loud roar in my head, I reminded myself which role I had drawn. What did I care now if Frederick lived or died?

The relief burned away. The atmosphere was unbearably tense. Of all of us, only Colm and Herm had yet to open their papers.

One death left.

Cat had become very still, as though it had only now occurred to her that in the extremities of her passion, she might just lose something. She was, simultaneously, a small creature waiting to be kicked, and a wildcat about to pounce.

Colm spoke, his words escaping in a rush of breath and with something like a sob, and I realised that by leaving his revelation this close to the end, he would now feel guilty, whatever the result.

"The Prince, Paris and incidentals," he said and then, "sorry." He buried his face in his hands.

Nobody moved.

Nobody looked at Herm.

Colm's torso quivered, his face crushed into his hands, his fingers squeezing at his temples as if trying to wring something out. Would he look at those faces on the wall of his caravan now, I wondered, and see accusation? Did he already?

Cat had not moved. She was white.

Herm remained expressionless. He shrugged a little, tossed the paper, unopened, into the fire and said, as if he had only just made the deduction.

"Well, I guess that makes me Mercutio."

There was absolute silence.

Then, and only then, the revelations finally being over, Cat drew a breath, Emily tensed her shoulders, and collectively, we prepared to roar.

Herm spoke into the midst of us, as if rebuking a collection of recalcitrant children. "It's what we signed up for," he said. "Right from the start. It's time."

Act Five

"Eyes, look your last.
Arms, take your last embrace.
And lips, O you the doors of breath,
seal with a righteous kiss
a dateless bargain to engrossing death."

Romeo
William Shakespeare, **Romeo and Juliet**

The Performance

(The interior of a barn. Hay bales create two lines of uncomfortable, raked seating. The place is dusty and cobwebbed, floorboards cracked and discoloured, moss and scattered weeds gathering in the crevices. Behind the seating, there is a narrow corridor leading to a heavy door. It is the only way in or out of the building. It is locked.

A wide balcony splits the stage area in two, the upper area lit with a bright-gold glow. The lower area is consumed by shadow, murky and unsettling, the backdrop a disconcertingly incongruous blend of bricks and forest. Dark faces peer out of it, subtly woven into bark and branches, knots and gnarls, and the cracks in the brickwork. In the corner, stage left, a wooden ladder leads up to the balcony. A creeping trail of ivy coils itself around the base, reaching up towards the first step.

At the balcony level the backdrop expands into a dappled canopy. Both sun and stars shine through it, but this incongruity, unlike the bricks and the trees below it, feels, somehow natural. A bird is depicted, perching in a tree. It is a nightingale. And not a lark.)

The stage was a masterpiece. Colm had outdone himself. He even had empty picture frames which, for the more sinister interior scenes, played out on the ground level, would be hung around those shadowy faces, like ghoulish family photographs. He had a mass of ivy piled at the stage entrance, which he would gradually arrange so that it crept up the ladder during the scene changes, so that by the time the performance was nearing its conclusion, the boundary between the upper and lower sections would be almost inaccessible, already too late. He had even painted spreading, rust coloured stains into the floorboards, as if to invoke the years of fighting, of blood already spilled in the name of

Montagues or of Capulets, long before the opening scene.

Now, the opening chords began to rise like a grim mist into the frozen atmosphere, and I heard the audience shift in anticipation. *'The Ride of the Valkyries'* by Richard Wagner.

So familiar and so chilling.

I pressed myself against the splintered wall backstage. I could feel Emily's breath on my neck, smell the sweat on Colm's costume. Nobody spoke.

As promised, there was a tiny corridor of space between the backdrop and the back wall of the barn that allowed one person at a time to squeeze themselves from one end of the stage to the other, back pressed against the snagging rough of the wall, carefully manoeuvring around the backdrop supports which waited, silently, to trip us in the dark.

Across the stage, in the smaller backstage area, the two new recruits played out their own private battles as they approached the moment of their entrance. There was a small flight risk, but it was unlikely. Their forms were resolute, stiff in the darkness.

The trumpets began their refrain. I remembered the whirl of emotion on my own first night, the bead of blood on the end of my finger, the weight of the knife, Herm, exposed and vulnerable beside me. It had not been a reprieve. Only a stay of execution.

The violins replaced the trumpets. I felt bile burn the back of my throat. There was a swish of air against my legs as Frederick quietly donned his cloak. He moved to the entrance, waiting for the violins to finish their climb and the trumpets to rejoin them. Somewhere in the shadows, Herm slid the volume dial to maximum.

The barn reverberated. The last, frenzied notes still rang through the walls as Frederick's measured footsteps replaced the orchestra.

My vision swam. I swallowed acid.

(A tall figure strides to the centre of the stage. He faces the audience, solemnly. For a moment, everybody holds their breath. Even the Valkyries are silent.

And then, his voice carrying easily in the instinctive hush, he begins to proclaim the famous opening words to William Shakespeare's 'Romeo and Juliet'.[5])

"Two households, both alike in dignity,
In fair Verona, where we lay our scene,
From ancient grudge break to new mutiny,
Where civil blood makes civil hands unclean."

Frederick had moved us fast. He had allowed us one night after the casting, one sleepless, agitated night in which I doubted that any of us even closed our eyes, but which was characterised by a silence so absolute that the birdsong at dawn seemed cacophonous and inconsiderate. Our camper vans were little blocks of light, haphazardly arranged in the darkness. We had paced and shifted inside them, made decisions, and over-ridden them. Several times that night I had made my way to the cab of my van, my hand shaking, hovering above the ignition. But I never turned the key. Herm's mild acceptance of his fate, his astounding rationality in the face of such madness, had somehow made it inconceivable that anyone else should try to leave.

And so, when we could turn over our options no longer, we had each begun, despite ourselves, to review our lines. And to discover again that spark, beneath those panicked reflexes – a sense of excitement, a quickening of the heart. Gone, I knew, were those early days, when a little bit of nudity, or a fist fight, was enough.

When the sun rose the next morning, we were, all of us, still there.

"From forth the fatal loins of these two foes,
A pair of star-crossed lovers take their lives."

Prop tables, one in each of the backstage areas, glowered at us in the darkness, each item outlined in luminous tape, like eerie phantoms. I took a sudden inhalation, realising that I had not been breathing, and heard Colm, beside me, do the same. The air smelled of sawdust and sick and fear.

"Whose misadventured, piteous overthrows;
Doth with their death bury their parents' strife."

I stared at the cracks in the floorboards on the stage. I thought of the weeds and the mud and the creeping, scuttling creatures that might live beneath them. I thought about blood, dark and thick in the blackness, dripping gently down upon them.

My blood. And Herm's.

"The fearful passage of their death-marked love,
And the continuance of their parents' rage,
Which, but their children's end, naught could remove,
Is now the two hours' traffic of our stage."

If Frederick had deliberately provided us with an opportunity to escape that first evening, he closed that door and locked it the next day. As soon as we emerged, drawn and grey-featured, he had us packed up, motors running. We followed him, like tiny, diesel-powered ants, as he led the way to the barn.

Perhaps we still thought it wasn't real. Certainly, a part of me, as I followed everyone numbly into the darkness of the building and heard the key turn in the lock behind us, had still thought it might have been a test. That we would prove our loyalty, and then the performance would be cancelled. It might all be just another initiation.

It wasn't.

So, we had learned our lines. Those of us who were playing several people practised the ability to step in and out of each character with minimal transition. We had set up prop tables, swept the floors.

"The which, if you will with patient ears attend,
What here shall miss, our toil shall strive to mend."

I watched Frederick turn and make his exit. His clock swung around him, revealing a flash of blood-red lining before Herm killed the lights and we were plunged into darkness. I could hear the audience waiting. Emily pushed past me to join Frederick, now cloakless, at the entrance and I caught a brief whiff of alcohol on her breath.

The lights went up. They sauntered onto the stage as Sampson and Gregory, servants of the house of Capulet. The rest of us, a grimly-assembled backstage audience, watched Colm collect his own weapon from the prop table, and disappear into the narrow backstage corridor. As one, we tracked his progress, reappearing in the darkness at the other entrance, a black silhouette, the metal of his sword glinting in the reflected light.

"I mean, if we be in choler, we'll draw."
"Ay, while you live, draw your neck o'th'collar."

(The costumes are simple but have clearly been carefully considered. The audience is still detached enough to notice. Sampson and Gregory wear red, as if their very clothes are steeped in the blood of centuries of fighting. Their eyes gleam with fond memories of wounds inflicted, valour and reputation won. As they speak, we watch the prospect of violence kindle gleefully in them, compensating for the drudgery of serving.)

It was stuffy in the barn. I could already see in the audience the glint of sweat on skin, the use of flyers as makeshift fans. The place was airless, dust floating thickly in the lights. Sharp-scented air freshener bonded thinly with the heavier undertones it was designed to remove.

We had spent two nights in this place.

When the lock on the barn door was not released, we had gradually accepted it and, one-by-one, bedded down on the floor or on the audience staging, simultaneously resentful and reassured by each other's presence. Emily was silent and sad. Cat was blank-faced, withdrawn into some strange, internal world into which no one, not even Herm, could follow. Colm had not spoken since the casting. He had begun work on the backdrop as soon as he had arrived, losing himself in this, his masterpiece, taking refuge in another fantasy. The only sounds in the place were the swish of his brush and the muted jangle of paint pots.

I had lain the dark, inhaling the paint fumes, the scent of dust particles which had burned in the heat of the lights, the acrid, musty smell of nervous bodies, their heavy breath in the night. I had curled, protectively around my stomach, swallowing little darts of acid, shifting uncomfortably, elbows and hip bones digging into the floor.

Frederick had studiously avoided me that night. His sleeping form was straight-backed and stiff. It was not the way he slept when he was with me. I longed for him, and I hated him, but the only thing I could really focus on was the never-ending nausea, and anyway, I didn't want to be touched.

Herm and Cat had slept close, entwined. They did not talk much, none of us wasted much energy speaking, but each was never far from the other's side. Even so, I could see Herm finding refuge in his character, becoming more and more Mercutio. She was losing him already.

"A dog of that house shall move me to stand," said Frederick from the stage, "I will take the wall of any man or maid of Montague's."

"That shows thee a weak slave; for the weakest goes to the wall."

"True; and therefore women, being the weaker vessels, are ever thrust to the wall: therefore I will push Montague's men from the wall, and thrust his maids to the wall."

Frederick was playing around with his sword, thrusting it and his pelvis into Emily's face. She giggled, gave a fake, girlish squeal, and then casually flicked her own up between Frederick's legs as she said, "The quarrel is between our masters", winking, "– and us their men."

The swords were loose in their hands, swung without thought from their fingers, as though only toys. As though Emily could not, with a slip of her wrist, castrate her playmate with a razor edge, or open a vein. Sampson and Gregory were eager for bloodshed. Their lives were cheap to them, the way mine was once.

"When I have fought with the men, I will be civil with the maids, and cut off their heads."

Emily gasped and covered her mouth dramatically, in mock shock.

"The heads of the maids?"

"Ay, the heads of the maids, or their maidenheads, take it in what sense thou wilt."

Frederick reached over to tweak her breast. She shrieked and jumped away.

"They must take it in sense that feel it."

At some point early in the morning, that first night, I had watched Colm pack away his brushes and drop, hollow-eyed and silent, into an exhausted stupor. I was still awake, in the grip of one of the violent waves of nausea which increasingly assaulted me, and I stumbled to the tiny makeshift toilet to retch and cough.

When I had finished, I spent some time hanging over the bowl, panting, then wiped my mouth and returned to my spot on the floor, only to find myself fixed by the glittering eyes of Cat in the darkness. I expected hatred, and perhaps I found it, but there was something else there too. A watchfulness, an observance of some detail.

I moved my bed out of the backstage area and re-established it on the stage, the only place I could find relative privacy. The irony of this did not escape me. I slept fitfully, awaking frequently and violently, alarmed from some real or imagined nightmare, and the eyes which peered out from the trees in the backdrop had seemed to sneer and judge me.

Frederick was posturing now, performing for his companion.

"Me they shall feel while I am able to stand, and 'tis known I am a pretty piece of flesh."

Emily laughed scornfully.

"Tis well thou art not fish: if thou hadst, thou hadst been poor John."

The audience tittered politely.

I watched Colm make his entrance as Abraham. He too wore red. A pale pink necktie proclaimed him of the house of Montague. He froze as soon as he saw Frederick and Emily, who braced herself immediately, sword out, on high alert.

"Draw thy tool," she hissed at Frederick, "here comes of the house of the Montagues." Frederick, who had been strutting about waving his sword in mimicry of a large and rather overactive penis, swung round in alarm, facing Colm, tightening his fist around the hilt.

There was a thin layer of sweat on the inside of my upper lip which had congealed to a white line. I bit it off and tasted blood.

(The two factions watch each other carefully, imitating a casual passing, but circling each other like wary animals, the Capulet servants discussing their tactics in excited hisses.)

"I will bite my thumb at him, which is a disgrace to him if he bear it."

Frederick locked eyes with Colm and from my frozen vantage point at the side of the stage, I could see in them both the anticipation of a fight. He brought his thumb up to his mouth, inserted it in a manner that managed to suggest both sex and violence, and bit down on it hard.

"Do you bite your thumb at me sir?"

"I do bite my thumb sir."

"Do you bite your thumb *at me* sir?"

I saw the danger, not only in their swords, but in their eyes.

"Do you quarrel sir?"

"Quarrel sir? No sir."

"If you do sir, I am for you. I serve as good a man as you."

"No better sir?"

"Well sir…"

Cat pushed past me and entered as Benvolio. I stared. Everything about her was mild-mannered and peaceful. She seemed to bring with her a cooling breeze. Even as the alarm started up in her face as Frederick and Emily tried to show off for her, a noblewoman of their house, she was possessed of a quietness I had never before seen in her, onstage or off. Frederick, Emily and Colm had drawn swords and I flinched as she walked calmly between them. Colm had a kind of madness in his eyes.

"Part, fools." she said. "Put up your swords, you know not what you do."

A figure entered swiftly from the far side. Tybalt. The first of our new recruits. He was broad and stocky, fizzing with vicious energy and dressed all in red.

"What?" he said to Cat, and his voice was icy sharp, "Art thou drawn among these heartless hinds?"

The other characters had scattered immediately, Frederick and Emily pushing past, then turning back, to watch with me.

All eyes were on Tybalt.

His face was florid, square-jawed, and clenched, a pulse in his temple throbbing already. He was filled with suspended violence. He was every inch Tybalt.

He drew his sword fast, not waiting to antagonise, skipping the formalities of law and foreplay.

"Turn thee, Benvolio, look upon thy death."

Cat was desperately trying to dodge his blows.

"I do but keep the peace," she said. "Put up thy sword or manage it to part these men with me."

I watched her look around, realising only now that the others had already fled the scene. Tybalt's lips curled in scorn, and behind the sneer I could see desperation.

"What?" he said, "drawn, and talk of peace? I hate the word, as I hate hell, all Montagues, and thee. Have at thee, coward."

They began to fight in earnest.

My mouth was dry as I watched, my own peril forgotten. Shakespeare's plot ceased to matter at this stage, the fact that the stage directions did not suggest that Tybalt would kill Benvolio now was irrelevant. This Tybalt fought with genuine intent, and he wasn't aware yet that this was his initiation, that he, at least, would not die tonight. He could kill Cat now with one false move.

She was darting about, genuine panic in her eyes, sometimes clashing swords like the expert fencer that she was, but more often her movements were clumsy and frightened, a duck or a dodge. Tybalt had not been trained the way we had, but he was fuelled by his passion. Where his sword missed, he used his feet or his fists, he tried to trip, or to punch. This Tybalt was pure energy and he fought dirty.

Frederick rushed past me and onto the stage as Lord Capulet, Juliet's father.

"What noise is this, get me my long sword, ho." His movements were older now, but stronger, born of experience and fired by ancient ire. Emily squeezed through the backstage corridor, swapping neckties as she went, to enter as Lord Montague from the other side, her sword drawn already.

My entrance was not for several more scenes. I held my breath and wondered, suddenly, what would happen if everyone else was dead by that point. I swallowed a mirthless little laugh.

I was intensely relieved when Colm made his entrance as the prince, moving lightly up the backstage stairs and appearing on the balcony, lit in gold like a gleaming god, the only actor clad in white rather than red. I moved a little way up the stairs myself, the better to see him. He was utterly beautiful. I felt a terrible wave of sadness, catching my breath so that it shuddered in my throat. Humans had evolved so much. And yet still we had not managed to choose correctly whom to love.

"Rebellious subjects, enemies of peace." Colm's voice was infused with undeniable power. "Profaners of this neighbour stained steel ... Throw your mistempered weapons to the ground."

(The stage is silent following the prince's command, and for a moment nobody moves, the audience tense and waiting. After a little too long, there is the clang and scrape of metal on wood as four swords land reluctantly on the rust-stained boards. Tybalt's is the last to fall, his hand twitching slightly. The prince, resplendent with power and anger, dismisses them, threatening death should they ever disturb his streets again.

Gradually the warring factions slope away, followed by the watchful prince, until the only characters left on stage are Lord Montague and Benvolio. Lord Montague's fire has gone with his sword and in its place is his fatherly concern for his son.)

The scene progressed. People pushed past me and collapsed, spent, backstage. Nobody was hurt, but the barn seemed still to reverberate with the after-effects, a rich concoction of high emotion and fear.

"See, where he comes," said Cat from the stage, and all of us snapped suddenly back to attention.

This was Romeo's cue. It was the last test, the final moment in which it still seemed possible that one of the new recruits might make a different choice, and unknowingly save the rest of us. I sensed Frederick behind me, watchful, Colm very still at the top of the stairs.

There was an uneasy pause.

Herm moved towards the entrance partition for the first time since the performance had opened, straining to get a better view.

And then Romeo stepped out onto the stage.

He was young, achingly young. His skin was still soft, his eyes still held something of innocence, even a hint of hope. I could see in him Romeo's great swell of feeling, his frustration and emptiness because he had not yet found anywhere to put it. This was a Romeo who knew no moderation, who had been raised in an atmosphere of anger and excess. He was capable of anything. He was a child only just stepping over the threshold of puberty, charged and impulsive.

Tears sprang to my eyes. I could love this Romeo.

But I did not want to die.

"Good morrow, cousin," said Cat, watching him.

There was a pause. Backstage, we collectively caught our breath and held it so tightly that its absence seemed to make an angry sound.

"Is the day so young?" he replied.

I felt a rush of air around me, as we breathed out again. Was it relief? Or something else?

If there was a second of hesitation before Cat's responding line, the audience did not notice it. The performance went on. And we, mute and cloistered in the dark, adjusted our costumes, checked the prop table, awaited our cues.

On the second night, the last before the performance, Frederick had relented slightly. He allowed Cat and Herm the privacy to say their goodbyes and, for once, afforded himself the same licence. We clung to one another on a mattress on the floor of his van, illuminated by a single, low-level spotlight on the floor of what had once been our stage. But I knew he had locked the door behind him.

His skin was smooth and as cool as always, but I felt hot and clammy in his arms. When he touched me, there was a tentative quality to it, as though he might break me, his muscles tense with restraint, and every nerve ending in my body set to hyper alert. I traced strands of his hair, very delicately, from root to tip with my little finger. I felt the strength at the base and the death at the ends.

We did not speak.

On stage, Cat was smiling gently at Romeo.

"Alas," she said, "that love, so gentle in his view, should be so tyrannous and rough in proof."

Cat had retreated into Benvolio. Of all the characters she was playing in this production, Benvolio was the most prevalent, and in Benvolio she would find both an outlet for her grief and a disguise for it. And I wondered as I watched her, not for the first time, why we had not tried harder to escape.

I had thought about it. Plans, wild and increasingly desperate had played on a loop, but were always consigned to the back of my mind, while I prepared, on autopilot, for my performance as Juliet.

I could have run when he let us out to move to his van or made some sort of effort to break down the barn door. I could have burned the barn down. It would have been dangerous, but it would not have been difficult. I could have pretended illness, could have pleaded, could have argued against Frederick using his own precious rhetoric about free choice. But he would say, as had Herm, that we did have a choice, but we had already made it. And it was not the kind of commitment which could be easily retracted.

I could have talked to the others, found weak points and uncertainties, played on them, banded us together in organised mutiny. There were real weapons in that barn. I could have used them to threaten him, the way I had considered once before against Herm.

I could even have called the police. But we were not a Company who allowed mobile phones and, as desperate as I might be, we had all broken laws, and I could not bring myself to betray them quite so entirely.

And so, I did nothing. You will think I was weak, or sick, or brainwashed. In fact, it was rather simpler. I just couldn't imagine what I would do with myself if not this. There was an urgency in me, a survival instinct, even a drive, (though I didn't like to acknowledge it), to protect. But no matter how many times I made plans, or how violently I tried to shake myself out of this stupor, I could never destroy the conviction that whatever I escaped to would prove only to be another, greyer, prison.

All my life I had longed for a straightforward fight. To stride out with confidence and slay a dragon. But there were no dragons, and the only thing I had ever met which barely approached one, I had loved.

"Love is a smoke," Romeo lamented, "made with the fume of sighs." Cat frowned at him, but he continued, "Being purged, a fire sparking in lover's eyes, being vexed, a sea nourished with loving tears."

He was petulant, an armed bundle of warring hormones. He scuffed around in his love as though looking for something to kick. My heart ached for his youthfulness.

"What is it else? A madness most discrete …"

I had at least pleaded with my dragon. I had done that much. All through the last few days, any time I could catch Frederick alone, and several times even though I could not, I raised the question of the law, the police, the practicality of disposing of two dead bodies. I voiced concerns about Cat, about Herm, about myself. I jabbed at him where it would catch at him the most, reminded him of the shadow this production would cast over the future of the Company. The greatly reduced numbers, the effect that losing Herm would have on his recruitment chances for audiences and members alike.

I ignored the other, more damning reason, because I had still not found a way to express it. It breathed itself through me, wove itself silently into every argument, but I did not let it speak. I spoke instead of the two new recruits and the unpredictable ways they might respond, at the point of casting and later, when they knew that their performances, at least, would not be for real. I talked of the trauma to the others, the effect on Colm. Would his mother loom larger as the number of other faces on the wall of his camper van dwindled?

Frederick had responded with a tremor to his mouth and a choke to his voice. But he did not move from his purpose. He was bound the way we were, in thrall to himself. And it was his fervour, his conviction, that steadied me in his arms that final night. So that, finally, silently, the fragile part of me which had fought for a freedom I did not wholly welcome, gave in. There were no words left for us then. We had spent them all in aimless flailing. We made love. Gently, and then with a need which bordered on violence. And when, finally, we could hold back time no longer, and the light prised long fingers through the edges of the blackout blinds at the windows, I had not even tried to hear the nightingale in the howl of lark song.

Centre stage, in front of an already rapt audience, Romeo declared his love for Rosalind. Only his superior and gentler love for Juliet would make him a man. And then the adults around him would make that man a corpse.

I turned, dashed into the small curtained-off area which served as our toilet, succumbing to the ever-present urge to vomit. My body felt foreign and dysfunctional.

I stared for a moment at the bile in the bowl, teaspoon sized and foaming at the edges, and pressed a hand to my stomach, as if to soothe some monster.

"Be ruled by me," said Cat from the stage, "forget to think of her."

"O teach me," Romeo replied, "how I should forget to think."

I emerged from the toilet, ignoring the gaze of my companions, watching me in the darkness, and leaned against the wall. I shut my eyes tight and concentrated on breathing without retching.

By the time I returned my attention to the stage, Benvolio had promised Romeo she would find another beauty to distract him, and Frederick and Colm were taking their places as Lord Capulet, my father, and Paris.

"My child is yet a stranger in the world," Frederick said, combining an iron authority with a gentleness he would not exhibit again until after he had lost his daughter. "She hath not seen the change of fourteen years, let two more summers wither in their pride, ere we may think her ripe to be a bride."

"Younger than she are happy mothers made." said Colm.

I turned and retched again.

I was only half-Juliet, still partly myself and I knew it was this latter part which would be my undoing. And so, just as I had done that moment so long ago, when I climbed into the back of a van to be driven to an unknown destination by two strangers, I told myself that the deed was done. The decision was made. There could be no half-measures.

I took a deep breath and closed my eyes and when I opened them again, I was Juliet.

I listened to Paris and my father on stage, making plans for my marriage, selling me on like a docile puppy. I waited, while Romeo and Benvolio, encountering my father's servant in the street, learned of the party my father would throw, and agreed to gatecrash it. I stepped aside to allow Cat, breathless and grim-faced, to squeeze past me and around behind the staging, shrug a rich velvet, fitted cape on over her clothes and race up the backstage steps to enter onto the balcony as Lady Capulet, my mother. Hands folded and demure, I waited for my entrance, while Emily, my nurse, bumbled and chattered her way around the stage, running along, panting slightly, behind her.

"Nurse, where's my daughter?" demanded Cat, with just the tiniest hint of accusation, as if my absence was a personal affront to her. "Call her forth to me."

"Now, by my maidenhead at twelve-year-old, I bade her come." Emily was flustered, blustering, "What, lamb?" she called, "What, ladybird?" and then, with a glance at my mother, she added, with a pretence of impatience, which even I knew was a performance, "God forbid, where's this girl? What, Juliet?"

Somewhere in the back of my mind, a memory stirred, of another call of this kind, another time.

But I was another person then.

I smoothed my dress, climbed the stairs, and hurried onto

the stage.

"How now?" I said. "Who calls?"

"Your mother," said the nurse, rather unnecessarily, and the flat delivery sent a shallow ripple of laughter through the audience. I hesitated, standing between the two of them, patient, but slightly perplexed as they proceeded to discuss me over my head, one fondly, one with a colder, more routine affection.

"I can tell her age unto an hour," said Emily.

"She's not fourteen," said Cat.

Emily was redoubtable, "I'll lay fourteen of my teeth – and yet to my teen be it spoken – I have but four." She cackled, and the audience laughed with her, grateful to her for this relief from the tension. I knew they would not choose to notice the full set of perfect dentistry in Emily's mouth. If she said she only had four teeth, then she only had four teeth.

"… and then my husband – God be with his soul, he was a merry man – took up the child. "Yea," quoth he, "dost thou fall upon thy face? Thou wilt fall backward when thou hast more wit, wilt thou not, Jule?"

My nurse was almost helpless with laughter, so amused by this memory she could barely get the words out.

"And … and … by my holidam, the pretty wretch left crying and said "Ay"."

She rocked back on her heels clutching her side and, forgetting herself for a moment, clapped her hand on Lady Capulet's arm.

"Ha ha … to see how such a jest should come about. I warrant, an' I should live a thousand years, I never should forget it …"

The audience were laughing too, less at the joke itself than at the nurse's infectious hilarity. Even I, my eyes on the floor, could not help but smile a little. But my mother, Cat, was not so amused. She shook Emily's hand from her arm with a quick, stiff movement. She wanted this done right and done swiftly.

"Enough of this, I pray thee," she said, "hold thy peace."

I felt my smile disappear at once. I looked up at my nurse, who was now retelling the entire story again, and felt myself simultaneously pleading and protective. I interrupted quickly.

"And stint thou too, I pray thee nurse, say I."

"Peace, I have done," my nurse smiled, put her hand over mine, "God mark thee to his Grace. Thou wast the prettiest babe that e'er I nursed. An' I might live to see thee married once, I have my wish."

Cat saw her opportunity, "Marry. That 'marry' is the very thing I came to talk of. Tell me, daughter Juliet, how stands your disposition to be married?"

My response was thoughtless and automatic.

"It is an honour that I dream not of."

"Well, think of marriage now," said my mother, with an edge in her voice which made me flush and bite my lip, "younger than you, here in Verona, ladies of esteem are already made mothers."

Something shifted inside me at those words, and I felt my heart quicken. The back of my neck was suddenly very hot. The nausea, never far away, threatened to return. I swallowed hard.

Cat was wheedling now, coaxing. "What say thou, can you love the gentleman?"

I hesitated. Images of Colm, as Paris, flooded my mind. I thought of his size, his muscle, of the half-understood things he would do to me as part of this contract of marriage. I thought of his good looks, and I thought of his power.

"So shall you share in all he doth possess," my mother was

still talking, betraying now the real driver for this arrangement, "by having him, making yourself no less."

"No less? Nay bigger," said the nurse, laughing in delight, and then, as she winked at me, I saw Emily within her. "Women grow by men," and she nudged me, playfully, in the ribs which felt suddenly as though they were on fire, my breath held unknowingly, so that I let it out in a quick, surprised puff.

"Speak briefly," said Cat, and there was a warning in her voice, "can you like of Paris' love?"

I gathered everything within myself and poured it, doggedly, into Juliet.

"I'll look to like," I said, quietly, "if looking liking move, but no more deep will I endart mine eye, than your consent gives strength to make it fly."

I turned and made my exit.

(As Lady Capulet and the nurse leave, hurrying after Juliet, the lighting dims. The wood floor of the barn becomes dusky and shadowed, a cold light like moonlight falling across it. The dark patches on the floor are black spaces. The balcony is barely visible at all.

A quiet, creeping beat begins. The first few bars for the corresponding scene of Prokofiev's Romeo and Juliet ballet score, played on a loop. It is an insidious sound, like a nagging thought, or a warning ignored.

Offstage, Romeo and Benvolio's voices are heard approaching. They have certainly been drinking, Romeo for comfort, Benvolio, perhaps for courage, as they prepare to crash the party. The quiet beat, still pulsing in the background, becomes just a little louder.)

"Give me a torch," said Romeo, "I am not for this ambling. Being but heavy, I will bear the light."

"Nay, gentle Romeo, we must have you dance." Herm, as Mercutio, was walking backwards onto the stage, bowing with exaggerated courtliness, and carrying a ridiculous mask with snake-headed horns and a nose nearly half a metre long and quite clearly fashioned to resemble a penis.

He turned, as if sensing the audience somehow, paused, eyes glinting and then grinned straight out into the stalls and his grin was so infectious, so full of laughter and so inextricably mixed up with tension and alcohol that the audience laughed too, though I knew that they were not sure what at, or why the laughter made them nervous.

(The beat grows louder.)

"You are a lover." said Mercutio to Romeo, "Borrow Cupid's wings."

(All of the actors are carrying masks, though neither Romeo's, nor Benvolio's are as daring as Mercutio's. But this does not matter, because the audience has eyes for no one else. Mercutio is jumping around lightly, from toe-to-toe, like a boxer, as if he is expecting attack. He dons his mask. The nose is so long that the others, laughing and a little embarrassed, keep having to duck out of the way when he turns his head, and so he does so, frequently. But sweat gleams in the gap between the mask and his hairline, and his hand, when he gestures, shivers slightly.

The beat is loud enough now that the actors have to raise their voices slightly above it.)

"I dreamt a dream tonight."
"And so did I."
"Well, what was yours?"
"That dreamers often lie."

Herm had been remarkable the first time round, and yet only a shadow of the Mercutio he was tonight – feverish, youthful, his voice breaking slightly over the beat, burning too fast and too bright. Too high, too tense, too much.

"Oh," he said, "then I see Queen Mab hath been with you."

(Mercutio removes his mask again with a flourish, sending it skimming across the stage. It lodges itself in the tangle of ivy at the bottom of the ladder to the darkened balcony.)

"She is the fairies' midwife, and she comes in shape no bigger than an agate-stone on the forefinger of an alderman, drawn with a team of little atomies athwart men's noses as they lie asleep…"

I watched from the wings as Cat stepped forward, as if to stem Herm's flow of words. He shifted, twitching out of the way, talking hard, and clipped, spit showering the stage. He swept up his abandoned mask and thrust it back onto his face with a snap of elastic. Tiny beads of sweat flew out from his damp hair.

(The beat of the music is very loud now, reverberating slightly through the stalls. Mercutio is shouting above it, suggestively stroking the protruding appendage of his mask as he describes his imaginary queen galloping across a courtier's nose.

Benvolio steps back, half in protest, half laughing, but there is a sadness too in this exchange. Perhaps she knows only too well her friend's unhappiness, the restless boredom which drives him to extremes. Or maybe she knows, as do most of the audience, that Mercutio will not survive.

And everybody loves Mercutio.)

"This is that very Mab that plaits the manes of horses in

the night, and bakes the elflocks in foul sluttish hairs, which once untangled, much misfortune bodes.

The background beat was no longer background. It filled the barn like a terrible repetitive thunder. Herm was screaming now above it.

"This is the hag, when maids lie on their backs, that presses them and learns them first to bear, making them women of good carriage. THIS IS SHE."

I swallowed and stepped out.

The second I entered, the looping beat finally finished looping and the music began, only gentle notes but at this volume it was mind numbing. I stumbled into Emily's waiting courtier's arms and began a dull and monotonous dance.

Juliet. At a party. A little nervous.

"Peace, Mercutio," Romeo shouted, and everything went suddenly and absolutely silent.

Emily and I continued to dance, mechanically, the ghost of the music still throbbing in our ears.

"True," said Herm, his body drooping. "I talk of dreams, which are the children of an idle brain, begot of nothing but vain fantasy, which is as thin of substance as the air."

Somewhere, in a flimsy part of me that could still peek through Juliet and remember Rose, I recalled that moment in the university theatre, Herm flopping into the armchair, spent and discouraged. I wanted to cry.

I felt Emily's grip tighten around my waist. For a quick, confusing moment, like strobe lighting, I remembered her stumbling, broken body at the end of *The Fiddler of the Reels*, that interminable run. I remembered the crack of Colm's ankle, his pale face in the bed.

I forced the images away, looked past Emily and met Romeo's gaze.

But it only made me remember Frederick.

(The audience watch as Romeo and Juliet catch sight of each other. The opening to Holst's 'Mars, the Bringer of War', unmistakable and ominous, begins to play, until Prokofiev is drowned into a whisper. Tybalt recognises Romeo, tries and fails to draw Juliet's father into a fight. Everyone, players and audience alike, draw a small breath of hope. Perhaps the inevitable ending could still be averted. But Mars clearly signals otherwise, and as the two young lovers press their hands together, the Prokofiev score disappears altogether.)

"Have not saints lips, and holy palmers too?"

"Aye pilgrim, lips that they must use in prayer."

I was flirtatious, giggly. Romeo and I had climbed the first, ivy covered rungs of the steps, leaves clinging a little to my dress, as if trying to hold me there, to catch young Juliet red-handed in this, the first and only act of passion in her stifled young life.

"Then have my lips the sin that they have took."

"Sin from my lips? O trespass, sweetly urged, give me thy sin again."

"You kiss by th' book."

Those famous lines. I spoke them with giddy nervousness. The audience loved it. The performance moved on.

We had rearranged the chorus scene that would normally come next, to use it later, and so when Romeo and I had been interrupted by the nurse, had learned of each other's identity and the party dispersed, I needed to re-enter almost immediately. I stepped around the ever-increasing creep of ivy at the foot of the stepladder, to enter the cramped, backstage exit to the left of the stage and sidestep my way through the tiny backstage corridor, behind Colm's painted forest. The backdrop was chipped and pitted this side, unadorned with paint or varnish. It was rough against my hands, splinters catching between my fingers. I brushed them on my dress. It did not matter. My dress would not stay white for the duration of this performance.

I shuffled out at the other end, Colm stepping aside to let me pass, and climbed the backstage stairs, like a child in a dream, to the balcony entrance.

(Juliet appears on the balcony. It is night, and yet she is bathed in a warming, golden light, as though she carries it in herself, transforming the moonlight from silver to gold. "Romeo", she breathes and there is something spellbinding in the way she says his name.)

It was no longer a stage. It was my bedroom. When I spoke the famous lines, so hackneyed now, such well-trodden territory, I felt only Juliet's youthful frustration, the unfairness of her parents' feuding now brought to bear, like a weapon, on her life.

"Romeo, doff thy name," I said, and meant it. I banged my fist on the balcony banister in exasperation.

"What's in a name?" I said, "that which we call a Rose…"

I hesitated. Only for a split second. It seemed as though everybody, backstage and in the audience, held their breath.

"…by any other word would smell as sweet."

We breathed out. All of us. We breathed together.

When Romeo spoke to me out of the darkness on the ground floor stage, I jumped, genuinely startled. As we talked, he moved towards me, into the light cast from my bedroom, so that he was pale and white. He had thick, dark lashes and floppy hair. I looked into his face, and he became a strange, dreamlike mixture of himself and Frederick. I looked at that vision and I fired all my love at it.

"Swear not by the moon," I cried, "th' inconstant moon, that monthly changes in her circled orb."

He moved closer, trod the lowest rung of the ladder, now so ensnared with ivy that he cried out a little and wobbled, gripping a high rung to pull his foot out from among its twines.

"What shall I swear by?"

"Do not swear at all, or if thou wilt, swear by thy gracious self."

I was bending over the rail, climbing out from my cossetted territory, reaching into the ivy to entangle his fingers in mine.

"My bounty is as boundless as the sea," I said, "my love as deep, the more I give to thee, the more I have."

I felt the desperation in the words. I had climbed over the balcony now, hanging from the ladder, my fingers sore from holding myself up, my other hand in his. There were thorns entwined among the ivy, a subtlety Colm had not revealed, and they tore at our clothes and through our skin, so that my arms bore a delicate cobweb of thin red scratches. He was bleeding from a deeper graze on his face. The distance we would have to traverse for this love was treacherous. The thorns were only to be expected. But he shielded my face from them with his palm when we kissed, gently disengaged my dress.

"Goodnight," I said. "Parting is such sweet sorrow, that I shall say goodnight till it be morrow."

"Sleep dwell upon thine eyes," he said, "peace in thy breast. Would I were sleep and peace, so sweet to rest."

But we moved apart with difficulty, and the ivy caught at him, possessive. I had a tear in my dress, and his blood on my face.

(The play continues. Romeo meets with Friar Lawrence and asks for his advice. The friar, like all well-meaning adults, sees youthful emotion and writes it off. It is a teenage crush, but it might just, finally, reunite the two families. This passing fixation might bring about peace. And so, he agrees secretly to marry the young lovers, and the children are used, as so often happens, to mend self-inflicted, adult wounds.

The audience are gripped. But they do not understand what it is they are watching.)

It was the dagger that undid me.

I had made my way down the backstage stairs from the balcony and felt my way behind the backdrop and when I rounded the corner, half-blinded by the light spilling in from the stage, it was the first thing I saw, like a call to reality. A slim, black shape, sheathed for now but there, at the point where the handle met the blade, a sliver of silver, winking at me in the reflected spotlights.

I was sweating with residual emotion and effort, my skin still stinging from the previous scene and for a moment, the dagger, the whole prop table in front of me, became strange and swirly. I felt a cold sensation where the flimsy, white fabric of my dress had stuck to the damp of my skin, as though a long-dead ghost had planted its palm flatly and deliberately onto the flesh of my back.

And then everything suddenly swung into focus and the dagger was there, like a shiny black monster. I was struck, once again, by its plainness, just as I had been all those lifetimes ago. Frederick wanted the knife's simplicity to be shocking and clinical, an unsympathetic weapon. Dazed, I felt myself reach out towards it, my fingers close over it.

"Rose."

Frederick. I felt it thrill through me, hot and visceral, the way he said my name.

He had just made his exit; the scene was over. On stage Herm and Cat and Romeo were gathering, waiting to be joined by Emily.

"Rose."

His voice was clear but pitched low so that it did not carry to the stage. I whirled round on him, knife in hand, my knuckles white around it.

"Rose." This time his voice was a whisper. I am not sure which one of us had moved but his arms were around me now, and I felt the pound of his chest. His hand traced the length of my arm very gently, until he reached my fingers, and prised them free of the knife. He put it back on the prop table behind me, redoubled his grip around my quivering body. I closed my eyes.

(Mercutio is swaggering around the stage, swishing with his sword at the air. He has told Benvolio, with an air of great importance, that Tybalt has sent a written challenge to Romeo via his father.)

"Romeo will answer it," said Cat, but there was fear on her face. Mercutio, who had been pacing and slashing at the air, turned back and gave her a cheerless, little grin.

"Any man that can write may answer a letter," he said, a shade of cruelty in his banter, forcing Benvolio to explain her fear that Romeo might rise to the challenge. Then he paused, his face sombre.

"Alas, poor Romeo," he said, "he is already dead."

I pulled away from Frederick. His cloak, as the friar, was large and too long, even on him. It had a heavy, broad hood which covered much of his head, casting his face in shadow so that his eyes were dark hollows and the rest of his slim figure indiscernible. He seemed ghostly, as though there might be nothing inside the cloak at all. As though he might slide through my fingers like a phantom.

Three more scenes and Herm would die.

"Frederick. We can't." It was all I could manage. He didn't question me, didn't ask me to elucidate. I reached up on an angry impulse and threw back his hood, felt the captured violence in the gesture. He submitted to it.

"Rose. Come on. What else could we do?"

"We could fake it. That's what everyone else does." My voice was bitter now, rising. On stage, Herm, who was making bawdy jokes at the expense of the nurse, raised his own volume to cover it. "That, Frederick, is what *literally* everyone else does. Everyone."

My voice was breaking, squeaking at the high points and scraping painfully across my throat at the low.

"That's the argument you're using?" said Frederick, "That what we do isn't normal? That we're not walking the same path, tramping through the same mud trails as everyone else? Is that what you want Rose? Is that what you want now?"

I thought about Herm's cocktails. The thick, dark sludge in the bottom of the shaker, a concoction made of coloured water.

He had swapped it that day for something else, something stronger.

Something real.

I felt my anger dissolve, a heavy inevitability in its place. I turned my face to Frederick, pulled him to me, and as we kissed, I tasted salt.

(Romeo, having with some difficulty persuaded his friends to leave him, talks earnestly with the nurse. He thrusts the ceremonial cords that will bind him to his love into the nurse's old, arthritic fingers, and they depart.)

The scene ended. There was a sudden silence.

I pulled away from Frederick, wiped my face. We looked at each other. We were wrecks, both of us. There was too much colour in our cheeks and too little everywhere else.

"I think it's your entrance." He did not touch me, made no attempt to insist. But I could no longer clearly remember why I had been resisting. Was this not what we were here for? We had never sought normality. We were actors. Fanatics.

This was just what we did.

(Juliet seems to enter too suddenly, as if her place on the stage had been a last-minute afterthought. She seems distracted and jumpy, but her nervous impatience at the tardiness of her nurse is real enough. She twitches with anticipation when the older woman enters, then with irritation when the news is not delivered immediately. This is the first time we have seen Juliet on the grimy stage floor. It is a sign of darker things to come.

The nurse sends Juliet to Friar Lawrence to be secretly married to Romeo and a church bell begins, as if in obedience, to toll. But as Juliet hurries off and the friar approaches, his face shadowed by the hood of his cloak, the cords in his hands, it seems as if the soundtrack is wrong, the toll of the bell too slow, too sombre, more fitted to a funeral than to a wedding.

The light fades, very slowly, until, as the script runs out and the friar begins to perform his ceremony, there is silence apart from the tolling bell, and darkness apart from a slender spotlight on Romeo and Juliet. Their faces are pale and blue-tinged in its beam. They hold hands, allow the friar to bind them. The spotlight grows smaller, until it fades into nothing as the bell makes its final, doleful toll.)

The stage was pitch black when we left it, and we felt our way in silence along the balcony and down the backstage stairs. Behind us, the empty stage was suffused suddenly with a blood-red light. There again, were the strains of the Valkyries, violins creeping and descending. Soon, Frederick's pre-recorded voice would begin to speak the words of the chorus which we had moved from Act 2, his voice sonorous and echoing, loud enough to make the barn vibrate.

It was terrifying, even from backstage, but there was another purpose to it. The scene after this would be Mercutio's last. It was a breath in the story, a breath in ours, to allow us a moment to say goodbye.

Everyone's cues had been carefully arranged so that we would all be together in the larger backstage area. In the smaller area opposite, only Romeo and Tybalt waited, knowing perhaps that we needed this space. Neither Tybalt nor Romeo shared this sorrow. They had not been with us long enough to have anything – or anyone – here to lose.

Herm looked up as we approached, and I saw that he was pale and sweating. Cat had his hand tightly in both of hers, but her expression was fierce rather than tender. Herm's sword was already fastened in his belt loop. He stood very still in the midst of us, his feet firmly planted in their boots. He met our eyes deliberately and grinned.

"Fancy meeting you all here," he said softly.

No one smiled. Cat was frozen, her small hands white with the grip she maintained on his hand. For a moment, nobody moved, and then Emily, gathering herself with visible effort, managed to match his grin with her own rough levity.

"Any last requests?" she said.

I saw Herm meet her eyes, saw his relief at the change of tone. He shrugged with painful nonchalance. "Maybe some of that nasty brandy, if you haven't drunk it all."

There was a sudden flurry, everyone trying to grasp this small chance to do something simple, something helpful. I was the only person who didn't move. I had no idea where the brandy was. For a long time now, I had felt too sick to touch it. There was an odd creeping sensation low in my abdomen, so that I checked, with a kind of delirious panic, that I hadn't somehow emptied my bladder.

Frederick stood still, his eyes on Herm's, and for a moment the two men locked gazes. There was sadness there, but mostly only that quiet, instinctive understanding that they had always seemed to share. Frederick inclined his head very briefly and I watched the almost imperceptible movement Herm gave in return. A nod. There was nothing more to say.

On-stage, Frederick's recorded voice still resonated around the barn, the music filling the exaggerated pauses he left between each slow, deliberate line. The audience, thankfully, was spellbound.

Someone passed Herm a brown bottle. He unscrewed the lid, tossed it behind him, tipped it to his lips and took a swig.

"Gargh." he said, wiping his mouth with the back of the hand that still held the bottle. "Nope. That stuff is officially still rank."

The laughter, what there was of it, was swift and shallow. Emily took the bottle just in time for Colm to launch himself forward, throwing his arms around Herm, who reciprocated without loosening himself from Cat, wrapping his free arm tightly around Colm's broad, shaking torso.

This could not happen. We could not go through with this. Herm could not die. I became consumed suddenly with an urgent need to find the lid of the brandy bottle. We might need it, I thought. Mercutio would be wounded onstage but would take his final breath out of sight. It might just be possible that we could use it to clean his wound, get him stable, staunch the blood, get him out to a hospital.

I knew as I looked, that it would not happen that way.

Frederick's chorus on stage continued, but it was nearing the end. The music for the Valkyries swelled again, the trumpets climbing and falling away, the heralders of death.

Colm backed away, still shuddering, and Emily stepped forward, mouth twisting, and squeezed Herm's shoulder with unnecessary force.

"Good luck girl," he said, saluting, and for a moment he was an army hero, an old, wise captain in some long-ago war, before it faded and Emily stepped aside and he became Herm again, pale but ready, hand in hand with the woman he had loved. I almost couldn't move. I felt Cat's eyes like heat on me, but she accepted the moment, flinching back a little, stiffly, as I made myself approach him.

"We can't … Herm … we can't do this." My voice was strangled. It barely carried above the noise on-stage. But he heard me, and he met my gaze.

"Rose," he said, and held out his free arm.

I stumbled forward. The others may have been ready for this, and to all accounts I should have been. I was not. I stepped into Herm's embrace.

"I'm sorry," I said. "I'm so, so, sorry."

But he gripped my dress in his fist, pulling me back so that I was forced to look at him.

"Rose," he said, "this isn't your fault."

It clearly was. I was certain of it. And I knew that Cat, her gaze on me now filled with open hostility, agreed. But he shook his head and I saw a sternness which I had never seen in Herm before.

"No," he said. "It is what we signed up for."

Frederick's voice on stage was nearing its conclusion. The music was slowing. I felt somebody pull me aside and Herm stepped forward so that he stood at the stage entrance and took Cat in his arms. Everyone else looked away, allowing them their moment. But my heart was pounding in my throat like an escaping animal, and I only watched dumbly, as they turned to each other. They had less than a minute.

She pulled him to her.

The ghostly Frederick spoke his last line. The trumpets and violins rose and fell, cymbals clashed, the music slowed. The red spotlight began to be replaced by something brighter, more akin to daylight. Across the stage at the opposite entrance, I saw Romeo and Tybalt watching, bowing their heads respectfully, poised for their cue. I wondered how Tybalt felt now, remembered Colm's words about it being as hard to bring about the death of another, as it would be to die, and swallowed.

Colm started up the stairs to the balcony, Emily pulled on her cloak for her entrance as Lord Montague, and Frederick donned his necktie for his, as Juliet's father.

"No." I said, "Please. We can't."

The music was playing its final chords. The lights were nearly fully up.

"We can't. We have to stop. This is madness." I was speaking into empty air, turning my head desperately, everyone around me sombrely dispersing.

Herm and Cat pulled apart and prepared to make their entrance. And I said the only thing I knew that might stop them, the last true thing I would say while I was still Rose.

"Please. We can't. I'm … I think I'm pregnant."

There was a stunned silence. Blood thundered in my ears

and my vision blurred with the heat of it. I was dimly aware of five frozen faces, each registering a different shade of shock. Was there knowledge there too? Had they suspected? I wasn't sure. I was struggling to focus properly.

The music had finished. The stage was set. Outside, somewhere, our rapt audience was waiting.

Nobody moved.

I staggered, and felt somebody's steadying hand on my back, Emily's perhaps, or Colm's. And then I was sitting on the floor, my head spinning, the nausea rising and settling again.

The stage was silent.

Somewhere in front of me was Frederick, his face a pale blur of my tears. I could not see his face, but I felt it like a punch. His love. And his anger.

Somebody in the audience coughed.

And then, like puppets, we sprang automatically to our entrances.

Mercutio and Benvolio, no longer kissing, strolled onto the stage, arm in arm, talking. On the balcony, Colm dragged his gaze away from me, changing grimly into his cloak as the prince. Frederick was a statue at the entrance to the narrow walkway behind the staging. For a moment we froze, our gazes locked, wild and staring. And then he turned with a sweep of his cloak and disappeared.

Emily helped me up the stairs to the balcony.

This was no longer about me. This was Mercutio's moment. It was simply too late now.

The show must go on.

(There has been a slight delay in their entrance, and some indistinguishable shouting backstage, but when Mercutio and Benvolio stroll out onto the stained floorboards, bleached in yellow

light, all is forgotten. The audience leans towards Mercutio, he is their favourite. Later, when they leave, shell-shocked and subdued, they will agree amongst themselves that it was a very memorable production, and that the actor playing Mercutio had been especially talented. He will go far, they will predict, he should be famous. It is a shame there were no programmes issued, so that they could have taken a note of his name.

Benvolio is a little nervous, she is concerned about the Capulets, she fears another encounter with Tybalt, and the dull, steady beat that was present in the first act has begun again in the background, quiet and ominous. But Mercutio teases her, almost dancing in his merriment, and she can only smile, and allow her friend, as always, to laugh at their lives, and make light of their deaths.

Music begins. The first strains of a familiar refrain. Holst again, 'Mars, the Bringer of War'. It is Tybalt's theme and, almost as if the music alerts her, Benvolio drops her laughter and clutches at her friend's arm.)

"By my head, here come the Capulets." Cat tried to pull Herm backwards, but he shrugged her off.

"By my heel," he said, "I care not."

Tybalt entered, the music growing a little louder in recognition. His initial politeness felt pained, as if physically difficult for him to restrain, as he enquired as to the whereabouts of Romeo, with whom his quarrel truly lay.

It could have gone another way, but it wasn't scripted, and Mercutio, at this stage, was too hot to stop. He had been bored for a long time, since long before the opening of the play's action, and was heartily tired of it. Herm portrayed it perfectly. Mercutio wanted to play. The deadlier the game, the better.

"And but one word?" he said. "Couple it with something, make it a word and a blow."

The audience held their breath with the rest of us. Tybalt tried again to enquire about Romeo, and Mercutio tried once more to break his resolve. There was a fragile thread between them now, an understanding. Tybalt the warmonger and Mercutio the clown. They were seeking the same thing.

But Benvolio's tone was sharp. "Either withdraw into some private place, and reason coldly of your grievances, or else depart, here all eyes gaze on us."

Mercutio turned to the audience and winked.

"Men's eyes were made to look, and let them gaze."

He stood, legs apart, facing the audience full on, strutted, puffed his chest out, grinned. I heard the audience laugh uneasily, shocked at this blatancy, afraid of its consequence.

Romeo made his entrance.

Tybalt rounded on him.

"Romeo, the hate I bear thee can afford no better term than this – thou art a villain."

Startled, Romeo stepped back. He put up a hand as if to shake Tybalt's, or to push him away, hastily retracting it when he took in Tybalt's reaction. He explained, a little dreamily in his love-cushioned state, that he had more reason to love Tybalt than to hate him, that he bore him no ill, that he would have no quarrel.

It was too much. Mercutio exploded with indignation.

"Vile submission," he cried.

(The music swells, but the beat behind it is louder now, reverberating through the barn like some dark, rumbling beast. It is a heartbeat, quick and deep and low.)

Herm drew his sword, and there was a quick, wild rush in him, which seemed to ripple through the barn.

"You rat-catcher", he said, "you king of cats. I want but

one of your nine lives. Make haste."

Mercutio was beautiful in that moment, every part of him alive and gleaming, light on his toes and ready for anything. It was a level of charisma that no one else on that stage could approximate. Everyone in the building was rooting for him.

And Tybalt could feel it.

We could do nothing. We could only watch.

(With an angry growl, Tybalt yanks his sword from its holder, almost forgetting himself in his haste, so that he has to take a moment to steady his posture, rock his weight onto his back leg, redouble his grip.

Mercutio smiles.

It is a slow, satisfied smile, like an overblown villain in a children's film. He glances at the audience, rolls his eyes, springs a little on his toes.

Tybalt lunges. Mercutio steps aside, balletic, hips out, like a dancer, twirls his free hand in something approximating a bow.

He steps back a little. In a flash of bright, knowing anachronism, he pretends, idly, to check his watch. Then he thrusts forward, his sword narrowly missing Tybalt's face. It meets Tybalt's own sword with some force. The clang of metal echoes around the building.

The drumbeat is louder now, drowning out the music. Tybalt whirls and swipes, Mercutio ducks. He twists from a low position, his sword neatly severing one of Tybalt's bootlaces. There is a wave of nervous laughter through the audience. Tybalt scowls. Mercutio grins.

Benvolio and Romeo are standing back, trying desperately to intervene.

"Draw Benvolio," Romeo shouts, "beat down their weapons." Mercutio throws him a look of scornful indulgence, and, by a series of running, jabbing thrusts, he drives the fighting further back across the stage, and away from his friend.

Tybalt allows this, that flash of understanding between the two men arising again. They are almost enjoying themselves now. They play like cats or puppies, but with claws unsheathed.

Tybalt swipes, Mercutio jumps. Mercutio springs, Tybalt skips aside.

All the while Mercutio has one eye on his audience, he winks and laughs, throws them knowing looks, as though letting them in on some private joke. Tybalt, on the other hand, is perfectly focused, he wastes no time garnering support, he knows he does not have it. Instead, he waits for a moment when Mercutio's natural showmanship will cause him to let down his guard.

Romeo has been shouting from the sidelines, trying to reason with the two avid swordsmen. But the drum beats its insistent, steady pulse. It fills the space. The air seems thick with it.

Mercutio jabs. Tybalt smashes Mercutio's sword, but Mercutio rides the momentum, swinging it around full circle and at speed. Tybalt ducks. Mercutio laughs.

Romeo leaps between them. "Hold Tybalt," he shouts. "Good Mercutio."

His voice breaks with the effort of speaking over the drumbeat.

Mercutio stumbles, caught on his front foot readying to strike, and wobbling a little with the effort of holding back for fear of harming his friend.

Romeo stands helpless with his arms out between them. Mercutio squints in exasperation, trying to see around him.

Tybalt thrusts.

Mercutio gasps.

And the deafening drumbeat stops.)

In the resulting silence it seemed that nobody, backstage or on-stage, moved. Emily was downstairs, frozen, head bent low over the switch which controlled the sound, fingers still clasped around the slider with which she had cut the drumbeat.

Behind me I could feel the heat of Colm's body. Neither of us breathed.

Tybalt was the first to recover. In the silence, there was a horrible, wet, schticking sound as he withdrew his sword. I heard Herm cry out, a brief, high cry of pain, as though he had been burned. Tybalt hesitated for one shocked moment. I saw Herm, his back to me, bend over, clutching his upper thigh. A seep of dark liquid, gleaming slick in the lights. Emily, fist pressed into her mouth, stabbed at the dimmer switch.

Tybalt turned and ran. I heard the pound of his boots as he fled the short distance from the stage to the tiny, cluttered corner which was the opposite backstage area. If I squinted, I could see Frederick there, a dark shape, white-faced, waiting. He would tell him now, Tybalt, our newest Company member, fresh from the horror of death, that he had killed another, but that he would not die himself.

Herm turned, so that I had a partial view of his face. He was blueish white, lips pale, his skin sheened with sweat.

I whirled around, in blind sorrow, and stumbled into Colm's hot chest. He held me tight, buried his own curly head in my hair. We gripped each other. On-stage, I could hear Herm now, speaking his lines. His voice was breathless.

"A plague," he said, "on both your houses." His voice was weak, he was gasping his lines out and the fervour with which that curse should have been made, was missing.

I pushed my head hard into Colm's chest, grateful for the solidity of him. I felt my knees shaking, redoubled my grip on his waist, and hung there.

Outside, the scene continued but the world seemed slowed now, mired in treacle.

"Courage, man," I heard Romeo say, the shock still

evident in his voice, "the hurt cannot be much."

But Herm was slurring his words, there were long, juddering pauses between his lines. "You shall find me a grave man tomorrow," he quipped but gone was that bright, bold humour, and I heard a stumble and a quick gasp from Cat as she stepped forward to support him. "A plague," he said again, "on both your houses" His voice was failing, the audience must have been struggling to hear him.

There was a long silence, punctuated only by laboured breathing, "A braggart," he stammered, and then, after an even longer pause, "A rogue."

He still had more lines before Cat could help him off the stage. I willed him to get through them, to abandon them even. It was over now anyway. Downstairs, Emily moved towards the costume rack, shrugged on a dark garment, like a cagoule, one of the cold details we had thought through previously, to protect our costumes.

She dragged out the mattress we had prepared backstage, placed it near to the stage entrance. She pulled out a selection of pillows, arranged them carefully, plumping them up with great attention, as though somehow, by making him comfortable, we could mend him.

We had a blanket prepared, and she spread it over the mattress, folded it back as though to welcome a reluctant child into bed. Then she stopped, leaned her head against the wall, closed her eyes.

We waited, all of us frozen, listening to the shambling conclusion of the scene, until, the relief evident even in his fading moments, Herm whispered, "Help me into some house, Benvolio, or I shall faint."

There was a scrambling and a stumbling and Cat half-fell through the backstage entrance, her jaw clenched and her face hard and white. Herm's arm was looped, heavy over her small, straining shoulder as he shouted back towards the stage, recovering his vocal chords as if realising only now that these would be his last words.

"A plague on both your houses … your … houses."

And then, faintly, the lines spilling out, muddled, and almost forgotten, as he and Cat collapsed onto the waiting mattress.

"I have it … and soundly too. They have … they have made worms meat of me …" He gave a skewed, wry smile, a tiny shadow of an earlier Herm, before his eyes rolled backward in his head and the weight of him seemed to sink, to seep into the mattress on the dirty floorboards of a disused barn, far from the bright, white lights of the stage area, the pathetic backdrop for his final breath.

Everything seemed to speed up. I watched, frozen in horror, as Cat wriggled out from beneath Herm, covered in his blood, put her hand on his forehead, stroked his hair. Emily was next to him, brandy bottle in hand, trying to dribble some between his lips. He spluttered.

Romeo had scant few lines before Cat's cue to re-enter. He was spinning them out, part in shock himself, but there was a limit to how long he could feasibly do that. Cat bent down very low, and kissed Herm's pale lips, flecked now with brandy spittle. Then, with an anguish held cruelly at bay, she stood up, and, allowing her grief out only in the guise of Benvolio, she took her cue and rushed back onto the stage.

"O Romeo, brave Mercutio's dead."

I pulled away from Colm and rushed down the stairs, pulling another cagoule off the rack and over Juliet's dress. I grabbed at the props box, pulled out any material I could, and ran towards Herm. He would die of blood loss, we had thought this through earlier, when planning seemed reasonable and not cold and hard. It would be, we had thought, a less painful death than a stomach wound, a little slower than the heart. The biggest arteries are in the thighs, when the moment was right, that was where Tybalt would aim. It seemed to me impossible that we had ever thought this way, that we could have planned these details. Now, faced with the reality, I could think only of how we could undo it.

Emily watched me. I don't believe she was so deluded as to expect we could save him, but she took my lead. The rules were gone now, he had played out his scene, he had fulfilled his contract, he could be allowed, surely after all, to live.

I pulled at the material, trying to rip it into strips, but it wouldn't give, I pulled again, bit it, cried out in frustration. Colm appeared behind me, tore at it from another angle, it came off in uneven, ragged ribbons. I grabbed it and tried to tie it, pressing hard around the wound. Blood seeped onto my hand, spilling over my fingers. It was warm and sticky and the heat and quantity of it shocked me.

Herm stirred and cried out, too loud, I was certain it would have been audible from the stage. I tried to tie the material tight like a tourniquet, a little above the wound, but he cried out again and struggled weakly.

"It's OK," I said and put my hand to his head.

His hair was drenched with sweat, plastered to his forehead, his lips blue now, his teeth chattering. The mattress was soaked. When I put my weight on it, dark, viscous liquid collected in the creases of my plastic cagoule. The stage must have been slippery with it.

On-stage, a grief-stricken, furious Romeo called out for Tybalt, drew his sword.

Emily tried again to feed brandy to Herm, but he was shaking uncontrollably now and it splashed onto his face. He screwed up his eyes against it, barely conscious, turned his head and vomited weakly. A thin stream of dark yellow brine and brownish brandy mingled with the blood and cut a slimy trail on the floor. I felt a reluctant disgust and then a terrible shame.

There was a clash of metal from the stage. Romeo and Tybalt were fighting. But Tybalt was off his game, still shocked by his own actions. It wouldn't be a long battle.

I tried to take Herm's pulse, but I couldn't feel it, my own thundered too loudly in my veins. There was a smell of sickness, the metallic scent of blood, and something else beneath that which reminded me, horribly, of unprepared meat. Gently, Emily pulled at Herm's eyelids. His eyes were white and unseeing.

I was vaguely aware of a flurry on stage. There was a sudden movement, a cry of shock. This was the scene in which Romeo would kill Tybalt. Both brothers by now were aware that they would survive this performance, and Romeo had the only blunt weapon. There hadn't been time to switch it for Tybalt.

There was another cry. It sounded as though it came from Romeo. I glanced back. The brothers were fighting furiously. They were a whirl of dust and angry breath. There was another cry from Romeo, a stifled "No!"

Tybalt was holding both swords. I felt my body grow a little colder, turned back, questioningly, to Emily. She was looking past me, her hands still on Herm's slack face, mouth open, eyes fixed on the stage. I remembered Frederick's words that night, about one of the brothers being convinced he had already contracted the illness. I thought of the sense of disappointment, of being somehow untethered when I sat down by the campfire that first night, when I knew that Juliet's death was no longer my own.

When I turned back, Romeo was standing, shuddering on stage, and Tybalt was motionless on the floor, a new and fresher pool of blood already seeping through the boards.

Had he stabbed himself with his own sword, still wet with Herm's blood? Or switched the weapons and impaled himself bodily, on a point held unwillingly by his horrified brother?

A surge of horror ran through me.

The truth was, I had almost forgotten about them. All of us had, they were new to us, we had other things to concern ourselves with, and anyway, they were going to survive. Maybe we even resented them a little.

But they had been brought to the edge and reprieved from it mid-performance. They'd had no time at all to process that. That was never the way we had done it before. Less than an hour earlier, Romeo had been expecting to kill his brother, then himself, and his brother had been willing for him to do it. More than willing. Now Romeo was an unwilling participant in a death he was still trying to process his own, last minute, release from.

And none of us even knew their real names.

Sorrow swelled in me like a physical force.

What had we done?

I felt Colm stand up behind me, trudge, still partially in shock, back up the stairs for his entrance as the prince. Emily stood up too, slowly, like a much older woman, pulled off her cagoule and picked her way carefully around the mattress, to her entrance.

On stage, Romeo gathered his character around him, dropped his sword and ran into the wings.

After all this time, all this posturing and proclaiming, none of us had really been ready for this. We were barely functioning. But now it was done, it seemed unthinkable for the rest of us not to play our part.

I tied more material around Herm's wound. This time,

there was no reaction. I felt my eyes fill, my head swirl.

"No. Come on." I said it between my teeth, an urgent hiss, a plea for a revival, but this was no fantasy. This was death. We could call it, we could cast lots about it, plan for it, gamble with it, welcome it in. But we did not have the power to send it away.

"Tybalt, oh my cousin, oh my brother's child." I heard Frederick, as Lord Capulet, from the stage. Cat, as Benvolio, was left once again, to explain who exactly had just killed who. I could hear Colm's deep tones as the prince.

It would soon be my cue. I was supposed to enter on the balcony, but I knew I wouldn't have time to climb the stairs now. I shrugged off my cagoule, but I did not leave Herm's side.

I slapped Herm gently on his ashen face. He did not even quiver. I shook him, he sank back into the sticky mattress.

"Stop that. Come on. Herm. Stop … stop *play-acting* …"

For an unconvincing moment, somewhere in the dregs of my remaining hope for him, I almost expected he might react at that, might open his eyes, and grin at me, and laugh. But he was limp, unresponsive. The Herm I knew had retreated somewhere I could not follow, and in his place was this object, this ageing, paunchy body which leaked and seeped. Lying there, my rags tied helplessly around the wound, his body seemed trussed up, humiliated. I did not recognise it.

I don't know what I had pictured. Something better, something a little more glamourous, something spotlit, stagey and heroic. I had forgotten that, sooner or later, the curtain would always have to fall. There would always be a backstage. It would always be dirtier, dingier, messier.

And through all my heady, feverish fantasies, I had never imagined it this way.

(*The audience watch in sombre silence as Tybalt's body is lifted onto a stretcher and carried backstage. This has been a stranger and more brutal enactment of this story than any they have seen before.*

The stage, for a moment, is empty. There has been no music since the death of Mercutio, and the silence, given the volume of the soundtrack when there is one, feels empty and strange. There is a place on the floor at the far side, where both fights took place, which is stained and wet. It gleams, drawing the audience's gaze towards it with morbid magnetism, until the lighting changes and the stage dims, and it becomes only a darker patch in the darkness.

Juliet enters. She is barely lit initially; the spotlight being trained on an empty balcony before the lighting seems to catch up and refocus on the floor. She paces like a wraith in her white dress, back and forth in the corner furthest from the bloodstain.

She is meant to be happy, hopeful, at least at the beginning of this scene, but she seems overly agitated and jumpy, as though, somehow, she already knows the terrible news her nurse is yet to bring her. When her nurse finally arrives, and Mercutio and Tybalt's deaths are revealed, along with news of Romeo's subsequent banishment, enforced by the prince as punishment for his actions, it is almost as if it comes as a relief.

Juliet collapses, easily, almost too quickly, into her grief. The nurse too, voices her lamentations with surprising fervour, and there is a moment in which they both abandon themselves so far to their anguish, that the script seems to be forgotten, and the action does not move on for some minutes.

Eventually, they recover themselves, the nurse rushes away to find Romeo at Friar Lawrence's cell, and Juliet exits, numb and spent, to the far exit, a trail of ivy from the top of the overgrown stairs to the balcony catching on her ankle as if to snare her as she leaves.

Music begins to creep back in, very faintly in the background, the Prokofiev theme again, but low and rumbling, base notes unbalanced with the melody.

The nurse meets Romeo and Friar Lawrence, and the two men seem to repeat the same pattern as the nurse and Juliet, their grief a little too hot, too heavy, available too early. By the time the scene is over, and Romeo has made plans to come to Juliet that evening, a sweet moment of stillness in the turbulent events, the consummation of his too brief marriage, everyone, audience included, are exhausted.)

I had entered from the wrong floor, and I exited at the wrong side, furthest from Herm's too-still form. It was automatic, some inner part of me wrapping myself in brittle armour.

I left before Emily could move, so that she had to adjust her own exit the same way she had needed, earlier, to adjust her entrance, and Colm the lighting. If I could change this much, I remember thinking, if I could adjust the course of fate this far, might it still be possible to change everything else?

But the play continued, Romeo and Frederick passing me to make their entrance, Romeo's grief palpable and hot, but lost now, grimly, in his role. The tiny backstage area was suddenly too crowded, and then, just as suddenly, too empty. I wanted to grab at them, to touch their warm, still living bodies. I wanted to hold Frederick, to be held, but he was late for his entrance, and he did not tarry now. We were past the point of no return.

I did not look at the dagger on the table. I moved through the narrow space behind the stage, for the first time grateful for its oppressive darkness. I didn't emerge until the very last moment, when I would have to climb the stairs for my cue.

I steeled myself for what I would find in that backstage area, but in the end, it wasn't necessary. The mattress, Herm, and Tybalt on his stretcher had been moved back from the entrance, and the white curtain we had previously erected around the makeshift toilet had been rearranged respectfully around them. Some morbid urge gripped me, and I paused on the stairs and looked down. Tybalt had been covered with a sheet. The body beside him was silent and unmoving. A small, thin shadow knelt at its side.

Cat.

Herm.

I turned and stumbled up the stairs.

(The Prokofiev music mellows and grows gentle in the background. The stage is lit by two spotlights. On the lower level, Paris and Juliet's parents doom her to a rapid marriage, the date set for Thursday, only two days from now. But nobody in the audience is watching them. All eyes are on Romeo and Juliet, making gentle, sweet love in the second spotlight, on the balcony.)

Romeo had exited on the lower level, white and breathless from the previous scenes. I was leaning, dizzy with grief and fear, on the banister at the top of the backstage stairs, at the entrance to the balcony. He looked up and we met each other's eyes. I saw his breath slow, his eyes grow gentle in his young face.

He came up the stairs and took my hand, as the music swelled, and the upper stage, lit warmly with its background of birds, sun and sky, seemed suddenly inviting. He had a sheet and a pillow and he led me so tenderly, the tears still drying on our faces, and laid me down with such care that everything in me seemed to melt and pool and I leaned into him, into this love, this acceptance. I looked at Romeo and transposed Frederick's face over his.

We did not have long, though the others had slowed their scene as much as possible, and begun it much later, my disappointment was real when they left the stage and the light changed.

Romeo disentangled himself from me, and I clutched at him.

"Wilt thou be gone?" I said. "It is not yet near day. It was the nightingale, and not the lark, that pierced the fearful hollow of thine ear."

And there it was, fantasy breeding with reality, a painted nightingale, plainly lit in the backdrop.

"Nightly she sings on yon pomegranate tree," I said, "believe me, love, it was the nightingale."

He smiled. "It was the lark."

Never before had these lines held such significance. I pulled him to me.

"Stay yet, thou needst not to be gone."

After this scene, I would be summoned downstairs again, onto the lower stage for the terrible confrontation with my parents, during which they would try to force me to marry, and I would refuse. Frederick was playing my father, Cat my mother. I had not, since Herm's death, exchanged a look or a word with either one of them.

But Romeo was lying down again, giving in to my embrace. "Let me be ta'en, let me be put to death, I am content, so Juliet wills it so."

I felt cold thrill through me. There was no turning back. Herm was dead. So was Tybalt. How could we stop this now without perjuring their memory?

"Let's talk," said Romeo. "It is not day."

I sat up so suddenly he almost fell away from me. My eyes were bright with unshed tears and, as they met mine, I saw his cloud over.

"It is," I said, and the urgency of the words was subsumed instead with resignation. "It is, hie hence, begone, away."

I walked us through the rest of the scene. He climbed, with

some difficulty, over the banister onto the top rung of the steps, struggling to find his footing through the ivy. I gripped his hands in mine, leaned my weight backwards, holding him there, pausing the inevitable for as long as I dared.

"Farewell," he said, "one kiss, and I'll descend."

We lingered over that kiss, but the thorns in the ivy had attached themselves to his clothes, and seemed to drag him downwards. He took a step down, slipped, grabbed at the ladder. A thin trail of blood appeared on his arm.

"Thinkst thou we shall ever meet again?" I said, and knew we would not. As he descended to the lowest rung, I spoke our final lines together.

"Methinks I see thee, now thou art so low, as one dead in the bottom of a tomb, either my eyesight fails, or thou lookst so pale."

I meant it. His face was white with grief and shock.

He stepped down, onto the bloodied stage, thorns and ivy catching and tearing at him. This ladder would not again be passable.

I had to fight an urge to throw myself down from the balcony, and physically grab him and drag him back.

(The music swells further as Juliet soliloquises briefly from the balcony, a level of heartbreak in her voice far beyond what might have been expected, but she is, the audience remind themselves, only really very young. The mood is broken suddenly by a call to Juliet from downstage.

Immediately the lilting, romantic music snaps into silence, the gentle light of the balcony replaced by a brighter, crueller light on the ground.

Lord Capulet, Juliet's father, a tall, dark figure in the light, stands on the red-stained boards of the lower half of the stage, looking up. He seems, given the way the shadow falls from him, to be almost as tall as the balcony itself, as if he could reach up and simply pluck her small, white form from her bedchamber.

Juliet hesitates for a moment, surprised. Then, she seems to collect herself and hurries off stage, disappearing briefly and reappearing below.)

That entrance should have been my mother. They had switched the lines around without telling me, and Frederick's voice, slicing now with such sharpness through my temporary refuge, threw me for a moment, so that it took me some time to recover my senses enough to respond.

I ran down the stairs backstage to reappear to his summons, a little shakily, unease building within me. The script was uncompromising in this scene. Lord Capulet's cruelty, his violence in the face of his daughter's reluctance to marry the man he had picked out for her, was clear. It was not left open to interpretation. By switching the lines, they had given Cat an opportunity. I was absolutely certain that it was deliberate and I quailed even as I felt the justice of it.

I entered, a little breathless, tried hard not to look at the stains on the boards. With a chill, I noticed that someone had hung two empty picture frames on the backdrop, from which two of the ghoulish faces which Colm had painted into the surroundings glared out. One for each departed player. How many more would they hang before the production was over? Just the one now? For me?

I gulped, turned away, looked up and into Frederick's face. He was solemn. I could see love in his eyes but it was overshadowed with something grim. His face was even paler than usual, his skin, so smooth and unmarked by beard or blemish, seemed almost reflective against the dark of his eyebrows, his brown eyes nearly black in the light. I wanted to reach up and trace his cheekbones with my finger, and I wanted to turn and run away.

I saw something reciprocal in his eyes but there was resignation too. He smiled. "Why, how now Juliet?"

There was an emphasis, very faint but clear, on the name 'Juliet', and I blinked in response, having nearly forgotten where and who I was.

"Sir," I said, only just remembering to adjust my line from 'madam', "I am not well."

"Evermore weeping for your cousin's death?" he said, and for a moment our shared grief flashed between us, forming Herm's face in the dusty air. But the moment was gone. I saw his face change, sarcasm sharpening his voice. "What, wilt though wash him from his grave with tears?"

Tears sprang to my eyes, as if summoned, and he reached out a hand and cupped it around my face. I closed my eyes and leaned into it, relishing this contact with him. It seemed an age since we had touched. I wanted to pull him to me and sob. He adjusted his hand, subtly, but enough to push my face away.

"Some grief shows much of love," he said, and there was a warning in his words, "but much of grief shows still some want of wit."

I had brought us to this. If I did not hold it together now, I would have no excuse. We were all of us suffering. I had been given a choice very deliberately, very carefully. And I had made it. I should have known all along that this was how it would end. *Never say never.* Herm had told me himself.

I reached inside and pulled at the threads of Juliet.

"Yet let me weep," I said, and I pleaded with him through the lines, "for such a feeling loss."

"So shall you feel the loss," he said, "but not the friend which you weep for."

Herm had made his choice too. He had never wavered. He

was a better man than me.

"Feeling so the loss," I said, "I cannot choose but ever weep the friend."

He was a better man than any of us.

I had been wiping at my eyes, my gaze downcast but now I looked up, suddenly, to face Frederick, and saw in his eyes the same sentiment. But his mouth only quivered a fraction, then set, a little harder, in his jaw-line. He picked up pace a little, as if to march us through the scene.

"Well girl," he said, "thou weepst not so much for his death, as that the villain lives which slaughtered him."

"What villain, sir?"

"That same villain, Romeo."

I felt a rush of anger, and when I spoke again, my words were too loud, too quick to be Juliet's muttered aside.

"'Villain' and he be many miles asunder."

Romeo was an innocent. We had brought him in with his brother, both of them vulnerable, and it was our actions that had brought his brother to his death. I wasn't sure how Tybalt had managed it, but he had died, if not quite at Romeo's hand, at least in his presence. Romeo would carry that trauma for ever. And the rest of us wouldn't mourn Tybalt with him, at least not the way we would each other.

Frederick's hand gripped my wrist suddenly, tightly enough to make me gasp and bring me back to my senses, or to Juliet's. I wasn't sure anymore where one began and when the other would end.

"God pardon him," I continued, the lines emerging without thinking. "I do with all my heart, and yet no man like he doth grieve my heart."

This began the double-speak which Juliet and her father would engage in, Juliet professing her love for Romeo at the same time as her father understood her to be demanding vengeance. But we paused, both of us, after that last sentence.

"With all my heart," I said again, and now it was as much as a statement as it was his cue. He seemed to collect himself before he spoke again.

"That is because the traitor lives," he said.

There was such vehemence in it that I searched his face in alarm, but no sooner had he spoken than he settled again into his role as Lord Capulet. He was only my father, come to commiserate with me, and to tell me his news. His grip on my wrist softened. Then I felt his fingers leave my skin, lingering just a little as they did.

I looked into his face and saw only Lord Capulet. I summoned Juliet – all that rigid obedience, that youthful passion masked and smothered with blind compliance. She mingled, messily, with Rose. I spoke my lines, heard his responses, let Shakespeare's clever wordplay carry the weight. The only way we could survive this sorrow was to bury the indignity, the mess and the spit of it, deep inside someone else's more elegant tragedy.

"But now, I'll tell thee joyful tidings, girl."

"And joy comes well at such a needy time," I said, "what are they, I beseech your Lordship?"

I am pregnant. I am carrying your child.

"Well, thou hast a careful mother, one whom, to put thee from thy heaviness, hath sorted out a sudden day of joy, that thou expects not, nor I looked not for."

"Sir," I said, "in happy time, what day is that?"

I have your baby inside me, and I am going to die.

"Marry, my child, early next Thursday morn, the gallant, young and noble gentlemen, The County Paris, at St Peter's Church, shall happily make thee there a joyful bride."

A subtle spite laced his words and I felt again that punch of fury that, I knew, surpassed any of Juliet's father, and grew entirely from Frederick. I was carrying his child and I had not given him a chance to consider or discuss it. Now, perhaps it was too late. Panic consumed me.

"Now, by St Peter's church and Peter too, he shall *not* make me there a joyful bride," I said. "I wonder at my mother's haste, that I should wed ere he that should be husband comes to woo."

I moved further away from him, met his gaze with a vehemence of my own, biting back the tears that were rising again.

"I pray you tell my mother, sir, I will not marry yet, and when I do, I swear it shall be Romeo."

There was a shocked pause. "… whom you know I hate," I added, "rather than Paris. These are news indeed."

Inside me Juliet merged with Rose in a dark concoction, and I had a sudden vision of that 'cocktail', sludge in the bottom of a metal shaker.

Would you really kill your baby? I demanded, silently, *would you kill us both?*

He was shaking his head with Lord Capulet's paternal condemnation, and as he spoke next, I saw again the warning in his eyes.

"Here comes your mother," he said. "Tell her so yourself and see how she will take it at your hands."

Cat strode onto the stage. She entered from the backstage area I had been avoiding, direct, perhaps, from her place by Herm's side. She walked fast towards us so that my instinct to step backwards pushed both Frederick and I further towards the far right of the stage.

She wore high-heeled boots and a cape as Lady Capulet, and she seemed larger than the Cat I had known, an ogre compared to the slight girl I had first met that night, handing Herm his glasses. She was nearly a head shorter than me without her shoes on, but now she seemed to tower above me with a power which had nothing to do with her heels.

"How now? A conduit, girl, what still in tears?"

The words were conciliatory, but her manner was not. The lines were imbued with impatience and scorn. "Evermore show'ring? In one little body thou counterfeits a bark, a sea, a wind."

She could have been describing herself. She was held together rigidly, every muscle quivering with the effort. At her temple, some pulse pumped visibly, her mouth was hard, and her teeth pressed fiercely together, so that she spoke through a tiny gap of air between her lips, which were newly made-up, and blood-red. But she had absolute control of her lines. Every word rang out with perfect clarity.

"The winds," she said, "thy sighs, who raging with thy tears and they with them, without a sudden calm, will overset thy tempest tossed body."

You have no right to be afraid, you have no cause for emotion which is greater than mine.

I felt her rage.

She turned to Frederick now, addressing him as though I was no longer there. "How now husband, have you delivered to her our decree?"

I wanted to call out to him, to stop him from answering.

"Ay madam," he said, "but she will none. She gives you thanks. I would the fool were married to her grave."

Cat met Frederick's eyes. He gave an almost imperceptible nod. She turned to me, and her face was filled with fire and ice.

I'll marry him. I wanted to shout in panic, *I'll do it.* Emily's laughing voice crept into my mind, unbidden, *'Of course, have you seen Colm?'* She was right, I thought, as Juliet and as Rose, I should have married Colm ages ago. Who would refuse him?

"Soft," said Cat in mock amazement, "take me with you, take me with you, husband, how will she none? Doth she not give us thanks?" Her voice became louder. She was talking to Frederick but she was looking at me. She took a step forward, her heels loud and sharp on the floorboards. I started to step back but somewhere during the previous lines, Frederick had moved behind me, so that my back met his chest. I gave a small cry of alarm.

"Is she not proud?" Cat continued, her voice still rising. "Does she not count her blest, unworthy as she is, that we have wrought so worthy a gentleman to be her bridegroom?"

The man I love is dead. What makes you think you have the right to resist now that the time has come for you?

Cat took another step towards me. Frederick was hard and unmoving at my back. Juliet's words tumbled out of me, tinged hopelessly with fear.

"Not proud you have, but thankful that you have," I stammered. "Proud can I never be of what I hate, but thankful even for hate, that is meant love."

It was a contradictory statement even as scripted, and I delivered it badly. Cat was standing so close that the sharp point of her boot met the tip of my bare toes, which curled back instinctively. With a jolt of horror, I realised I was standing in the sticky residue of Herm and Tybalt's mingled blood.

"How now? How now? Chopped logic? What is this?"

Cat's hand shot out and gripped the back of my head, her small fingers tight in my hair. I gasped a little. Frederick, behind me, did not move. I felt his gaze on Cat. I felt him give her permission.

"'Proud' and 'I thank you' and 'I thank you not'," with every sarcastic repetition, she jerked my head by my hair, like a puppet, "and yet 'not proud' mistress minion, you?"

With each jerk, my hair pulled painfully at the roots. My hand shot up to clutch at hers. She yanked it away with her other hand, keeping hold of my wrist, whirled me round, twisting my hair, and pushed her face close to mine. I felt her spit on my skin.

"Thank me no thankings nor proud me no prouds, but fettle your fine joints against Thursday next, to go with Paris to St Peter's Church, or I will drag thee on a hurdle thither."

And with that last sentence she stepped around me, releasing my wrist and pushing me hard so that I fell forward onto my knees.

"Out," she screamed, "you green-sickness carrion."

I cried out in pain and alarm, scrabbling round, to face her. She pulled back her arm and hit me, open-handed, on the side of the face with such force I felt my vision spark, and I fell to one side, pushing myself up dazedly on one elbow.

"Out. You baggage." I saw her pull her foot back, aiming a kick at me. "You tallow-face." I curled myself protectively around my stomach. But the blow didn't come.

"Fie, fie, what are you mad?"

Frederick had stepped past me, interjected himself between her foot and my body, his arm on her shoulder, husbandly, calming, but I could feel the force in it and Cat could too.

Hope rose in me. "Good mother," I said, struggling to pull myself up. "I beseech you on my knees, hear me with patience, but to speak a word." I wasn't on my knees, I was propped on my elbows, breathless and still a little dizzy. I shook my head to clear it. Refocused. Saw blood on the floor.

"Hang thee, young baggage, disobedient wretch." Cat bent and grabbed my arm hard, whipping it out from beneath me and yanking me upright so that I looked up into her face, and saw her grief laser-hot in her eyes. Beside her, Frederick had stepped away. This was Cat's moment. She needed to have it.

"I tell thee what," she spat, "get thee to church on Thursday, or never after look me in the face."

I'm sorry. I hung there, the grip of her hand burning into my muscle.

"Speak not," she shouted, and I realised I had been about to say it. "Reply not, do not answer me."

I closed my mouth. Tears sprang to my eyes, and I began, pathetically, like a child to cry. Her face hardened further. Deliberately, she pulled her other arm up, hand open. I waited for the blow to come. If I was carrying a baby, that was only further proof of my breaking the rules. My actions had been instrumental in bringing about the death of her love. I was kneeling in his blood.

A life for a life.

She brought her hand down across the other side of my face and my vision blurred and span wildly. Only her iron grip on my other arm kept me from falling.

There was a tense pause. The tears ran down my face unheeded. I did not sob, I only swayed there. Frederick stood, very still, in the edge of my swimming vision, silent but watchful.

"My fingers itch." Cat let go of my arm and I fell onto all fours, like some unwanted, crawling creature, scraping about in the blood at their feet. "Husband, we scarce thought us blest that God had lent us but this only child, but now I see this one is one too much, and that we have a curse in having her. Out on her, hilding."

She hooked her boot in my elbow, pulled upwards, so that I stumbled forward, blindly turning, trying to crawl away, to forget the performance, to exit the stage.

"God in heaven, bless her."

Emily.

I had forgotten her entrance. She knelt in front of me, and I stumbled forward, sobbing, into her lap.

"You are to blame, my Lady, to rate her so."

But she knelt very firmly between me and the exit.

"And why, my lady wisdom?" Cat was dismissive, her voice dripping with scorn. "Hold your tongue, good prudence, smatter with your gossips, go."

Emily was very still. The only movement she made was to move one hand and, very gently, stroke my hair. My sobs softened. I breathed the warmth of her.

"I speak no treason," she said, and her voice was calmer than she should have been.

"O God gi' good e'en." Cat was barely making sense, her words spattering out onto the stage between us.

"May not one speak?" said Emily. But she put her hands either side of my head, pushing me upright, disengaging herself. She stood up.

"Peace, you mumbling fool," snapped Cat. "Utter your gravity e'er a gossips bowl, for here we need it not."

"You are too hot," said Emily, and there was warning in her voice. But she did not move from her position, blocking the exit, and Cat was already too far gone.

I felt a rough hand at my shoulder, spinning me round so that I skidded on my knees on the slick of the boards.

"God's bread," said Cat, with biting enunciation, the words spat out like daggers. She was crouching now, her face close to mine, gripping my shoulders. "It makes me mad. Day, night, hour, time, tide, work, play." With every word she shook me violently by the shoulders, so that my teeth rattled, and the sides of my face throbbed in time with it. "Alone, in company, still my care hath been to have her matched." She stopped shaking me, her hands still squeezing at my shoulders, and looked up at Frederick, as if to convince him of my guilt. "And having now provided a gentlemen of noble parentage, of fair lands[6], youthful, and nobly allied, stuffed, as they say, with honourable parts," and at this she turned her gaze to catch Emily's eye, recalling her to their earlier alliance, my nurse's innocent agreement of Paris' desirability. "Proportioned as one's thought would wish a man. And then to have a wretched, puling fool," she turned back to me now, returned her hand again to my hair, "a whining mammet, in her fortune's tender, to answer. 'I'll not wed, I cannot love'."

She began jerking my head again, puppet-like, but harder. I cried out and brought both hands up to my hairline, but her grip was too hard and the jerk she gave with each phrase unbalanced me so that I had to bring them back down to steady myself. She affected a silly, high, mocking voice. "'I am too young, I pray you, pardon me'."

She paused to catch her breath. For a moment, we both hung there, Frederick and Emily silent and still in the background. Then she said, in a voice so quiet and laced with such hatred, I struggled to make out the words beneath it, "But, an you will wed I'll pardon you."

She pulled my hands out so that I smashed forward onto the boards, her hand in my hair just preventing my head from hitting the floor. She held me there, so that I could not help but look down at the blood, congealing. I was close enough to hear it, intermittently dripping down between the boards into the darkness below.

"Gaze where you will," she said, very softly, and her meaning was clear. "You shall not house with me. LOOK TO IT." The shout was so sudden that I jumped in alarm, my head hitting her knuckles, still holding my hair, and she pushed me downwards, so that the side of my face connected with the blood. "THINK UPON IT."

We breathed, the two of us together. For a moment we were utterly connected. I felt her pain.

She held my face in the blood. I smelled metal and damp. "I do not use to jest," she said, calmer now, "Thursday is near, lay hand on heart, advise, an you be mine."

She softened her grip just a little, to allow me to pull my face up, then changed the angle of her grip and slowly, almost gently, pushed it back down so that I grazed the boards with my other cheek.

"I'll give you to my friend, an you be not, hang."

She released me and stepped back. I sat up too quickly and felt the adrenaline spike and rush to my head. When my vision cleared, I met her gaze, but my face was smeared with Herm's blood, and as she looked at me, there was only grief and a terrible, hopeless anger in her eyes.

"Beg," she said. "Starve. Die in the streets. By my soul, I'll not acknowledge thee, nor what is mine shall never do thee good. Trust to it, bethink you. I'll not be foresworn."

She left, her heels like thunder on the boards, so that we all stayed frozen for a moment, poised, listening to the sound of them backstage.

I staggered to my feet. I wiped at my face. Met Frederick's eyes.

"Is there no pity," I said, "sitting in the clouds that sees to the bottom of my grief?" I stepped towards him, reached my arms out. "O sweet my father, cast me not away."

He did not step into my arms. But he brought his hand up gently, and wiped my cheeks.

"Delay this marriage," I said to him desperately, "for a month, a week. Or if you do not, make the bridal bed in that dim monument where Tybalt lies."

But Herm was also a bloodied shell on a mattress. And in the silence, none of us could fail to hear Cat's sobs, released now and clearly audible from backstage.

Frederick's hand fell from my cheek as if it had burned him.

"Talk not to me," he said, "for I'll not speak a word."

Please.

But he turned without meeting my gaze, swung on his heels to stride offstage, the shadow of that earlier ringmaster persona reappearing, then fading as he left.

"Do as thou wilt," he said over his shoulder, "I have done with thee."

(In the wake of Lord Capulet's exit, the audience is hushed. The action has been steadily rising, the violence and passion of this play visceral and wounding. They long for an interval, to sip wine and eat ice cream, to lose themselves a little in mundanities, small talk, and text messages – and the queue for the toilets.

It will not be granted to them.

Instead, they can only watch as Juliet brokenly begs her nurse for her counsel, receiving only the misguided suggestion that Juliet give up on Romeo, and marry Paris after all. They hear the sarcasm in Juliet's response. They feel her indignation, but they are as powerless as she is. Less naïve than the nurse, they hear the lie in Juliet's proposal that she visit the friar to 'make her confession'.

There is a pause in which it seems Juliet is supposed to continue, to make some aside to confide her real plans to the audience but at the word 'confession' she seems somehow undone. Instead, the nurse, hesitating to make her own exit, simply puts her arm around her young charge and guides her, gently, off the stage.)

I missed out Juliet's soliloquy, but Emily showed no concern for the script. She led me to the larger backstage area, where there was water. I sat as she soaked a flannel, dabbed at the blood on my cheeks, the water cold and shocking, in the hope it might lessen any swelling. For what that was worth.

On stage, Colm, as Paris, met with Frederick, now robed up as the friar, to make arrangements for his forthcoming nuptials, unaware of the turmoil this intention had caused.

The scene was barely over before Emily gently pushed me to my feet and I stumbled back onto the stage, to be greeted by Colm, his jarring jubilance striking a discordant note on an already heavily discordant stage.

I spoke the lines, more double-speak, a politeness to Paris and a message of desperation to the friar. Eventually, the friar rescued me from my courtesies, entreating time alone and sending Paris away.

Colm left as bidden, but the kiss he planted on my forehead as he left had more of Colm in it than Paris, and I felt the gentleness of it like a spike to my senses.

"O shut the door," I said to the friar, when he'd gone, "and when thou hast done so, come weep with me, past hope, past care, past help."

I meant it. But when I looked into Frederick's face, I saw now only love.

"O Juliet," he said, and for a moment it was as though he had called me Rose. "I already know thy grief, it strains me past the compass of my wits."

I felt my mouth twitch violently downward, the tears, always so close now, threatening to reappear. There was a pause in which we seemed to lean on each other, the love Frederick showed me as the kindly friar transported into something of the love we had known on those furtive evenings on the stage of his van.

"I hear thou must," he said, "and nothing may prorogue

it …" The pause was too long. We were staring into each other's eyes. "… on Thursday next be married to this Paris."

"Tell me not, friar," I responded with Juliet's words and both our desperation, "that thou hearest of this, unless thou tell me how I may prevent it. If in thy wisdom thou canst give no help, do thou but call my resolution wise, and with this knife …"

I stopped, looking down at my hands. I did not have the dagger. I had exited in the wrong place with Emily and left it on the table at the smaller exit. The one I should have retreated to after the soliloquy I had failed to deliver.

I felt Frederick's eyes on my empty hands. And then, some long-held actor's instinct woke in me, and I covered my error, almost without thinking.

"… With the knife … which I have in my chamber, I'll help it presently. God joined my heart and Romeo's, thou our hands."

The show, as always, must go on.

(The audience watch. The friar lays out the plan that will eventually cost both young lovers their lives.

He passes her a vial of liquid, tells her to agree, temporarily, to her parents' wishes, then drink the liquid alone that night. Its effect, a sleep so deep she will appear to be dead, will cause her to be laid in the family tomb, where Romeo, after the friar has sent a message to him, will meet her.

From there, they can elope together, and, in the friar's most hopeful imaginings, the grief and shock of their parents might manifest itself into the final resolution of their feud.

It is a thin plan, pitted with uncertainties and danger, but it is all Juliet has. She holds the friar's gaze for a moment, and then closes her fingers over the vial, pressing it to her heart.

For a long time, there is no further movement, Juliet and the friar seem frozen in place. Then the actors exit the way they entered, Juliet reappearing almost immediately with her parents and nurse, full of insincere obedience. She plays her part. She hangs her head.

She will be married in the morning.

Mollified, her parents leave the stage, but not before Lord Capulet places a golden wedding ring on the boards in the very centre of the stage. It lies there on the rust-stained boards, the lights fading around it very slowly until it is the only thing visible on the empty stage, lit by a thin red spotlight.

At first quietly, and then, gradually, more loudly, a single bell begins to toll.)

They were there, all of them, gathered and waiting for me. But as I exited the stage, my eyes were drawn first to the curtained-off area for Tybalt and Herm. A terrible silence emanated from it. I wanted to turn and run.

But this was my moment.

They had planned it like this, the wedding ring on the stage was another breath in the action, a space for me to say goodbye. This would be the last time I would see them. I would enter, drink the contents of the vial and when I awoke again, I would be alone on the stage except for Romeo's body. They had written out the brief entrance of the friar into the tomb. Nobody else would touch me until I was dead. And we didn't have much time.

I dragged my gaze away from Herm and Tybalt's bodies to meet five pairs of eyes, and all of us hung there, suspended in that moment, the air thick with emotion. I felt their love, their fear and their regret. But I did not feel their anger.

On-stage, the bell tolled again, loud enough for the sound to reverberate palpably through the boards. And then suddenly, they launched themselves towards me, and I stepped back a little, anticipating an attack.

I closed my eyes in irrational panic, but whatever I expected, it never arrived. Instead, as I opened my eyes again, I found myself held, tightly, Emily's breasts pressed up against mine, her arms around my shoulders, Colm's firm chest at my back, his head bowed in, leaning on mine, Cat, at the other side, one small hand fiercely gripping mine. She was the Cat I had first met, the one I had grown to love, perhaps, of all of them, the one I understood best. Even Romeo was at my side, his gentle hand shaking slightly at my waist. All of them, holding me, holding each other. And over the tops of their heads, Frederick. He stood slightly apart, jaw clenched and there were tears in his eyes.

We stayed like that, silently, until the bell seemed to chime from very far away and I felt myself sway in the warmth and the strength of them. They let me go then and stepped back, so that I caught my breath slightly in the sudden cool air. Only Emily did not retreat all the way, only pulled a little apart from me, her hands still gripping my shoulders, hard enough that I could feel a shot of pain in the places where Cat's fingers had been in that previous scene. She was struggling with herself, her mouth spasming and twitching.

"You bloody … you …" Her voice broke. Love for her rose in me like fire and my arms flew up to cover her trembling hands with mine.

The bell tolled and the audience began to fidget.

"Just … just get out there and fucking knock them dead," she said, let go of my hands and stepped back.

Herm would have raised his eyebrow at that phrase. Would have made some comment about breaking a leg being marginally more appropriate given the circumstances. He would have passed me the brandy. But it would have made me sick. And anyway, Herm was dead.

Maybe I wasn't the only one who was thinking it, because

there was a pause, a hiatus in which nobody moved. But there was only so long that we could keep the bell tolling before the audience grew more restless.

Colm stepped forward and wrapped me in a kind of bear hug, but there was great gentleness in it, as though, he, of all of them, understood how bruised my body was, how fragile my resolve. He didn't try to speak, only pressed his lips to my forehead, smoothed my hair, and stepped away.

Romeo only shook my hand rather formally, kissed me on both cheeks, like a shy child, as though he had not made love with me half an hour before. But I understood. We had said our goodbyes already, as different people, and there was no better way.

Someone in the audience coughed.

I saw Frederick catch Colm's eye and he nodded, he and Romeo disappearing to collect a stretcher. It would be Juliet's bed, deliberately undisguised, clearly a vehicle for bearing the dead.

I stood, dazed in the wake of these simple expressions of love, so painfully inadequate in the circumstances, and yet which meant so much. The others had tactfully melted away, leaving Frederick and I facing each other, while the world spun around us.

I looked at him. His eyes were black. I saw him standing barefoot, violin on his shoulder. I saw his face in the spotlight in his van, soft after lovemaking, frowning as he puzzled over the next production. I saw our passion, our selfish, heady fervour. That compulsive mixture of kindness and cruelty. I saw the narcissist in him, and the circus ringmaster, and I saw the fear behind it.

"Rose." He said it very quietly and without either of us moving. We stared at each other until my eyes stung, and I couldn't breathe.

"Frederick." I whispered.

Romeo, understanding, watching us from the controls, slid a switch and the lights went up.

Cat moved beside me to take her place. I closed my eyes for a moment, unable to contemplate what I was about to do. When I opened my eyes, I saw Emily, alone in one corner, facing away from us, wiping at her eyes.

A small hand gripped mine. Cat pulled me to stand next to her.

"We never got our goodbye," she said.

On-stage, Colm and Romeo entered, carrying the stretcher between them, moving in time with the still tolling bell. A funeral march.

I stared out at them. I did not look at Cat. Tears rose in my eyes and bile in my throat. I swallowed.

"I'm … I'm so sorry," I said.

I felt her turn and look at me. Then she laughed, sharply and without mirth.

"It wasn't actually all your fault."

Amazed, I whirled around to look at her, but now she was watching the stage, her face taut. In the corner of my vision, I could see the shapes of Romeo and Colm, standing over the stretcher they had placed centre stage, bowing their heads, as if paying their respects.

I couldn't think of anything to say. I opened my mouth, but no sound emerged and even in my mind, the words were only part-formed, uncertain.

I turned back to the stage. Romeo and Colm raised their heads again, met each other eyes.

The bell tolled. It was making my head hurt.

"This baby," said Cat, "I assume it's Frederick's?"

I nodded, dumbfounded. My throat felt dry. Nobody had asked me this question. Nobody had talked at all about the baby.

"Well then," said Cat. Romeo and Colm turned their backs to us in unison, like soldiers, and began their slow pace offstage, towards the other exit. "I suggest you consider it quite carefully." She sounded practical, matter of fact.

Quite carefully.

"Are you trying to protect it? Or are you using it to try and protect yourself?"

Colm and Romeo disappeared. The bell stopped.

She dropped my hand, nodded at Emily who had appeared at my side, and gave me a little push onto the stage.

(Dazed and distracted, Juliet seems to stumble through the curtain, her nurse at her side, as the last reverberations of the clanging bell echo like departing ghosts through the barn.)

"Ay," I said, my voice tight, "those attires are best, but, gentle nurse ..." My voice thickened as I turned to face Emily. I took her hand and held it between my own. There was a long silence.

"I pray thee," I said, eventually, "leave me to myself tonight."

Emily was standing, trembling, her eyes fixed on me. We stood there, and it seemed as though the air on the stage had filled with honey, and it was barely possible to breathe. The actor inside me sensed the need for pace, and I pulled myself up a little straighter.

"For I have need of many orisons," I said, "to move the heavens to smile upon my state, which, as well thou knowst, is cross and full of sin."

It was a little too close to the truth. There was a passing beat, in which Juliet and I shared some private moment, and then,

"What, are you busy, ho?"

Cat swept onto the stage as my mother, full of bustle and brisk efficiency. I felt like a sleepwalker shaken unceremoniously awake. I dragged my focus away from Emily and met Cat's eyes, bright and sharp and questioning.

Are you trying to protect it? Or are you using it to try to protect yourself?

I dropped Emily's hands. Cat stepped forward, eyes locked on mine.

"I ..."

I stopped in confusion, realising I didn't have the next line.

Cat gripped my arm, would not drop my gaze.

"Need you my help?" she said.

I was trying to protect myself.

I felt it, a dark realisation, and with it my guts twisted and settled heavily, as if mounting some protest, and then giving up.

I knew nothing of this baby. Only that it was Frederick's. Even then, given the choice, I knew, deep down, that I would have saved Frederick without a thought in its place. Or I would have saved myself. What chance would a baby have with such a mother? And if I wasn't protecting the baby, did I, who had, unintentionally or otherwise, brought about the death of a friend, a brother, have any right to protect myself? I met Cat's eyes. The man she loved had already sacrificed himself for this.

A cold resignation set within me. Very deliberately, I shook my head.

"No madam," I said, my voice gathering strength, "we have culled such necessities as are behoveful for our state tomorrow. So please you, let me now be left alone."

I saw a reluctant admiration in Cat's face. She nodded once. Adrenaline shot through me. This may or may not be the right thing to do. But it was the only thing.

"And let the nurse this night sit up with you," I said, and I placed a hand, steadier now the decision was made, in the small of their backs, hustling them physically off the stage.

"I am sure you have your hands full all in this so sudden business."

For a moment, I thought they might both refuse to leave me. But they only turned to face me, resisting, for a moment, the push of my hands.

"Goodnight," said Cat, so softly it was almost a whisper. "Get thee to bed and rest, for thou hast need."

And with that she turned and they left me, so that I stood alone watching their departing backs, until the curtain fell behind them and I could no longer see into the darkness backstage.

"Farewell," I said, "God knows when we shall meet again."

Did I believe in God? I felt myself and Juliet rise together within me with a terrible, paralysing panic.

"I have a faint cold fear thrills through my veins," I said, and my voice grated painfully in my throat, "that almost freezes up the heat of life. I'll call them back again to comfort me."

I would be alone until the end now. Romeo would not drink poison, not this time at least, but to be certain, I knew they had procured something instead that would render him unconscious. His unresponsive body would be the only other occupant in this bloodied space, so public and yet so lonely.

"Nurse!" it came out a strangled cry. But as soon as I said it, I felt Juliet move within me and clap her hand across my mouth.

"What should she do here? My dismal scene I needs must act alone."

I forced myself to turn away from the exit and look downstage. I could see the stretcher on the floor.

"Come, vial." I said. I untied it from the thin belt cord at my waist, where Emily had secured it for me earlier, and dropped to my knees to examine it.

A small glass bottle. I could see liquid inside but whatever it was, it did not seem to have any colour of its own. If I held it to the light it took on the black of the curtain, the white of the stretcher, the shadows at the edge of the spotlight. I had no idea what exactly it was, a sleeping drug? Something similar to the one they would give Romeo? Or something stronger?

Frederick and Herm would have chosen it carefully. They would have had it ready as far back as my first initiation, everything done exactly right. It had always been only a matter of time.

Had they tested it? Were they sure?

"What if this mixture do not work at all?" I said. "Shall I be married then tomorrow morning?"

Juliet surged within me, in fierce rebellion, "No." I cried. "No, this shall forbid it—"

I gestured, without thinking, to my empty hand. But once again, I didn't have the knife. I should have had it for this scene, but there still hadn't been an opportunity to collect it from the far exit.

"My dagger," I corrected. "My dagger shall forbid it."

I glanced, despite myself, towards the smaller backstage area, at the rickety little props table that held the instrument of my death. Its contents were a collection of small dark shapes in the shadows. What would I do in the last scene, if I didn't have the knife?

Somewhere, deep inside me, something gave a bitter, mirthless little laugh. I needn't worry. I'd have the knife beside me by the time I woke up. The others would make sure of it. We were professionals.

I turned my attention back to the vial, unscrewed it, sniffed. It was completely odourless.

"What if it be a poison which the friar subtly have ministered to have me dead, lest in this marriage he should be dishonoured, because he married me before to Romeo? I fear it is."

What would it do to my baby?

I corrected myself quickly, harshly, *the* baby. It was not *mine*. I had no right to it.

"And yet ... no. Methinks it should not, for he hath still been tried a holy man."

Grimly, I walked with Juliet through her lonely terrors, her last minute regrets.

"How if, when I am laid into the tomb, I wake before the time that Romeo comes to redeem me? There's a fearful point ... Shall I not then be stifled in the vault, to whose foul mouth no healthsome air breathes in, and there die strangled ere my Romeo comes? Or if I live –"

It occurred to us, Juliet and I, that death by suffocation was not our greatest concern, given the circumstances. Juliet did not value her life without Romeo. And I would die anyway. The thought struck fear into us and we rose together in mounting hysteria.

"Or if I live, is it not very like, the horrible conceit of death and night – together with the terror of the place – as in a vault, an ancient receptacle where, for these many hundred years the bones of all my ancestors are packed ..."

In my mind's eye, I saw the packed bones, white and glistening with decay or gristle, like bricks built into the walls of the barn. I looked out at the audience and their faces glowed, white and grinning in the darkness, like congregated skulls. The picture frames, hung around ghostly faces, peering out between the painted trees on a backdrop crafted out of their real counterparts, hacked and felled before their time.

"... Where bloody Tybalt, yet but green in earth, lies festering in his shroud ...?"

Tybalt.

"... The vault where – as they say – at some hours in the night – spirits resort ..."

Choked with fear, I was looking around feverishly, searching the stage, expecting it to be suddenly filled with accusing phantoms. But the boards were empty, the backdrop darker now in the narrowing spotlight, and the faces within it hidden. But I could feel them, watching me in the blackness. My senses screamed. I could hear the creep and prickle of the ivy entwined around the balcony ladder, could feel the sting of buried thorns, the sweep of the heavy curtain at the larger backstage exit.

"Alack, alack."

I was losing sense of what I was saying, the fear so strong my vision wavered.

"Is it not like that I, so early waking, what with loathsome smells and shrieks like mandrakes torn out of the earth, that living mortals, hearing them, run mad ..."

Out of the corner of my eye, I caught a furtive movement.

I whipped round, scrambled to my feet, eyes wide and blinking, fists balled, the open vial still in my hand.

The small backstage area. The props table. There was somebody there.

"Or ... or if I wake ..." I stuttered, stalling in my speech. I squinted offstage, trying to see in the dark. No one had any need to be waiting at that entrance, not at this point in the play.

The figure was bent over the prop table, wearing a monk's habit, the oversized hood pulled up and over, obscuring any detail of face or features, and the bent posture serving to give away nothing of its height or stature. I couldn't see in the darkness what it was doing.

I blinked. There was a slight sound, a faint swishing of material. And whoever it was had gone.

I almost dropped the vial. I recalled myself, and at the same time, Juliet's fear crashed over me, like a breaking wave, sweeping me into a kind of delirium of terror.

"He...help," I squeaked, barely able to control what I was doing. I turned to the audience, still and silent in the stalls. The lighting was so dim on them now, so bright in my eyes, they might not have been there.

"Help," I said again, in a high whisper, my voice breaking and tears building in my eyes so fast I could no longer see.

The audience waited, uncomfortable but admiring. Such clever direction, such an original touch, to bring them into the drama, to break the fourth wall.

I waited.

So did they.

Puck's Legacy.

Terror mingling with resignation, I swallowed. I breathed in, my lungs and windpipe so tight and narrow I could barely summon in the air.

"... Or if I wake," I said, the script and Juliet taking me over, "shall I not be distraught, environed with all these hideous fears and madly play with my forefathers joints, and pluck — "

My voice was rising to something close to a scream, but strangled at its climax so that it cracked and scraped, sobs and gasps and words alternately reaching for air,

" — and pluck the mangled Tybalt from his shroud. And in

this rage, with some great kinsman's bone, as with a club dash out my desperate brains?"

I could barely see my surroundings now, even the parts of the stage which were lit brightly, I could see nothing more clearly than the images my own mind had conjured with my words. I had fallen sideways, crashing onto my knees on the boards, next to the stretcher.

I crouched there, panting, looking down at the wooden boards, the black gaps between them through which, not so long ago, blood had flowed.

"O look. Methinks I see my cousin's ghost seeking out Romeo that did spit his body upon a rapier's point."

When I raised my head I really saw it. A bloodied sceptre I had painted for myself, part ghost, part shadow, bleeding, black and gruesome.

Herm.

I shuffled backwards, stumbling across the stretcher, held up a shaking hand, and just about held onto my lines.

"Stay ... Tybalt. Stay."

I'm sorry.

I had almost forgotten the vial, and I still gripped it, unstoppered, in my flailing hand. A tiny splash escaped from the top of it, soaking, invisible, into the bloodied grey-white of my sleeve. I steadied it immediately.

The ghost disappeared.

"Romeo, Romeo, Romeo," combined desperation and resignation seemed to flush the blood from my veins so that, even before the vial touched my lips, I felt light-headed and dizzy. The room swam around me.

"Here's drink," I howled, raising the vial as if in toast. "I drink to thee."

I tipped my head back and drank.

Memory did not come to me at once. When I drifted, almost lazily, back into consciousness, I was aware only of a strangeness in the silence around me. There was a weight to it. It seemed expectant and unhappy, and I lay, for a moment, eyes closed, my mind empty, as if I were awakening from sleep. A Sunday morning, or a weekend lie in after a heavy night before.

But I had never really lived that life. And it was that which made my fingers twitch, my eyelids flicker. I felt a great mental heave within me as I tried to recall myself to my surroundings. I peered out through a slim opening beneath my eyelids, eyelashes darkening my vision.

It was dim and shadowy. I could see no one, but there was something, a breathing, in that silence. I could sense eyes upon me.

I felt a little rush of panic and pushed on my elbows to try to sit myself up. There was something heavy across my chest, and over my legs, something still and warm against my shoulder.

It was an embrace. But there was something wrong with it.

I panted a little, sank back down. I seemed to be lying low on the ground, on some sort of canvas, which, with the weight of me, pressed down into the ground, rough and hard through the flimsy material I wore, the bones of my back protruding and digging into something flat and unyielding.

Adrenaline surged through me and forced my eyes fully open. A bright light, shining directly onto me from somewhere above me, shot straight into my pupils and I squeaked in pain and screwed them shut again.

I lifted my head, kept my gaze downward and saw, through my streaming vision, an arm across my waist, a leg curled, foetal style, around the lower part of my body, which was encased in a grimy off-white dress. The top of a dark head resting on my chest.

Romeo.

I remembered.

I gasped in fear, scrambled upright, pushing the weight of him away from me. I tried to stand, but my body was still a little drugged and my limbs failed me. I fell back onto the boards, just outside of the spotlight and stared, like a trapped animal, around the stage.

There was a thick tangle of ivy now, entirely obscuring the steps upwards. The balcony was unlit. Ghoulish faces glared at me from the backdrop. In the shadowy light, they seemed to grow limbs and bodies, reaching out to me from their deadly forest. There were picture frames hung around them.

Tybalt. Mercutio.

Me.

Frederick, by now, would be waiting in the slim corridor behind the audience stalls. He would unlock the barn door before he slipped outside noiselessly to re-enter through the backstage area and become the friar again.

But only after my death.

I yanked my gaze away from the picture frames so quickly I felt something click in my neck. Romeo lay on the floor where I had left him. He looked small and limp, like a child. He must have cuddled up to me in those final moments, before whatever they had given him took its effect. He had probably been thankful for it, a brief reprieve. Perhaps he would have preferred the poison. He had curled himself around me for comfort, this coltish man-child who had just witnessed the death of his brother. But I would have been dead to him, floppy and unyielding, unresponsive to his kiss. My heart flipped within me and I felt my throat close in grief.

"Romeo."

I whispered it, forgetting the script.

I slid my arms around his body, laid his tousled dark head on my chest, rocked him gently in my arms.

What had we done here? To ourselves and each other? What had all of us done?

"Romeo," I said, and this time it was a moan, of grief and regret. I felt my body begin to shake and I pulled him closer, squeezed him to me. I stayed that way for a long time, script and show forgotten.

But not quite.

As I had anticipated, someone in the scene change had left me my dagger. It lay quiet and expectant on the floorboards, the silver sliver between sheath and handle glinting in the spotlight. There was no fight left in me. I deserved to die now. It was time.

"What's here?" I said, stroking his head like a baby. "A cup closed in my true love's hand? Poison I see hath been his timeless end."

At least we had afforded him some respite. Sleep would be an unlikely visitor to him for a long time after this performance.

"O churl," I teased him, curling the loose ends of his fear-dampened hair between my fingers, "drunk all and left no friendly drop to help me after? I will kiss thy lips. Haply some poison yet doth hang on them, to make me die with a restorative."

I meant it. I was afraid of that dagger. The sharp point and gleam on it, the need to place it exactly right so that I wouldn't die in agony.

I turned away from the knife and, bending my head to Romeo's, I placed my lips on his. I tasted salt. Fear and tears, his and mine.

"Thy lips are warm," I said, and my voice broke. I don't

know how long I stayed there, rocking him against me, while the audience and the ghosts in the picture frames watched me in silence. Then there was a noise, above me and offstage, at the entrance to the balcony. Emily or Colm, preparing for their cue, recalling me to mine.

Numb, I rose to it.

"Yea, noise?" I said, "Then I'll be brief."

I laid Romeo down on the ground with great care, I made sure that no part of his body would jolt against the floorboards as I released him from my embrace. I moved his arms so that they did not lie unnaturally beneath him, removed his jacket, and used it to cushion his head. I turned back to face the audience, ready – finally, to perform the act that Rose had been born for. I reached for the knife.

It felt cold, so cold against the fever of my palm. So very disinterested in its terrible purpose.

With a quick rush of anger, I yanked off the sheath and dropped it. The blade gleamed silver. Terror gripped me but it was overwhelmed, quickly, by a cold resignation. I raised the blade, aimed its point just a little below my ribs, angled upwards. I knew that I would need to do this quickly, before I entirely lost my nerve.

"Oh happy dagger," I said, "this is thy sheath: there rust and let me die."

I brought the knife down and thrust upward as hard as I could. Plunged it exactly where I had been taught to. Into my heart.

It retracted.

(It seems, for a moment, that nobody breathes. Even Juliet seems to pause as though shocked at her own action, the knife still held tightly in position, her eyes wide and surprised. Then she falls, face forward, across Romeo's body, knife and wound lost to view beneath

her, and lies still.

The audience are as still as she is. This has been a harrowing performance, even for them, who do not know what it is they have witnessed.

The other actors enter the balcony, looking down on the scene, their motionless colleagues. The air is heavy with grief. Together, they recount the events of the play, the feuds and prejudices, the minor mistakes and their terrible consequences, and bring the script to its sorrowful conclusion.)

"For never was a story of more woe, than this of Juliet, and her Romeo."

(There is a long pause. The audience begin to applaud. They wait for a curtain call, the tacit agreement between audience and actors, to release the pent-up anguish of this play, and welcome in a brighter aftermath.

But it does not come.

All the players on stage bow their heads, as if in homage to the title characters, lying on the lower stage. They turn and walk quietly away.

Only the broken lovers remain.

The audience realise that the performance is over. The applause falters and dies.

There is a small moment of stillness.

And then, somewhat subdued, the audience begin to murmur and shift, gathering handbags and coats, in preparation to leave.

And the girl playing Juliet lifts her head, staring wildly about her, scrambles to her feet, and runs headlong off the stage, past the audience. And out of the door.)

Act Six

"A glooming peace this morrow with it brings,
The sun, for sorrow, will not show his head.
Go hence to have more talk of these sad things:
Some shall be pardoned, and some punished,
For never was a story of more woe
Than this of Juliet and her Romeo."

The Prince
William Shakespeare, *Romeo and Juliet*

Scene One

(*A little under two years later.*

The inside of a house, silent except for a steadily ticking carriage clock on the mantlepiece. The room is decorated conservatively in brown and a bland sort of pale orange. There is a sofa to the side, with a couple of plain cushions, two armchairs facing each other across a low coffee table in the centre stage, and a cheap wooden mantelpiece above a fake gas fire, containing the clock and a couple of dull, wooden ornaments.

There is a strong resemblance to another set, staged years ago now, in a shabby university theatre. A penance, perhaps. Even the cocktail table is there in the corner, complete with shaker, glasses, and empty bottles.

But nobody ever visits to mix the drinks. The master cocktail-maker is dead. And there is no audience here.

There is only a woman sitting in an armchair, staring into space. If she is Rose, she is almost unrecognisable. She wears loose, grey trousers, a faded black jumper and thick woollen socks against the obvious cold, which the fake gas fire has done nothing to relieve. She holds a mug of congealing tea. She has dyed her hair brown.

Next to her, close to the fire, there is a child in a little toddler's chair. She is asleep, her small face lolling slightly to one side. Her eyelashes are very dark, a soft halo of black hair spread and spiked against the cushion. Her hands twitch slightly in her sleep, opening and closing as if trying to capture her dreams. Or to emulate a star.

She is the most colourful thing in the room.)

It's like suspended animation. When she stops, I do. I sit in this brown world I have painted for myself, and those heady days, with their spotlights, and their colour, their blood, and their laughter, seem to echo back to me over a chasm of incredulity. I don't know if I intended this saturation of brown as a disguise or an antidote. If the latter, it doesn't work.

Camper vans, campfires, rehearsals, and injuries. Colm apologising, Emily rolling her eyes. Herm shimmying up ladders to fix bits of staging, winking at me and swigging brandy. The acid taste of it, burning at the back of my throat. The rough wood in the tangle of beams in the barn, the stars above us, the ground so far below. Herm's blood on the mattress, Romeo's limp body. Thorns catching and tearing at our skin. Frederick.

Frederick.

They visit me in every idle moment, and they are simultaneously terrifying and alluring. A dream to escape to, a nightmare to claw myself awake from.

I ran out of that barn wild with terror, and without any idea what I was going to do next. I was not anticipating running; I was supposed to be dead.

I had stumbled over my own feet in my urge to get out but then, unbelievably, I paused in that field and looked back. The barn in the moonlight, the audience beginning to file out. Then something inside me jolted into action and I turned again and ran, barefeet skidding in the wet, brown grass, towards my van.

It seemed barely possible anymore to make important decisions without a script. I might have sat there, paralysed, in the cab and simply waited for them to find me if it hadn't been for the neat pile of papers on the passenger seat. My passport, an envelope with a wad of cash inside it, my original clothes. The door was unlocked, the keys in the ignition. Somebody had prepared my props for me. And so, I did as I was supposed to. I drove away.

I expected to see them in the wing mirror, a collection of

figures growing smaller on the horizon, my lover, my captor, my judges, my friends. But it was dark, and the road was bumpy. I could not tell if they were watching. I wasn't sure if they might be pursuing.

    I drove the van as far as I dared, then abandoned it in a carpark. I swapped my bloodied costume for the jeans I'd been wearing the day I arrived and crushed it deep into a nearby bin. I left everything else except the money and the passport and I walked to the nearest train station.

    I wonder if they found it. I hope somebody did. My van with its bells, its dreamcatchers, and ribbons. With its dreams and its pretentions. Gypsy skirts and red hair. Somebody should have it.

    I took three trains and two buses, doubling back on myself, making sure that I took the least predictable route.

    I ended up here.

    It was the most boring minor town I could find, with a big enough population for me to blend in with, but little enough amenities to be satisfyingly insignificant. There is a small theatre which alternates between panto and musicals, largely amateur, and poorly attended.

    I have never been inside its doors.

    I found a dingy little place with a lazy landlord who was lax on his identity checks. I did not use my real name. I did not use 'Rose'. I gave him a new name, the blandest I could think of, and he did not bother verifying it against my documents.

    There is no real paper trail that could lead anyone to me. I have no internet presence. I am not on social media.

    I wear grey and beige and brown.

    I walk heavily, as though I am a decade older. I pitch my voice a little lower, give it a hint of an accent, but avoid making it too interesting. I do not speak much. I cultivate a dour disinterest in everything, so that I will not, (though it seems unlikely anyway), be tempted to laugh, because real laughter is harder to change.

I could have used my birth name. Only two of them ever knew it. And one of those is dead. But I know how to become another person, I have done it so many times before. After a while I felt myself begin to cleave to it. True disguise has very little to do with appearance, and everything to do with what you believe in your head.

I know this. I am trained to know it.

The irony does not escape me, that even now, I am perpetually acting.

She stirs, in her sleeping chair beside me, and her movement moves me. I stand, walk to the tiny kitchen, and begin the unremarkable process of washing up.

I still see them. Everywhere. In crowds and at bus stations, driving camper vans or in queues. Cat mostly, with her sly, feline face, twisted in resentment at my betrayal. I catch my breath, look again, and the face resolves itself into somebody else's, some slight, pale stranger, a teenage boy, or a child.

I see Colm too sometimes, his face tense and focused, the way it sometimes was in his more violent or erratic acting personas.

Or Emily, grinning and drinking, smoking, or swearing at some shop assistant somewhere. But none of them are really there or, if they are, they retreat before I can decide whether to approach them or to run.

Most of all I see Herm. His ghost or his likeness. Watching me or winking at me. Accusing or patient. Sometimes, if I lean on the doorpost to my living room, narrow my gaze just a little, I can almost see him mixing cocktails. A slender, faded shadow against the splash of colour that he was. He melts into the walls almost as soon as I picture him.

*Herm, do you wish you had never recruited me? Do **I** wish it? Are you there?*

I long to see Frederick. I long for it and I dread it, but mostly I long. I want to talk with him, to wake up with him on his stage in his camper van and realise the whole thing was just a performance.

But it had always been real. And that was the point.

Maybe I never wanted it, really. Maybe I never understood. Maybe I was always just a bored child, throwing a tantrum.

(The washing up is done. For a moment the brown-haired woman stands, hands in the water, scraps of food and soap scum floating against her skin, staring into space. As if moved by some ancient clockwork inside, she moves automatically into a cupboard-sized bedroom, taken up almost entirely with a rusting clothes-horse. And begins to fold laundry.)

Once I abandoned my loose skirts, I was more obviously pregnant. I did not dare to see a doctor or have a scan, I thought maybe that was where they would look for me first.

I am afraid even now, that they are looking for me.

And I am afraid that they are not. That I am no longer important enough for them to care. Just another automaton, living the life I had once so dreaded.

(The child stirs, and the woman leaves the bedroom, moves to the lounge to check on her. She goes to the fridge, gets out margarine, opens the cupboard for peanut butter, and begins to spread it on cheap, white bread. She cuts the sandwich into tiny triangles, cuts off the crusts. She turns back to the child, crosses the room on gentle footsteps, bends down to her daughter. For a moment, she watches her, a tenderness spreading across her face. She reaches out a hand

to the child and, very gently, strokes her cheek. It is the first time any expression has reached her eyes and, fleetingly, we can still see Rose.)

Evie was born on the first of September, amidst the usual blood and turmoil. I refused drugs and insisted on the birth being natural, less from a desire to avoid chemicals, though heaven knows I had already subjected my body to enough of that, but because the pain, though worse than anything I had ever experienced, somehow made me feel alive.

I called an ambulance when I felt my waters break and they took me to hospital, where I gave them the details they needed, but told them I preferred to be known by another name. Midwives like a name. They use it a lot, repeat it in every sentence. *"Come on, Jenny"*, *"You can do it Samantha,"* *"You're doing wonderfully Hannah."* Until the baby emerges, and they only call you *"Mum"*.

I lay there, sweating and screaming and pushing, and the pain filled me and occupied me until I was no longer present. I closed my eyes and saw tableaus, scenes from my previous existence, like flashes of colour in the dark. Spotlights and costumes and backdrops and greasepaint. And all the while I lay on an identical white bed, surrounded by rooms and rooms of identical beds in a blue-white hospital, where the lights never dimmed and the scene never finished, and the only audience was a dutiful doctor who had seen it all before. And the soundtrack was my screams and the rasp of my breath and the terrible fear that the drugs I had taken as Juliet, which I did not know the identity of and could tell no one about, might have done something awful to my child.

There was one moment, amidst all the rush and the drama, nurses pressing oxygen into my nostrils, my back arched in a scream and sweat dripping into my eyes, when I could have sworn, I saw him. A dark head, in a doctor's pressed white coat, worn ironically, like another costume, his pale skin stretched across cheekbones, dark, gentle eyes.

Time slowed.

It was just the oxygen. But as I closed my eyes, succumbed, for a moment, to my body's exhaustion, I was sure I heard him whisper, "*Rose.*"

There are very few books on the psychological after-effects of returning recruits from a fanatical theatre group, though there are plenty on the subject of cults. Perhaps my love for them had been only a confused illusion. A kind of Stockholm syndrome and they had been nothing more than my captors.

But the fact is, somebody switched that knife.

You will want to know who, and I will disappoint you. I have disappointed you all the way through. But I don't know. To this day, I do not know who did it. Maybe it was Frederick, there was something in the quiet arrangement of the papers in my van which had his touch in it, and he was certainly the only one with access to cash. But however, I imagine it, I can't quite see him betraying the purity of his own production. Perhaps he only prepared my exit, predicted, correctly, that somebody else would do the rest. Colm? Emily?

I do not know. And I know now that I probably never will.

By the time they laid Evie on my chest, I had spent months just hiding, not thinking much about my pregnancy, too full of my flight. But when the midwife pulled her out of me, howling and writhing, they held her up and she hung there for a moment, looking at me, silent suddenly and watchful. I held out my arms and pressed her to my skin. I breathed it all in, held her to my sweat-sheened breasts, saw the bright-red blood on her, her eyes, already so dark beneath tufts of slick, wet, black hair.

And I realised that both of us had survived.

As if aware that I am thinking of her, she opens her eyes now and meets mine. There is something uncanny in her, already, she is her father's daughter, she has a changeling, sprite-like quality. I can believe she is special. I can believe she is magic.

"Do you want a sandwich?" I ask her. "It's only peanut butter, we're on our last reserves I'm afraid. I should really go shopping."

I have never patronised Evie. There is something knowing about her. When she was a tiny baby, she would cry only until she could see that whatever she wanted was being prepared. Then she would return to her quiet watchfulness.

Now she smiles and, unexpectedly, reaches up to wrap her arms around my neck. I hug her back, fiercely, and urgently, and she releases me and rolls herself out of the chair, pulling herself to a standing position, one small hand gripping the sofa for balance. There is an other-worldly grace to her.

"Sandwich?" she says, as if reminding me.

"Sandwich." I agree and lead the way to the kitchen.

I love this child more than anything else in the world.

Epilogue

(A grey-tarmac playground, outside a grey breeze-block school.)

Maybe the swallow knows.

I watch it, circling above the dusty playground, wings spread, neck stretched, beady eyes watching. There's nothing much for it to see, of course. I have made sure of that. We are only a handful of hot, squat figures dotted across the tarmac. Waiting.

I am wearing a rather tired, brown jumper and faded, black jeans which went out of fashion before I bought them. I have brown hair and a brown shopping bag. A pint of milk, a loaf of bread, a block of cheddar. I walked here in solid, flat, brown shoes. I have been wearing this costume for the last nine years and it is dissolving me slowly.

We stand in silence, mostly, except for Millicent, who has always been skittish. You notice a lot when you've been trained the way I have. You know the things normal people do which betray them. Millicent hums sporadically, a cross between Beethoven's *Ode to Joy* and *Yankee Doodle*. The rest of us remain quiet, except for the odd sigh or cough, and the continual 'blip blip' of the pelican crossing, which serenades us, blandly, in the distance. The humming fades. You can't expect much from someone called Millicent.

I *want* the swallow to know. It nears us now, circling downwards, considering a landing point.

"Well," says Mr. Adams, filling the silence, "I guess this is our summer then."

"Hope it lasts," says Janey.

"The thing is," says Millicent, "It's a bit *too* hot …"

The swallow despises us. But it lands anyway.

I am just another blob on the tarmac. I am a greyish-brown lump.

Because of me two people are dead.

It only takes the thought in my head. Just a moment, a heartbeat and I am there again, just for a second. The rush of colour, the heat of the lights, the smoky smell of nervous sweat. A sort of misplaced sensation, like going on holiday.

A woman, blank-faced and pale, holding her lover limp in her arms.

Dust in the footlights.

Blood on the boards.

There is a miniature commotion, and a stream of small life forms pour out of doors and rush towards us like jubilant water. All around me, other grey-brown figures are stooping, greeting, scolding, embracing. There is a crescendo of excited voices, a hundred mingled, mixed-up narratives.

She emerges, drawing a sort of involuntary cry from me by simply appearing, carrying a piece of paper carefully in one hand and her school bag in the other, looped carelessly over one small finger. It drags on the ground behind her as she skids to a halt, steadies herself on my shopping bag and looks up at me with eyes that are filled with stories.

"Guess what, Mummy ...?" she says. She is holding some sort of brochure or poster. I can see a flash of red on it.

She doesn't know my real name. I left it behind. I'm not sure I can exactly remember it myself.

The swallow knows. But it's telling nobody.

If any of these parents, with whom I stand in a playground and discuss the weather, had any idea of the things I have done, of the people I have been, they would have me arrested. Perhaps, so will you.

"Mummy?"

That's who I am now.

The brochure is oddly familiar. I frown, put my head on one side, try to focus on the design on the flapping paper. I see triumph in her eyes as she catches me looking, she puffs her small chest out just a little.

Something suddenly chills inside me.

"MUMMY! I have a message for you." She changes her voice now, it becomes lower, conspiratorial. "I have a message. From a *man*."

She hands me the brochure with just a little flourish, subtle enough not to be ridiculous, big enough to have an effect. She is, and always will be, her father's daughter.

The paper is slightly crumpled. I smooth it, but my hand is shaking, and the world seems to have become very slow around me.

It is not a brochure. It is a flyer for a performance.

Romeo and Juliet.

It's a very simple design, just a drawing of a flower, but artfully rendered. You could pick it right off the page.

"He says to make sure you get it," she says, "because it's important."

The flower is a rose.

And the play is for one night only.

"He says he loves you very much. And he says that he's sorry."

Her voice seems to travel miles to reach me. Beneath it, I am vaguely aware of a muted noise, as though the playground and its occupants are going about their business from the bottom of a deep, grey, undulating ocean.

"There's a note on the back," she says, and I glance at her sharply, because there is something a little too innocent in her tone, like a line which has been rehearsed too often. She flushes, as though she knows she misjudged it, gestures quickly back at the note. I watch her for a little longer because I know she has already read it. Perhaps I could read it instead in her face and avoid looking again at that piece of paper, and maybe, just maybe, that would make it disappear.

But I don't want it to.

I breathe in and refocus. I turn the flyer over.

'Rose.'

I stop breathing. And somewhere, in some parallel world, another part of me, another me altogether, inhales deeply.

'I'm sorry.

It's time to stop. It's been time for years. And I'm sure you understand, as I do, that there is only really one way to do so.

I love you. This will be my last performance.'

I cannot speak. I concentrate very hard on breathing.

"Mummy?"

I grip the flyer in one hand, my child in the other. The playground has emptied.

The stage is set.

But don't worry. This was only a story. A clever succession of words and mirrors. There's no reason at all to believe it is real.

But you *want* to.

People Who Helped Behind the Scenes

A SPECIAL THANK YOU to *Emma Rinaldi*, without whom I wouldn't have thought the idea for this book was worth writing, for her incredible enthusiasm over a cup of coffee, in a lunch-break which really should have been over by then, for reading as I wrote it, and, above all, for naming my Rose.

THANK YOU very warmly to *Charlotte Cox, Kate Pogson, Laura Grove, Claire Rutter, Maike Kraus, Julia Boddy, Clarissa Pattern* and *Vicky Audley* who all read some or all of my work, (in some cases as I wrote it) and made me feel as though I had an audience and might even have the right to call myself a writer.

THANK YOU to my wonderful husband, *Martin Hall-May*, who has encouraged, loved, cherished, and generally put up with me.

THANK YOU to *Nicole Anson* for her advice on Aikido, to *Hollie Swift* for giving me time off work to write my earliest drafts, to *Nicolas Gregoriadas, Heather Langley,* and *Ashley Pearson* for being endlessly supportive and (at least appearing) endlessly interested and to *Alex MacArthur, Gareth Bottomley,* and *Jane Twell* for sitting in The Pulsing Loft and listening to me bang on about my characters' 'slow descent into madness' whilst descending fairly swiftly myself.

THANK YOU to *Lisa Cagnacci* for her fascinating and informative conversation about acting, directing and theatre in general over a lovely dinner that was a brilliant excuse for a long-overdue catch-up. Thank you also to Lisa for her recommendation of *Mike Alfreds'* book <u>Different Every Night:</u>

Freeing the Actor which helped me to understand the many ways in which my actors might prepare.

THANK YOU also to the myriad of people who answered Facebook requests for advice, including *Sarah Hall, Owen Kingston,* and *John Hardy* and notably *Jon Riley*, for his advice on theatrical lighting and sound cue set up.

THANK YOU to *Bubblecow* whose editing services and friendly advice made this book, to *Georgette Harrison* for her cheerful, collaborative proofreading, which strayed very welcomely into copy-editing territory, and to the team at *BeBookSharp* for lending me a level of media savvy which I don't (and will never) have of my own.

THANK YOU to *Kindle Direct Publishing* for opening the door to self-publishing and making it cool and affordable, and, last but not least, to *Claire Rutter*, for her amazing cover design.

THANK YOU

About the Cover Designer

I can't speak for the content, but I'd at least like to shout about the cover design of this novel, which was designed and produced with great patience and skill by my sister, Claire Rutter.

Somehow managing to fit this around a warm but hectic family life, a responsible job and about a hundred other important commitments, Claire is a talented photographic illustrator. To create her pieces, she first builds a miniature, shoebox-sized 'set', which she tweaks, recreates, tears down, starts again and then – finally – photographs.

Each 'set' is painstakingly lit to reflect the appropriate mood, weather, or time of day. This design is constructed so that it tells its own story from front cover to back, neatly allowing you to avoid having to read all those tiresome words in-between.

If you'd like to congratulate Claire on her brilliance you can email me on katie.hallmay.authorcontact@gmail.com and I will be pleased and proud to pass it on.

About the Author

My name is Katie Hall-May, and I am a writer. Aside from that, I have very few vices other than alcohol, chocolate, crisps and lying about how many vices I have.

Memories of a Lost Thesaurus was my debut novel and *Puck's Legacy* is my second (if you can technically have a second 'debut').

I have another in the 'editing' tray and a fourth being planned. They do tend to take their time in gestation, but I don't mind that because writing makes me happy (though sometimes in a teeth-grinding, grumbly sort of way).

If you would like to get in touch, you can email me at katie.hallmay.authorcontact@gmail.com, visit my website at www.katiehallmay.co.uk or rate this book online and leave me some feedback.

Best wishes, and whatever you're doing, good luck with it. I hope you enjoy reading this, and that it somehow lives up to its cover design.

References:

[1] All references are to William Shakespeare's *Romeo and Juliet*, and any and all lines quoted are taken from the original text. I used the RSC Shakespeare version, 2009, edited by Jonathan Bate and Eric Rasmussen

[2] Adapted from Mary's speech in Act 4, from *Long Day's Journey into Night*, by Eugene O'Neill

[3] Adapted from Act 4, *Long Day's Journey into Night*, by Eugene O'Neill, all speech taken exactly from the original, only descriptors and character names have been adjusted for the narrative flow.

[4] From George Bernard Shaw's *Arms and the Man* – all text taken from actual lines in the original play. Please note I feel rather less antipathy to this play than my character expresses!

[5] All references are to William Shakespeare's *Romeo and Juliet*, and any and all lines quoted are taken from the original text.

[6] Original text: 'demenses' – translated for clarity to 'lands'

All other works have been referenced clearly in the text where they appear.

Printed in Great Britain
by Amazon